THORNS OF DEATH

*To all the ladies looking for that mysterious older guy.
Daddy Marchetti is here.*

THORNS OF OMERTÀ SERIES

Each book in the Thorns of Omertà series can be read as a standalone with the exception of Thorns of Lust and Thorns of Love, which is the story of Tatiana Nikolaev.

If you'd like the preview of the next standalone book in this series, Thorns of Silence, keep reading after this duet ending.

All rights reserved.
No part of this book may be reproduced in any form or by any electronic or mechanical means, including information storage and retrieval systems, without written permission from the author, except for the use of brief quotations in a book review.
Visit www.evawinners.com and subscribe to my newsletter.
FB group: https://bit.ly/3gHEe0e
FB page: https://bit.ly/30DzP8Q
Insta: http://Instagram.com/evawinners
BookBub: https://www.bookbub.com/authors/eva-winners
Amazon: http://amazon.com/author/evawinners
Goodreads: http://goodreads.com/evawinners
Tiktok: https://vm.tiktok.com/ZMeETK7pq/

THORNS OF OMERTÀ PLAYLIST

https://spoti.fi/3CB11r1

AUTHOR NOTE

Hello readers,

Please note that this book has some dark elements and disturbing scenes to it. Please proceed with caution. It is not for the faint of heart.

Don't forget to sign up to Eva Winners' Newsletter (www.evawinners.com) for news about future releases.

BLURB

Enrico Marchetti.
One of the five Italian mafia kings.
Powerful. Untouchable. Corrupt.

It started with one innocent look across a room in Paris. He was a lot older than me. A Roman god dressed in an Italian suit, surrounded by an aura I couldn't resist.

When I ran into him again, he effortlessly pulled me under his spell. But little did I know, a night full of carnal pleasure would cost me everything.

When Enrico Marchetti wanted something, he didn't just take it. He possessed it. Now, his sights were set on me.

There were secrets this man was keeping. They surrounded him, his dead wife, his children.

I wanted no part of it, but there was no escaping him. He had taken me to his kingdom, locked the doors, and thrown away the key.

Now the only thing left to do was fight. Even if it killed me.

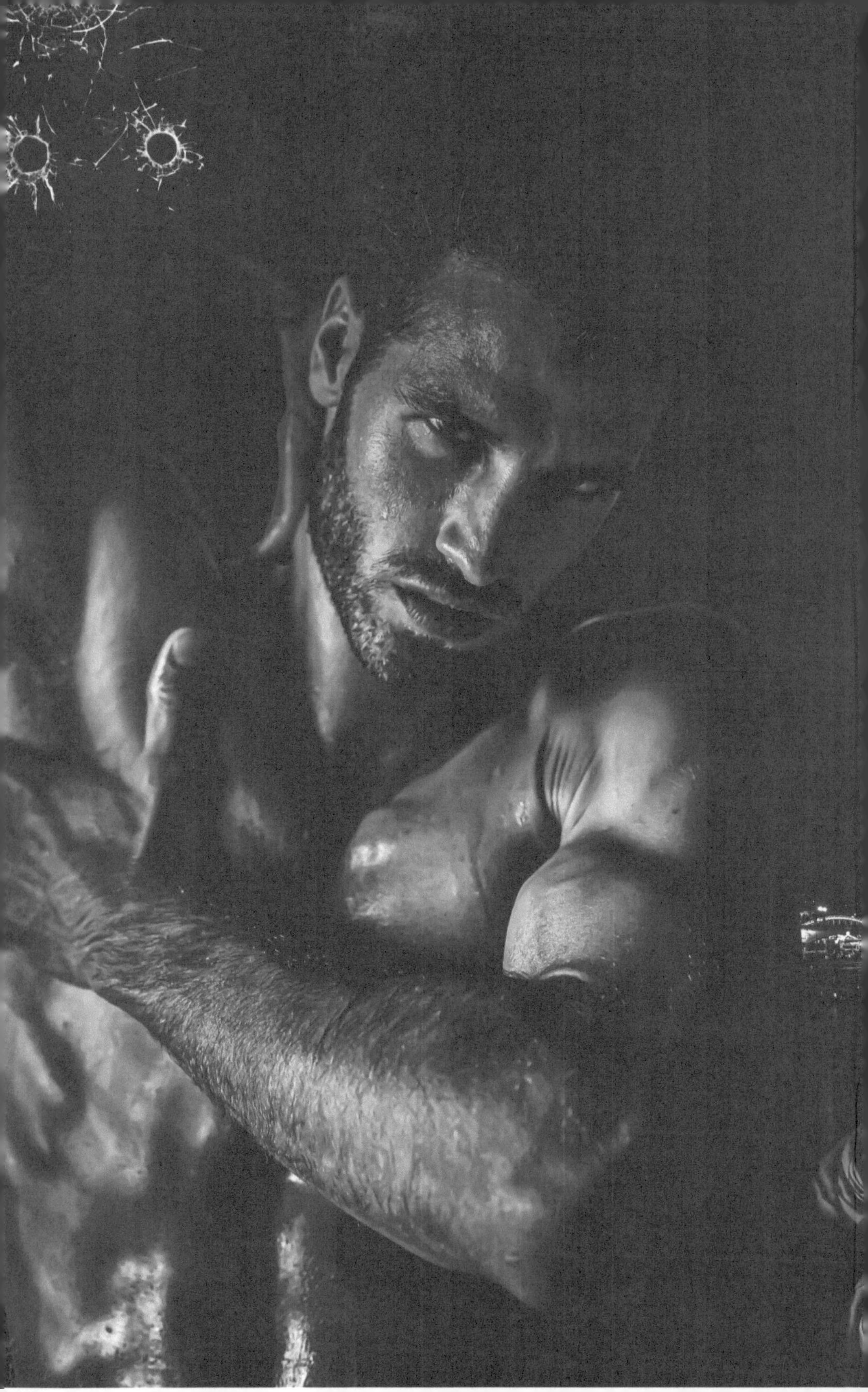

PROLOGUE
ENRICO

Past

I watched the life ending right in front of my eyes.
    I'd seen it so many times before, you'd think I'd be numb to it by now. Yet right now, it touched me down to my soul. To my bones. And fear settled there.

A fear that I'd lose another person I loved. First it was my mother. Then my father. Now my brother.

Panic momentarily froze me in place and suffocated me, slowly but surely.

"It was an ambush. They had twenty men waiting for us," my uncle shouted.

I ran to the car decorated with bullet holes and ripped the door open, pulling out my brother's slumped body. He was the same size as me. Except his face, so similar to mine, was now deathly pale.

His body lay sprawled on the grass as it quickly turned crimson. With the vineyards affording us shelter, I ripped open my brother's shirt and listened for a heartbeat.

The world moved in slow motion yet still too fast while I waited for signs of life. When it didn't come, I rushed to perform CPR.

One. Two. Three. Breathe.

One. Two. Three. Breathe.

Repeat. Fucking repeat. As many times as it required to bring him back to life. I felt again for a pulse, and it was there, so faint and unsteady that I almost missed it.

I inhaled a relieved breath.

My ears buzzed with adrenaline. My heart thundered with fear.

Manuel and another shadow lingered behind me, blocking us from view.

"He won't make it." I recognized Kingston's voice. "That slash in his abdomen and bullet in his chest... You shouldn't try to save him. It's too late."

I shook my head, my hands bloodied. Soon they'd be soaked in it.

My brother lay on the soft ground like a broken leaf. My men's voices grew nearer, and Manuel barked orders as he sent all the guards to the front gate of the property. They'd ensure nobody else was killed tonight.

I grabbed my brother's cold hand. "Don't you fucking die," I shouted. If I had any say in it, he'd stay alive. For the *famiglia*. "Wake the fuck up!"

His eyelids peeled open. "You know what to do." His words were breathy, each a futile struggle.

Those were his last words, and my heart bled as I watched the light in his eyes extinguish. But the fucking world continued to turn. The waves continued hitting the shore, seagulls sounded high in the sky, celebrating their freedom.

Somehow, I fucking knew we'd end up here. His impulsiveness, his sense of entitlement and invincibility... they were his damnation all along. I just hoped it'd strike much later in life.

"You know what he means, don't you, *nipote*?" Manuel usually used that word, *nephew*, when things were bad or when he wanted to annoy me. The latter wasn't the case this time. As his hand came to rest on my shoulder, my heart twisted.

I knew what he meant. The burden became mine, and it turned my heart to stone.

THORNS OF DEATH

Maybe it was that day I lost myself, and I became one and the same with the thorns of death.

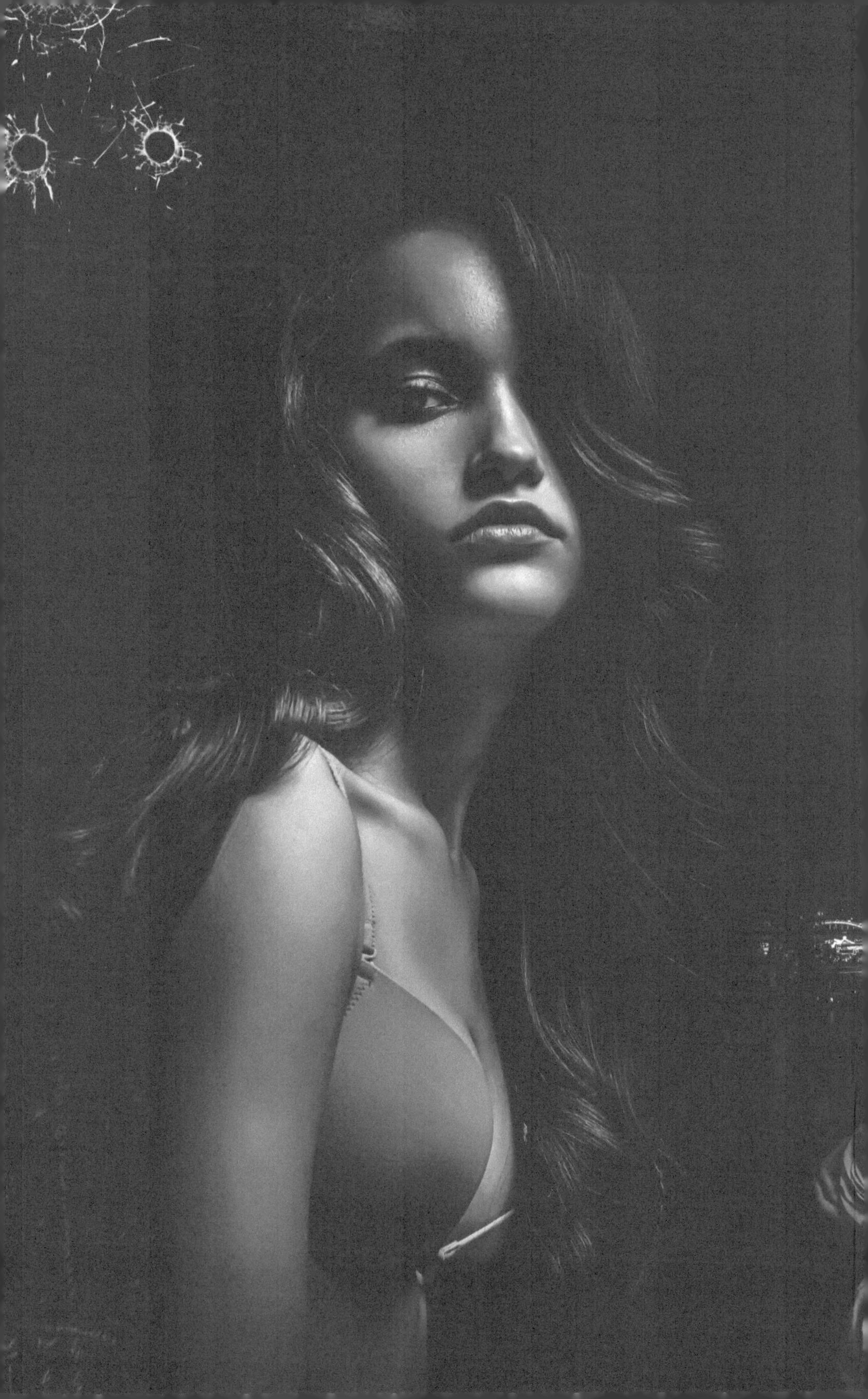

ONE
ISLA

Present

I caught him looking at me before the show started.

Dark eyes. A sprinkling of silver in his jet-black hair. A thin layer of stubble. And the ghost of a smile that could bring you to your knees.

The air caught in my lungs as I felt his eyes on me like a cool breeze against my heated skin. Usually men—the ones in my field at least—watched me with a single purpose. To get me into bed and brag about it to their fellow symphonists. I could never quite pinpoint what drew their eyes to me. Was it the unconventional, vibrant dresses I wore while I played the violin? The spotlight I got while on the stage? Or maybe it was simply the way I let myself feel the music.

But this guy looked at me like he wanted to consume me. Devour me. Own me.

And I'd let him.

The term "hot daddy" never made sense until this very moment. He was older, but definitely not *old*. Maybe double my age, if I had to guess.

I inhaled deeply, but there wasn't enough oxygen to loosen up this knot in my chest. His black eyes burned through me, tracing down my body and studying my every curve. Did he like what he saw? God, I hoped so.

Arousal shot through me, sending a shiver down my spine. I should look away. I should turn my back to him. But I didn't.

Instead, with a thundering heart and excitement running through my veins, I blew him a kiss and winked playfully. What the heck? We only live once.

"Isla, are you ready?"

Athena's voice pulled my attention away from the stranger. I turned to find her staring at me, right along with Phoenix.

"Ready for what?" I asked, confused.

"We agreed you'd play before Reina's fashion show starts," she muttered. "I swear, everyone is losing their minds." I didn't get to answer, because she continued with her ranting. "I know I have good organizational skills, but the least you could do is follow directions."

I bit the inside of my cheek. Athena was a control freak. She hated disorganization. And broken schedules sent her over the edge, but it worked well for all of us because the rest of our group was a mess. Well, aside from Reina.

"Where is your violin?" she squealed, snapping her fingers to get my attention.

I lowered my eyes and realized it wasn't in my hand. Then I remembered. With the handsome stranger capturing my attention, I'd completely forgotten about it.

"Let me grab it," I said, rushing to where I had left it.

As if pulled by a force, my eyes flickered to where the man had been, but he was no longer there. An empty void lingered where he once stood.

Disappointment washed over me, which made no sense. I didn't even know him. He could be a complete douche for all I knew.

"Okay, I'm ready. What's the first song we're playing?" I asked, signing in ASL at the same time so Phoenix would understand me too. I learned it shortly after meeting her and Reina. I hated seeing her excluded from conversation when Reina wasn't around. It was one of the best decisions I'd ever made.

When I first ran into Phoenix in my music class, I'd marveled at the thought of someone playing the piano while not being able to hear a single note. Yet, she never let her disability hold her back and had taught me so much through the way she embraced other senses, and about what music meant to her.

And her dedication put mine to shame. She and her younger sister, Reina, were super close. With almost two years between them, Reina had taken extra classes in high school to graduate alongside her older sister. Whenever a professor argued about having a deaf child in their music class, Reina had stepped in like a little firecracker and argued until they accepted Phoenix, even at the cost of sacrificing her own time.

It was how we'd all ended up in the same college. Reina wanted Phoenix to get everything she wanted—namely, the best musical education in the world. But none of us were ready to let Reina give up her own passion: fashion design. So we'd all settled for the best of both worlds.

The Royal College of Arts and Music. In Paris, the City of Love.

After all, it allowed us to remain together.

"Okay, let's get this party started!" I exclaimed enthusiastically, taking my violin out of its case. "Reina Romero, mere human today, fashion goddess tomorrow."

We rushed around the large podium. It was hectic, everyone making last-minute changes to arrange for everything to be perfect. The venue was magnificent. I had no idea how Reina had gotten so lucky to have the infamous Enrico freaking Marchetti let us use it. He'd even extended invitations to some of his key contacts.

Yikes! More pressure.

It was important that it all went well. For all of us. It would open the world of fashion to Reina, the world of top musicians to Phoenix and me, and expose Athena and Raven to artists and buyers.

I found Reina running around like a chicken with her head cut off in the back room, getting all the models ready. Shoes for this one. Ribbon for that one. Makeup touch-ups on that one.

Geez. I'd just kill them all. Much easier.

"Where have you been?" she exclaimed in her over-the-top "mother" voice. The girls and I shared a knowing look. "Stop rolling your eyes," she grumbled. "Get to your spots," she ordered in her sternest voice.

She may have been the youngest of us all, but that definitely didn't stop her from being the bossiest.

The three of us snapped to attention, stifling our grins. "Aye, aye, Captain." The salute we gave almost made me lose it and burst into laughter.

TWO
ISLA

Three hours later, we clinked our crystal glasses in celebration, alcohol swishing and drops spilling over the table.

"To us," we exclaimed in unison. "Today Paris, tomorrow the world."

We found our way back to the dance floor, swaying our hips and laughing. For the first time in over two years, I felt lighter. The murder we'd committed didn't feel as heavy on my soul tonight, and by the looks on my friends' faces and the way they let their bodies flow with the music, they felt the same.

I didn't like to remember how death looked, although sometimes it felt impossible to forget the frosted, blank eyes devoid of life. A ghost of a shiver rolled through me, but I shook my head, chasing the memories away. Tonight it was all about celebrating our achievements.

Letting my gaze travel over the crowded bar, I spotted *him* again. My hot daddy. The incredibly gorgeous stranger, only a few feet away from me. And—oh my gosh, he was coming my way. My friends all but forgotten, I took a step toward him and the scent of sin and citrus wafted into my nostrils.

Fuck, I'd always been a sucker for citrus.

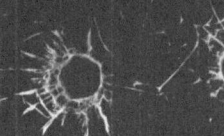

The corner of his lips tugged up. "Ciao."

Oh my wet panties. That Italian accent. Smooth and raspy. God, yes. Take me. Ravish me. Do something, *anything*.

"Hello," I greeted him, appearing cool and sophisticated, at least in my mind. All the while, my heart bounced within the walls of my rib cage like it was on steroids. Jesus Christ, so much hotness couldn't be healthy.

"Celebrating?" he asked, his eyebrows arching in mild interest. "By the looks of it, the fashion show went well."

Forget the fashion show, Daddy. If this man could just scoop me up and take me into a dark corner and make me come, I'd have something to celebrate. *Good God, get yourself together, Isla! No sex on the first date.* Although, technically this was the second time I saw him—in the same night, sure, but hey, just minor details. I tended not to get hung up on those.

"Yeah," I breathed, wondering what exactly he wanted. Somehow, it struck me that I wasn't his usual type. My eyes flickered past him to where he'd left his date. Thirties. Blonde hair. Legs that went on and on, almost reaching the sky, while mine stopped too close to the earth. God, she had to be, like, over six-four at least. Meanwhile little ol' me was barely pushing five foot four, and my ginger hair only screamed wild and untamed. Sure men had pursued me before, and I'd turned down my fair share of eligible bachelors who offered me riches on a silver platter, but that was just the way it was when you were constantly surrounded by the arts. You always had to read between the lines. They wanted to sample something new and exotic.

Yeah, something was fishy here. Why was this guy talking to me?

He closed the rest of the distance between us and my chest squeezed. I could feel the heat radiating from beneath his sophisticated tailored suit. He reminded me of my brothers, in some ways. Dark, brooding, intimidating.

None of which I cared for very much. Luckily for my brothers, I loved them anyway. This guy, however, had some crazy magnetic pull on me that I definitely didn't need. Just one look from him could steal the breath from my lungs.

I was S.C.R.E.W.E.D.

This was what all the stupid Disney movies were about. Handsome men who swooped in, made you do dumb, reckless stuff, and then left you. Disney just conveniently decided not to cover the last part.

As if he read my thoughts, his beautiful and oh-so-kissable lips curved into a smile, and every part of me melted into a puddle.

"Isla, we're gonna head to another bar," Athena shouted. "You coming?"

I waved my hand noncommittally, drowning in this stranger's dark gaze. "Yeah, I'll meet you there."

I didn't bother sparing her a look. I feared if I tore my eyes off this man, he'd disappear again and I'd miss my chance. For whatever ridiculous reason, it felt like I *needed* this chance.

I had to keep him in my vicinity.

To keep his heat. To keep his darkness. Just for a little while longer.

He studied me with the same interest, and I wondered what he saw. A drip of darkness that slithered through my light, slowly suffocating it? Or was it the sins I'd committed? The ghost of a smile passed his lips, and his dimples turned my stomach into warm goo. God, I had never been much into anatomy, but there was something so bewitching about his sharp jawline. The curves and edges of his face were ruthless. Between those cutthroat cheekbones and square chin was a mouth that must have been made for saying filthy things in the romance language. Even his straight nose was attractive.

Leisurely, I let my gaze travel down his tall, strong frame. I couldn't find a single flaw. His navy suit made him look severe. When my eyes wandered back up to his face, he cocked his head to the side, as if waiting for me to render my judgment.

I remained silent. Because really, what could I say? The man looked like a Roman god.

I averted my gaze to his hand, checking for a wedding band. At the confirmation of his bare fingers, silent relief washed over me. I'd never get involved with a married man, no matter how strongly our attraction brewed. That was a hard pass for me.

"Did I pass the test?" he mused, his accent sending tremors through me. I was a sad case if the sexy Italian accent alone was turning me on.

"I haven't decided yet," I quipped, lying through my teeth.

He jerked his arm, allowing the sleeve of his blazer to slide up as he glanced at his vintage Rolex. Growing up around wealth and living in Paris for the past several years, I was no stranger to opulence and spotted quality over gaudy easily. This man, he came from old money. He didn't need to flash it to emphasize his power. Maybe it was exactly that which attracted me.

"Better hurry up, little one," he mused, confident that he could make any woman's dreams come true. He probably could. "The sooner we get started, the sooner we'll both get to feel pleasure."

Oh. My. Freaking. God.

The way he was all businesslike talking about pleasure? That was an Italian man for you, it would seem. God, I needed to get laid. My first boyfriend was a disaster. I swore he almost shoved his penis in the wrong hole and scarred me for life. Obviously since then, I hadn't ventured to second, let alone third base with a boy. I'd been busy with shit and trying not to make the same mistakes again.

Either way, I'd bet my violin—my most precious possession—that this man knew exactly how to give and take pleasure.

My eyes darted around him to where the blonde bombshell stood. "Aren't you on a date?" I asked him, narrowing my eyes. "The last thing I need is a scene with a scorned woman screaming at me. God forbid it be in Italian. I wouldn't even know how to respond."

He offered me his hand. His poise unnerved yet fascinated me at the same time. "She didn't come with me, and she won't be leaving with me," he responded.

Fuck it. I wasn't usually the impulsive type, but tonight the stars were aligning. This was meant to be, I was certain of it.

So I slid my hand into his, his warmth instantly seeping into me and spreading all the way down to my toes. He leaned toward me, entering my personal space, and brushed his thumb along the column of my throat. A simple touch, but it sent my body into overdrive. Shudders rolled through me, and my entire body broke out in goose bumps.

His smile was predatory, and in response, my insides clenched, my panties dampening between my thighs. He leaned forward, his lips close to my ear, and whispered, "I'll make it good for you."

Without a single doubt in my mind, I knew he would.

Ten minutes later, we entered a fancy home. No, not a home. A mansion in the middle of Paris. Knowing what I knew about real estate in this city, I couldn't believe anyone aside from the French prime minister could afford something like this in the heart of Paris.

"What do you do, exactly?" I asked as my heels clicked against the marble. The whole house was dimly lit and soft Italian music drifted through the air. As if he'd always planned to bring someone home. Irrational jealousy slithered through me, but I smothered it down and focused on this incredibly gorgeous man, letting his presence bolster my spontaneous decision rather than make me second-guess it.

The moon glimmered in the sky, probably looking down and witnessing many one-night stands, laughing at all the ridiculous people looking for pleasure. Well, let the moon laugh. I'd be the one laughing when the sun rose as the most sated woman on this planet.

We climbed the stairs silently while my heart screamed, nearly bursting from my chest. My phone buzzed, or maybe it was his, but neither one of us paid it any mind. My knees trembled under the flirty yellow dress that Reina had designed for me.

Last night she handed it to me with the words, "I think it'll bring you good luck."

She was so fucking right.

Oh my gosh, I was doing this. I was really having a one-night stand. There was nothing unusual about a twenty-three-year-old having a one-night stand at least once in her lifetime. It was on everyone's bucket list, surely.

We entered the large dimly lit bedroom with accents of black and white everywhere. The door glided shut with a soft click, and before my next breath, he stalked toward me, his eyes cool and detached.

He cornered me against the wall, every step more eager than the last. My back pressed against the wall when a thought pushed through my desire.

"Hold on," I breathed nervously. He instantly stilled, which worked to reassure me, if only slightly. I could sense he wouldn't force me to do anything I didn't want. My pulse wrestled inside my throat while he watched me with that dark gaze that made me feel like I was drowning in deep waters. "I—I don't even know your name," I murmured.

He considered me with those eyes. "Enrico."

Was he—

No, he couldn't be. Enrico was a very common Italian name… right?

"Any other questions before we get started?" he asked in that deep accented voice.

My nostrils flared. He probably considered me a chick that flirted and had sex with strangers all the time. I wasn't, but it didn't really matter. I'd probably never see him again.

"No more questions," I answered. "You may proceed, *Enrico*."

Dark amusement flashed in his eyes, and something about seeing his mouth curve into a half-smile made my insides clench. Maybe I'd waited way too long to give sex another try, and now everything about this man made me want to orgasm. I wasn't a prude by any means. Nor shy. I'd been on plenty of dates, but the touching and kissing left me feeling flat. Until now. Nobody had ever sparked this flame within me and then fanned it into a full-blown inferno like this Italian stallion.

No wonder women went bananas for Italian men.

He cupped me through my dress and I whimpered, my body arching against the wall behind me. His thumb found my clit and dug its way through the fabric, pressing hard and massaging it in lazy circles.

A moan climbed up my throat and filled the space between us.

"Fuck, you're eager, *dolcezza*," he murmured, his lips skimming my throat.

"My name is Isla," I snapped back. "Not dolce-whatever."

A dark chuckle vibrated in his chest. "It means sweetheart in Italian."

"Oh." Fuck, if all Italian men looked like him, I should definitely learn the language.

He pulled away, studying my face as he removed his blazer. He kicked off his shoes next, and I anxiously waited for his shirt and pants to come off. They didn't. Not yet, anyhow, and his next move made me forget everything.

His body slammed against mine and our lips fused together. He was so much taller than me that it felt like I'd been swallowed whole by him. My eyes rolled into the back of my head from the pleasure that shot through me. Stars exploded behind my eyelids, and I wrapped my hands around his neck, clutching the collar of his shirt, pulling him closer. Needing more of him.

He hoisted me into his arms, and my legs wrapped around his waist. My heels fell against the hardwood floor with a thump. His fingers dug into my ass as I ground against him, lust igniting in my lower belly. When he rubbed his length against me, I lost all control. His body was like marble under my touch. I moaned, sinking my claws into him, needing so much more from him.

Enrico's lips were as soft as velvet when he slipped his tongue into my mouth. Another moan bubbled in my throat and he swallowed it, his hips rolling against my hot core. And by the feel of his hard—very hard—cock, he was well-endowed.

Each roll of his hips against my slit sent a shot of pleasure through me. We kissed like two needy humans. Maybe he'd been just as starved for touch as I was. Or maybe he just gave it his all when he fucked. Right now, it didn't matter to me. Like a greedy woman, I took everything.

He bit my lower lip hard before sucking the pain away. I cried out for more, grinding my body shamelessly against his. He slipped his hand between us and under my dress. He nudged my panties aside before slipping two fingers into me as my head fell back against the wall. An obscenely erotic noise filled the room. A noise that came from *me,* from how *wet* I was.

He growled, murmuring something in Italian. I was so far gone that I couldn't have cared less what he said. I just needed him to see this through. An involuntary groan escaped my lips when he dug his fingers deeper into me. Each time he thrust them in, he curled them and hit my G-spot.

He pulled his fingers out, and a whimper escaped me. My eyes shot open to find him staring at me. He looked put together, almost unaffected, but there was a dark gleam in his eyes that had my soul shaking from its dark promises.

His other hand traveled up to my breasts, twisting one nipple roughly through the thin fabric of my dress. "Isla," he drawled, bringing his fingers up and smearing my desire over my bottom lip. "Is that Russian?"

"Yes," I breathed. "No." I couldn't think straight. My brothers always insisted on keeping my Russian heritage a secret. "I grew up in California."

He returned his fingers to my pussy while he tasted me on my lips. "Your mouth tastes like sweetness, my *dolcezza*."

He skimmed his mouth over my lips, my jawline, and then down to my neck. Ignoring my inexperience, I brought my hand down to his zipper and pushed my palm against his huge cock. Jesus H. Christ.

There was no way he'd fit. He was built like one of those dicks in my favorite alien romance novels.

He must have sensed my panic, because he purred, "I set the pace, but you get the pleasure first."

It sounded like a good deal. Fuck if I knew. I was still hung up on his huge alien cock.

He slipped another finger into me—most of his hand—and I was so full I thought I was going to explode. He swallowed my moans with our filthy kiss as he kept thrusting his fingers into me until pleasure shot through me like a lightning bolt. I came all over his hand, shudders rolling down my spine, my body quickly turning into mush.

Enrico steadied me, taking my chin between his fingers and holding our gazes locked. "We have barely gotten started," he growled. "Are you ready for the next round?"

I watched him through half-lidded eyes. "I was born ready," I murmured, my voice hoarse.

"*Bene*." He seemed pleased with my answer, his eyes lasering in on me. "Now, I'm going to eat your pussy. You better taste as good as you look." Then he smiled smugly. "Although judging by the sweetness on your lips, I won't be disappointed."

Before I could even process his words, he braced me securely against the wall, then slid to his knees. Effortless and agile, like he was in his prime. Well, duh. The man *was* in his prime. In one swift movement, he flipped my dress up and pulled my panties down my legs and tossed them aside. He threw one of my legs over his shoulder and drove his tongue into me.

"Holy shit," I breathed, my eyes squeezing shut. He licked and sucked, rolling his tongue around my clit like it was a lollipop. "Oh my... God!"

His rumbled chuckle vibrated to my core as my hips arched into his mouth of their own will. Then he started fucking me with his tongue. I threaded my fingers through his hair and gripped it like both our sanities depended on it. It was my first experience with oral sex, and I swore to God right then and there, it wouldn't be my last.

I had been missing-the-fuck-out.

My head rolled against the wall as Enrico's mouth devoured me, and every noise from his throat brought me closer and closer to another orgasm. I clamped my thighs around his face, grinding against him like a wanton hussy. The sounds he made vibrated through me, making me think he might actually enjoy eating my pussy.

That thought alone pushed me over the edge. I felt it from the tips of my toes to the hairs on my head. It was like an electric shock, sending waves through my body and shipping me to heaven.

This man was a walking, talking, orgasm-producing phenom.

He closed his lips over my swollen clit and sucked it with force.

"Enrico!" I cried out, my entire body shaking violently as waves of pleasure smashed through me. This had to be sex-heaven.

My feet met the hardwood, the coolness standing in stark contrast to my heated skin. With a seductive zipping sound, my dress loosened and fell down my legs, pooling around my feet. I'd foregone a bra since the dress had a built-in one, and now I stood naked in front of him while he was still dressed.

Then, as I watched him under my lashes, my breathing labored, he stood up and got rid of his socks, followed by his dress pants and shirt. God, he'd been commando this whole time! My mouth watered at the sight of him naked. Olive skin covered every hard plane of muscle, making me salivate. I wanted to lick every inch of him.

I had no idea from where he produced a condom, but I was grateful at least one of us was thinking. The damn thing hadn't even crossed my mind. I watched him rip the wrapper with his teeth and roll it onto his length, and just the act of it was a whole new brand of porn.

"You know, if you recorded yourself rolling on a condom, I bet you'd make millions on an OnlyFans page," I rasped, my eyes locked on his shaft. "Or TikTok," I noted reluctantly.

"Don't worry about how I make my millions, little one." Crap, why did that turn me on even more?

Might as well. I hated the idea of anyone else seeing this man's naked body. I wanted to claim it as my own. Claw any bitch's eyes out if they dared look his way.

Jesus, that's kind of violent for a one-night stand, I mused in my head.

"Okay, then," I breathed, anticipation buzzing underneath my skin. "All for me and for free," I murmured, bringing my half-lidded, lust-filled gaze up to his.

His finger trailed over my breasts, twisting one nipple, then the other. My back arched into his touch. His musky scent overwhelmed me, and I realized I'd never be able to eat or smell anything citrusy without thinking about this. *Him!*

"Get on the chair," he ordered. The sound of his low, gravelly voice made my heart stutter.

My gaze flicked around the room until I saw the cream-colored chaise lounge he was referring to. It was close to the window and my heart hammered against my rib cage. I opened my mouth to question him, whether he really wanted me there, but the intense look in his eyes told me everything.

With my heartbeat drumming, I padded across the room and lowered myself onto the chair, its cool material like ice against my searing hot skin. Never removing my gaze from him, I scooted backward, watching him approach me like a predator ready to devour its prey.

"Open your legs."

A faint trickle of arousal made its way down my inner thighs. Good God. The man had made me climax twice already, and my pussy was still greedy for more.

"Don't make me repeat myself, *dolcezza*," he purred with a dark warning.

Fuck it. He wanted evidence of my arousal, he'd get it. I spread my legs wide open, leaning against the soft back of the chair.

"You going to get down on your knees for me again, Enrico?" I drawled lazily, my voice huskier than I'd like it to be. "Are you sure you're ready for the next round?"

Enrico's lips tugged up as though he actually found my temper amusing. Isla the Goddess. Or Isla the Temptress. *Lovely*. I, Isla, had officially lost my mind. Isla the Looney.

Despite being naked, he looked like a king as he walked toward me and, to my shock, proceeded to get down on his knees.

"Anything for my queen," he purred before burying his face into my pussy.

He ate my pussy like a starved man who knew this was his last meal. Again. He reached up and pinched my nipple, and a shudder rolled through me. My head fell back and my hips arched into his mouth.

We'd barely spoken six words to each other but here he was, down on his knees, telling me everything I needed to know. This man was a god on his knees and magnificent with his mouth. A flicker of moonlight sliced through the windows and cast sharp shadows across his face, highlighting the blaze of lust in his dark eyes. Wetness slicked my thighs, and every touch of his tongue on my oversensitive clit triggered another needy shiver. My core clenched and I panted, needing more than his mouth on my pussy.

He thrust two fingers inside me. In, out, in, out, faster and faster until my orgasm was impending. It gathered at the base of my spine before it exploded, just like that. He rose and leaned over me, grabbing my thighs and wrapping them around his waist. He slammed into me, all the way. A scream ripped from my throat, his big cock stretching me. My insides clenched around him as he fucked me through my orgasm. Tears sprung to my eyes at the intense pleasure building inside me.

He kept fucking me, my mindless whimpers and moans flowing as he pounded into me, mixing with his grunts.

"Ohhh... my... fucking... God."

His dark chuckle reverberated through me. "Not God, *dolcezza*. Say my name."

His left hand came to my throat, pressing me against the chair while he popped my left leg on his shoulder. On his next thrust, I screamed his name. Over and over again.

My nails dug into his forearms, clinging to him—or maybe to push him away, the pleasure too intense—but it only made him fuck me harder. Tension lined Enrico's face. Our groans and pants danced through the air, our bodies furiously slapping against each other. I registered the window once more, and just thinking about the whole of Paris watching us as we fucked like rabbits was enough to set me alight. Heat blazed hotter in my body, that familiar feeling building again. Holy fuck! Was it really possible to orgasm more than three times in one night?

This was like a catch-up for all the years of not giving sex another try. So freaking worth the wait.

I clenched around his length. He pressed harder against my throat, faint spots dancing across my vision, as his thrusts turned savage. Brutal. So fucking consuming, I felt ruined. For any other man.

Friction between our bodies built. Sweat gleamed on Enrico's forehead, and taut muscles corded his neck. He fucked me with full force, hitting my G-spot over and over again.

"Enrico, please," I sobbed as I fell apart.

"Your pussy feels so good," he growled. "I think I'll make it mine."

"Yes. Fuck, yes." I gasped. "Please... I'm going to... *Fuck!*"

I screamed as white-hot pleasure blazed through me. Every thought drifted away, leaving a numbness in its wake. He kept fucking me, hard and brutal, wringing another orgasm out of me, leaving me a boneless heap under him. My pussy convulsed around him with my third—maybe fourth, I didn't know—orgasm when Enrico finally came, his cock twitching and pulsing inside me.

We lay there—my leg still hooked on his shoulder—our breaths heavy, and him deep inside me. My eyes drooped, grinning like a fool, when his dark chuckle had my eyelids suddenly opening.

He scooped me up and carried me to the bed. As he laid me down, his big body hovered over mine, heating me like a blanket. Burying my face into his warm, tanned chest, I peppered it with kisses.

"I'm so happy you knew where to stick it," I murmured, smiling blissfully while a languid sensation pulled on my muscles. I'd never felt such peace come over me. Even when I played the violin.

"Excuse me?"

"Ugh, my first... ummm, sexual encounter. The guy didn't know what to do with his dick."

His hand—which I just realized was still wrapped around my neck—tightened its squeeze, and I found his dark gaze. "*Dolcezza*, this is your first and last warning. Never mention another man again."

I chuckled, slightly uncomfortable. I couldn't tell whether he was serious or not. "I guess it's true what they say about Italian men. You are a possessive bunch, huh?"

"You have no idea." He grinned seductively. Dangerously. "Now, I'm going to make you scream—again—and you'll never remember anyone else before me."

I barely had the energy to raise my eyebrow, although that didn't stop my mouth. "Bring. It. On."

When we finally collapsed into bed five hours later, I was thoroughly fucked. My lips were swollen and stubble marks covered every inch of my fair skin. Not to mention bite marks. I was sure the look on my face was testament to the fact that I had been to sex-heaven and back.

I woke up to dark eyes staring me down, five inches from my face. I screeched. She didn't. I scooted away like she was the plague, pulling the sheets up to my chin.

"What the fuck?" I hissed.

She didn't answer. In fact, she didn't even flinch. My eyes darted next to me to find the bed empty. Jesus, where in the hell was Enrico?

"Who are you?" I spat, glaring at the woman. She was pretty. Dark hair. Even darker eyes. Petite. Olive skin that made you jealous. It was easier to hide your emotions with that kind of skin complexion.

Again, no answer. "Where is Enrico?" I asked tiredly.

She reached over to the nightstand and all the wrong scenarios twisted in my mind. She was going to kill me. She was a psycho. I could see the front page already: "Jealous Ex-Lover Kills One-Night Stand."

Get yourself together, Isla, I scolded myself mentally.

I startled, jumping out of my skin, when she pulled a photograph out of her bag.

She flipped it over, and my heart stopped.

It was a wedding photo, the surface grainy and creased. And this woman... she was Enrico's wife.

Oh. My. Fucking. God.

THREE
ENRICO

I tapped my fingers impatiently against the mahogany table.
Cazzo, I didn't want to be here. I'd slept like a baby for the first time in almost three decades and then *this*.

Flicking a glance at Giulio, I gave him a barely noticeable nod, dismissing him. He'd been with our family for almost fifteen years, but I never kept any of my men in the room when discussing business with the other family heads.

Manuel, my uncle, being the only exception. *Cazzo*, at barely five years older than me, it pained me to call him my uncle. We were practically raised together, more like cousins.

"What is so urgent that it couldn't wait until tomorrow, Costello?" My tone was annoyed, but fuck, I left Botticelli's muse naked and sprawled out in my home because of this "urgent" request to meet.

Costello held a cigar in one hand, his dark hair and eyes holding my annoyance. Contrary to common belief, Costello wasn't Italian. Lykos Costello was the head of the Greek mob. Ever since his wife passed away, he spent most of his time in southern Greece with his children. His youngest, Aria Costello, had the biggest crush on my youngest son, Amadeo. At thirteen years old, he already believed himself to be a hustler when it came to the ladies. During Luca DiMauro's wedding to Margaret Callahan, she even went so far as to beat up some boys to defend him. It was something Enzo, my oldest, should have done. Family first. Always.

"Don't get pissy with me," he muttered. "I wouldn't have bothered you if it wasn't urgent."

Lykos wasn't usually the type to stir up drama. He kept to himself and focused on running his empire and raising his children. His sons were as old as mine, but his daughter was young and vulnerable.

"Okay, what's so urgent? I hope it's not your children." Being a single parent, I understood that vulnerability all too well.

"No, no. They're fine. Back in Greece."

I nodded, tapping my fingers and thinking again of the ginger-haired woman I left in my bed. I'd kept Isla up into the early morning hours, and I was certain she would be there, probably still asleep, when I got back.

I didn't dare ask myself why I didn't kick her out of my bed. I never let women sleep over, yet I didn't have the heart to wake this one up.

"The Corsican mafia intercepted my shipment from the States." He hated the French in general, and the Corsican mafia in particular.

"Were you planning on docking it here and taking the land route to Greece?" It seemed odd, but theoretically his shipment shouldn't have been so close to the shoreline for the Corsicans to intercept.

"When do I ever want to dock it in France?" he grumbled. "The ship had some technical issues and had to make an emergency stop. Just as we were within ten miles from the shoreline, the fuckers snatched the boat."

Well, that was the Corsican mafia for you. "What do you want me to do? I don't work with them."

"But you have docks in France," he remarked wryly. "I'm going to attack them and take it back. I'll need a temporary port here in France and one in Italy for ship repairs before it continues its way to Greece."

"That's a lot of favors," I deadpanned.

"I'll make it worth your while." Damn straight he would.

"What's on the ship?" It didn't escape me that he'd failed to mention that. When he remained silent, I narrowed my eyes on him. "It better not be flesh trading." Although I didn't think it would be.

His late wife had worked with victims of sex trafficking; she would have murdered him in his sleep if she even suspected he was involved in anything like this while she was still around. Nobody knew how the late Mrs. Costello died because everyone in the underworld knew better than to ask.

"It's not flesh," he assured me, then scoffed. "I must say, I find it a bit hypocritical, considering what Romero's into."

I shook my head. "He ended that shit." Only recently, but he didn't need to know that.

He furrowed his brows, then a thought must have occurred to him. "Well, shit. I didn't think many people could still surprise me." It turned out, he could. Truthfully, Romero had surprised me too. Only weeks ago, he'd come to me with the request to arrange a marriage between his youngest and Dante Leone. When I told him my condition—to end flesh trading—he admitted to what he'd been doing for the past few years. He feigned his involvement so he could easily eliminate those who actually were. The man was fucking brilliant, although it made me wonder what prompted the change of heart. "I didn't think he had it in him."

I shrugged, not echoing the sentiment. "Okay, so what's on the ship?"

"Drugs and guns."

"Twenty percent fee," I told him. "Ten upfront and ten when you get your shipment back."

He let out an incredulous laugh. "Damn Italians."

"Damn Greeks."

"Okay, deal."

We shook on it. "Is Aria still infatuated with Amadeo?" I mused, teasingly.

He rolled his eyes. "You better keep your sons away from my

daughter. One she wants to kill. One she wants to marry. Neither is acceptable."

I chuckled. "Best keep her locked up in Greece." Thank fuck I didn't have daughters to worry about.

It was another hour before I was home and making my way up the stairs, tugging on my tie and picturing how I'd take Botticelli's goddess—in my bed, on her hands and knees. I'd listen to her moan and scream my—

I came to a sudden stop. The bed was made, the room freshened up, and the scent of the woman I'd spent hours fucking was nowhere to be found.

"Manuel," I bellowed, agitated that I wasn't already climbing into my bed and finding heaven between the thighs of the ginger-haired goddess.

My right-hand man—and coincidentally my uncle—sauntered into the room like he didn't have a care in the world. And he probably didn't, which only increased my frustration more.

"Where is the woman?"

His brows furrowed. "What woman?"

"The one who was sleeping here," I gritted, clenching my teeth.

His eyebrow shot up. "You never let them spend the night."

My jaw clenched so hard, I could hear my teeth grinding. Why did he have to point out the obvious? "I let this one spend the night," I snapped. "Where the fuck is she?"

"How in the fuck should I know, *nipote*?" He rolled his eyes. "I just got in ten minutes ago."

My brows furrowed. "Where did you go?"

He shrugged. "That bitch Donatella showed up. I had to take her back to the nuthouse."

"Donatella was here?" My voice was eerily calm, but underneath that calmness, my fury thundered. He nodded his confirmation. "Did she come before or after the woman left?"

"Must have been after," he muttered, but it was clear by his expression that he didn't know. "I didn't see a woman here. If that psycho bitch saw her, she'd be dead."

Suspicion crawled up my spine, but I had bigger problems to deal with than a Renaissance goddess.

Donatella! Damn her, because her shit was the last thing I needed right now.

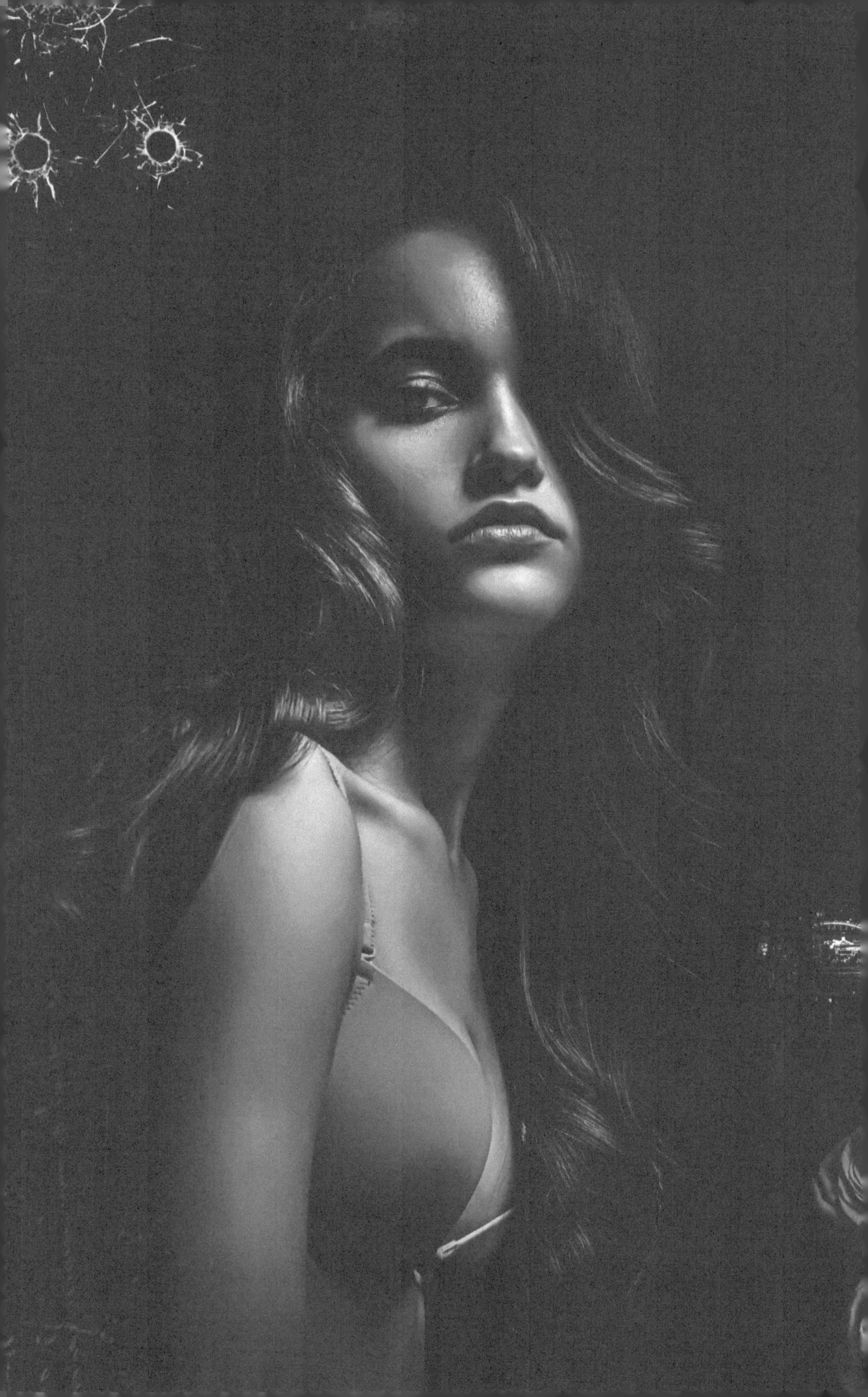

FOUR
ISLA

Walk of shame.

I experienced it for the first time in my life, and even the beautiful morning could do nothing to ease the sting of my sins. I had broken my rule: Never sleep with a man promised to another. I should have asked the question outright. I should have been more thorough.

I didn't want to end up like my mother, being second best to a man. I didn't know much about her, but what little I knew made me determined not to find myself in her shoes. Ever.

When I was a little girl, I questioned Illias, my big brother, why our father had never married my mother. He avoided the answer for years until I finally built up the courage to corner him.

The memory from when he'd visited me at boarding school came back to me as though it were yesterday.

"Isla, just drop it," he grumbled. My hand tugged on my brother's suit sleeve, making him groan in annoyance. Even at fifteen, my hand looked small and childlike on Illias's. "The dead deserve some peace, too, and talking about them won't bring you any answers."

"I should be the judge of that," I protested, my voice whiny. "I'm certain you know something, but you're being a stubborn pig."

"That's my job."

I shook my head. "No, your job is to tell me everything you know about our father. My mother. I deserve to know." His jaw clenched, but before he could say anything, I continued, "You know how shitty it feels not to know anything about your parents." I took a deep breath into my lungs. "Even a simple biological test on trait similarities to your parents. I don't know if I have them or not."

I could see the dark expression cross his features, and I thought I heard my brother's teeth grind.

Silence stretched. Other parents came and went, throwing us curious glances but neither one of us acknowledged them. As always, Illias had come to this parent-teacher conference as my guardian. Almost twenty years my senior, Illias had been my brother, my mother, and my father. My entire family. Our other brother, Maxim, helped too, but Illias always managed to fill the role more effectively. He had the aura of a god—tall, strong, and powerful. His dark hair and piercing obsidian gaze made it difficult for women to resist.

So of course, female teachers swooned over him and male teachers felt uneasy around him.

A soft breeze swept over the grounds of my school. I only had another ten minutes or so before he left and I'd have to get back to my dorm room. Reina and Phoenix were there already. Their father had come and gone, both of them relieved to be left alone.

I didn't mind it here, but I loved being home with my brothers. I loved being anywhere with them.

"You look like her," he finally said. "In fact, you're the spitting image of her."

My eyes widened. "Really?" A terse nod was my answer. "But you didn't like her?"

A muscle in his jaw tightened, and something bitter passed through his eyes.

"I didn't know her well enough or long enough."

I let out a frustrated breath. "Well, you knew her for at least nine months."

After all, it was at least that long that I cooked in her tummy, and I knew Father brought her home to Russia because that was where I was born. Plus, Illias was the one who helped the doctor deliver me.

"I didn't interact with her much," Illias retorted back dryly. "I was busy with running..." He faltered, and it felt like he almost slipped, but he quickly got himself together. "...the businesses Father neglected."

My shoulders slumped. Illias was always so in control, and I really wished he'd slip so I could get information. Any information, because I was certain he was hiding something.

He'd pulled me into a hug and his familiar scent seeped into my lungs. "Let it go, sestra. If not for you, then do it for me."

After that day, I never asked him again. I tried to learn some information about my mother when it was time to apply for my passport, but Illias had it magically worked up for me. And the renewals.

Thrusting my attention back to the present, I shoved the memory away. It didn't matter that I didn't know my parents. I had realized over my twenty-three years that I was luckier than most girls. At least I had protective brothers growing up who would've burned the world down for me.

I took a deep breath into my lungs, letting the fresh air and the distant notes of a familiar song seep into my blood. Paris in the morning was the best Paris. Locals sang old melodies as they prepared their shops for yet another day. The scent of croissants drifted along the cobblestone paths. The soft buzz of the city as it was just waking up. Fall was in the air, and the month of October didn't draw tourists as much as the summer months did. In my humble opinion, it was the best time to visit this city. The crowds started to thin in September, but by October, it was as if they were never here.

The smell of fall in the air, cooler temperatures, and the rustle of leaves under your feet made the city feel softer... more romantic. The drizzling, rainy days—like today—gave the impression that the city was weeping with you.

Not that I was crying or anything. It wasn't like I'd just had the best sex of my entire life, or anything. I knew that didn't mean much since it was only my second time, but something told me it'd be impossible to compare anyone else to him.

Enrico. *The cheating bastard.*

I wasn't entirely certain what pissed me off more: the fact that he was married, or that I couldn't have more time with him. To have him inside me. To have his mouth on me. Good Lord, the man fucked like a stallion. My insides clenched, already craving another taste of him.

I sound like a sex addict already, I thought as I entered the apartment building.

I saw the doors slide open, along with the telltale *Up* arrow flashing, and picked up speed so I wouldn't have to share the ride with anyone. A minute later, I tumbled out of the elevator that had to date at least a hundred years back. One of these days, it'd stop working. Hopefully when I was nowhere near it.

Feeling exhausted—from physical exertion and multiple orgasms—and smelling like him, I hoped for a way to sneak past everyone's rooms and into my own so I could have the morning to myself.

And re-evaluate what I had done. I sighed. What a fucking shame not to have one more night of Enrico. That had to be better sex than all my alien romances put together, and the fucker was married. Un-fucking-believable.

I pulled my key out of the secret compartment built into my dress. Thank God for Reina and her clever and practical designs that made me still look gorgeous. When I went to slide it into the keyhole, the door swung open, revealing a very pissed-off best friend whose eyes flashed like a thundering sky.

"Where have you been?"

I groaned. Wearing nothing but a tank top and shorts, Reina had her hands fisted on her waist and her eyes narrowed on me. Her heart-shaped face was framed by wild, golden curls that fell down her lower back. Her face free of makeup and her hair loose, she looked even younger than her twenty-one years. It reminded me of our boarding school days, except she was always up for parties back then. That was before Amon. This version of Reina was the result of Amon.

It made me want to strangle the man.

"Oh, hey," I greeted her sheepishly, hoping she couldn't see the markings of wild sex on me.

My best friend—incredibly beautiful and caring to a fault—was a do-gooder. And right now, she had nothing but worry on her face as she took me in, her eyes roaming all over me. She tended to concern herself with all of us girls, but I knew she was a subtle rebel. Although after what had happened with Amon, she hadn't been the same.

I kept waiting for the old Reina to come back, eager to see her bright smiles and carefree self appear. But as days, months, and years passed, I'd started to think we'd never see that version of her again.

"What is it with all of you disappearing one by one last night and then strolling in one by one at dawn?" My eyebrows shot up my hairline. Did we all get some last night?

"Phoenix too?" I asked.

"Yes, her too," she grumbled. "I was worried sick."

"Sorry. Is everyone sleeping, then?" God, I hoped so. I needed to take a shower, crawl into bed, and sleep for the next twenty-four hours straight. I had a solo performance tomorrow, and I couldn't afford to fall asleep midway through.

"No, we're having a family meeting."

Oh boy.

"Are you sure that's necessary?" I asked. Reina screwed up her little nose in response and gave me a "what do you think" look. I sighed tiredly. "All right. Let's go have this family meeting."

I kicked off my heels by the door as a relieved breath slipped through my lips. My feet were killing me. Instead of hitching a cab, I'd walked the ten blocks in an attempt to clear my head. It may have been the most amazing night of my life, but morning had brought the bitter truth to light.

It turned out I wasn't the last one laughing.

"You coming?" Reina glanced over her shoulder, flicking me a curious look. Probably because I stood like a statue staring into the wall.

"Yeah."

I followed her barefoot into our living room. We found Raven, Phoenix, and Athena sitting on the couch all huddled together and still wearing the same outfits from last night. At least I wasn't the only one who'd done the walk of shame today. Well, except for Reina.

"Okay, we have to establish some rules," Reina announced, while signing at the same time. She sat on the round ottoman by the window, her back to it. Sunrays flickered against her hair, casting hues of gold and making her appear like an angry angel. "I was up all fucking night worried about you four. I messaged you, attempted to track your phones. I almost called the police."

"Gosh, you are taking this mother thing too far," Raven muttered around a yawn. "We promise, next time—if there is one—we shall send a message in the middle of sex to ensure you know we're safe." She made sure to sign her declaration for Phoenix's sake.

Athena and I choked out a strangled laugh. At least we knew Raven had gotten laid.

"Can you imagine?" Athena muttered, stifling a yawn. "Please pause your ejaculation, I've got to send a message to my friend to let her know if I die, it's from an orgasm. Not a slit throat."

Another round of snickers followed.

"Stop it, all of you." Reina used her sternest voice. It was as if she'd lost her sense of humor overnight. "I'm not asking for anything so drastic. But a text letting me know you're hooking up would have been nice. You left me all alone, and then seeing—"

She cut herself off, her eyes widening a bit. Whatever had her upset must have happened last night.

"I'm sorry, Reina." I signed the words, my voice a whisper on my lips. I sat up straight and really looked at her. "Tell us what happened. Something—or someone—clearly upset you. We want to help."

She shook her head, blinking hard. Her shoulders slumped. She was too innocent for the heartache that always seemed to go her way. The past few years had been hard. She was the sunshine of our group. She loved hard, played hard, and was usually the most hopeful.

Until she ended up heartbroken and empty.

"Dad arranged a marriage between me and Dante." Barely a whisper as her shaking hands came up to follow her words. "Amon was there too." Her demeanor clearly spoke of the heaviness she carried. On both matters.

I swallowed. "Did he... Amon... did he say anything?"

She shook her head, her golden curls catching the light, and my heart hurt for her. It fucking hurt. If she married Dante, she'd be forced to see Amon. All. The. Fucking. Time. Because the Leone brothers were as close as the Romero sisters.

A thick silence gripped our throats, engulfing us.

"Are you going to go through with it?" I didn't know who asked, but we all thought it. "Considering what happened?"

"I don't have a choice," she stated.

"*Isn't that going a bit too far?*" Phoenix signed. She looked like she had been crying too. What the heck was going on? Phoenix wasn't easily upset. She'd developed a thick skin over the years, especially when she was younger and she first lost her hearing. Kids could be cruel sometimes, although they quickly learned if they fucked with Phoenix, they fucked with Reina and me. We didn't hesitate to get even. So if anyone had hurt Phoenix now, there'd be hell to pay, and we might have to resort to another murder. Geez, this shit was getting out of hand.

"Want to kill him?" Reina challenged her sister. "Because that's the only alternative."

"*No more killing.*" I'd have to agree with Phoenix. We still had nightmares from what we'd all done.

Reina sighed. "I'm not killing him, Phoenix. I'll marry Dante. I told you, I agreed to it."

Emotion flickered through Phoenix's eyes. It almost looked like... jealousy? No, it couldn't be. The sisters were close and always had each other's backs. But something was definitely up. Reina was more tense than a rubber band. Her face was pale, and if I didn't know any better, I'd say her swollen eyes had to do with more than her late night.

"What is truly going on?" I asked, my gaze darting between the Romero sisters. "There's something more at stake here." I was signing aggressively at this point, probably fucking up some of the meaning. I tended to do that when I was flustered. Or pissed off. "One of you is holding something back. And you'd both better tell me what, or I swear to God, I'll drag it out of you."

Phoenix's eyes, filled with so much sadness, darted to her sister. We all waited for her to say something. But Reina said nothing.

"*It's nothing*," Phoenix ended up answering.

I shook my head. "No, don't give me that. We're friends. A family. We've killed together, and damn it, we'll cry together too."

"Why can't we just all be happy together?" Raven muttered.

"Or eat together," Athena chimed in. "It always has to be 'kill together' like that's all we do."

"*Maybe we're sinners like our father*," Phoenix signed. Reina twisted her hands in her lap so hard her knuckles turned white, but she refused to take the bait. The Romero sisters were close with their father and loved him, despite some discord once in a while. When one said something against him, the other always—fucking always—defended him.

Reina covered her face and my heart clenched for her. The firecracker's light was dimming, slowly but surely, and it was difficult to watch.

I made my way to her, lowered to my knees, and wrapped my hands around her.

"You know what my brother Illias always says?" I murmured softly. From the corner of my eye, I saw Athena signing for Phoenix. "Strength is silent. Your resilience, Reina, is stellar, and I've seen your determination. You, Reina Romero, don't give up. So whether you marry Dante Leone or not, give that fucker your silence. It's the best response to people who don't deserve you."

"How do I marry Dante and want his brother at the same time?" Her shoulders shook gently, and I felt helpless. My morning's problems paled in comparison to this shit.

"Easy." It wasn't, but I wouldn't add more fuel to her misery. "You pretend you don't want him anymore until it starts to feel real. Show Amon what the fuck he lost."

The unfortunate part was that Dante would be the one to get her.

If you asked me, neither one of those assholes deserved her.

When I woke up later the same day to the sound of the vacuum cleaner, I knew everyone but Reina was asleep. That girl would start renovating our apartment if someone didn't get to her soon.

Phoenix couldn't hear her, and I had a feeling Athena and Raven had earbuds or earplugs in, so it left me to deal with Reina.

I walked into the living room, bleary-eyed and stifling a yawn, only to be shocked by the scene in front of me. My best friend had transformed the entire living room. The furniture wasn't where it had been before, the rugs had been moved, and the windows sparkled. Yes—they sparkled, even with the rain pattering against them.

Reina was going all wild, vacuuming like her life depended on it. Maybe it did, fuck if I knew. I padded over the rugs and hardwood, careful not to mess anything up or leave footprints. God forbid she started to clean all over again.

I patted her on the back and a soft squeal escaped her.

"Sorry, sorry," I muttered as she whirled around, holding the cord tight to her chest. It made it look like she was plugged in too—which would explain her manic energy.

"Fuck, Isla," she breathed. "You scared the living daylights out of me."

"Sorry."

Her curls were pulled up into a messy bun, and a white scarf was wrapped around it to keep her flying hair from her sweaty forehead. She wore blue jean overalls with a white T-shirt underneath, which made her look like a girl barely out of high school. Not a soon-to-be famous fashion designer. *And a wife,* my mind whispered. I cringed at the last thought and swiftly pushed it out of my mind. Whatever she'd end up being, she'd still pull it off. She could be smeared in coal and wearing rags and she'd still look stunning.

I took the vacuum from her hand and turned it off as she smiled sheepishly. "Too early for vacuuming?"

I didn't say anything, instead I just made my way to the couch and patted the seat next to me. "Sit here and talk to me."

She let out a choked laugh, but there was no humor in it. "You should have been a shrink," she grumbled under her breath as she reluctantly joined me. She threw herself on the couch, her head landing on the back cushions. "Okay, hit me."

She looked tired as I watched her eyelids flutter closed. It had been like this ever since Amon. Almost two years. She should have moved on by now, and looking in from the outside, you'd think she had. Except she wasn't the same. The girls and I had yet to figure out what happened. Even her sister didn't truly know. All we knew was that he broke her heart. Maybe even broke her. Or maybe it was that accident?

"What do you want to talk about?" I asked instead. Honestly, I didn't know where to start with her. Was she upset about Dante? Or Amon? Probably both.

She let out a heavy sigh and opened her eyes. Staring into them always made me think of the ocean. She and her sister had identical blue eyes, and not the kind you saw every day. Their depths were only matched by the Mediterranean Sea in Southern Italy.

"How about we talk about you?" Her response threw me and I tilted my head. "You were gone all night and came in this morning looking like you'd been to heaven and back." It was an accurate description. It felt like I'd gone to heaven, only to wake up in hell. With a scorned wife. "Unless you don't want to talk about it."

I shrugged. "There isn't much to tell. I saw this gorgeous guy at the fashion show yesterday…"

Reina perked up, her problems forgotten. "Who?"

I blushed a bit at the thought of him. "Well, I have his first name. Enrico."

Reina's mouth parted. "Marchetti?"

My brows scrunched. I had heard of Enrico Marchetti. Aside from him letting Reina use the venue for the fashion show, I, like most of Europe, knew him as the reclusive mogul who owned one of the most prestigious fashion houses of Italy. Among many other things.

No, that didn't seem right. He'd have been surrounded by fashion models and high-society women.

I shook my head. "We never got to last names, but it couldn't be

Enrico Marchetti. Anyhow, he kept staring and I blew him a kiss. You know, for staring. Besides, he was hot, and I didn't think I'd ever see him again. Unfortunately"—or fortunately, since the man was a freaking god in bed—"I saw him again. You girls called out to me, ready to go to the next club, and I told you I'd catch up."

"And you never did," she noted dryly. "You know, he could have been a serial killer."

I rolled my eyes. "Well, luckily he wasn't. Instead he was just a lousy cheater with an incredible dick."

Reina flushed red but waved her hand, dismissing my comment. "Okay, back to your night. Why unfortunately?" she inquired. When I gave her a blank stare, she clarified, "You said you ran into him again unfortunately."

I waved my hand. "Did you miss where I said 'a lousy cheater'? Anyhow, it doesn't matter. I'm certain it wasn't Enrico Marchetti. You always refer to him as older."

"Well, he is older. The man you are describing sounds older too."

I rolled my eyes at her rationale. "Not *that* old."

She shrugged her slim shoulders. "Enrico Marchetti might be in his forties, but he doesn't look it. And women throw themselves at him at every turn."

I gave her a pointed look. "Exactly. This guy was alone at the fashion show and again at the nightclub." He did have a gorgeous blonde there, but I left that part out. No sense in wasting time on minor details.

She tilted her head pensively. "That first nightclub we went to belongs to Enrico Marchetti," she muttered. "What does your Enrico look like?"

My heart raced in an unhealthy way before I could remind myself we were in Europe—names like his were a dime a dozen. And I didn't know much about Enrico Marchetti aside from what Reina told me when he'd granted her his venue, but apparently, he owned, like, half of Italy.

"Well, he was hot." Okay, that didn't say much. "He was tall. Dark hair, dark eyes. Slightly older. Strong jaw. Beautiful mouth." Reina giggled, but she didn't stop me. "Tiny bit of gray over his temples. But it only contributed to his persona, you know? Honestly, I have never seen a man so well dressed, aside from Illias." I mentally slapped myself, because I forgot the most important part. "Oh, and he's a cheater. I woke up naked to his wife staring me down."

Reina's expression turned puzzled. "Well, I was going to say with certainty that's Enrico Marchetti until you made that last statement. His wife died years ago."

"Well, I slept with a different Enrico, then. The married one." I drew my hand through my red curls. "It was amazing, Reina." My voice lowered a few notches, turning into a whisper. "This guy… oh my gosh… He knew what he was doing. I lost count of the number of orgasms I had. But waking up to that scene this morning… yeah, it was bad."

She didn't look sold. "Isla, there was only one Enrico in attendance at the fashion show yesterday. Enrico Marchetti. Older, tall, about six foot four. Super dark eyes. Kind of moody, intimidating. Navy custom-made suit with diamond cufflinks. It was Armani, by the way."

My mouth gaped as I stared at her in shock. Every piece of new information she gave me had me nodding my head so excessively I was worried I'd get whiplash. Well, everything but the Armani three-piece suit. I never got around to checking the label on it.

"Oh my gosh. I got laid by Enrico freaking Marchetti."

Reina chuckled. "And he's single. A father to two boys, but single."

Single father didn't bother me. Married man totally did.

I shook my head. "I'm telling you, Reina. The woman was his wife. She even showed me their wedding photo."

She shrugged. "I don't know. All I can tell you is that there was a funeral for Donatella Marchetti. In fact, there's kind of a sad tale going that the wives of Marchetti men end up dead. Killed. It goes back like four or five generations. It's the reason why some of them refuse to marry."

Good thing marriage wasn't on my mind. Only sex. If only it was sex with a single man.

"Hmmm." That made no sense. Maybe the woman photoshopped

the image. After all, anything was doable in today's day and age. "Do you have a photo of his dead wife?"

She shot me a wry look. "Yeah, I walk around with it in my wallet."

I pushed her playfully. "Wiseass."

Reaching to the side table, she grabbed her phone and pulled up Google. She typed, then typed again until an image came up.

"Here. This is her obituary."

I took her phone into my trembling hand and my eyes widened. "That's her!" My voice pitched higher. "Reina, this is the woman that was there. His wife."

My best friend's gaze darted between the screen and me, looking at me like I had lost my mind.

"She's dead, Isla," she whispered. "She couldn't have been there. She was killed alongside Marchetti's brother"—she looked down at the article again and read from the screen—"Enzo Lucian Marchetti."

"Enzo Marchetti," I murmured.

"Don't forget his middle name," she reminded me in a teasing tone.

"What's with that name?" I muttered, shaking my head. Then I realized how little it really mattered. "Never mind about their fancy names. I'm telling you, this woman," I said, pointing to the screen, "is her spitting fucking image. She was there this morning. Alive and well." And crazy, but whatever.

None of this made any sense. I didn't have a lengthy conversation with the crazy woman because I stormed out of there, slipping on my dress on-the-go. She screamed obscenities after me—in Italian—so I *knew* I saw her and heard her, yet the obituary was clear as day. She was dead.

My eyes skimmed over it once more. The death of Donatella Maria Marchetti, wife of Enrico Fausto Marchetti. Right next to it was the obituary for Enrico's brother, Enzo Marchetti. I skimmed the date. He died on the same day as Enrico's wife.

Reina took her phone back, her eyes skimming over the obituary while I tried to wrap my head around all of this. "It couldn't be a sister,

Donatella was an only child. Unless—" Her voice faltered and our gazes met.

"Unless?" I urged. She didn't seem too keen on finishing her thought. "Reina, what are you trying to say? Unless what? Don't make me drag it out of you."

"Well, the Marchettis are known for their connections to the mafia. Some even say they *are* the mafia."

My eyes widened. "I'm assuming you know this because of your dad?"

She nodded. "Of course, he thinks Phoenix and I are oblivious to it all."

Men were just idiots. Plain and simple. They thought these types of things could remain hidden forever. Everything—fucking everything—eventually came out. Just as I knew the deed my best friends and I did to protect Reina would come back to haunt us one day.

"But what does that have to do with his dead wife?" I rasped, my ears buzzing and my head spinning.

She chewed on her bottom lip, emotions flickering in her eyes. Almost as if she didn't want to say the next words.

"Maybe they made it look like she was dead to keep her protected." *That motherfucking, lying, gorgeous Italian!* "If she was considered dead, it'd be easier to keep her alive."

I should have been alarmed at the possibility that he was involved with the mafia. But no. My mind and my body railed against the fact that I couldn't have him again, and even more importantly that I'd slept with a married fucking man, no matter what the story was.

Jealousy and anger were a bad combo for someone with my temper. And Enrico Marchetti would learn just how bad if he ever crossed my path again.

FIVE
ENRICO

I watched the streets of Paris blur past, lampposts beginning to flicker on as night settled in. I was on my way to the Philharmonie de Paris. My mood was sour, and it matched the current weather, throwing gray shadows over this city of love.

But my mind was elsewhere. It searched for the ginger-haired woman who'd slipped through my fingers. It wasn't often—never, actually—that women walked away from me without bothering to get in touch. It piqued my interest. I wanted to taste her again. Feel her lips on mine. I needed to drink her sighs and swallow her whimpers.

Giulio drove swiftly in and out of traffic while my faded reflection stared back. Was it my face, or a stranger's face? It had all started to blur. It didn't really matter though, did it? It was for the good of our *famiglia*. A dynasty. The kings of Italy.

Except lately, it felt like a gold chain wrapped around my neck. Suffocating me.

My phone buzzed and I retrieved it out of my pocket. It was from my uncle.

Donatella secured.

I typed my message back.

>> Make sure she can't slip out again.

Of course.

Then my phone buzzed again.

See you at the Philharmonie.

Putting my phone away, I leaned back in my seat and pinched the bridge of my nose to ease this pressure behind my eyes. Maybe I was tired or maybe this anticipation that shit would blow up any minute was taking its toll on me.

I pushed my hand through my hair. Years ago, when it started to gray, I thought it'd dissuade women from hooking up with me. It didn't. Apparently, it was "in" to have salt-and-pepper hair, and women found it more appealing.

I inhaled a lungful of air. If they knew the fucked-up shit our family was into, they'd probably run screaming. The image of the girl with emerald eyes and ginger curls cascading down her back flashed in my mind. She seemed innocent. Pure. Even though the woman's sexual appetite matched my own, much to my delight.

Yet something about her intrigued me. A quiet, rebellious strength she projected without even trying.

Unlike another woman I knew.

Donatella Marchetti was a fucking curse on our family. Weak. Clingy. And catastrophic for everyone around her.

Like a goddamn leech, she refused to die. Instead, she made everyone's lives hell. Including her own. A fucking psycho. The only reason I kept her alive was for the fact she was Enzo and Amadeo's mother. I had hoped she'd get better with time and professional help, but she hadn't, and I couldn't help the bitterness that crept up whenever I thought of everything she'd done.

Having her locked away kept me from killing her, but it didn't stop me from wishing her dead. She stood on thin ice, very much like the mafia—with one major difference. She could be killed, the mafia couldn't.

Over the last ten years, the mafia organization in Italy had changed and adapted to the times. We as the five ruling families—Marchetti, DiMauro, Agosti, Romero, Leone—had developed a finely honed sense of loyalty among our citizens. At the cost of ourselves and our own families.

But now, we fucking thrived.

We divided Italy into five territories and worked together rather than against each other. But not only that, we went a step further and built ties with other powerful families. Konstantins. Callahans. Even the Ashfords through Kingston. The infamous Ghost.

It made us stronger and together we ran one of the most successful organizations in the world. The Thorns of Omertà.

Except nobody knew that little cracks had started to appear. First in the Marchetti family. Then with Luca DiMauro. Romero wasn't far behind, hence his eagerness to tie his youngest to Dante Leone. Agosti's presence in Italy was steady… enough.

Still we were stronger together than apart. We were powerful men and ruled with iron fists. United we could fend off the Bratva—good thing Illias Konstantin was part of our organization—the Corsican mafia, the Yakuza… and the list went on. Set apart, we'd be specs of dust against rival criminals in the underworld.

No matter what, together we would fight. Our children would merge bloodlines and we'd grow even more powerful. Nobody would dare turn on another family if their own children were involved.

The car came to a stop and my driver, who also happened to be my bodyguard, came around and opened the door for me. I gave Giulio a swift nod and made my way out of the car, straightening my jacket and heading up the stairs into one of the most esteemed concert halls in Paris, famous for its architecture. The Philharmonie de Paris.

People parted for me, some even shouting my name, each hoping for a glimpse of my attention as I made my way to my private box. I ignored them. It was just white fucking noise. To them, I was Enrico Marchetti, owner of one of the fashion powerhouses in Italy, as well as a few in France. They'd shit their pants if they knew about the other side of the Marchetti business.

I sensed Manuel's presence as he joined me, his steps in sync with mine, and his left hand in his pocket. For some reason, he never put both his hands in his pockets. My guess was it had to do with his paranoia of not being able to reach his gun in time. We all dealt with the death of my brother differently.

"I didn't take you for a symphony kind of guy," he remarked dryly. "Why the sudden change?"

I didn't bother shooting the coy fucker a look. We both knew well enough that I wasn't. My preferred pastime was listening to Bocelli in my home in Italy and drinking scotch or fine Italian wine, not coming to a crowded symphony and being gawked at.

But I hoped—against all odds—that the wild ginger-haired woman who had left my bed without a single note would be playing with this orchestra. Old man Romero mentioned that Reina's friend played with the orchestra and was highly sought after. It was a shot in the dark, but I was desperate to get her back into my bed.

One night wasn't enough. My dick demanded more of her tight pussy.

Fucking sue me.

"Were you able to find anything out?" I asked. "She was there with friends. Someone must know her. Did you ask other men from the Omertà who attended the show? I saw her talking to Reina Romero."

"Niente," Manuel muttered under his breath. *Nothing.* I bet it killed him, but it killed me more. I had tasked him with finding intel on the woman for me. It seemed everything about Isla kept coming back blank. "Aiden Callahan ran into an old acquaintance at the fashion show and disappeared. Romero had to deal with his daughters. Apparently he decided to drop the bomb about the arranged marriage the night of the fashion show."

"I'm guessing the girl wasn't too happy?"

Manuel shrugged, his brow arching and cutting thick creases into his broad forehead. "She agreed, so she must not have been too unhappy."

Even though Manuel was my uncle on my father's side, he was only five years older than me. But he never let me forget he was "wiser and older" than the rest of us. He'd been with my brother and me through thick and thin. He'd done a lot for us. For me. Without questions, without qualms.

That was what family meant to Italians: protect our own at all costs. And that was exactly what Zio Manuel did.

"How hard is it to find a woman?" Agitation suddenly coursed through me. The image of Isla came into my mind. She was... unexpected. Different. Fresh. After a lifetime of deceitful, greedy, and ruthless partners, she stood out like a fresh flower in a meadow. Or maybe a treasure.

She didn't have the typical beauty I was accustomed to. Hers was untainted and pure... but wild. Definitely wild. The vibrant hair and green eyes that sparkled with delight as she challenged me to get down on my knees. As if it was a hardship. Eating her pussy could easily be put in the top three favorite things I'd ever done. The first being the sensation of her folds strangling my cock. The second would be watching her suck my dick. I'd been too greedy for her pussy, though, and we never got around to her sucking me off.

A heady rush consumed me and something in my chest tightened with a warning. *Never get too close to a woman.* Our family and women didn't go hand in hand. Every woman who'd fallen in love and married a Marchetti man over the last five generations had ended up dead. *Or dead to me*, I thought bitterly. It was safer—for them and for us—to keep them at arm's length.

Our family was riddled with the thorns of death.

Or blood. Same goddamned thing. I recalled my father's heart-wrenching howls when he lost our mother. I'd heard the pain in Nonno Amadeo's voice every time he'd spoken about my nonna, but still he never regretted a moment of that pain.

Amore, my boy, is a blessing. We are what we love, mio figlio.

My brother never understood those words. I never understood it. But our father did. It was never more apparent than the day we buried my mamma who was shot while at the beach. Death came for our women everywhere.

Yet, I couldn't keep away from this one. I couldn't handle the distance from her with a clear mind. And the thought of never seeing her again sent a hollow ache throughout my chest.

It was no wonder though. I liked everything about her.

Her sassiness. Her submission. The way she challenged me and stirred something inside me without even trying. I didn't know what it was. Either way, I got a sense that challenges were as much her weakness as they were mine. And I was up for uncovering hers. The more mystery surrounding her identity, the more enticed I was.

Hence the reason for looking for her. I wasn't fucking done with her.

"In my humble opinion, maybe the woman doesn't want to be found," Manuel reasoned. This time I shot him a glare, which only drew a smile from him. "What? I kept talking and you weren't listening. I needed your attention."

My lips twisted wryly. "You sure know how to get it."

"I do," he agreed with that leisurely Italian gesture, a barely noticeable shrug. "The look on your face worries me though."

"What look?"

"The same look you get when you decide to take on a challenge. Or to solve a puzzle. The one that will get you into trouble. Whether with this woman or the entire underworld."

"Contrary to your belief," I drawled, "I'm never in trouble with women. It's the other way around. And secondly, that girl has nothing to do with the underworld, so we're safe there."

"How can you be so certain?" he challenged.

"She's too direct. Outspoken. Women in our world are usually wary of men like us. They have instincts to stay away from anyone like us. Isla didn't portray any of that fear."

Manuel laughed as we made our way into the box. "This woman intrigues you, but apparently you don't intrigue her, because she slipped out of the house without so much as a phone number or a love note."

He referred to the many previous times when love notes were left with a phone number, email, address—you name it—in hopes of a repeated rendezvous. I guessed payback was indeed a bitch, because I was fucking ready to throw a fucking rock with my phone number through Isla's window.

Wherever the fuck she was.

Both of us took our seats as I said, "I will find her. I might even bring her back to Italy with me."

Manuel's grin spread across his broad face as he clapped a hand on my shoulder, chuckling darkly.

"I can't wait to meet the woman who has broken that steel armor of yours without even trying."

"She hasn't broken anything," I noted, feigning nonchalance. "I just want to play with her a little bit longer."

A glimmer of intrigue flashed in his eyes, but I didn't think he bought my words.

Hell, I didn't think I bought them either.

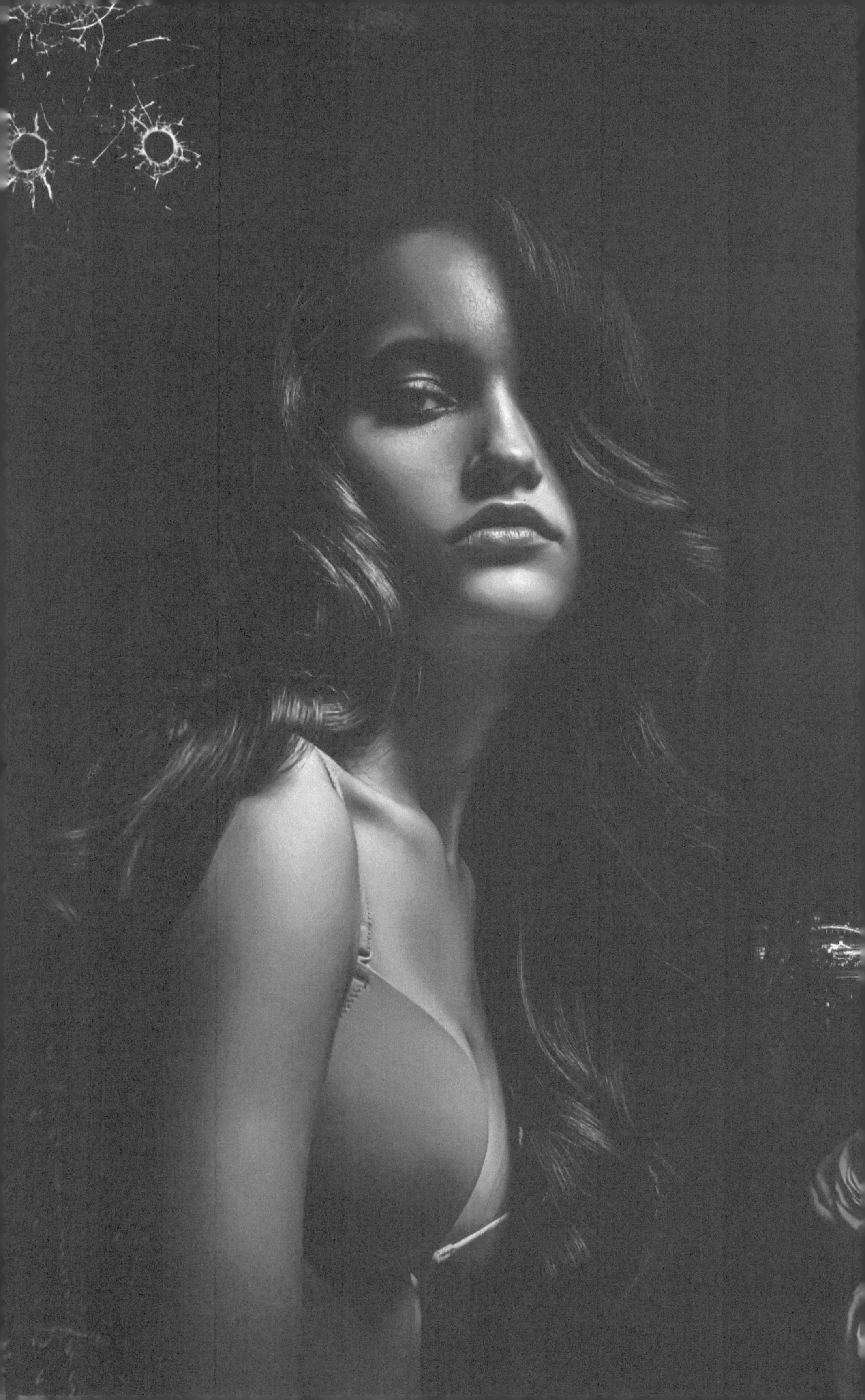

SIX
ISLA

Music was a big part of who I was.

From the moment a violin was put in my hands and I played my first note, I was sold on it. There was nothing else I wanted to do, and I spent hours, days, and weeks practicing. My brothers—Illias in particular—encouraged me to follow my passion.

I was seven when I received my first violin.

My music teacher just about had a heart attack when I strolled into class holding my very own Stradivarius violin.

Of course, Illias had done detailed research and got me the best out there. I wouldn't have known the difference. I still had it, and hoped that one day I'd get to pass it on to my children. The truth was that I couldn't bear to part with it. Nor the next one, or the one after that.

Drip. Drip. Drip.

My thoughts came to a halt as the rain droplets started—soft and cool. My friends and I ran inside the Philharmonie de Paris. The back entrance, of course. The manager of the building would have a cow if he saw me enter through the grand entrance.

The moment we were in the dark hallway, my friends whispered softly, "Break a leg." The only one who couldn't come tonight was

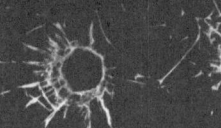

Reina. She had to meet with her fiancé. Phoenix offered to go along with her, but much to my surprise, Reina refused.

Just as Phoenix turned to leave, I tugged on her sleeve. Athena and Raven kept walking, unaware that I'd pulled Phoenix back.

"*Are you okay?*" I signed.

She nodded. "*I'm just worried about my sister.*"

My brows furrowed. It felt like a half-truth.

"*Are you sure it's just that?*" She nodded again, but I didn't believe her. The despair was etched in her expression and sadness lurked in her blue eyes. "*You can talk to me.*" I hated to see her unhappy. We'd been friends for a long time now. Almost a decade. It was a gradual friendship, but was sealed in blood two years ago. Now, it was ride or die, baby. "*When you're ready to talk, I'm here. All of us. No matter what it is.*"

We stood for a moment, and I thought she'd say something, but then she shook her head, as if convincing herself not to say another word.

"*I'm fine. Break a leg. I'll see you later.*"

With that, she turned around and went in search of our friends. People often wondered why Phoenix bothered coming to these events. Yes, she was legally deaf, but she could feel the vibrations from the sound waves. She could feel it roll over her skin and down to her bones, and I knew she enjoyed being surrounded by the beauty of it.

"Miss Evans, hurry up, this way." The event manager's panicked voice spurred me into action. I made my way down the long corridor to the backstage area and waited my turn in the wings. As I reached my position, the concertmaster walked on stage and led the orchestra in the tuning session that happened before any concert. Once everyone settled, the conductor took his place in front of me in preparation for our entrance.

"Are you ready, Miss Evans?" he asked with a smile. He was my favorite conductor. It was so much easier to work with him than some of the other pricks in the industry who thought themselves gods. This one was more down-to-earth.

I smiled in return. "Yes, I am."

I secured my violin in my hand and stepped onto the stage, taking my spot as the crowd burst into applause.

When the hall quieted, my mind shifted back to the first time I played—truly played—the violin. I refused to stop practicing until I could get one whole song right.

And I didn't go for "Ode to Joy" like everyone had suggested. I went for Beethoven's "Allegretto" and refused to stop until I got it perfect.

I still remembered that feeling; it came back each time I played.

The conductor nodded towards me to see if I was ready. I nodded back with a confident smile. Then...*Tap. Tap. Tap.*

The conductor announced the start, and I placed my instrument in position. The bow became part of me, and I closed my eyes as the notes danced in my mind. The first piece's melody echoed and everything left my body. The shift in the air swirled all around. Soft, peaceful feelings washed over me and my lips stretched into a smile.

A free, happy smile.

The violin felt like an extension of my soul as I played with all my heart. I didn't know how to play it any other way.

The notes sent a chill through my bones. When I played "Adagio" by Albinoni in G minor, I felt the heartbreak as if it were my own. I absorbed the sorrow and pain, sending shudders through me. I let go completely and thoroughly. It was the only time—aside from a few nights ago—when it felt like I was free-falling, drifting through the air along with the melody.

As the last note left my string, the sudden roaring applause startled me out of my dreamlike state. The spell was broken, interrupted by the loud cheers filling the hall. I opened my eyes and found the audience on their feet, some clapping vigorously while others discreetly wiped under their eyes.

My senses awoke. Even though I hadn't taken a step since I started playing, I needed to catch my breath. The musicians in the orchestra behind me released what sounded like a collective exhale, patting each other on the back while waving their bows in tribute as I acknowledged the audience. When I left the stage, the conductor, who had followed me off, walked over to me, took my hand, and smiled.

"You're a marvelous musical prodigy, Isla Evans. *Brava.*" He spoke with a heavy French accent, and my mind flitted to the man from two nights ago. *Enrico.*

A delightful shudder rolled down my spine. *Damn him.* How I'd felt that night was as close to playing a violin as I'd ever gotten. To taste something so close to perfection, only to realize it was tainted.

"You were magnificent," the conductor continued as he took my hand in his and kissed it. "I have yet to find another muse like you."

I smiled uncomfortably, fighting the urge to wipe my hand on my black knee-length dress—another one of Reina's designs. Black was my least favorite color, but it was flattering, and Reina had a way of adding a little creativity into her dresses. Like sunflower designs over the skirts. Or like the wide, white belt this one was styled with.

As the conductor talked and talked, I became vaguely aware of a presence in my periphery. I sensed eyes on me, so I turned around, nearly losing my breath.

Enrico was *here*.

I blinked once, twice. He didn't disappear. The man I slept with—a cheater—was entering the backstage area behind me, wearing a black three-piece suit with diamond cufflinks that glimmered. He looked composed, but there was a vibe around him that I'd missed before.

Danger. Ruthlessness.

It emanated from him in waves. I'd seen it before. In Mr. Romero. Even in my brother, although he tried to hide it. This man—just like them—was lethal.

How could I have missed that?

Probably because I was blinded by his beauty. That strong jaw. Sun-kissed skin. That body that put twenty-year-olds to shame.

Reina's words echoed through my mind, warning me. This man was involved with the mafia. His whole persona screamed trouble.

Shit, I had to get out of here.

"*Ma chérie,* you played exquisitely," the conductor continued, beaming as he took both my hands into his and squeezed them. I was sure my smile resembled a grimace more than anything.

"Thank you."

"You make grown men cry." He sniffled. "It hits me right in the heart."

Oh my gosh, I had to get out of here, or I might hit someone in their balls. I couldn't see that man again, or I wouldn't be liable for my actions.

"I hope you don't mind, Maestro Andrea. I couldn't resist meeting such a talented violinist."

I bit my tongue to stop a snarky comment like "I'd never met such a talented cheating bastard" escaping and letting the whole music community know I slept with the douchebag. Andrea's penchant for gossip made that of any grandma, housewife, and bored socialite combined look mild.

"Ah, Mr. Marchetti—" Oh, fuck me! Just like that, confirmation that Reina had been right. Not that I doubted her. I'd just hoped more than anything that she was wrong. God, why couldn't it be anyone else but Marchetti. Shit!

Two sets of eyes stared at me in anticipation as if I was supposed to say something. Maybe acknowledge his cheating ass? Well, I didn't want to. I wanted to smash my violin on his gorgeous head, and maybe dig his eyes out with my bow for good measure.

Jesus, violence had never been my thing. Until today apparently. Or that one time with Reina, but I refused to think about that right now. Or at all, as a matter of fact. It was the pact we made that night. Never to speak of it, and never to utter *his* name.

"Did you hear that, Miss Evans?" Andrea beamed like a 1000-watt light bulb.

I blinked. "Hear what?"

"Mr. Marchetti said he has never heard anyone play 'Albinoni' so exquisitely." I bet he wouldn't say that if I smacked him upside the head. The ringing in his ears would then be the best music he'd ever heard.

I wished I knew Italian curse words to utter, but I had to settle for

Russian as I flitted through every single one I had in my mental arsenal. And how dare he show up here looking so fucking hot. "Enrico Marchetti is one of our biggest donors," he added.

I bet he was. Fucking criminal.

"How lovely." I tilted my head, my lips twisting into something resembling a smile. I'd bet my life he could see it exactly for what it was. "Please excuse me."

Displeasure flashed in the conductor's eyes. I didn't give a shit. It was better than me saying something rude. Like calling him a deceitful, cheating scumbag. Without waiting for a response, I turned on my heel and headed for my friends. I had to get out of here.

Each step away from Enrico drew another relieved breath into my lungs. Every so often, I was stopped, congratulated, and asked to join an after-party. I nodded, answered with vague "maybes," and kept going.

My limbs shook, whether from the shock of seeing him again or the memories of that incredible night, I didn't know. All I knew was that seeing him had made me feel lightheaded. And not in a good way.

My thoughts scrambled and my mind elsewhere, I turned the corner and collided into a wall of muscle. I winced, taking a step back.

"Excuse me," I muttered at the same time that the masculine, citrusy scent registered. It was so unique, there was no misinterpreting who it was. Lifting my head slowly, I met his dark gaze, and then without a second thought, I turned and headed in the opposite direction.

"I wouldn't recommend you leave me for a third time, Isla," he stated casually. Fuck, why did his accent have to be so hot? "It will make me chase you all the more."

The sound of my name on his lips sent yet another shudder rolling through me. It reminded me of the ways he grunted my name as he—

I shook my head. No, I couldn't go there. That night had to be erased out of my mind like it never existed.

If only I didn't have to see him. It was hard not to notice how good he looked. One hand in the pocket of his black pants and the other by his side, he towered over me. The pose was casual, but it reminded me of a predator's. I could try and run, but he'd catch me. Sooner or later.

I'd have to deal with it. With him.

"Mr. Marchetti, what can I do for you?" I asked, thankful my voice didn't betray my scattered emotions. The way his lips curved in a sensual way had me cursing at my stupid question. "Actually, scratch that. I'm busy and my time is limited. There's nothing I will ever do for you. Now, why are you here?"

This guy could wreck me with a single strike, but I refused to play meek and nice. Fuck that shit. I'd go down fighting, even if it made me an idiot.

"Tick-tock," I said, tapping my foot impatiently. "I have many fans to give my time to, Mr. Marchetti."

Displeasure flickered across his expression every time I said his name so formally. So I kept doing it. Was I being petty? Probably. He should have thought about that before sleeping around on his wife. With me.

"Wrong, *dolcezza*. Your only fan is—and will be—me. From here on out." My jaw slackened and possibly landed on the floor as he added, "Don't act so surprised. You didn't think we were finished, did you?"

The scariest thing about this guy wasn't that ruthless, lethal energy that I could see clearly now. It was his deranged mental state. Because the Italian was L-O-C-O. Shit, was that Spanish? Either way, Spanish or Italian, it made him extremely dangerous.

"Listen, it was one night." *And you are married, you crazy fucking dipshit.* "I have standards, and there are certain lines I don't cross. I don't knowingly sleep with married or unavailable men," I spat. Nor criminals, but it was better not to push it too far. Criminals killed; cheaters didn't. I had a good enough excuse already. "To each their own, but you and I *are* finished. Finito!"

That had to be Italian, goddamn it!

"So you *have* met Donatella." Yes, that was his dead wife's name. Fuck this bullshit, I wanted out of this goddamn triangle. I didn't need more problems in my life.

"Excuse me, my friends—"

"No."

My eyebrows rose to my hairline. "No?"

"We are not finished." Something about him thinking that it was okay to use me as his disposable pleasure toy had my spine snapping into a painful line.

"Yes, we are," I hissed. "I don't have time for this shit, nor your deranged ass."

It was as if I hadn't spoken at all. "Have dinner with me, Isla."

"I'm not interested in having dinner with you," I sputtered.

Did he not hear that I wanted nothing to do with him? His face remained an inscrutable mask.

"Fine, then let's go straight to fucking."

"What?" I snapped, bewildered. Did I sleep with a lunatic? "I don't think so. You go... go and do your thing. As long as it's not with me. I am not the 'other woman,' and I'm not interested in being one," I said with as much dignity as I could muster.

"You won't be the other woman."

I bared my teeth, my patience running thin. "My answer remains the same." Then, in case he hadn't grasped it yet, "I. Am. Not. Interested."

I went to sidestep him when his hand wrapped around my wrist. My eyes lowered to where his strong fingers gripped me like a band of fire. Unlike most of the men I'd met, Enrico's hand wasn't smooth nor soft. It was rough, calloused, and it sent something boiling hot leaking into my bloodstream.

His touch—just like two nights ago—was heavy, firm, and experienced. It made me hyper aware of his proximity. The aftershave he used had my body tingling with sensations that I knew only he could extinguish. Or ignite into worse flames.

No, no, no.

I shook my head. He was married. It was a hard line for me. Everything in me revolted at the idea of being the other woman. I was an illegitimate daughter—an Evans, not a Konstantin, because my father had refused to marry my mother—and although I had no intention of having kids, we were nothing if not made of principles. *Right?*

He closed the small distance between us, towering over me, and it took all my courage not to cower. My senses were so heightened that his scent shot straight to my head and goose bumps broke out over my bare arms. He smelled so damn good—like citrus and spice. And I knew the man was spicy.

"Tell me what you want." His voice was dark. Seductive. It made it hard to process his words.

"What do you mean?" I breathed, blinking. He was intoxicating. If I didn't get away from the cheating devil, I'd ravish him in the first dark corner I could find.

"I want another night." I had no doubt this man got everything—fucking everything—he ever wanted. All he had to do was snap his fingers, and people obliged. I refused to be one of them, if not for the simple reason that it was wrong.

"Well, go have another night," I said sweetly. "With your wife. Or someone else. But it won't be with me." His grip on my wrist tightened. "Let go of me, or I'll make a scene."

The moment the words slipped through my lips, I knew it wouldn't matter to him. If he was in the mafia, I'd wager causing scenes was right up his alley.

His gaze traveled over me, slowly and sensually, and damn it, my body responded to the heat radiating from every inch of his big, muscled frame. My pulse kicked into high gear, and I watched as his gaze locked on the throbbing vein in my neck.

He smiled, those full lips curving smugly, but still his eyes flashed with darkness. The consuming kind that would refuse to let me go. I shivered in response. My eyes, half-lidded, met his, unable to break this pull he had on me. I imagined he knew it too.

He took a step closer, his sculpted body barely brushing against mine. Unable to move, I held my breath—waiting—as a hazy rush of lust pooled in my lower stomach. It pulled at my muscles, stretching me thin, and suddenly I worried whether I was strong enough to resist this man.

"Enrico, we have a—" The interruption was welcome. By me, at least. Judging by Enrico's expression, it wasn't perceived well by him. He was pissed off at the intruder. Fucker thought he got me.

He almost did.

I gave his chest a pat. *Bad move, Isla.* The feel of his hard, muscular chest under my palm lit sparks beneath my skin, sizzling me to my core.

"Mr. Marchetti, stop crowding me and annoying the shit out of me," I said sweetly, pulling my wrist from his grasp. I batted my eyelashes, ignoring the way my body burned. "Or I'll cut your balls off. *Capisce?*"

Now that was Italian, I was certain of it. God, where did that *Godfather* voice come from? All I had left to do was scratch my chin and I'd be a shoo-in for the role.

A spark of surprise and a touch of amusement lit in his dark gaze.

Not waiting for his comeback, I turned on my heel and rushed out of there like the entire mafia was on my heel. Probably was.

SEVEN
ENRICO

My heart was doing an odd little twisting thing. Or maybe it was my balls.

I didn't fucking know, but I knew that Isla scurrying away from me was not how I envisioned this. She was supposed to blush and let me take her home so I could ravish her soft, welcoming body all over again. The caveman in me wanted to listen to her whimpering and panting before screaming my name.

Jesus H. Christ. What the fuck happened?

While I stared after her, the red-haired minx didn't even glance back. That was fucking unacceptable.

"Ah, I see why you're obsessed, *nipote*."

I snorted. "Listen, *vecchio*." I knew he hated when I called him "old man" as much as I hated when he called me "nephew." We were more like cousins or even brothers, considering my parents had raised him. He was practically still in diapers—or running around naked at five years old, knowing my mother—when I was born, but he still found ways to remind me of our age disparity. "I am not obsessed with her." Fucking lies. By the look he gave me, he knew it too. As a rule of thumb, I never obsessed over women, but something about Isla intrigued me. "I want you to dig up everything there is on Miss Evans. Fucking everything."

At least we now had her last name. An identity. Ties to the symphony. Although, it should have been alarming that it hadn't come up when we searched through guest lists and entrants into my nightclub.

Manuel snickered, a cunning glimmer shining in his eyes. "And you claim you're not obsessed with her."

There was something about Isla that was unlike any other woman I had ever met. It made me want to drown in her. Maybe it was her innocence, or the way she shone when she played that fucking violin, but I wanted to let her fill every inch of my soul. I needed her to consume me.

"I just need ammunition to break through her resolve." I shot him a side glance. "Which brings me to the next concern. Donatella must have gotten to her."

"*Puttana*," he muttered. "I told you we should have killed her."

And I should have listened.

That fuckwit woman was determined to wreak havoc on Enzo and Amadeo, never mind me. In her delusional state, she thought she could fuck with all of us. Manuel would never know how much I wished I'd ended her that fucking night. I should have listened to him and planted a bullet between the whore's eyes right after she birthed Amadeo.

"What's done is done," I stated matter-of-factly. There wasn't much point in regret. "The issue at hand is that if Miss Evans talks, there will be a problem. To the world, Donatella is dead."

He was already typing a message to our contact who'd dig up everything there was on Isla for me. Best part, the contact was a woman, so there was little danger of her being fascinated by my red-haired *dolcezza*. I could ask Konstantin, but there were certain things I liked to keep private. Like my women. And if I knew the Russian at all, he was slightly preoccupied right now with chasing the wild Tatiana Nikolaev, so he'd be no good to me.

My phone buzzed, and I retrieved it.

"Ah, we have Lykos's shipment. No deaths. Must be a saint's day."

I spoke too soon, because another message came through. "*Figlia di puttana bastarda,*" I cursed savagely. "It seems it wasn't the Corsicans who intercepted the shipment. It was Sofia Volkov and her men."

Manuel let out a few curses of his own. "Did they catch anyone?"

I nodded. "Let's pay a visit to the bastard."

After a short flight on my private plane, we arrived at the docks in Le Havre—one of the few docks I owned in France. I found the Russian bastard strung up from the ceiling by his ankles.

After World War II, my great-grandfather bought seaside docks along the French coastline for strategic purposes. He'd had enough foresight to understand the value of its position during cross-Atlantic journeys. This particular dock was beneficial because Le Havre went on to become a UNESCO-listed port city, sitting at the mouth of the Seine. The properties had more than tripled in value.

On days such as this one, the docks came in handy for different reasons.

Back to the strung-up Russian hanging like a damn cow carcass five feet off the ground. He was bleeding from multiple knife wounds, which told me it was Kingston who'd been working on him. There was nobody like Kingston when it came to knives.

He knew exactly where to cut so the victim would bleed out, slowly and carefully. The victim could suffer a thousand cuts but he wouldn't die until Kingston was ready to slice his throat.

"Someone had too much fun," I muttered, flicking a curious look at Kingston. He leaned against the single column, wearing jeans, combat boots, and a leather jacket. There wasn't a speck of blood on him. He was that efficient.

"He kept speaking Russian," he said coolly. "Annoying the shit out of me."

Lykos Costello stood expressionless with his hands in his pockets as he studied the scene. Much like myself, he rarely did the torturing himself anymore. Only when there was a point to be made.

"Seems fair that you strung him up, then."

Kingston, also known within the Omertà as the Ghost and one of the best killers and trackers we had, wouldn't give a shit if I agreed or not. Funnily enough, Kingston and I made an alliance years ago. I'd have his back, and he'd have mine. He knew my secret—one of only two men on this planet who did—and I knew his.

I stepped through the cooling pool of blood as I crossed the concrete floor of the warehouse, stopping before the hanging Russian's head. His clothes hung off him, stained with blood. This was what happened to anyone who fucked with the Thorns of Omertà, and any families that had sworn allegiance to us.

My hand smashed against the Russian's skull, hitting him so hard he woke up from his unconscious state. His head jerked back as a painful yelp tore from his lips.

"Oh, I'm sorry, brutto figlio di puttana." *Ugly son of a bitch.* "Did I wake you up?" A sinister smile curved around my lips.

The Russian's pupils dilated with terror as his bloodshot eyes darted to me, then behind me to where Kingston stood casually.

I turned to address Kingston. "How long has he been hanging upside down? I'll be pissed off if he dies on us too soon."

Kingston shrugged his shoulders. "A minute or two."

Clearly, he didn't give a shit if he died on us in the next minute or not. Not that I could blame him. This hate for Sofia Volkov was his life's sole purpose.

"You ready to talk to us?" I asked the *stronzo* in front of me.

Before my father's untimely death, he'd taught me that our most powerful motivators when facing an enemy were fear and love. This guy was a coward, so pain would work just fine in getting information out of him. And if it didn't, we had a backup plan.

Manuel already had someone chasing it down.

"I don't know anything," he whimpered.

"We'll start easy, then," I drawled. "Your name."

"Fedor... Fedor Dostov."

"Excellent. I didn't feel like starting this conversation with lies," I deadpanned. Kingston had secured his name and his whole life story within the first five minutes of his capture. It was amazing how easy digging up people's information could be these days. All you needed was the digital image of a face.

Well, except when it came to Isla Evans, I thought wryly. Then you kept running into roadblocks.

"Who do you work for?"

"The Pakhan."

I grabbed him by the hair and tugged on it. "Wrong. She's not the Pakhan. Wannabe, maybe."

Fedor shook his head. "She... sh-she is."

What the fuck was with these men that followed her? What did she have that they found so appealing? It was like a goddamn cult, and she had them all convinced that she was the head of Bratva.

"Illias Konstantin is the Pakhan. Before him, it was his father who had overthrown the old Volkov. Sofia Volkov was never, in any fucking scenario, a Pakhan. Except maybe in her own head."

Manuel snickered beside me. "Nothing stinks worse than a desperate woman."

And Sofia Volkov stunk to high heaven.

I glanced over my shoulder. "Kingston, want to have another go at him?"

It had been only over the last few years that he reverted back to using his birth name. For the past two decades, he was known as the Ghost. Lethal. Deadly.

He pushed off the column and produced a knife out of somewhere. "I'm game."

I stepped back and watched with an indifferent expression as Kingston worked him expertly. The Russian screamed and yelled, but it was clear twenty minutes in that he wouldn't cave. It wasn't unusual for men who grew up in the underworld to be resistant to torture.

I studied Kingston inflicting pain on Fedor without emotion. A psychologist might have called us all psychopaths. Or suffering from dissociative behavior. They might have been right, but you had to dissociate to survive in the mafia. It was how Kingston had survived

Ivan Petrov and Sofia Volkov's years of imprisonment and torture. It was how I dealt with my brother's death.

Dissociation.

Manuel's phone buzzed and his eyes found mine as he nodded.

"Kingston, let's try another approach." I snapped my fingers, and Manuel stepped forward and presented the screen. I grabbed Fedor by the chin and forced him to look at it. "This is your daughter, isn't it?" I purred as I forced him to watch the footage that one of our men recorded of her through the window, completely oblivious of the danger lurking outside her home.

I didn't need to turn around to know Kingston had become a statue behind me. Of course we'd never hurt the girl. From all the information we had, she didn't even keep in touch with her father.

"You motherfucker," Fedor barked, finding the energy to jerk against the ropes. "You fucking motherfucker! She has nothing to do with this."

He thrashed against the ropes, the coarse material cutting into his wounds. More blood dripped onto the ground.

"You have all the power here, Fedor. Tell us why she attacked the ship and what her plan is."

To ensure he understood I meant it, I brought the screen closer to him. Fedor coughed as the knife Kingston had twisted in his ribs, fighting to breathe through the pain.

"Stop," he hissed, glaring at all of us.

"Save your daughter." Fedor slumped at my simple instruction, and I could tell we were finally getting somewhere. "Tell us what Sofia is planning, and what she wants"

"I don't know." He sighed, exhaustion seeping from his voice. "Not much, anyhow."

"I'll be the judge of that. Tell us what you know," I demanded. "Why attack this ship?" I gripped his hair, making sure the handful was taut against his scalp.

"End the underworld." He coughed up some blood, then repeated, "She wants to end the underworld, for her kid. That's all I know."

That was fucking bullshit. Someone who wanted to end organizations like ours didn't try to take power. Nor did they claim to be the Pakhan. And what was this shit about a kid? Sofia Volkov was just playing a game, and if my guess was right, she wanted all the fucking power.

I drew my gun from its holster and held it loosely as I studied Fedor's bloody face. "Give me the names of who else is involved, hmm?"

His eyes were trained on the heavy gun in my hand.

I inclined my head and cocked the gun. "In that case—"

"Wait, wait," he balked. "The Yakuza," he confessed on a shaky breath. "Itsuki Takahashi. That's all I know. I promise."

The fucking head of the Yakuza. Amon Takahashi-Leone's cousin. As cruel and sick as Itsuki Takahashi was, Amon was the opposite. He was the older, smarter, illegitimate cousin—the true heir to the Yakuza empire. Yes, he was the illegitimate son and settled for the second-in-command of the Yakuza organization, but it didn't erase the fact that he was the true heir to that organization. If only he'd seize it. Amon was also the slightly older—albeit by a few weeks—illegitimate brother to Dante Leone. Amon was owed a double crown, but he remained crownless. A Bitter Prince.

I narrowed my gaze at Fedor as I gestured with my matte black Glock G19.

"End him."

"Wait, wait," he pleaded, sucking in a deep, shuddering breath, before he whispered, "She has a mole in your organization. That's how she operates. She has moles everywhere."

Rage shot through me, fast and hot. It ripped my chest to shreds.

"Name," I gritted.

He shook his head. "I don't have it. Only Sofia knows the names, and she doesn't share them with anyone."

Then he was of no use to me. A shot rang out, echoing through the dark dock.

"Tell them not to touch his daughter," I instructed Manuel while flicking a look at Kingston. The frigid air rolled off him in waves. I kept my eyes on him as I switched to Italian and said, *"Stai bene?"* You good?

"Sì." Kingston was a man of few words.

It was the wrong time for him to have one of his episodes. Not that he could control them. I waited, studying his features to ensure his complexion didn't pale further. It was usually the first sign of his seizures. The episodes weren't pleasant to witness.

"I'm good," he repeated, his voice steadier this time.

I nodded.

"We have to find the mole," I declared. "Before it costs us all we've built. Only the four of us know about it." I fixed my gaze on Lykos, Kingston, and Manuel. "It doesn't leave this room until we find whoever it is."

And then that damn mole would pay with every drop of their blood.

EIGHT
ISLA

My life went on.

Somehow, I had divided my life into two sections: before Enrico and after him. Before the most incredible sex of my existence, and after... Damn him! It was almost worse knowing it was actually possible, and not just a thing of steamy novels.

It had been a week since I last saw him, but I couldn't shake off the feeling that I was being watched.

A few times, I swore I caught a glimpse of Donatella Marchetti on the street. But when I went after the person, they'd disappear, or turn out to be an innocent bystander simply roaming the streets of Paris. It made me edgy, but I was unsure what to do about it. I could call my big brother, but that seemed extreme. Besides, I'd have to admit to Illias that I slept with Enrico Marchetti, and that was a hard pass.

Instead, I just went on with my normal routine. Winter was approaching and the rehearsals at Opéra National de Paris for the upcoming performance of Tchaikovsky's *Swan Lake* took up most of my time. It would be performed over and over again over the holidays. It was my least favorite piece of his. The *1812 Overture* was my favorite. Not because it was the story of Napoleon's defeat at the hands of the Russian army, but because it portrayed so many complicated emotions. The distraught mood of the people after Napoleon declared war, that sorrowful harmony declaring the end was near.

It was late in the night, and all the girls were asleep. Except for me. I tossed and turned, unable to find rest. Usually, playing my violin soothed me, but it'd wake up the entire building, never mind my friends.

It left me staring at the dark ceiling, my mind scrambling with random thoughts, but always circling back to my mother.

Some girls grew up with daddy issues, but I didn't have that problem. Illias filled that hole with the role he played in my childhood. He was my brother, my father, my uncle. He even tried to fill the impossible role of my mother. Of course, I'd never tell him that he'd failed. He'd tried so fucking hard.

My mother.

She was an enigma. While Illias told me plenty about our father who was a ruthless businessman and had become unnecessarily cruel as he got older, he kept tightlipped about my mother. About who she was. Her lineage. Her parentage. She must have had one, yet he refused to share it with me.

I always had a sense he did it to protect me.

It was hard to just brush off. She was my mother. Every girl should know certain things about her mother. Did she love Father? Was she satisfied being second best? Because knowing bits and pieces that my brother Maxim had let slip, our father lost his mind when his and Illias's mother died. It made me wonder if he'd sought solace in my mother.

I sighed and turned to my side, staring at the landscape of Paris glimmering under the full moon.

All in all, I was a happy girl. I had great friends. We'd been through thick and thin. We always had each other's backs. And even though life might get complicated now that Reina was getting married, we were a unit. Always would be.

And I had wonderful brothers. I immediately winced. *One brother*. I had one brother left. Maxim died last summer, and while it hadn't come as a surprise—not after he'd been struggling for so many years with addiction issues—it still hurt. It still saddened me. I remembered him as he was before he fell into the abyss of drug abuse.

A soft knock against my door startled me, and I shot up on the mattress.

The door creaked—sounding much louder in the dead of the night—and Reina's curls of spun gold peeked through.

"Did I wake you?" she whispered.

I shook my head and patted a spot next to me on my queen-sized bed. "Nope. I can't sleep."

Shutting the door behind her with a soft click, she padded barefoot over to me. Reina was the youngest of us, appearing even younger now wearing her boy shorts and a white tank top. We all viewed her like a little sister we had to protect, even when she often acted more like our mother with her controlling ways. I wondered if maybe she wasn't the strongest one of all of us, while also the most vulnerable.

The mattress shifted as she climbed onto the bed. "I can't sleep either," she admitted.

I smiled sympathetically. "Engagement jitters?"

She shrugged. "I guess."

Watching her, I waited for her to say something. She pulled her knees to her chest and wrapped her arms around them, closing her eyes softly.

"Reina?"

"Hmmm."

I swallowed. "A-aren't you worried that Dante will find out what we did if you marry him?"

Under the light of the full moon, her blue eyes found mine in the dark and I could see anguish in them. The pained expression that flickered on her face.

"I should be worried about that," she whispered. "But all I worry about is Phoenix."

My brows furrowed, confusion washing over me.

"Your sister, Phoenix?" I asked stupidly, as if I knew another Phoenix.

She nodded, yet I still couldn't grasp the meaning behind it. What did Phoenix have to do with it?

"I don't follow," I admitted.

She let out a heavy sigh, her shoulders slumping. "She has a thing for Dante."

My eyes widened. "No," I gasped.

"Yes," she countered. She'd know. Reina and her sister were very close; sometimes it felt like they were twins. "I fucking hate it," she muttered. "I fell for Dante's brother and it almost killed me. Now my own sister is in love with Dante." She inhaled a deep breath, then slowly exhaled it.

"Dante—whom you're marrying," I stated incredulously. She nodded her head. Damn, talk about coincidences.

"This will end well," she added wryly, her tone full of sarcasm. "Anyhow, better me than her." Reina's voice was firm, but the tremor in her hands didn't escape me. "Dante would smother her. Destroy her. So I'll do this. We need the Leones' protection."

That didn't bode well for Reina either. Why was she always sacrificing herself? She and Phoenix should push back. Tell their father to fuck off. They didn't need him. They didn't need the Leone brothers either. Fucking pricks!

I knew things were different in the Romero family. Reina and Phoenix rarely discussed their father, but the little they said painted a fairly clear picture of the criminal organizations he belonged to. He kept them away from it all, probably to protect them, but Reina and Phoenix were a lot stronger than all three of the men combined.

I pushed my hand through my unruly hair. "Fuck. I never saw this coming."

"I wish I could say the same thing," she whispered absentmindedly.

"What do you mean?" I questioned her. "You knew Dante Leone was going to ask to marry you?"

"I had a feeling over the last few months that Papà was planning to marry one of us."

I watched her sympathetically. "And you knew it'd be you, not your sister."

"Yeah." Her fingers traced the threads of the bedsheets. Left and right. Up and down.

"Why don't you refuse?" I said softly. The question was dumb, because I knew the answer. "Maybe it will put the marriage on Phoenix, and since she already has a thing for him…"

She shook her head sadly. "Men like Dante consider anything less than perfection a fault. Papà said Dante found Phoenix lacking."

Red steam shot through my system, threatening to explode. I had to take several calming breaths before saying anything that I might regret. Like *Let's murder Dante and Amon.* Might as well wipe out the entire Leone family. We were nothing if not overachievers.

"That pisses me off so much," I grumbled under my breath. "You know, 'cause they are *so* fucking perfect. That tells me that Dante Leone is a fucking moron."

"I know."

"And Amon?" I questioned.

Reina's shoulders stiffened and the temperature in the room lowered a few degrees.

"What about him?" Her voice was as cold as winter in Siberia.

"You'll have to see him all the time," I pointed out. "What if Dante finds out about the history you two share? Or that you killed—"

Her hand shot to my mouth, her fingers pressing firmly, stopping the words from coming out. "Don't say it, Isla. Never utter those words."

I nodded and she removed her fingers from my lips. "I'm worried about you. He could use you as some kind of leverage. He could come after all of us."

She shook her head, those curls bouncing. "I'll never—fucking ever—tell anyone about your involvement in that mess. If it comes out, I did it all on my own. Do you hear what I'm saying?"

I let out a sardonic breath. "And you think I'd let you take the fall? You must not know me very well."

"It can't be any other way. Besides, I did it. I killed him. The rest of it—" She gulped, her delicate neck bobbing as she swallowed the lump in her throat. "Well, everything else is meaningless."

"Not exactly." I wouldn't call chopping up a man's body meaningless. "What if they find… the pieces?"

She chewed on her bottom lip. "Let's hope it doesn't happen. But if it does, you take care of Phoenix."

"Reina, nothing will—"

She shifted around so she was facing me on her knees as she took my face between her hands. Our eyes met, and while physically she looked so much younger than her twenty-one years, the look in her eyes was ancient. Exhausted.

"You promise me you'll watch over Phoenix," she whispered. "I mean it, Isla. No matter what happens, if any part of that body is found, I did it. Understood?"

The panic and anguish in her eyes had my heart squeezing. She deserved happiness after everything that happened. Yet it seemed as though life kept kicking her down. And by the expression on her face, she expected it to.

"I promise," I assured her.

But I'd find a way to ensure that body was never fucking found.

NINE
ENRICO

My phone buzzed. The dreaded number.

"*Cazzo*," I muttered as I grabbed it and slid it open.

The familiar scene started playing. Messy. Distorted. Parts of it were blocked by Manuel's and Kingston's bodies. My gut wrenched and my blood froze each time I watched it. I knew it by heart. I'd fucking lived it. It was always the same video. Yet, every time this fucking video came, I held my breath. I didn't pray. There was no saving the likes of me.

A red mist coated my vision as my eyes traced the movements on the surveillance. I saw the familiar body in the vehicle, and then the massive explosion that left nothing of it. Just memories and ash.

Violent anger shot through me, and I threw the phone across the room, where it hit the wall and cracked open. The pieces of it scattered all over the floor just as the door to my office flung open.

Manuel entered my office without knocking. As per usual.

Giulio was right behind him. Manuel grimaced before tracing the broken pieces with his eyes. He shook his head, but to his credit, he didn't comment.

"The file on your mystery woman," he said instead.

I glanced up from the desk. There was only one mystery woman. Isla Evans. Instantly, the haze in my brain began to clear.

Without delay, I dismissed Giulio. He was the guy in charge of cybersecurity and made sure every message coming in and out of my network was coded. I'd even gone so far as to test it with Illias Konstantin and Nico Morrelli. Neither one of the men were able to decode it. That was when I knew our network was secured, with Manuel and I being the only two who owned the passwords. Not even Giulio could access it, and he was the one who'd designed it.

"What took you so long?" I grumbled. I usually received information back in a day. It had been seven fucking days.

Manuel held out a folder that looked suspiciously thin and dropped into the chair across from my desk while I looked over the file. *Isla Evans*: *Mother unknown. Father unknown. Raised by a relative—again,* unknown. My brows furrowed as I skimmed through the pages that told me nothing.

"This cannot be all," I muttered, staring at the photos. The pictures portrayed a petite woman with a beautiful smile and wild ginger hair. But it was the mischief and quiet strength in her emerald gaze that pulled my attention.

Manuel shrugged. "I thought so too. Or maybe there isn't much to the girl."

There was so much to the girl that it threatened to steal my breath. So yeah, that comment made no fucking sense. Manuel had to be blind and deaf not to see there was so much more to her.

So I shook my head. "There has to be more," I hissed, shuffling through the photos and information. "She's friends with Reina and Phoenix Romero. Why isn't that in the file?"

"I don't know. We ran checks from all angles. Our contact even made it inside their apartment and snapped a few photographs."

My eyes darted through the photos until I locked on one and I froze.

"It can't be," I muttered. "No fucking way."

The photograph in my hand was taken inside Isla's apartment. I narrowed my eyes, bringing it closer. *No, it couldn't be.* Although it sure as shit looked like it. In my hands I held the photo of a frame that sat on Isla's bedside table.

In it, Isla stood holding a violin... between Maxim and Illias Konstantin. Barely reaching their chests, her grin was free and the happiness on her face was evident. Maybe the Konstantins were her sponsors. Albeit, it'd make it a small, very fucked-up world.

"What is it?"

I opened my drawer and dug around until I felt what I was looking for. "Check the frame in the photo," I told him, handing him the photograph and the magnifying glass. "Bottom right corner."

It took exactly four seconds for his eyes to widen. He met my gaze, and neither one of us uttered a word. The silence between us spoke volumes. There had been rumors circulating for decades that the Konstantin brothers had a sister. But it was always just that—a rumor.

Until now.

"Do you think Illias Konstantin is making a play at her?" he questioned, handing me the photo back. "Or is that his woman? She looks way too young for him, but if he groomed her from an early age, I'd say he's fucked up like his father."

I shook my head.

"No, that man is playing at Tatiana Nikolaev. He was ready to go to war if I didn't let her live." And from what I knew about Illias, he was nothing like his father. I'd stake my life on it. "I've known Illias for years, he's part of the Omertà for fuck's sake. How did he manage to keep this from us all?"

Manuel scoffed. "Everyone in Omertà has secrets. Big ones." He looked at me pointedly, referring to the one we shared.

"I want everything dug up on these two," I barked, annoyed that Isla had a connection to the Pakhan. It was an obstacle I didn't need. "Maybe the blackmail messages we've all been getting revolve around this girl."

"Or maybe he's using this girl to get to you." Manuel was suspicious of everyone outside our small circle. Just as I was. But I had good instincts, and they told me that wasn't the case. All of us in the Omertà had been getting scripted messages, threatening to expose us.

Ultimately, we all had secrets that we'd kill to keep exactly that. Secrets.

Illias was the Pakhan for good reason. He was whip-smart and powerful, and he didn't need to use anyone to get to me. If that was what he wanted, he would come after me head-on. No, there was something else at play here.

Besides, Isla had written me off when she learned of Donatella. If she was trying to get close to me, that wouldn't have mattered to her.

"So he raised her and then sent her into the lion's den?" I asked in a dry tone. That theory didn't make any sense, even if it explained why we couldn't find anything on Isla. Konstantin would know how to hide someone, and he was surely hiding Isla Evans. "I don't think so. She refused to have anything to do with me when I saw her again."

Manuel's lips tugged. "I admit, it's unusual to see a woman refuse you. I'm enjoying it."

"Is that jealousy I hear?" I snapped dryly. He was right, women never refused me, but it was the same with Manuel. He was forever a bachelor, sticking to short affairs with some of the most beautiful women in the world. "And I assure you, *vecchio*, I'd enjoy breaking your fingers."

He chuckled, completely unperturbed. "Why would I be jealous? I certainly don't want to experience a woman refusing me."

Wiseass.

"I know you're used to it, old man," I mocked, lowering my eyes back to one of the photographs of Isla Evans sitting in a folder on my desk. It was taken in the early days of her career. Jesus, she was young. Too young for me. It didn't stop me from wanting her though. To hell with age, I didn't give a shit who her connections were and who protected her, she'd be mine.

"Well, this old man isn't obsessed. You are." Manuel was having way too much fun with this shit.

Somehow it felt like obsession didn't even scratch the surface on this thing between that young woman and me. Each second and breath since I met her fed my fascination to the point of no return. I'd have her again, Konstantin or no. Even if it killed me.

But it might kill her, my mind whispered. I promptly shut it down.

"I'll have to pay Miss Evans a visit and see what her connection to Illias Konstantin is."

At least the other Konstantin—the weak one—was dead and gone.

"I'm sure it'll be a hardship." His tone was full of sarcasm. "Just watch your balls, *capisce*? She did warn you that she would cut them off."

"Maybe I should take your balls with me," I threatened half-seriously.

Manuel got up and walked away, flipping me the bird over his shoulder. "Try and get them, *nipote*."

"Watch it, old man."

The door shut behind him, taking the sound of his laughter all the way down the hallway with him.

Returning my attention to the photos, I hardened my resolve. It was inevitable we'd cross paths again. I'd wanted to see her for days. Now I had an excuse. Except, this wasn't the most pleasant reason for it.

One thing was for sure. If there was a connection between Isla and the Pakhan, the news of Donatella being alive could easily slip into the world.

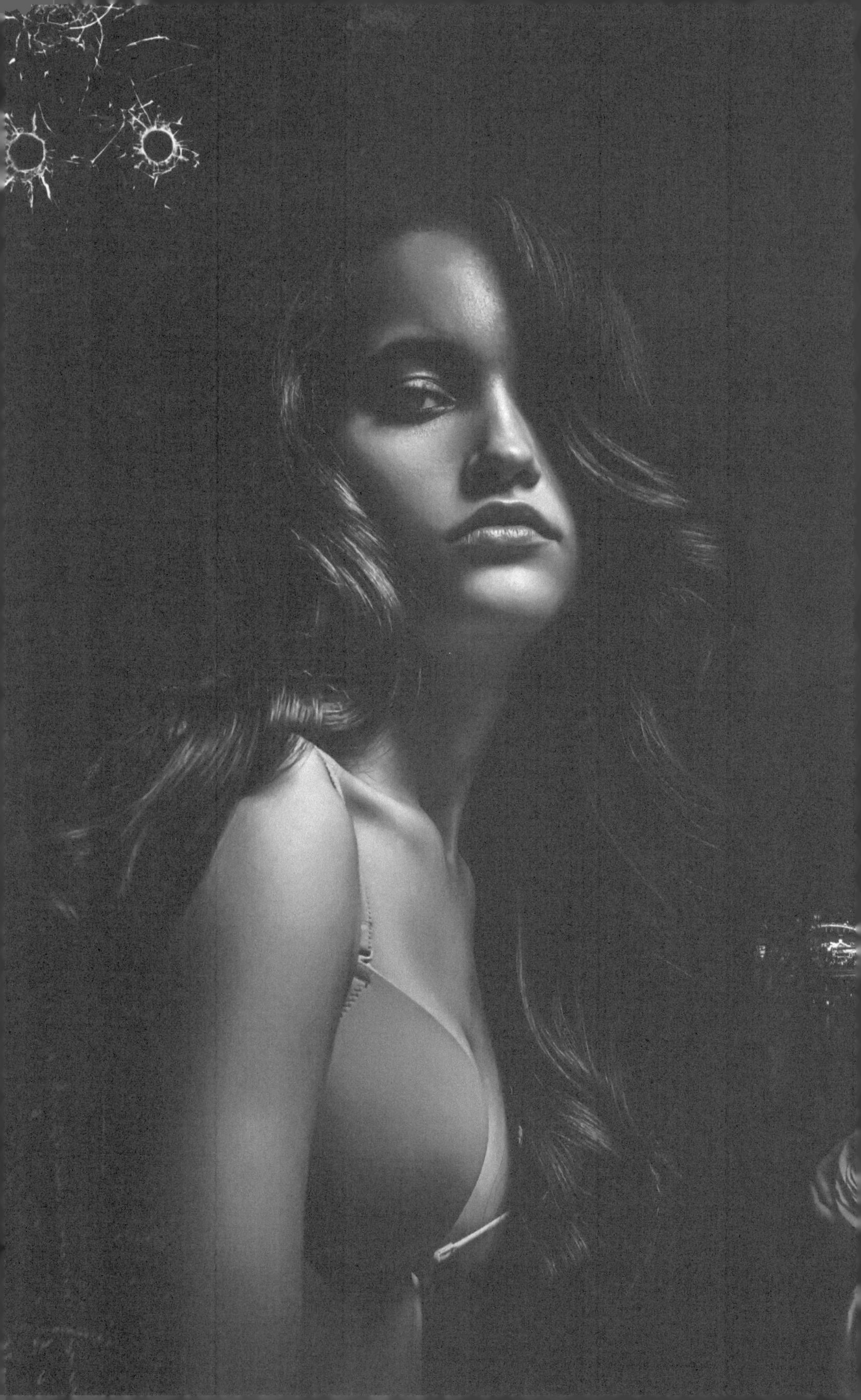

TEN
ISLA

I struggled with the two bags in my right hand as I reached into my pocket for my key.

If I stayed at my brother's place like he always insisted, I could get the doorman to bring all my groceries up. But then where would be the fun in that? This apartment belonged to me and my friends, and nobody could tell us what to do.

Except for the landlord, I thought dryly. And he was a creep. Just one of his many faults.

"Shit!" The two bags in my right hand slipped from my hold, apples rolling around the polished floors as I attempted to get the key in the door. "Why in the fuck is nobody home when I need them to be," I muttered under my breath.

"Need help?"

The familiar, deep, husky voice came from behind me—the one I'd been dreaming about ever since I bolted from him at the Philharmonie—and I whirled around coming face-to-face with him. *Him!*

Big dark eyes stared back at me, the ghost of a smile playing around his lips. It didn't strike me that he would smile a lot, but he should. It transformed his face into a Roman god. Like the Roman equivalent of Zeus. Shit… what was its name again?

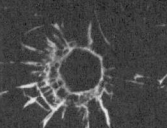

I shook my head. As if it mattered.

"What are you doing here?" I asked, kneeling down to collect my spilled groceries. He did the same, uncaring of his expensive suit as he knelt beside me. "I thought I made it quite clear last time that I wasn't interested in seeing you again."

Some men thrived on challenges, and I'd stake my life on Enrico being one of those. My refusal probably only pushed him to try harder.

"I came to see you." He handed me an apple, his fingers brushing against my palm. I could feel my cheeks flush, the images of the last time he touched me dancing through my mind. The way he'd watched from his knees, his head between my legs, eating my pussy. Our eyes locked and a smile crossed his face as if he could read my thoughts. The air crackled between us, and I felt ready to burst into flames.

Shit, I needed this guy gone. Stat.

"I'd rather you hadn't," I muttered. When his eyebrow shot up, I clarified, "Come to see me."

He didn't seem fazed by my statement. In fact, I'd bet my life and violin—my most prized possession—that this man never got frazzled.

"And why is that?"

Was he fucking with me? Suddenly my swooning was replaced with anger, and I shot up, my skull hitting his chin.

"Fuck," we both muttered at the same time. He rubbed his chin while I massaged my scalp.

"You okay?" He seemed genuinely concerned, but I refused to fall for it. That suave, handsome Italian face, strong body and—fuck, that mouth. It was all a mask. The guy was a cheater.

"I'd be better if you weren't here," I hissed, pissed off that my body warmed up under his scrutiny.

He ignored my biting comment, picked up the rest of the items from the ground, and took the bags out of my hand.

"You'll excuse me if I don't believe that," he remarked calmly. "Open the door, Isla, or we'll end up fucking in this hallway, and I don't really feel like giving your neighbors a show."

My cheeks burned. The nerve of this man. Yes, he had charisma, and I knew the most mouthwatering body hid under that custom-made suit. But the cheater was a scumbag no matter what body you put him into.

"Mr. Marchetti—"

"Enrico," he said, cutting me off and dipping his head with a breathtaking smile. "Please call me Enrico. You've screamed it plenty of times before. Too late to revert to formalities now."

I blinked, my mouth parting in shock. I couldn't decide whether that was being crude or hot. I needed to be smacked so reason would return. But there was nobody else around, and I couldn't very well smack myself. That might just send off some weird alarms—to this Italian daddy and to my own self-respect.

Someone cleared their throat and both of us lifted our heads to find Louis, my odd-as-fuck, creeper-peeper landlord watching our exchange with interest. All he needed was a chair and some popcorn.

Shaking my head and muttering under my breath, I finally pushed the key into the lock and opened the door. I kicked off my flats and continued into the apartment. Enrico shut the door behind him with his foot and followed me into the small kitchen with my bags.

I could feel him scoping the place out. It wasn't luxurious like the place my brother kept in the city, but this was mine and my best friends' home. It was our sanctuary—paid for with our own money—and nobody could tell us what we could or couldn't do.

He set the bags on the kitchen counter. I started to unpack them, hyper aware of the presence behind me.

"What do you want, Mr. Marchetti?" I asked, never pausing my movements. I didn't bother to look at him. It was too tempting to drown in his dark gaze. Maybe I was a weak woman, or maybe I was too susceptible to his practiced charm, but I couldn't risk standing chest to chest and falling into his arms.

The oddest part was that nobody had ever impacted me like this man.

"How much longer are you going to ignore me?" His deep voice carried a cold tenor, giving me a glimpse of the ruthless man Reina believed him to be. I silently cursed myself for being impulsive and falling into his bed.

I'd been so damn eager and willing.

I shut the fridge door and slowly turned around, facing him. My eyes skimmed over his broad shoulders and down his impeccable suit. He studied me, his gaze burning with lust as it singed my insides while butterflies fluttered in the pit of my stomach. My heart stilled for several beats, then sped into an unnatural rhythm.

"You have my attention, Mr. Marchetti," I said, keeping my voice toneless and sticking to formalities. I didn't want him to see the impact he had on me. "Now what?"

He stepped closer, the scent of his cologne reaching me. Instinctively, I took a step back, my back pressing against the fridge door. He took another step, and suddenly, all I could feel and smell was him. The scent of his aftershave seeped into my lungs, intoxicating and overwhelming. It was worse knowing how his mouth felt on my skin. How good he felt inside me.

His hand slid up my neck, fisting in my hair. He watched me through eyes too obscure to read, and though there was this lethal energy surrounding him, there was so much sex appeal too. I could taste it on my tongue. I could feel it in every fiber of my bones. I feared I'd combust into an orgasm just from the light brush of his body against mine.

"Now, we'll talk," he said, his mouth brushing against my earlobe. A hazy wave swarmed my mind and my eyelids grew heavy. "And then we'll fuck." A shiver ghosted my spine, and to my horror, I tilted my head to allow him better access.

His lips skimmed down my neck and a moan climbed up my throat. My heart was beating in my ears, and I hated myself for feeling this incredible desire for this man. His heat overwhelmed me while his touch seared through my skin, leaving my pulse crackling like sparks on the pavement.

"No." My voice was weak. He was too close. Not close enough. I turned my head to the side so I could breathe in air that wasn't *him*.

His mouth stopped trailing a burning path over my skin, and I hated myself for the pang of regret I felt. I didn't want him to stop, but I *needed* him to stop. I didn't want scraps. I wanted a love so deep that

I'd feel it in every cell of my body. And being the other woman never led to being the love of someone's life.

Enrico's lips pressed against my ear, words rough and his accent thick. "Tell me, *dolcezza*. What is stopping us?"

I let out a frustrated breath. "For starters, your wife." I couldn't even believe he'd ask the question. "I already told you I don't fuck around with married men."

He pulled away, his dark eyes finding mine. "I'm not married. There is no wife in my life that you need to worry about."

Disbelief filled me, and I fought an eye roll. "Right." I scoffed. There was still a small—very small—part of me that hoped Enrico Marchetti's wife was indeed dead and this was her delusional evil twin sister. Did it make me a good person to wish for something like that? Fuck no. Did it stop me from wishing for it? Unfortunately not, and fuck if I'd apologize. So I tested the fucker. "That's why your wife has been following me around all week. Because I have 'nothing' to worry about."

His shoulders stiffened and his gaze flickered with so much loathing that I felt myself pause at his strange reaction. He focused on my face, but something dark and dangerous in his eyes had me reeling.

"Who's been following you?" he asked in a controlled voice, but the vehemence of his voice touched my skin with a roughness that had goose bumps breaking out all over my body.

The change in him alarmed me, but I tried not to let it show.

"Your wife," I said, sarcasm lacing my voice. "The one that doesn't exist. Yet somehow the psycho bitch is following me."

Without warning, he released me and took a step back, leaving me disoriented and feeling raw. But it was his gaze that gave me chills. It was cold and dark. Downright terrifying.

He reached into his pocket and pulled out his phone. I watched as his fingers flew across the screen, and even dared to peek from the corner of my eye. Disappointment swelled inside me. He was typing in Italian. Damn him.

Maybe learning Italian should be in my distant future's plans.

Then he put his phone back in his pocket.

He lifted his gaze and cupped my face. "I'm taking care of it, and that woman will never bother you again."

"Not your wife, huh?" I asked, my voice deadpan.

Jesus, why did it bother me so much? It was just one night of hot, incredible sex. It wasn't as if I'd fallen in love with the man. I barely knew anything about him.

"I swear to you on the lives of my children, Amadeo and Enzo, that she is not my wife," he said, causing me to pause as uncertainty slithered through me, making me question myself. Nobody sane would ever swear on the lives of their children. He must have sensed an opening, because he continued. "That woman is sick and has been institutionalized, and she's not my wife."

The sincerity in his voice and those dark eyes fooled me.

ELEVEN
ENRICO

Porca puttana.

Donatella was turning into a major problem. I shot a message to Manuel instructing him to personally go check the facility where we had the woman stashed. If she was there, how in the fuck could she be following Isla?

The fury rang in my ears at the idea that Donatella would dare get close to my woman. *My fucking woman.*

Cazzo, that bitch was always in the way.

I—the head of the Marchetti family—had waited outside Isla's apartment for thirty minutes. I'd started to feel like a predator stalking its prey. Not that it had stopped me.

Just as I was about to call Manuel for a location on Isla, I saw her and followed her into the building. She looked so young wearing a casual outfit. Her flats gave her no extra height, and at five foot four, her small frame seemed swallowed by that wild hair of hers flying in the breeze. She was completely unaware of her surroundings; I couldn't picture her as the Pakhan's puppet to get information on me. The woman seemed too… angelic. Pure.

And that was how we found ourselves here. In her little apartment she shared with her friends.

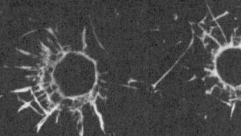

"I am *not* married." I emphasized the word "not," needing her to hear the truth in it.

She let out a heavy sigh. "But… I don't understand. I saw the wedding photo."

My chest twisted. Only Kingston and Manuel knew what happened that night. They were the only ones who knew the whole truth. I couldn't tell her… Not until she was part of the Omertà and bound to my family.

Enzo and Amadeo only knew that their mother was crazier than usual. Much to my dismay, I hadn't killed her. But still, I had to protect them.

I moved away from the kitchen and made my way back to her, crowding her space. She didn't seem to mind it at all. Instead she leaned into my palm like a cat seeking to be petted.

Isla's skin felt soft under my rough palms as I cupped her face, and I let myself drown in her deep green eyes. She was so damn young, although something in the way she carried herself seemed beyond her age. Her twenty-three to my forty-three. Despite everyone believing me to be forty-five. Fucking close enough. Age was just a number, wasn't that right?

Isla stood facing me, her defiance wilted a bit by my vow. I never fucked around with the lives of my family, and especially not when it came to Amadeo and Enzo. I was all they had left.

The slim column of her graceful throat worked as she swallowed, watching me as if deciding whether she should believe me. Finally she bit her lip. "So, you're not married?"

"Do you trust me?"

She let out a choked laugh. "I don't really know you."

"Sure you do," I said, brushing my lips over hers. "After all, you've seen every inch of me."

She gulped, a flush working its way over her creamy skin. "That night is kind of hazy."

I chuckled.

"A reminder, then."

It was a half-teasing, half-serious attempt to break this tension that brewed between us. It would be better for both of us if this sizzling attraction were nonexistent. But here we were, drowning in it like it was our lifeline. At least, I knew it was my lifeline. A reason that I had been searching for.

"So is it true?" she muttered, her eyes cautiously on me.

"What's that, *dolcezza*?"

"That you're mafia."

The Marchetti empire was built on our history in the underworld and, while we'd established many legitimate businesses, we were still heavily involved. Once in Omertà, the only way out was through death. What they failed to tell you was that they meant death *of the entire bloodline*. It wasn't what I wanted for myself nor my children. I had never signed up for this life, yet it found me. And when I was dead and gone, it'd find Amadeo and Enzo. It was the way of life in Omertà. Those were the thorns.

I couldn't admit it to her, even though she obviously had her own connections to it. Maybe unknowingly, or maybe she was just a phenomenal actress.

"Don't be afraid. I'll never hurt you, Isla." Then because I couldn't resist, I added, "Not unless it involves giving you mind-blowing pleasure."

Isla's eyes widened and her mouth gaped, tempting me with the image of my cock sliding between those plump lips. Her cheeks flushed crimson, almost matching the shade of her beautiful bright hair. My fingers itched to touch her long locks, spilling in waves of coppery silk down her back and wrapping them around my fist.

I forced that vivid image out of my mind. I didn't need a hard-on while trying to work this out with her. We might not end up in a church with wedding bells, but like a schoolboy, I wanted to keep her as mine.

I really needed to pull my head out of my ass, but I feared it was too late. This minx cast a spell on me, and there was no getting away. Her small palms came to my chest and she gently nudged me away.

"Umm, want to sit down?" she offered. "I was going to fix myself some lunch. Do you want some?"

My lips tugged up. "I'd rather have *you* for lunch."

Her beautiful face turned an even deeper shade of red, and I fucking loved it. I couldn't remember the last time I enjoyed seeing a woman's reaction so much. She was so close to me that I could count every little freckle as she stared up at me.

Reaching out, I twirled a piece of her hair around my finger, marveling at its softness and the variation of lights reflecting in it.

Her gaze locked on my face, pure innocence and marvel in her features. If I were a better man, I'd let her go. Move on. But I was far from a good man. And when it came to her, I was selfish as fuck.

I released her ginger curl, throwing off the colors of a burning sunset, and watched in fascination as it bounced softly. Slowly, I dragged my thumb across her lips. Our first night together was rushed, filled with hunger and lust. Today, I wanted to worship her and see those emerald depths haze over with pleasure.

I wanted to take care of her and wreck her at the same time, only to put her back together so she'd learn who she belonged to.

"We can arrange that," she said in a breathy voice. Fuck, the way my heart tripped should have been my warning. I'd had plenty of women in my life. They never had my pulse racing, not like this. Yet this young woman had all these unfamiliar emotions bouncing around in my chest. "But first you're going to eat the lunch that I prepare for you."

My chest grew warm at the playful expression in her eyes, and I smiled at her eagerness to cook for me.

"You know, in my country, cooking is synonymous with care," I drawled.

She rolled her eyes. "Well, Enrico. We're in France now. Lunch is the time to converse and learn things about each other."

A sardonic breath left me. "Very well, *dolcezza*. Let's converse, and then we'll fuck."

Her blush disappeared under her clothes. My gaze trailed down her neck over her one exposed shoulder and I watched in fascination as her blush disappeared, hidden by her white, off-the-shoulder sweater. It hung loosely over the black leggings she paired it with.

I slid off my jacket and hung it on one of the five chairs that sat around the island.

"Okay, Isla," I said. "Tell me what we're fixing for lunch. I'll let you boss me around in the kitchen."

She chuckled, her eyes glimmering. "Damn straight, Mr. Marchetti. You're at my place; you follow my rules."

"You live here alone?" I asked curiously, although I already knew the answer. I wanted to see what Isla Evans was about.

"No, my best friends and I rent this place. We wanted something of our own."

"Ah."

She tilted her head, studying me. "And you? Live alone?"

"Here in Paris, for the most part. Back in Italy, I have two sons and a few other family members"—and guards, but I kept that to myself—"who all live on my property."

"That would drive me nuts," she muttered. "Aside from the kids. I bet somebody's always in your business."

"No, not really." Aside from Manuel, nobody dared get into my business. I kept my tone light and casual, but there was so much that hung in the air. Secrets. Questions. It was clear she was testing me when she asked questions about Donatella. It was my turn to test her. "How about you? Any family?"

She opened the fridge door and bent over, her hand holding on to the handle as she started grabbing contents with her free hand. "Yeah, I have two bro—" Her movements paused and her voice faltered before she gave her head a subtle shake. "One brother."

I still couldn't believe the rumors that had been circling the underworld for years about an illegitimate daughter by the old Konstantin were true. There were no signs of her, so I chalked it up to being just that. Rumors. Except now... Could Isla be their sister? She didn't resemble them at all, yet my instinct warned.

I was rarely wrong. It was how I stayed alive for so long, despite the odds. I was certain now that Isla was Illias's little sister. It turned out the rumors running around all those years were true after all.

"You close with him? Or them, is it?"

She turned her head, and the sadness in her eyes was like a punch in the gut. Her eyes glazed over and her delicate throat bobbed as she gave me a shaky smile.

"I had a brother who passed away." Her bottom lip trembled, and it was another confirmation that Isla was Konstantin's little sister. Me sleeping with his sister wouldn't go over well. Not that I planned on enlightening him. The man was busy with his woman, Tatiana Nikolaev, for now. "I still have Illias, and I've always been closer with him."

Ah, fuck! There was my confirmation.

"I'm sorry," I murmured. Maxim was a loose cannon, and it was only a matter of time before he got himself killed. The drugs just about fried his brain. And then he had to go fuck with Sasha Nikolaev. "I know how much it hurts to lose a sibling."

Her hand reached out and came to rest on mine. The tenderness of her touch softened something inside my chest. Something I desperately wished would stay hard as stone.

"How long ago did you lose your brother?"

"Long time," I muttered. "But it still hurts. I see us in my sons' faces. They remind me of us when we were children."

She smiled, compassion shimmering off of her. "Were you and your brother close in age?"

I nodded. "Just a year and a half apart. Kind of like Enzo and Amadeo."

"I'm sorry," she murmured, squeezing my hand. "You must have been close, growing up like that. Mine were much older than me. They acted more like my parents."

Another confirmation. *I'd taken Isla Konstantin to bed.* Shit, this would start a war. But before I could let myself spiral, a thought popped in my head.

Marriage.

It was never something I contemplated, considering every Marchetti's marriage ended in death, but now it could bring dual benefits. This woman would be tied to me and my bed, and Illias would be my ally.

I studied her pensively, something about all that perfection wrapped up in that petite body made me eager to claim her. Own her. Even break her, only to put her back together.

But underneath it all, my reason warned. *Every wife that loves a Marchetti dies.* I didn't want anything to happen to Isla. Her sunshine shone brightly, from the way she took up space in the room, to the way she stood her ground with me. I didn't want to see it extinguished.

There was a reason not many families were eager to tie themselves to ours. The last bride—Donatella—was mentally unstable. Evil, even. Her family did a good job of hiding it, and it took several years for our family to catch on.

"Okay, let's get our lunch going," I offered, switching to a lighter topic.

She handed me an avocado, and for the next ten minutes, we worked in tandem. It was clear Isla had no qualms in the kitchen and was used to taking care of herself.

"You often cook?" I asked her as I cut the celery she handed me.

She shrugged her one bare shoulder. "I try, but I'm not great at it. Maybe I need more practice."

She slid on a pair of funny-looking glasses—more like goggles—and started chopping onions with a serious expression, all businesslike.

"What are you doing?" I asked, staring at her in shock. She looked like she was about to jump into a pool with those things on her face. Like a kid playing grown-up.

She lifted her face and gave me a sheepish smile. "I don't want to cry."

Silence stretched for two heartbeats. I threw my head back and laughed. She burst into a giggle too. It evolved into a full-blown, happy laugh, and I smiled as I listened to it, my own chest shaking.

She pulled her goggles off, still grinning. "I have to say, I've seen a lot of women cook," I mused. "But nobody—fucking ever—comes close to you."

She winked, chuckling. "I'm a special kind of woman."

I smirked. "The best kind. Now, how about plates?"

She reached into the cabinet, pulled out two plates, and set them on the counter. "Want some wine?" she offered.

"Sure, what kind do you have?"

Her eyes darted to the little corner that served as a liquor section. "Well, there's generic white and red wine, and some stronger stuff. For emergencies." She gave me a sheepish smile. "The girls and I usually go out to drink."

My eyebrow twitched. I had seen her do shots with friends firsthand, making me wonder how many times she'd come home with a man after one of these so-called girls' nights. It wasn't jealousy, but something inside me burned with the need to possess her.

Ever since I read that file on her, I'd been obsessing over her. I couldn't concentrate on anything else.

"Red," I said, pushing down my infuriating thoughts. She nodded and went to retrieve the bottle and two wineglasses before setting them alongside our plates. She moved efficiently, her bare feet quiet against the tile. Her gaze flicked my way as she pulled out a drawer and found a corkscrew.

"Where are your roommates?" I extended my hand, and she dropped the bottle and the opener wordlessly.

"Gone," she answered, watching me open the wine and pour some into both of our glasses. "I probably won't see them today."

Good. It meant we wouldn't be interrupted. I'd ensure Donatella was out of the city—if it was indeed her following Isla—before the insane woman hurt my woman.

My woman. Mia donna. Goddamn! Nothing had ever sounded so fucking good. So perfect. Isla é mia donna. *Yes, she was my woman.* And nobody would take her away from me.

She reached for the plate with little, ridiculous-looking sandwiches. "Cucumber and avocado sandwiches. Healthy. I think."

I took one, although I had no interest in eating cucumber sandwiches. Whatever the fuck that was. We ate salami and prosciutto on our bread. Even olive oil, but definitely not cucumbers.

She added two onto her own plate.

She bit into her sandwich and winced. I'd be foregoing the sandwich for sure. "We should probably stick to the salad," she muttered, throwing it back onto her plate. "These are disgusting."

The corners of my lips tugged up.

"How many times have you gone home with a man?" I asked abruptly. The question had been burning on my tongue.

My question must have thrown her off because she raised her eyebrows. She took a seat and extended her hand to grip the one opposite to hers as if to steady herself.

"Well, if you must know, you were the first," she muttered, her tone slightly bratty. "Now, instead of asking personal questions, want to do the honors of tossing the salad, Mr. Marchetti?"

"I'd love to toss your salad," I remarked. I wondered if she'd be up for ass play. I wanted to spank her ass red, ignite this simmering attraction into a full-blown volcano and see where it took us.

"Mr. Marchetti!" Her face turned beet red as desire shimmered in her eyes. "I'm not sure what you're insinuating, but I'm not that kind of girl. Besides, come anywhere near my asshole and you'll see what a woman's wrath is."

My chest shook with laughter. Jesus, this woman was unlike any I had met before. In the best possible sense.

"We'll see." I smiled wolfishly. "Now stop with the Mr. Marchetti bullshit."

Another eye roll. "Fine, fine. And you stop thinking about my asshole."

"Ah, but I already have," I said, smirking. "Which must mean you are thinking about it, because *you* want me playing with your ass, *dolcezza*."

She let out an exasperated breath, then put both her hands on my arms and manhandled me—only because I loved her hands on me and let her—to stand in front of the salad.

"Start mixing, mister, or there'll be hell to pay."

Goddamn it, I could already picture the way she'd be, bossing everyone around in our own household. Yes, marrying her was sounding better and better by the second.

Once the salad was tossed, we both put some on our plates and dug in. I waited until she put a forkful in her mouth before I said, "You're an accomplished violinist. Have you been playing for a long time?"

Her gaze met mine. She finished chewing before answering. "Thirteen years or so." She thought for a moment. "Maybe a bit more. I'm bad at math."

"How did you get into it?"

Her eyes darted to the large windows framed with tasteful draperies drawn open. "By accident," she admitted. "I was taking piano lessons and got to my lesson half an hour early. There was this boy there playing the violin, and I fell in love."

"With the boy?"

She scoffed. "Heck no. I don't even remember the boy. But the music he made with that violin." The dreamy smile on her face had my heart turning over. "It was magic. When my lesson started, I told Mrs. Chekov I wanted to play the violin. She had a spare one. The violin and bow felt so perfect in my hands. Like a limb I didn't know I was missing."

Shit, why did that make me feel jealous of her damn violin?

"What would you do instead if you didn't play?"

She brought the wineglass to her lips, pausing for a moment, then grinned.

"Maybe I'd be a world-famous model." I cocked my eyebrow as she tucked the hair behind her ear, mischief shining in her eyes. "Yeah, yeah. I know, I'm not tall enough. Nor slim enough."

"You're enough." My voice came out on a grunt. "You are perfect, just the way you are. Your height. Your weight. Every single inch of you is flawless. Exquisite." I watched as a blush spread over her porcelain skin. I couldn't stop looking at her. She was the perfect size for me. Soft, rounded curves. Creamy skin. And an ass I couldn't wait to hold in my palms. I longed to bite those cheeks from the moment I saw her at Reina Romero's fashion show. Then she blew me a kiss and I actually got a hard-on. "I'd let you model lingerie for me."

Isla laughed, and it sounded like the sweetest symphony. "Hmm, okay, I'll consider modeling lingerie, then."

A growl vibrated in my chest. She must have misunderstood me.

"You'll model only for me, *dolcezza*. Anyone else sees you in lingerie, and you'll be signing their death warrant."

Her eyebrows rose up to her hairline. "So are you saying you wouldn't hire me to model for anyone but you?" She gestured to herself, her hands waving up and down her body. "You'd hide all this from the world?"

"I'd hire you to wear other stuff," I grumbled.

She chuckled again. "Like what? Men's suits?"

I threw my head back and laughed for the second time today, and the sound sounded strange after going so long without hearing it. She kept throwing me off guard.

"That's a good idea," I admitted. "You can model men's suits. That way every inch of your creamy, silky skin is completely hidden from hungry eyes."

She shook her head, but was still smiling. "Men."

"Women," I retorted back, amused.

Silence followed and we continued eating. She seemed to be contemplating what to ask me next. I'd give it to her, she was clever. Maybe not in the same brutal way as her big brother, but she had a different kind of wisdom about her. And compassion always lurked in her eyes, ready to offer a hand to the world. I wondered if it was part of her, or if she'd been through something that made her this way.

I wanted to know everything there was to know about her.

"So, you're not married..." she started.

"I'm not."

"A widower, then." I nodded, although something in my gut twisted. Warned, even. I should tell her, except I couldn't. Not until she was my wife. Not until I was certain I could trust her. It was my sons' lives that depended on it. "And you have two sons," she continued, and I confirmed with a nod. "That must be hard. Being a single dad."

It was better than having Donatella in their lives. She destroyed everything she touched. I wouldn't allow her to ruin their lives too.

"They're good kids," I murmured, unaccustomed to talking about my children to anyone outside my family. "Amadeo and Enzo are their names. Thirteen and fourteen."

"Hopefully boys endure teenage years better than girls."

"Mainly with fists. Lots and lots of fighting," I remarked dryly, then switched subjects to a safer topic. "How long have you lived in Paris?"

We spent over an hour eating and talking. In my entire life, I'd never had such a good time with another woman just talking, and certainly never while eating salad and drinking budget wine. It was usually only about sex as a transaction, but with Isla—even with the years between us—we could talk. It wasn't just about the sizzling attraction that crackled whenever she was in my vicinity. It was about the serenity that she seemed to convey.

She stood up, reaching for both of our plates, and took them to the sink. I did the same with our glasses.

"Might as well chuck those sandwiches," she remarked. "They are awful."

I chuckled. "I'm sure they weren't so bad."

Her eyes twinkled as the corners of her lips tugged up. "Then I dare you to eat one."

I grinned, watching her hungrily. Two could play this game. "I'm saving my appetite for dessert."

Her breath hitched. She hadn't backed off and every signal she sent my way told me she wanted me as much as I wanted her.

She turned away from the sink and faced me, her eyes shimmering full of lust. She seemed to be waiting to see what I would do.

"Are you going to get on your knees again?" she finally said. My dick pulsed, thickening in my trousers. Fuck, I wanted her badly. I brought my hand up to touch her and, in fascination, watched a shiver race down her body.

Isla's cheeks flushed, and her hooded eyes glazed with desire. Her breaths came hard, mine came ragged.

As my hands continued up her body, under her sweater—*madre di Cristo*. She felt so fucking good, smelled even better... like sun-drenched coconut. Her skin was soft under my rough palms.

"Take me to your bedroom." She didn't hesitate taking my hand and leading me down the hallway and past several doors before opening the one that I recognized from the photo. White furniture. Lacy covers. The only splash of color was the peach rug and miniature paintings she had hanging on the wall. The scent of her in this room was stronger than in the rest of the apartment.

"Take your clothes off," I rasped. "I'm dying to taste you. To feel your pussy clench around my dick. It has been way too fucking long without it."

"Ditto," she breathed her admission. Fuck, I loved how she didn't play coy. Her desire was in the palm of her hands and she owned it. If she wanted to, she could easily own me too.

Her fingers trembled slightly as she pulled the sweater over her head and shimmied out of her yoga pants, leaving her in a black bra and lacy panties.

The view stole the breath from my lungs. Her nipples beaded behind her lacy bra, and her chest rose and fell rapidly. My cock was rock hard, eager for her.

"Should I get rid of these?" she whispered, tugging on the material, goose bumps breaking out over her skin. She reached behind her, but I closed the distance between us, my hand stopping her.

"That's my job."

I bent my head and skimmed my mouth over her soft skin. "You smell and taste like coconuts," I told her as I unhooked her bra, letting it fall on the floor. Next, my fingers trailed over her inner thigh and between her legs, cupping her pussy. "But the scent is the strongest here."

A soft moan vibrated through the room. Her body swayed as she arched into my touch, grinding herself shamelessly against my palm. She was soaked already.

I couldn't wait to taste her again. When I pulled my hand away from her, she whimpered in protest. "Please, Enrico. I haven't been able to get off since that night."

A smug kind of satisfaction washed over me. To know she needed me to get off. I hooked my fingers in her panties and pulled them down her beautiful legs, lowering myself onto my knees in the process.

"Get on the bed," I instructed. "I'm going to reward you for your honesty."

Her lips curved into a bright smile. Fuck, this girl was like a magnificent sunrise, beaming with all the colors of the burning sun and igniting an inferno inside me.

She got on the bed and crawled up to the headboard, giving me a magnificent show of her swaying, seductive hips. The view of her in that position nearly made me come. I wanted to fuck her like that, face down and ass up in the air.

Later, I promised myself.

She turned and lay on her back. I let my gaze travel over her pale skin. She might not be tall, but in all the ways that mattered, she was fucking gorgeous. In a Botticelli kind of way. If she'd lived during the Renaissance, artists would've fallen over themselves to paint her.

"Spread your legs, *dolcezza*," I ordered. She complied eagerly, showing me her glistening arousal smeared all over her inner thighs. I dropped my knee on the bed and wedged myself between her thighs, lowering my head until I was eye level with her pussy. "I'm ready for my dessert."

TWELVE
ISLA

I had lost my mind. Clearly.

The second Enrico kissed my folds, I lost my ability to think or talk. When the tip of his tongue touched my pussy, I just about orgasmed. My hips bucked, arching into his mouth.

His dark chuckle vibrated down to my core. "Fuck, you're so eager. Have you missed me, too, my *bellissima dolcezza*?"

God, hearing that Italian accent in that low tone, oozing with sex, didn't help me to control my libido. This man was the definition of sex.

"I didn't miss you," I croaked, grinding my pussy against his face. "Just your mouth and your dick."

Another chuckle filled the space, the air brushing against my wet folds. "I'm going to fill that mouth with something more useful than lies, Isla." Holy fucking shit! Why did I like the sound of that? "Now touch your breasts," he ordered.

I cupped my breast, heavy and aching, and squeezed my nipple while I ran my other hand through his hair. As he licked me from my entrance to my clit, pleasure shot through me, my panting breaths traveling through the bedroom.

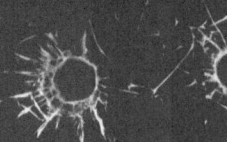

Enrico groaned, repeated the movement, and then pushed his tongue inside me. I threw my head back. My eyes slammed shut and electricity shot through me. My thighs instinctively closed, shifting backward, overwhelmed with so many sensations.

He let out a feral growl.

"Don't you dare keep me away from this pussy," he rasped, grabbing the back of my thighs and hooking them over his shoulders. He pressed his face closer to my folds and tongued my entrance. Then he began moving his lips and tongue, exploring, until he reached my clit.

He swept his tongue over the sensitive bud and another shudder of pleasure shot through me. Around this man, it was like the setting for pleasure switched "on" and stayed that way. Just for him.

Did it make sense? Fuck no. Was it smart what I was doing? Double fuck no.

Yet, I feared I'd kill any man—or woman—who tried to take him from me at this very moment. I needed him to see my pleasure through.

Tingles ran up and down my legs as he flicked and circled my nub with his tongue. The pressure inside me wound tighter, coiled until I could barely breathe. He ate me out like he was starving, swirling and sucking. My thighs started shaking.

His finger worked its way into my pussy, stretching me, and I moaned. "Oh... ohhhh... my God."

I was almost there, hovering on the edge of the cliff, ready to spiral over. God, I wanted to feel his tongue inside my entrance. Even more, I wanted his cock inside me.

"Not even God would dare touch you," he grunted as he slid another finger inside me. "Because you're mine now."

He closed his mouth around my clit and pulled on it with his teeth. My toes curled, and I could feel the orgasm building in my belly. My hips rocked against his face, my body desperate for release.

He thrust his tongue inside me again and I gasped. Toe-curling pleasure vibrated through me. He fucked me with his tongue, growling against my folds. *In and out. In and out. In and out.* My eyes rolled back in my head, my spine arching off the bed. The growl of satisfaction that escaped him vibrated through me.

"I'm so close," I breathed. "Please..." I thrashed my head back and forth, rocking against him. Grabbing a handful of his hair, I moved my hips, keeping his attention there. "Don't stop."

He nipped at my clit and immediately afterward continued sucking at it. My entire body was on fire. Sparks burned hot, then without warning, euphoria burst through me. The pressure exploded, my orgasm so loud it made my ears ring.

A scream tore through the room as my walls convulsed around his fingers. I could feel my limbs shaking with pleasure so intense, it dragged me into the dark, depraved depths. I opened my eyes to find his obsidian gaze on me, carnal and hungry. Feral.

He continued to lap at my juices, never breaking eye contact. My muscles lax, I watched him, arousal flaring inside me again. Then he crawled up, his strong body hovering over me, trailing kisses over my skin, until he reached my breasts. He took a nipple into his mouth and sucked hard. He switched to my other breast, his tongue flicking my nipple, then biting it before bringing it into his mouth to suck. I was a shuddering, mindless mess unable to stop moaning.

The throbbing between my thighs pulsed, and I writhed under him, panting. I clutched his expensive suit, the stark contrast between us evident. I was completely naked, and he was still fully dressed. I was exposed. He wasn't.

"*Magnifica*," he murmured, his mouth moving up my neck.

His breathing was uneven and his gaze filled with something soft yet striking. I brought my hands to his chest, pressing them against his white shirt. I tried to undo his tie, but my fingers trembled. Hell, my entire body shuddered from the intensity of that orgasm.

He took over and shed his clothes in record time. A Roman god stood in front of me. Strong. Powerful. And judging by his big, thick shaft, he was so fucking ready for me.

Enrico got back on the bed, wrapped both hands around my waist, and flipped me over.

"I want your ass up and your head on the pillow."

My body instantly obeyed.

"You want to be mine, don't you?" His purr had goose bumps

rising all over my skin. His calloused palm rubbed my ass, liquifying my desire further. "Mine to fuck. Mine to own. Mine to deprave."

My back arched and my ass pushed into his palm. "In the bedroom." I breathed the correction, my words muffled by the pillow. "Only in the bedroom."

His dark chuckle filled the space. Full of promises of dark pleasure and dark possession. Worst of all, it didn't scare me. It fucking excited me.

Enrico grabbed my hair, tugging my head back. His hot breath against my face, his mouth against my ear. "We shall see, *dolcezza*."

This physical connection and incredible chemistry was thrilling. I didn't lie when I said I couldn't get off without him. It was agonizing to crave someone's touch this much.

My heart hammered so loudly, I was scared it'd break out of my body. His large palm kneaded my ass, then carefully parted my thighs as far as they could go. The moment his fingers brushed against my soaked folds, a moan escaped me.

He thrust two fingers inside me, and I burrowed into the pillow. My ass ground against him, needing the friction. I was so close already. Again.

He pulled out his fingers and cupped my pussy. "This belongs to me." Then he gently tapped my ass. "This ass also belongs to me."

"Please, Enrico," I begged, my breathing choppy and frantic. "I need you."

"First give me the words," he demanded. "Who do you belong to?"

"You," I sobbed desperately. "Please…"

Enrico grabbed my hips and held me tightly as his cock thrust inside me in one forceful move, filling me to the hilt. Despite being wet and more than ready, his entrance into my body was a mixture of pain and pleasure.

"Ahhh… you're so big."

He pulled out, only to fill me again. His groin slapped against my ass. Again and again. Carnal pleasure buzzed through my veins. He thrust inside me, hitting that spot until I saw stars.

"Ohhh… yes… yes…"

"That's it," he grunted, thrusting into me. His pace built to a maddening level. The slap of flesh against flesh and my own arousal echoed through the air as his fingers dug into my hips. "Scream for me."

I turned my face to the side, taking in my Italian's rigid muscles as he thrust into me. His darkness was hidden behind hooded eyelids. My harsh breaths and pants mixed with his grunts.

His pace was becoming steadier, rougher. My orgasm hit me with a wrecking force, and I screamed his name.

His hold tightened on my hips as his head fell back, pleasure washing over his features and making for the most magnificent sight I had ever seen. He stilled at my back as warm liquid filled my walls. He remained inside me, his cock twitching and my pussy throbbing.

We remained like that, our harsh breathing and the scent of our exertion filling the space.

My ears buzzed from the intensity of what we shared. His big, rough palm skimmed over my body, petting me. Touching me. Murmuring a stream of words into my ear I couldn't make any sense of.

He pulled out of me, then surprised me by slamming back into me again. I gasped, unprepared, and twisted my head to find his gaze.

The devilish grin on his face made him appear younger, and my heart fluttered. Why, oh why, did my heart flutter?

"Already?" My question came out on a moan.

"I want more of your screams, *dolcezza*." He got them. Screams and so much more.

It was obvious this man was used to getting whatever and whoever he wanted.

An hour later, we were both breathing heavily, panting and grunting. Our bodies were slick with sweat.

Enrico had finished inside me several times and I'd lost count of my own orgasms. The sweet exhaustion overtook my body, and all I knew was I needed sleep.

"One more time," he rasped against my ear, his body like a weighted blanket on me.

I watched him through sleepy eyelids. "It's impossible for you to be hard again."

He chuckled, thrusting his hips and sliding his hard cock inside me. I gasped in shock, shaking my head in disbelief.

"Not impossible. See what you do to me?" He took my bottom lip between his teeth and nipped it. He pulled out, only to slam back inside. I moaned. The familiar throbbing started, but I couldn't move.

I wrapped my hands around his neck, gripping his hair. A smarter woman would have pushed him off, but my body was already responding to him. Needing him to finish what he'd started even if it killed me.

"Are all Italians like you?"

He thrust inside me roughly.

"You don't worry about any other Italians," he warned darkly, his accent heavy. "Only me."

I attempted to laugh at his jealousy, but instead a moan slipped through my lips. So he slammed inside me again.

The ringing of a phone cut through the air, and we both stilled.

Rrrring. Rrrring.

"Ignore it," I rasped, clutching his shoulders. I wasn't ready for this to be over.

Rrrring. Rrrring. Rrrring

He kissed the tip of my nose. "It might be important."

He pulled out of me, and I moaned my protest as he walked out of the room. I fell back on the mattress, my breasts bouncing. Here I was, panting, and this man was already breathing normally, despite the sweat glistening over his sculpted body.

I rolled over to lie on my stomach—naked as the day I was born—watching him down the hallway as he answered the phone.

"*Pronto?*" His eyes remained on me, his tall, strong frame looking even bigger in our small hallway.

"*Quando?*" I thought it meant "when" in Italian, but I wasn't certain. Silence swept through the apartment, the tension in his shoulders visible as he listened to whoever was on the other end of the line. "I'll be there in two hours."

He hung up, and disappointment flooded me. He was leaving.

In five long strides, he was back in my bedroom and standing in front of me. He pulled on his pants and finished getting dressed. When he slipped his suit jacket on, he came to kneel in front of me.

"You keep kneeling down, Enrico," I teased, "and I'm going to get ideas."

He didn't seem scared at all. He cupped my face, then kissed me. "I have to go."

"I figured." He watched me with a peculiar expression on his face, but I couldn't decipher it. "Everything okay?"

He ran a thumb across my cheek.

"It will be." The hard edge to his voice told me he'd ensure it. Although, it was hard to stop the disappointment from washing over me when I realized he didn't plan on sharing what was driving his sudden departure.

The ruthlessness of this man reminded me of Illias. I couldn't pinpoint any particular quality, but it was there. In the lethal energy around him.

I kept waiting for Enrico to explain, but he didn't. Nor would he. I'd seen that look plenty of times in my brother's eyes, like when he decided to handle that senator who got a bit too handsy with me. One day, I ran crying to my big brother that the senator touched my bare legs and tried to push his hand up my skirt. The next day, he was dead. I wasn't an idiot, and I certainly didn't believe in coincidences. Not that I'd ever voice it.

But I never inquired further. Sometimes ignorance was bliss. Bottom line was that my brother was a good man, and he had probably spared other women and girls of the senator's attention. So, like a coward, I buried my head in the sand and pretended my assumptions were wrong and irrational.

"Do you have any travel plans?" His question caught me by

surprise. I had been contemplating going back to Russia and staying at my brother's place, but I wouldn't share that with this man. He could keep his secrets, and I'd keep mine.

"No."

"Good," he said, still cupping my cheeks. "We'll talk about us when I get back. I won't be gone long."

I frowned. "Us?"

He smacked me lightly on the ass. "Yes, Isla. Us."

"Okay, Father. Whatever you say."

He smacked my ass again, this time slightly harder.

"You're really striving for punishment." Then he smiled smugly, his gaze flaring with something hot and dark that sent shivers rolling down my back. "Although if you're taking that route, *dolcezza*, I must insist you call me Daddy."

My cheeks flushed, sending heat through every inch of my body. "Daddy," I repeated, tasting the word on my lips. He must have liked it, because his eyes darkened and his fingers—still on my ass—squeezed my cheek.

"Good girl." I just about purred at the praise. Jesus, what the hell was going on here? His gaze darted around the room until it landed on the pad of paper. He reached for the pen next to it, and wrote something down. "That's my number. Text me yours."

Then he walked out of my apartment with a soft click behind him.

THIRTEEN
ENRICO

The Marchetti empire was built on blood, women, and drugs.

It wasn't until about twenty years ago that I had started building the legal side up. My legitimate empire didn't happen nor did it thrive through sheer luck. I had made strategic movements and used certain manipulation skills to ensure the expansion of the Marchetti empire.

All with one purpose in mind.

To cease any involvement with human trafficking and illegal brothels.

I succeeded in that not long after I'd taken over as the head of the *famiglia*.

Except now, as I stood in my home in Paris and read the report that Manuel was able to extract, I knew my success had come too late. I already had big obstacles to overcome with the red-haired young woman, but if Isla learned of this one, I'd bet my life on it being a hard ending.

"You're sure about this?" I questioned Manuel. I trusted him with my life. My children's lives. He wouldn't be fucking around with information like this. Yet, it seemed so unbelievable.

"I'm afraid so."

He moved to the little bar in the corner of my office and started preparing a drink. He strode back to the desk and handed me a glass of scotch. I shook my head, so he put it on the coaster in front of me before downing his drink in one go.

I returned my attention to the document, reading through her family's information. On her mother's side.

Mother: Louisa Maria Cortes.

The youngest daughter of the Cortes family, she was sold to my father to settle a debt twenty-four years ago. A lost drug shipment. A debt owed and settled by the flesh of a young cartel princess. Jesus Christ. Why would any parent give their child up like that? Yes, the Corteses were known for their ruthlessness and usually used their women to advance their position, but this was beyond normal behavior we'd seen from them.

My father had put her in one of the brothels, which was where Konstantin Sr. fucked her and got her pregnant.

Fuck! Make that double fuck.

Brazilian cartel princess. *Santo cazzo. Madre di Cristo.*

"She's the niece of the Brazilian cartel boss." That piece of information was disturbing. "Kian Cortes's niece." Manuel was pointing out the obvious. I didn't need that shit right now. "If we are able to connect the dots, *nipote*, others will too. The moment they learn of her, they'll come for her."

"They'll get her over my dead body." I had a taste of her, and I'd be damned if I let anyone take her away from me. Especially not some oppressive head of a cartel. That fucker would destroy someone as soft and beautiful as Isla. There was a reason Kian Cortes kept away from his brother.

Isla wasn't just beautiful. She was warm, funny, and so full of life. I found her, and I would keep her. She was mine. She was mine to ruin. Mine to put back together.

"I want eyes on her at all times," I said, my gaze still on the skyline. But it wasn't the city I was seeing now. It was the ginger-haired woman naked, lying on her bed, her wild mane cascading down her back as she watched me take the call that led me here.

Jesus, who else knew? Konstantin had to know. There was no way he was ignorant of that fact. It was a miracle he'd been able to keep it hidden from his sister, from the world.

"Is she that important to you?" Manuel questioned. I could feel his inquisitive eyes on me, trying to decipher my motivations.

"I have a plan," I announced, ignoring his question.

"I have a feeling I'll need another drink to stomach this plan," Manuel muttered as he reached for the drink he just made me, throwing himself back into a chair. "Let's hear it."

My eyes traveled to the large window that displayed the magnificent view of the Paris skyline. I could glimpse the bell towers of the Notre-Dame Cathedral from my window, and the river Seine flowing seamlessly downstream as it had for hundreds of years. It was one of the most romantic cities in the world, but I'd dare say, it had nothing on my country.

Even better was that I could protect Isla in my country. Here, she was up for grabs.

I turned my head and met Manuel's eyes. "I'm going to marry her." *I'm going to make her my wife. My partner. The mother of my future children. My everything.*

Surprise flickered in his gaze. "Just like that?"

I nodded. "I am. I was going to take her as my mistress, but this is better."

After all, I fucked her without a condom, and I never do that. No matter how much a woman swore up and down she was on the pill, I always sheathed, but for some stupid reason, I didn't earlier. And God, when I felt her warm pussy strangling my dick with nothing separating us, I swore I had gone to heaven.

"And Donatella?" he questioned, frowning.

We locked eyes, his as dark as mine. It was the Marchetti signature coloring. Dark hair and even darker eyes. Tanned skin.

"I'll take care of it."

"You should let me do it," he grumbled.

I shook my head. "No. I'll do it. It's about time she paid for the shit she's caused. I also learned she has been following Isla around." He stiffened, apprehension entering his features. We both knew that was not good. Donatella was a crazy bitch willing to murder her own sons, never mind a stranger.

"How in the fuck did she get out of that place?" he said, echoing my thoughts. "I just locked her up in there. There has to be someone helping her."

"It won't matter soon. The moment I find her, I'll wring her neck."

"About time," he muttered. "Will you talk to the boys?"

"Yes." My jaw clenched. The sad part was that Enzo and Amadeo had no connection to their mother. We'd tried to build it—it was the reason I'd kept her alive, after all—but she couldn't be trusted to be left alone with them.

I should have known if she was willing to end her unborn child, it'd only get worse the older they got. The memory yanked me back, pulling me under.

Fourteen Years Ago...

The bitter taste bloomed in my mouth. My brother was buried six feet under. An empty casket full of dirt, because there was nothing left of his body but ash and dust.

I walked into my home and toward the stairs, my feet heavy as lead. I felt like I was slowly drowning and the shitshow had barely started.

"Stai bene?" Manuel's hand was on my shoulder, squeezing it firmly. "We had to do this."

I nodded. It didn't make me feel any better. It felt like we'd both aged a few years since my brother died in my arms.

At least I'd had a taste of freedom. Until now.

I made my way up the stairs to go check on Donatella. She hadn't gotten out of bed since we brought her home. She was still angry and bitter at not being allowed to be free. Since the world now believed her to be dead, we couldn't risk her exposure. Her growing belly gave her the excuse for locking herself away in her room, although I suspected it was a pretense. She didn't truly care. Something about her apathy rubbed me the wrong way.

In front of Donatella's bedroom, I stopped and listened. The pitch of a woman's voice. Struggling cries from a baby that was turning into high-pitched screams by the second.

I pushed on the door, but it was locked. So I kicked it open. It smashed against the wall behind it with a loud thud.

Fury slithered through my veins at the sight before me. Donatella, heavily pregnant, held infant Enzo by his feet, dangling him off the balcony.

Her eyes, hazed with hate and full of madness, darted to me. For a second, neither one of us moved.

Then fury roared through me. I lunged for her and wrapped my arm around her rib cage—above her belly to ensure I didn't hurt the baby. Her grip on the baby's small feet loosened and she let go.

My free hand shot out and caught him, scooping him up and holding him like a football. Thank fuck he was nine months old, or his neck would have snapped.

Donatella shrieked, struggling in my hold. "No! Die, die, die! He has to die."

She thrashed, unhinged madness in her eyes. She reached for the gun secured in my holster and I had to jam my elbow into her ribs.

"Let me go," she shrieked, kicking her feet and her legs, uncaring if she hit the baby in my arms. I was tempted to headbutt her to shut her up. Enzo's screams increased in volume, probably sensing my fear.

"Stop screaming and kicking," I growled. "You're scaring Enzo."

She didn't care, continuing to fight against me. Hammering against my chest. Again, she tried for my gun.

"I'll kill the child in my womb."

I froze, my eyes narrowing on her and seeing her—really seeing her—for the first time. Something crazy in the depths of her eyes that was rooted in her soul.

"Che cazzo." Manuel's voice came from the door and my gaze found him.

"Take the baby," I barked.

He didn't hesitate, prowling through the room and taking little Enzo from me. I wrapped both my hands around her and dragged her to the old radiator, which was left over from the old days when the castello was first built.

Without looking behind me, I said, "Give me your handcuffs."

He threw them my way and I shackled both her hands before grabbing the rope hanging from the curtain and tied her to the radiator.

"I won't allow you to hurt the baby in your belly," I growled, a red mist taking over my vision. "Consider yourself lucky you are Enzo's mother and have that baby in your belly." I took her chin between my fingers, gripping it tightly, ensuring she met my eyes. I let her see all the darkness swirling inside my soul. "Or I would have sliced your throat already."

It was what finally got through to her, and she stilled.

That had been the last straw. I had to have her committed to a private institution known for their discretion, but throughout the years, I'd tried to help her build a connection with the boys. Why didn't I kill her after I let the world believe she died right alongside my brother? I'd wondered that many times over the years. Maybe there was some shred of decency left in me, although it started to feel like it was for naught. I had her thought dead to protect her, and it turned out we all needed protection from her crazy ass. "I sent for them and will keep them with me until we can eliminate the threat."

They were at home, attending school within the bounds of my territory with teachers and principals that were on my payroll. My zia, who lived with us full-time, watched over them along with my most trusted *soldati*. Zia Ludovica was my mother's sister, and after her husband passed away, I took her in. It helped that her cooking skills were incomparable. She fed us and we took care of her. That was what family was for.

"That might be best," he agreed.

"You just ensure Isla is safe. Keep our most trusted men on her."

He scratched his chin pensively.

"Kingston might be best for that." I didn't like it. Kingston was a good-looking guy. Younger than me. Shit, this jealousy when it came to the wild woman would be the death of me. As if sensing my thoughts, he added, "He won't be interested in her. They'll never even meet."

"Fine," I conceded. Isla's safety was of the utmost importance. "Put him on her. Money is no object."

Silence followed while a heavy weight in the pit of my stomach warned of a shitstorm brewing. There were too many moving parts. Way too many unknowns. But none of it mattered.

As long as she was safe. As long as she was mine for good.

Enzo and Amadeo were in my Parisian home three hours later. It was one benefit of having my own jet.

I came out of my office to go in search of them and get the conversation over with.

"Boys are in the back garden," Manuel said, appearing out of nowhere. His steps synched up with mine. "Each one is sporting a black eye."

I slid my hands into my pockets. "What happened this time?"

"They refuse to say."

"At least they stick together," I pointed out.

My brother and I always had each other's backs. Just like Manuel and I had. In our world, it was important to have a family that wouldn't stab you in the back. Enzo and Amadeo might fight and give each other a few black eyes, but regardless of what caused the fight, they were there for one another.

"Remember when you, your brother, and—" He paused for a flicker of a moment, then continued, "And I got into fights?"

I nodded. "I remember you beating us up for the first ten years of our lives because you were older and bigger."

He chuckled. "Just admit it. I'm better and stronger."

I shot him a wry look. "Not anymore, old man."

"Bring it on, *nipote*," he challenged, grinning like an old fool. "And once you're married, definitely bring it on. You'll be too busy to keep up your workout routine."

This time I couldn't contain the grin. "I'll work out more to keep my young wife happy."

He slapped me on the shoulder. "The girl has you by the balls, and she hasn't even married you yet."

The garden came into view where my sons stood under a single tree, their heads bent over a device as they muttered amongst themselves. It seemed they were back on speaking terms.

"I'll wait for the day when a woman has your balls, *vecchio*," I said, then left him before he could utter another smart-ass comment. I went through the large French doors and two sets of blackened eyes lifted. Thank fuck they didn't have any physical nor mental traits of their mother.

They both greeted me at the same time. "Papà."

I smiled and made my way over, pulling them both into a hug. My father was always too busy for physical affection, but my brother and I had our mother. However brief. Enzo and Amadeo didn't have their mother's affection. So it was on me to ensure they got mine.

I stared down at both of them, each only coming up to my shoulders. Another year or two and they'd be as tall as me. It seemed like only yesterday when they were born. The blink of an eye had seen the years fly by. Enzo and Amadeo were no longer boys; they were young men. Another few years, and they'd be active members of the Marchetti empire. And just like I had a choice, so will they. One would run the underworld, the other would run the legal side. Unless he wanted to be part of the Omertà, and I suspected Amadeo would be all in.

"How are my boys?" I asked, unable to keep the pride out of my voice. I held them on the day they were born. I had been with them through every stage of their childhood. They were fucking *mine*. Not Donatella's.

They both shrugged. "Good."

"Are we going to get in trouble missing school?" Amadeo asked. I had to stifle a scoff. My sons only went to school for the socializing aspect. They couldn't care less if they got into trouble. In fact, more often than not, they *were* the trouble.

"I sent a note to your teachers. Just do your homework and turn it in on time. When we're back home, you'll be back in school and it will be like you haven't missed a day." The two shared a look. "Which one of you is going to tell me what's with the black eyes?"

Another shared look, wordless messages that only they could understand.

"It's nothing," they both answered at the same time. I studied them. Their dark hair and dark eyes mirrored my own. Enzo was the strategic one, while Amadeo was more impulsive. They had the Marchetti traits for sure.

"If you need my help, you'll come to me. Si?"

They nodded. "What's happening?" Enzo asked. "Is it Donatella?"

It was fucking sad that my sons knew she was usually the problem.

"Yes. I want to keep you close to me until we settle the threat." A terse nod by both of them. "I also have news that I want to share with you." They waited for me to continue, slight interest in their eyes. "This remains between us. Only Manuel and you two will know."

They both straightened up, watching me attentively. Most parents liked to shelter their children until they were blindsided. I never took that approach. I let them be children for as long as I could, but once they were old enough to understand right from wrong, I kept them in the loop with things that concerned them. Like their safety. Their mother. Our family business, to some extent.

The latter was needed to ensure they stayed wary of strangers, keeping them safe from potential threats. They had guards with them at all times, but it'd be stupid not to make them aware of the dangers that came with being a Marchetti.

"I will be married soon." Curiosity flickered in their dark eyes. Good, at least there wasn't resentment or anger. "How do you feel about that?"

Amadeo just shrugged and remained silent.

"Is she pretty?" Of course Enzo was already too interested in girls. I had already instilled in him the importance of protection—for himself and his girl—for whenever his first time happened. "Old?"

I shook my head. "Well, I think she's pretty. And she's older than you, yes."

"What about—" Amadeo's voice faltered as questions soared in his big, dark eyes. "Donatella?"

I focused on my youngest son. "What about her?" I asked carefully.

Amadeo puffed his chest. "That's why you called us here. She's trying to kill us again, isn't she?"

"Yes, she's out there somewhere," I confirmed. "I want you safe and with me. Once I'm married, we'll all return to the castello."

"What are you going to do with Donatella?" Enzo asked, his voice squeaking slightly as he uttered his mother's name. His vocal cords were going through puberty, switching from deep to high-pitched and he had no control over it. I noticed it was more prone to fluctuation when he was emotional, although he tried to hide this side of himself.

I met my son's gaze and held it. I wished they could be spared. I'd hoped Donatella would come around and be the mother Enzo and Amadeo needed. But, like always, the woman only cared about herself. She never cared about the boys, not when they were born. Not today.

"I can't risk her hurting you or your brother."

Enzo turned his head away, huffing. "About time."

His words made my chest squeeze. I wanted so desperately for them to experience their mother's love. To know they were loved and cherished.

"I'm sorry, *mio figlio*," I murmured. "If I could fix it, I would."

Enzo gave me a terse nod and stomped away, his body emanating the energy of a twenty-year-old. Amadeo and I stared after him until he disappeared into the house.

"Don't worry, Papà," Amadeo assured. "He's mad that Donatella doesn't love us."

I faced my youngest. "And you?"

He tilted his head pensively. Amadeo might have had a temper on him, but he was also reasonable. When his temper didn't get the best of him, that was.

"Sometimes it's stressful to think about a crazy woman always lurking about trying to kill us," he admitted.

"I won't let her harm a single hair on your head," I vowed. "She keeps escaping the institution. Her condition must have worsened, but I don't want either of you to worry about it." I took my youngest son by his shoulders and pulled him into a hug. "I'm going to handle her."

Amadeo nodded, a serious expression on his face. "I understand what you're saying, Papà."

The sad part was that he really did.

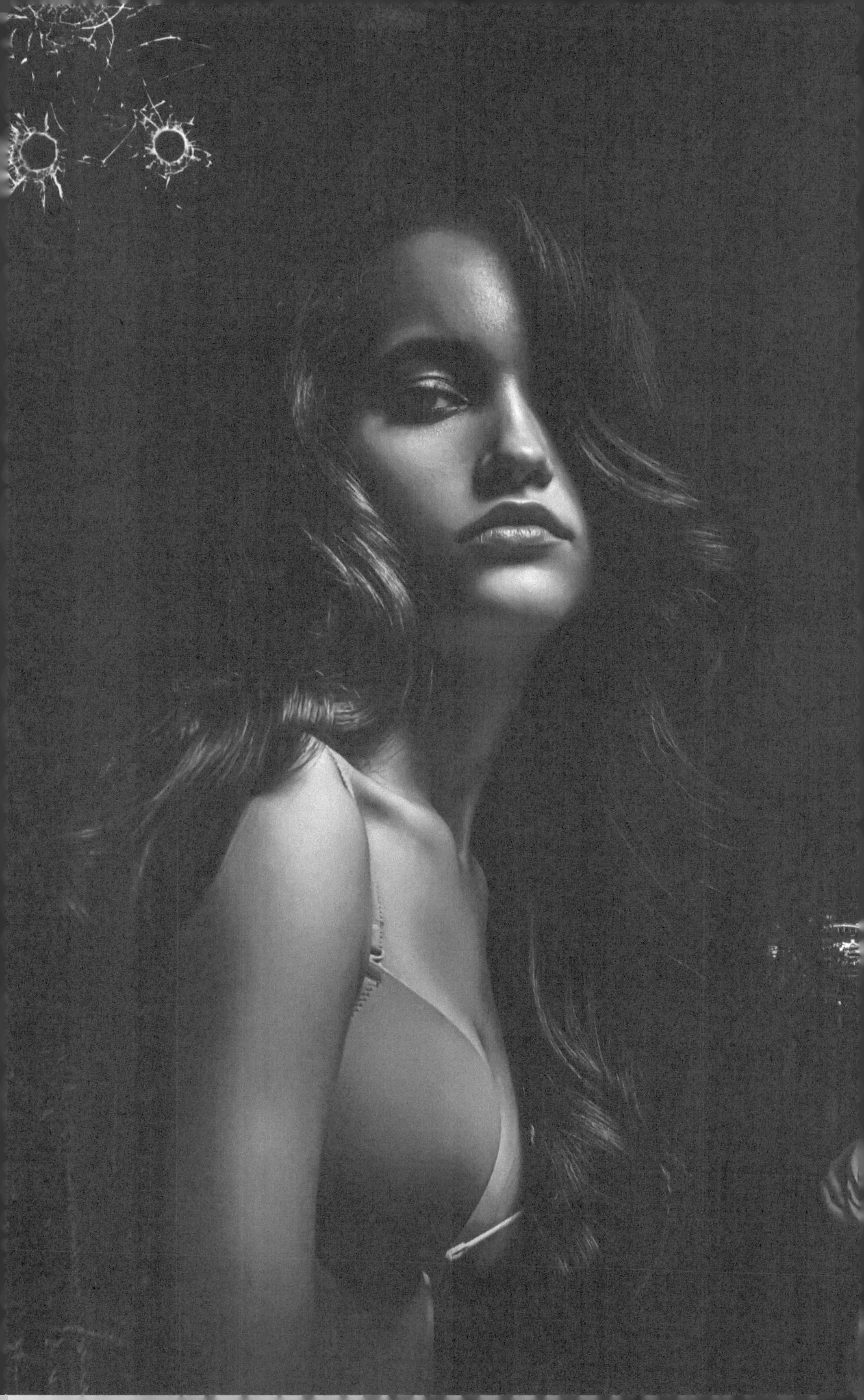

FOURTEEN
ISLA

I walked down Rue Lepic, a lively street that wound through Montmartre—from the Moulin Rouge and ending at Place Jean-Baptiste-Clément. It had been two days since I'd seen Enrico.

Reina and I struggled to balance our cappuccinos, bags full of fruits and vegetables from the market, my violin, her fashion portfolio, and our purses.

"Why don't you text him again?" Reina asked, balancing her portfolio under her armpit while scrolling through her fashion blog on her phone.

"He said he won't be long. I sent him a text so he'd have my number; it's on him to return it. I don't want to come off clingy and desperate."

She rolled her eyes.

"You're thinking too much." I didn't agree. For the past two days, I'd waited and waited for Enrico to reach out. He hadn't. He said he wouldn't be long, yet a simple response to my text shouldn't have been that hard. "I still cannot believe you hooked up with him."

I shrugged. "We all do something reckless once in our lives," I muttered. I knew Reina could relate. "This will be my wild moment. I'll get it out of my system and everything will be back to normal."

At least, I hoped so. It wouldn't be easy to forget him. The man fucked like a beast, and I thrived on it. Apparently, I wasn't frigid nor a saint when it came to carnal pleasure. Thank fuck. I should call that lame-ass ex-boyfriend that didn't know where to stick his penis and tell him how Daddy Enrico made me come screaming his name. Or better yet, I could record us and maybe that little "boy" could learn how to fuck women.

"What did he say about the woman who looked like his wife?" she asked curiously, pulling me away from the petty revenge thoughts.

I let out a heavy sigh.

This was the part that bothered me the most. Enrico swore he didn't have a wife, but he never really explained who the woman was that looked like his dead wife. It felt stupid to admit it, though.

"Never mind Marchetti and me," I said instead. "Tell me how things are going with you."

"Fine." Her voice was clipped, which meant she was the opposite of fine. "Perfect, in fact."

I took a sip of my cappuccino and shot her a curious glance. "That bad, huh?"

I thought I saw a flicker of anxiety flare in her big blue eyes, but she hid it behind a fake smile.

"Listen—" I broke off, my heart lodging in my throat. We just managed to dodge a cyclist at the last second, but not before Reina could shoot out some French obscenities at him. My best friend cursed only when she was furious or down in the dumps. I gave her a knowing look.

"Ugh, it's not as bad as you think," she started explaining. I tilted my head, studying her. Was she lying to herself, too? "It's not," she assured, the protest weak on her lips. "Dante is trying to be—" She searched for the word but apparently failed to find it. "He wants to have a few dates so we can get *acquainted*," she muttered.

She grimaced as she said "dates," and it didn't take a genius to know she didn't want to get to know Dante better.

"Shouldn't you say no to this farce?" I said. "I hate to see you like this."

She shrugged, her golden hair blowing in the breeze. "It seems the Leone brothers will be the end of me after all."

I stopped in the middle of the sidewalk, anxiety for my friend fluttering in my throat. She stopped too, but her eyes weren't on me. They were on her phone screen. She was throwing herself into work, drowning in it, rather than dealing with this fucked-up arranged marriage.

"Reina, look at me." Her beautiful eyes glimmered like the Mediterranean Sea under the bright sun. "Call the wedding off. I'm sure your dad will understand."

She shook her head, sad and resigned. "No, I can't. I gave my word. It's to keep us safe."

I was tempted to drop all the bags and grab her by the shoulders and shake her. To shake some sense into her.

"People change their minds all the time," I told her. "Engagements end. It's not the end of the world. It's a bad idea for you to be around either Leone brother. Puts your secret at risk. It definitely doesn't keep *you* safe."

"Stop. It." Two words, but there was so much anger in them. "I made my mind up and that's it."

She resumed walking again as I stared blankly after her. Her posture was rigid, tension in her slim shoulders evident.

Someone bumped into my shoulder, waking me out of stupor, and I rushed after her.

"You never struck me as the type to give up, Reina," I said, our steps synchronized as we made our way to our apartment. "So don't start now."

She flicked me a glance. "Oh, I am *not* giving up."

Somehow I believed it, but before I could ask her about it, a familiar face caught my attention. The woman who looked like Enrico's dead wife stood across the street, her eyes—full of raw hate —on me.

My steps faltered, and to my horror, I realized the woman was crossing the street, headed straight for me.

Before I could react, she lunged for my arm, digging her nails into my wrist. "I know who you are, whore," she hissed.

"I beg your pardon," I spat out.

"You look just like your mother." Shock rolled through me. I barely knew anything about my mother, so how in the heck would *she* know anything about her? She cackled, something unhinged and truly terrifying in her laugh. "A brothel whore." A shiver of unease climbed up my spine. "Unless you want the world to know, you'll get out of this city."

"How do you know my mother?" I rasped, staring into her crazed dark eyes. Something wasn't right with this woman. "From where?"

"She was in one of my husband's whorehouses," she snickered. "The Marchettis' brothel."

My breath hitched, cutting off oxygen to my lungs. A whorehouse? No, it couldn't be. My mother died in childbirth. My brother told me so.

"What do you mean?" My voice was hoarse, and I could feel my pulse racing in my ears.

She scoffed, the look in her eyes hateful. Scary. "How do you think your father met your mother, stupid girl?" I swallowed. Nobody had ever told me how my father and mother met. She continued, her words the only thing I could focus on in the middle of this busy street. "By visiting one of the Marchetti family's famous brothels."

Her words felt like a whip against my skin. My soul.

"How do you know that?" My voice cracked, sounding strange and distant to my own ears.

She sneered, her lips curving with distaste. "I've seen her. She was their main brothel's most prized whore. They called her Pixie."

Reina's quick steps took her further away from me, unaware I was cornered by this madwoman.

"You got it wrong." My voice came out stronger than I felt at this moment. After all, it was what my brothers taught me: never show your weaknesses to the enemy. I didn't really understand it. Until now. Deep down, I knew this woman was an enemy. "I have no fucking idea who you're talking about. Now get the fuck away from me."

She cackled—actually cackled. It sounded witchy. Slightly mad too.

"I'm never wrong. She looked like you. Full of fire that men wanted to tame. A fucking savage." I gasped. Maybe my backbone wasn't all Konstantin's blood. Maybe some of my mother's heritage gave me my strength too. If only I knew what that heritage was. "She tried to kill every man who paid for her, so they had to sedate her before her working hours so she'd be compliant."

Dread settled somewhere deep in the pit of my belly. My stomach hurled, but I refused to react as a weak woman. Instead I opted for boiling fury. Anger—red and hot—ignited in my veins. I didn't believe her. I couldn't. It was obvious she was threatened by me and was probably acting out for attention.

My eyes darted to my best friend who was oblivious to what was happening as she continued to berate the poor cyclist farther up the path.

"Take your hands off me, you crazy bitch," I said, yanking my wrist from her grip.

I knew at that moment, I'd be making a trip to Russia.

My father's home in Russia—Konstantin Castle as I liked to call it—was an impressive building. It dated back to the Romanovs in the 17th century, and it was entirely too big. I didn't consider this my home. Although I was born in Russia, I was a California girl through and through. Whenever I said the words "I'm going home," never in a million years did I mean Russia.

I landed in Moscow two days later, thanks to a last-minute cancellation, my reward miles, and my well-funded bank account. Despite my big brother's disdain, I often flew commercial. Although, now was not one of those times I could claim this to be one of my favorites. I was squashed between two teenage girls bickering back and forth, throwing insults and popcorn. So damn immature.

Stepping off the plane cranky as fuck, I was met with cold

Moscow temperatures. I shivered, letting out a breath and creating a cloud in front of me. It was another thing I didn't care for about Russia; the cold stole the heat from your body and left your teeth chattering.

At least I had plenty of warm clothes at the castle. Throwing my Lily Pulitzer overnight bag over my shoulder, I made a quick exit out of the airport. I flagged down the first taxi driver and recited the address.

Once in the seat, I leaned back and sighed tiredly. Ever since Enrico's maybe-wife-slash-stalker uttered those words about my mother, I hadn't been able to shake them off. I had always been curious about my mother, but the details were vague. Aside from her first name and that she had red hair and green eyes like me, I hardly had anything to go by. But every time I asked Illias about her, something dark and uneasy—almost painful—passed his expression, so eventually I stopped asking.

But now I had to know. I was sick and tired of being left in the dark. About my mother. About my father. Even my brothers. Because if Illias thought for one minute that I still believed Maxim was shot by a stray bullet in the middle of an abandoned warehouse, he didn't know me at all. He didn't know what I'd discovered the day of Maxim's funeral.

My mind shifted to last summer, to the private funeral that only Illias and I attended in Russia before he was buried next to his mother in New Orleans.

Gray clouds gathered in the distance, forming thick layers that darkened until they were nearly black. Just like this day.

Maxim's issues had been known for years. As much as Illias had tried to hide them from me, I'd lived enough to know the signs.

"Why is the casket closed?" I asked again.

"It's for the best."

Illias's expression was somber. Despite the fact that Maxim and Illias drifted apart and had completely different personalities, they still had that connection. They were twins after all.

I slid my hand into my big brother's. He wore a black suit, making him appear like a dark angel. Almost as if he were prepared to exact revenge. But that was a silly thought. Right?

My sixth sense warned me that it wasn't.

"He's in a better place," I croaked, my voice breaking. "And we'll never forget him."

I'd barely eaten today, my stomach twisted in knots. It was the first death in our family that I lived through. It hit differently. So fucking hard that it had my soul trembling.

He squeezed my palm. "We won't, baby sister."

It was lonely and so damn heart-wrenching seeing Maxim off without anyone else. I was certain there were more people who loved him. The two of us couldn't be the only ones.

The church was damp and cloaked in darkness. The priest had said his blessings, yet neither one of us could find the strength to move. To say our final goodbyes. For a long stretch, we remained silent as we huddled close together.

It was the priest who broke the silence.

"Mr. Konstantin, may I have a word?"

"Yes." *Illias pressed a kiss on my forehead.* "Wait for me outside. I'll meet you there."

I nodded, watching him join the priest in the back of the church before they disappeared from my sight.

Staring at the fancy ebony casket, I meant to turn around and leave. It was time to say goodbye, to let Maxim find the peace he'd craved for so long. But instead, I took a step, then another, until my hand came to rest atop of the coffin.

Don't do it, *my mind warned.*

It was too late. The top was lifted and my gasp echoed through the silence of the church.

Maxim's face was beaten black and blue and no amount of makeup could hide the truth.

"Stray bullet," *I rasped numbly.* "Fucking bullshit." *A bullet-sized hole had pierced cleanly though my big brother's temple.*

The end was always the start, wasn't it? Maybe not for Maxim, but certainly for those around him.

The sound of a horn and a string of Russian curses pulled me away from the memory and returned my attention to my surroundings.

It took over three hours—past the glitter of the city and busy industrial areas, and down long, windy roads—for the taxi to arrive at the grand estate. The sun was setting behind the trees already, warning of a freezing night.

It was an expensive cab ride, but it beat calling my brother's driver.

Unfortunately for me, the taxi driver had to park at the iron gates, a bit aways from the building. I knew none of Illias's guards would let him pass through.

"*Vosem tysyacha pyat'sot rubley.*" Eight thousand five hundred rubles.

My eyes flickered to the dash, where a clear amount of only four thousand rubles flashed back at me. Yet another tiresome thing whenever I visited Russia: being treated as a tourist. Much like most of Eastern Europe, it was standard for Russians to set a price for locals and a completely different price for outsiders.

I paid the man, then reached for the handle. Stepping out of the car, I was just about to close the door when I said in fluent Russian, "If you hadn't ripped me off, I would have called you for my ride back too."

I slammed the door, holding my duffle bag in my other hand. Without a second thought, I pushed the iron gate that blocked the rest of the country from the estate and it squeaked, alerting the guards to my presence.

I waved to them casually. "Hey, I'm home for the holidays."

It was a bullshit excuse. The holidays were another two months away. Not unless you counted Halloween, which was a week away. But the men—my brother's guards—were used to me coming and going, so they just waved me through.

I walked up the long, winding driveway as the wind howled through trees. My boots creaked against the snow, leaving the footprints behind me, which I knew would disappear by the morning. It always fucking snowed in Russia.

I walked up the stairs that had once upon a time seen kings and queens, and pushed on the large mahogany door.

"I'm home," I yelled to nobody in particular. My voice traveled through the foyer and up the stairs. But there was no reply.

Good, Illias wasn't here. Not that I expected him to be, but you never knew with my brother.

My boots squeaked against the polished marble floors as I made my way through the castle and toward my brother's office.

No time like the present to dig through our family's secrets.

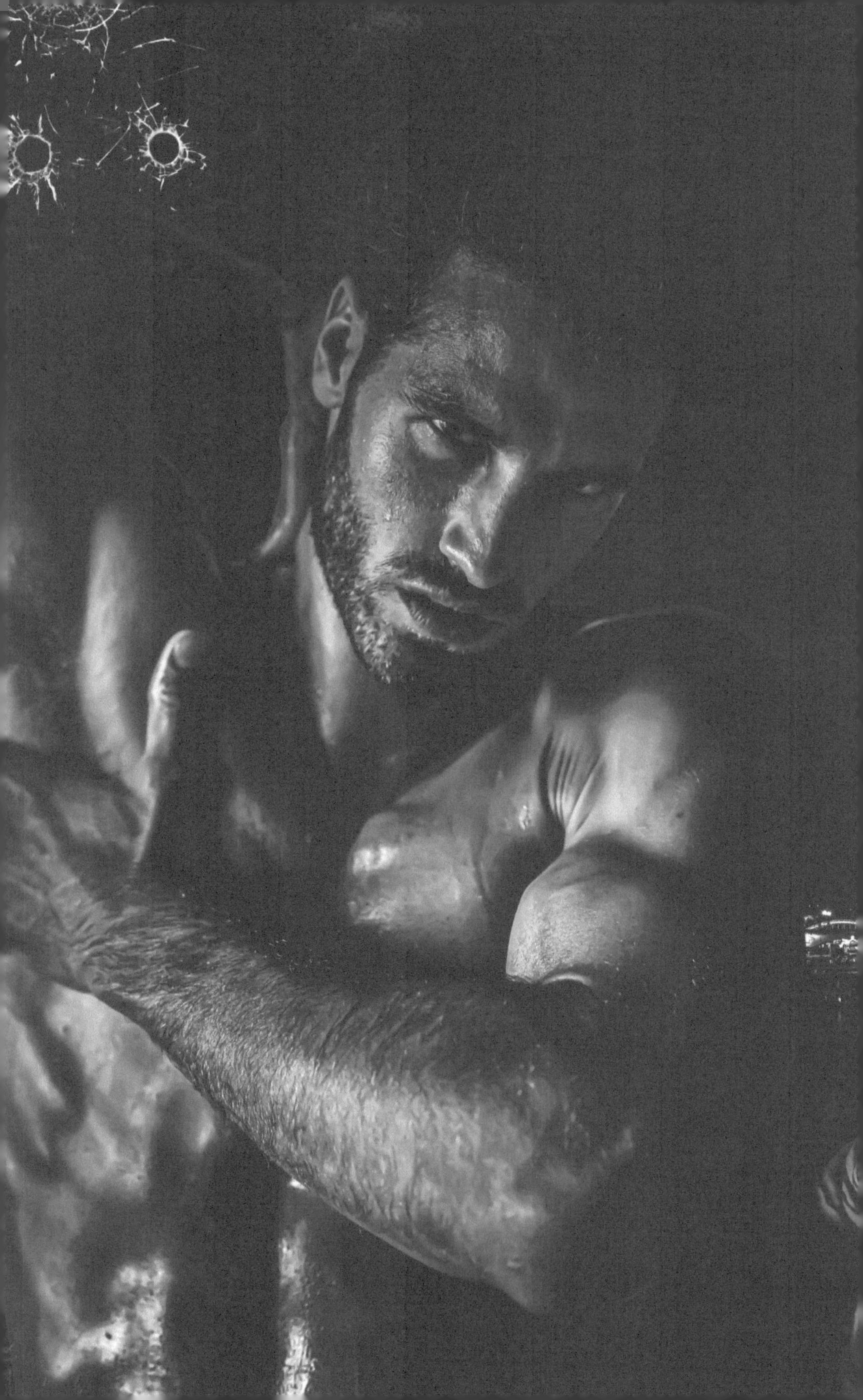

FIFTEEN
ENRICO

I stared out the window at two of my discrete guards patrolling as if they were passersby. There were also a handful in the security room, monitoring the area through the security feeds.

Kingston's text kept playing on repeat in my mind.

> She's in Russia. In Konstantin's home. I don't linger in Russia.

I fucking knew that. The man would set fire to the country if he could, and I wouldn't even blame him.

So here I was considering my next step with the ginger-haired beauty instead of focusing on the files strewn across my desk. One of the Marchetti legal entities had finally secured the billion-dollar contract for the French government building we'd been pursuing for months. It was a key location for both our legal empire and our smuggling business. Despite what this would mean for my legacy as the head of this family, I couldn't get Isla's smiling face out of my mind. The way she looked when I got that call. I swore I got blue balls as I walked away from her even though I had fucked her mere minutes before.

And now, she was in Russia.

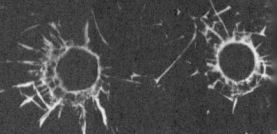

Goddamn it. I should have answered her text. Made some concrete plans with her so she wouldn't leave the city. Although I didn't think it was my non-responsiveness that overwhelmed her. It had to be something else.

As if the universe were sending me a message, my phone buzzed. My eyes flitted to the phone screen and my heart squeezed in a weird way. Discounting it as stress, I slid the message open.

> Fool me once; shame on you. Fool me twice; shame on me. We are done. Don't contact me again.

I typed a message back.

> Are we back to that again? Whatever is the matter, we will talk about it and solve it.

The reply was very mature. A line of twenty "fuck you" emojis. My cell buzzed again.

> Thanks for the experience. Our time has expired. Now exit my life. Capisce?

Once it was clear I wouldn't be dragging anything out of this woman via texts, I dialed up Kingston. He answered on the first ring.

"Marchetti."

"Kingston, did Donatella approach Isla while you were tailing her?"

"No, but there was a short window where I didn't have eyes on her."

"Why?" I barked.

"A moron cyclist almost ran into her and her friend. Had to teach him how to ride a bike."

I shook my head. Sometimes Kingston was a mirror image of Alexei Nikolaev. "Is he still alive?"

"Depends on what you consider alive."

"I wonder about you," I muttered under my breath.

"Ditto."

He ended the call without another word.

I was too old for this shit. Too old for her. Maybe I just needed to pull my head out of my ass.

Fuck—*no*. I wasn't too old for her, and my head was fine where it was. Isla Evans would be mine, old or not.

But first, I had to solve the Donatella situation. She was another problem entirely, and more than a mild frustration. The fucking woman was nowhere to be found. I half expected her to make her way into my home again. That would make it easy to end her, but she must have learned she had used up her last chance.

Grabbing my phone, I typed a message to Kingston.

> Find Donatella while Isla's in Russia.

Konstantin better keep his baby sister safe, or I'd be the one to destroy his country, not Kingston.

Work was a waste of time today. A conference call was in progress, with all Omertà families participating. Even Luca DiMauro, although he kept mostly quiet.

I couldn't concentrate, my mind still stuck on Isla. I hadn't seen her in a week and sleep was hard to chase. Even after jacking off in the shower, furiously stroking myself. It was as if my cock had zeroed in on the woman with freckles and an emerald gaze and refused to give in unless it could bury itself within her tight folds.

My cock would chafe if I kept this up. I had to fuck her soon.

Oddly enough, the more I thought about marrying her, the more I fucking loved the idea. The thought had always been repelling. Until her.

But there was also underlying fear. The whispers weren't off base when they claimed every woman who married a Marchetti male ended up dead. Well, almost any. Donatella was still alive, at least for now.

"Are you paying attention, Enrico?" Manuel's voice snapped me out of my thoughts. I found his eyes on me, studying me curiously. It was out of character for me to get sidetracked.

"Yes."

We were on a conference call, but our side was muted. The discussion about what to do with our portion of the Costello product had been cycling through each of the families' respective offices.

Lykos, the Greek don, got his shipment, which was docked in one of my ports in Italy. His product would be secure until he made the necessary repairs to his yacht and then sailed back to Greece. He had been running a successful operation for decades, and this favor I had done for him would prove to be very lucrative.

The easiest fifteen million I had ever earned, and by distributing the product over the Omertà territories, it would make me another hefty profit while barely lifting a finger. Business was booming.

Except, I couldn't shake off the worry about the supposed mole within our organization. I was always extra careful to select only the men I trusted with my life into our organization. My brother and father had been the same. The children of men who'd worked for my father came to work for me. We rarely went outside the circle of confidants who had proved themselves to the Omertà over the generations.

Moles usually cost the lives of the entire family, not only the head of it. The worry for my sons always lingered. I taught them from a young age how to defend themselves. Shoot a gun. Fight with not only their strength but with their minds. But it hardly earned me any peace. I didn't want them to end up dead like my brother.

"It might be good to tie the Costello and Marchetti lines," I remarked as Romero droned on about some territory dispute in Northern Italy. "Lykos's youngest is already infatuated with Amadeo."

And if the arrangement was in place, it'd secure my son's life if something happened to me. He'd also be under Costello's protection, not only the Omertà's.

Manuel gave me a pensive look. "Not a bad idea, but you know he's a wolf when it comes to his children."

"As he should be."

"The Marchetti reputation and dead wives dating back five generations won't speak well for this union."

I shrugged. "When I marry Konstantin's sister and keep her alive, it will be proof enough."

"So you still plan on going through with it?"

My dick might not survive if I didn't. I was so fucking infatuated with the young woman that Manuel would make fun of me if he only knew.

"Yes." The moment I decided to marry Isla I'd begun to put everything in motion, and nothing would hold me back. Not her big brother. Not Donatella. Fucking *nothing*. The world might burn. The Omertà might crack... but Isla Evans would still become my wife. "Merging the two families will appeal to Lykos."

"I think keeping his children alive appeals to him more," Manuel noted dryly.

"Well, I'll put a clause in." My uncle's brows lifted. "If I manage to keep my wife alive"—and I fully intended to—"the arrangement stands. If I don't, he can break it off."

Something in my chest twisted at the thought of anything happening to Isla. It was so volatile that I feared it'd stop my black heart, catching me by surprise.

"So I guess that leaves Enzo to marry Luca DiMauro's daughter," he said, stating the obvious. The marriage arrangement was put in place when Luca's wife was pregnant. "You know, nephew, a lot could happen in the years those children have to grow up."

"True, but the arrangements will remain."

"Are you sure it's wise to pair little Penelope with Enzo?"

"He'll be the head of our family one day. It's the only thing that makes sense. Luca DiMauro might still be angry at the way things played out, but he'll be pleased to know his daughter will continue to be mafia royalty once she marries Enzo. Rather than some third-class wannabe."

I'd convince Luca to see things my way. He was still steaming, refusing to participate in the Omertà meetings. His brothers-in-law stepped in and it had worked so far, but he couldn't continue that indefinitely.

"Somehow I don't get the feeling that Luca nor his wife are thinking the same way," Marco noted, tilting his head to the phone.

"Probably, but until his access supersedes ours, he won't be running the show." He knew I meant access to the drugs that came in through our ports. The only ones that had the means to bypass us were the Yakuza. If Amon Leone decided to take over his stolen empire, his organization would be more powerful than most in the world.

"True."

I pushed out of my chair, reaching for my suit jacket. "I'm going to call Costello. Handle the rest of the call."

My cousin's jaw fell open. "You never leave work."

I shrugged. "It's business. And some wedding arrangements."

I wanted Isla to wear a dress designed by my fashion house. The one I approved of. And I had to go fetch my mother's ring that was stored among my other assets in Switzerland. I'd be prepared, and the moment she was back, I'd put that ring on her finger and fuck her within an inch of her life. Or mine.

It'd be a good way to die, that's for sure.

SIXTEEN
ISLA

I sat behind the wheel of my brother's Land Rover at the arrivals lane of Moscow Airport, typing vigorously on my phone. The end of October was fast approaching and the busy season for violinists—the dreaded holidays—was almost here. I knew people would be pissed I took off, but this was important. I had to uncover the truth about my mother.

So here I was making excuses to my bosses. It wasn't very responsible, but I refused to feel guilty for doing this. I wanted information on my mother.

A loud squeal had me raising my head to find four familiar figures lugging their fashionable and colorful luggage behind them.

"We're here," Raven yelled loud enough to wake the dead as well as draw the attention of every person around.

I rolled my window down despite the cold outside and waved them over before pressing the button to open the trunk. The men here were used to me coming and going. Although I preferred to go rather than come to the cold Russia.

"Put your shit in the back," I instructed.

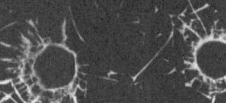

Prancing like they were on a runway, they looked like movie stars walking the red carpet. Men and women alike flicked gazes their way,

probably wondering whether those four women were someone they knew. Or should know.

Reina wore her Gucci sunglasses, her blonde curls bouncing with each step she took. Decked in a pink sweater dress, white Ugg boots, and a white faux-fur hat, she looked like a Hollywood movie star going incognito—much like her mother and grandmother were. Phoenix wasn't far off with her dark hair and white sweater dress. Raven and Athena, much like me, opted for black leggings and long sweaters, finishing off their looks with flats.

I'd been back at my brother's place for only a couple of days, but frustration bubbled inside me. I hadn't been able to find anything. I searched and searched Illias's office, library, and even his bedroom. Absolutely nothing.

With all of their suitcases secured, the hatchback started lowering. Before it clicked shut, the doors of the Land Rover opened and my girlfriends piled in like a ton of bricks.

"Do you have any idea how much we love you to make this journey to Russia?" Athena grumbled. "We might not get out of here alive."

Raven blew a raspberry. "Stop exaggerating. We might find ourselves a hot Russian," she said, her glove-covered hands coming up to sign.

"*I prefer Italian men*," Phoenix signed, confirming once again what Reina had shared with me. Not that I doubted her, but I hoped she was wrong, because it could only mean both sisters would wind up unhappy.

I left my parking spot, glancing over my shoulder to ensure there weren't any crazy Russians ready to slam into me.

"Clearly Isla prefers Italian men too. An *Italian daddy* to be more specific," Reina replied, facing Phoenix to sign. "She just refuses to admit it."

Slamming on the gas pedal, the Land Rover revved into the next gear, causing a few honks to blare behind us. I laughed happily for the first time in days, then pushed my hand out the window and waved the car forward. It sped up to pass me but stopped parallel to me.

I turned my head and gave him a sweet smile. The old man sitting in the passenger seat rolled down the windows and then let out a string of Russian curses.

Another wave and he was forgotten as he sped up ahead of us.

"I'm just happy to get some time away from my investigative work," I remarked dryly. "Apparently I suck at snooping."

"Have you checked his underwear drawer?" Raven asked.

"Or his sock drawer?" Athena chimed in.

"*If I were you, I'd find his safe and break into it,*" Phoenix suggested. It was Raven who translated since I had to keep my eyes on the road.

"I'm good with stealing," Raven told Phoenix. "I can handle that. Killing, not so much. My stomach is too weak. I can't handle blood."

Then as if to emphasize it, she gagged.

Silence filled the car and the ghost creeped through the air until Athena put a stop to it.

"Forget the fucker who's dead." She talked and signed at the same time. "Now, Isla, did you or did you not go through your brother's stuff? We have to work using the process of elimination here."

I held my hand up. "No, I didn't go through my brother's underwear and socks. Yikes!" I flicked a glance in the rearview mirror to meet Phoenix's gaze and confirmed that Raven was signing for her since I was driving and needed both hands. "And my safe-cracking skills are slightly rusty, so there's that."

"So you know where his safes are?" Reina asked. I nodded. "Then he wouldn't have it there. It'd be a spot that nobody but him would know."

I rolled my eyes. "Lovely. Not sure how I'll find it if nobody knows about it but him."

Athena waved her hand. "Let's worry about that some other day. Tonight is our break time."

"*Where are we staying?*" Phoenix asked. "*Please don't say some motel.*"

I chuckled. Reina, Phoenix, and I went on a girls' trip once, and I'd been in charge of booking the hotel. Phoenix never let me live down my mistake in booking a motel instead of a hotel. How was I supposed to know a motel wouldn't have any amenities aside from maybe a toothbrush and tiny bottles of shampoo and conditioner? I'd never stayed in one until that time.

And Phoenix liked her amenities apparently.

"I booked us at The Carlton." I switched lanes so I'd make my exit. Reina signed to her sister, snickering. "It has all the fucking amenities. Best of all, there's a club right next to it. We can walk to it, have fun, and be back in our room in no time. No drinking and driving."

I never took anyone to Illias's castle in Russia. I could take my friends to any other home but this one. It was one of the hard rules he'd given me early on. It was okay with me though. Nobody I knew was Russia-bound crazy. Besides, there was nothing for miles in the countryside where our home was. So this was a win-win.

Squeals of excitement filled the closed space of the Land Rover.

"Tonight we shall have music, food, and lots of drinks," Raven exclaimed.

"I hoped you'd say sex," Athena remarked. "I want to try some wild shit. Spanking. Oral. Ass play." Enrico's smirk and the dark glimmer of his eyes flashed in my mind. I'd bet my violin he was into ass play. Dirty man.

"I tried spanking, it just didn't do it for me." Reina stiffened, realizing she slipped, and we all watched her as she turned beet red. It just so happened that she'd conveniently forgotten to sign for her sister's benefit. But Athena came swiftly to the rescue and filled Phoenix in.

"*Tell me you did not let Amon spank you during sex!*" Phoenix demanded to know, her eyes bulging out of her head. We all knew Reina and Amon's history. She'd fallen for him hard. I was so fucking sure that he fell for her too. After all, he fucking waited for her to become of age to touch her. "*I didn't think he was into rough sex.*"

I certainly wouldn't have thought Reina was into it either.

Although it was interesting that Phoenix didn't think it was Dante who spanked her, considering she was engaged to him. Unless Phoenix knew Dante's preferences. Interesting.

"What?" Reina's tone was defensive, her eyes darting out the window. "I wanted to see how it felt."

I chuckled. "Good for you. I just think it's sad for the rest of us that you have more sexual experience than all four of us combined."

"Speak for yourself, woman," Raven chimed in. "I have some freaky stuff in my bag too."

For the rest of the ride, we discussed *hypothetical* sexual experiences.

At least, I hoped they were.

Three hours later, we entered the club.

The bass of the loud music thumped, vibrations traveling up my body and deafening my ears. The bright lights flashed above the dance floor. Bodies ground against each other. Young. Beautiful.

Forgetting all our troubles for a while, the five of us made our way to the dance floor. For the night, we forgot Reina's engagement. We ignored the haunting ghost of my mother and the secrets surrounding her. And we certainly didn't talk about any men. We made the best of our time together.

We jumped and lip-synced, writhing and moving sensually but staying close together. Letting my eyes close, I swayed and felt the music envelop me. The songs blurred together. We danced our asses off.

Phoenix's deafness was categorically profound, but she did have a sliver of hearing left. She could hear some loud music and feel its vibrations. When she danced, you'd never guess that she was deaf. Until they would see us sign to each other and found her lacking. It certainly didn't deter men from ogling her, but she'd simply smile sweetly to them before flipping them off with both middle fingers.

She said she'd either be accepted as she was or she'd remain single for the remainder of her life.

All of us wore high heels and short sparkling dresses, and it took no time for our feet to start hurting. When a familiar song came on, we froze. Reina signed to her sister, letting her know it was "Truth Hurts" by Lizzo blasting through the speakers.

We spun and twirled, screamed the lyrics and laughed. We let the music carry us off to a place where nothing and nobody mattered. Where it was just us. Where we were free.

Phoenix grabbed my cell and started recording us while we shook our asses, limbs jiving and hips rolling. The words to the song were our bible, and we were having a blast studying it. Yet I couldn't help but think of the dark eyes and rough hands that knew how to touch me.

Shoving the thoughts of a handsome Italian man out of my mind, I enjoyed the moment. We continued on as one song after another blared, and it almost felt like old times. Before college. Before Reina's accident. Before the murder. Before the secrets and the pact. And definitely before Enrico Marchetti and his supposedly dead wife.

Many songs and even more drinks later, I needed a break. I leaned over and tugged on Reina's arm.

"I have to use the bathroom; I'll be right back."

She nodded and gave me a thumbs-up.

My feet throbbing and my head slightly woozy, I made my way down the long hallway to the stairs to the VIP section. The bathrooms were usually cleaner there. The man guarding the stairs threw a glance my way and instantly dismissed me.

"Hello, can I use the VIP bathrooms, please?" I said loudly, sticking to English. They were usually nicer to tourists. I smiled sweetly, smoothing my hands down my minidress, hoping he'd give me another look and decide I belonged in the exclusive bathrooms.

The man didn't even look my way. "Use the ones downstairs."

I let out a groan. "Where is the famous Russian hospitality?"

"You're in the wrong country."

I narrowed my eyes on him. What a dick!

Turning on my heel, I headed back down the dark, empty hallway. My mind whispered that it was the classic way to get murdered. A dimly lit sign flickered, and while I tried to decide whether it looked like a toilet or exit, I heard a faint moan.

My feet were moving before I could stop myself. Tiptoeing and keeping my heels from hitting the marble floor, I kept to the wall as I made my way to the door. The heavy metal door was slightly ajar, the sound of music less intense here and I peeked through the crack.

The cool night air washed over my face and bare shoulders, sending a shiver through me.

Another moan.

My eyes followed the sound and I saw two figures in the darkness. A woman leaned against the wall, her legs parted and her long skirt bunched up. *She was being pleasured.* My lips curved up into a grin. Good for her.

Just as I was about to move, a muffled voice sounded. A familiar one.

"I'm yours forever, Sofia." Holy… shit. It was two women. Then, just in case I was unsure, the woman who was getting serviced gathered an abundance of the other woman's dark hair between her hands and gripped it tightly. "Get rid of her and I'll eat you out. Day. Night. I'll do anything you want."

I didn't want to know what that meant.

"I'm the Pakhan. I decide who we get rid of. Now get back to eating my pussy and make me come."

Gripping the other woman's dark hair, Sofia arched off the wall and at the same time brought the woman's head back to her entrance. The woman on her knees must have gotten straight to work because the moans instantly started. Wild. Sensual. Erotic.

Oookaaaayyy. It was time to go.

I tried to shift away without making a noise, but failed. The soft click of my heel sounded, barely audible, but the couple looked over.

It was only then that I saw the face of the woman on her knees. No wonder it sounded familiar. It was Donatella. Enrico's "dead" wife.

For a moment, I found myself unable to breathe. I covered my mouth with my palm, staring at her. The wife of the man I wanted. Yes, I wanted him. I could admit it to myself, if nobody else. Who in their right mind wouldn't?

Apparently Donatella, my mind whispered. Maybe that was the reason the two of them lived separate lives and she was considered dead. He protected her from the underworld so she could pursue her extra-curricular activities that didn't involve men. I was confused as heck.

It still didn't excuse his lies. Or this woman's behavior toward me. I wanted to make her pay—for her lies and the doubts she planted about my mother. Maybe even for the simple fact that she had a man like Enrico Marchetti tied to her and she didn't want him, while I craved him even from Russia.

Goddamn it!

We remained staring at each other for what felt like hours. Yet, only mere seconds passed.

Neither of the women seemed concerned at being caught, judging by their evil grins. And I knew without a doubt that Donatella recognized me, although she didn't seem surprised to see me. Was the woman stalking me all the way here, in Russia?

My heart started racing as I recalled the look swirling in her eyes just a few days before. Fear wrapped around my throat and I whirled around. Acting on instinct, I raced back the same dark hallway I came through, trying to put distance between them and me. My pulse raced and my ears buzzed from the terror.

Was I the one Donatella was talking about getting rid of?

I swallowed hard, fear giving me extra speed and allowing me to ignore my aching feet. My instinct warned those women were cold-blooded killers. Maybe I was exaggerating, but Donatella was definitely nuts, and more than slightly mentally unstable. It wouldn't bode well for me if she'd followed me all the way to Russia.

Heels—not mine—clicked not far behind me. I glanced over my shoulder to see them closing in on me. Jesus, those women were older than me and ran like experts in heels. I cursed myself for leaving my phone with Phoenix. I couldn't even call them and ask them to meet me at the exit.

I was almost by the dance floor when I slammed into a body. I whipped my head around and saw a young woman. Younger than me. Maybe Reina's age, with light brown eyes.

"I'm sorry," both of us said at the same time.

A heartbeat passed when an order was barked.

"Liana, get away from her." It was Sofia's voice.

A man's deep voice came from behind the young woman—Liana—and the way he hurried toward her, breathing heavily, made me think he was chasing her. My eyes scanned over his features. Dark hair. Tall. Olive skin.

"This girl doesn't understand the definition of bodyguard, Sofia," he hissed, his accent heavy. To my surprise, it was an Italian accent. I studied his face. So he was Liana's security detail. Yet, his eyes flicked over her head and darted past me and his charge. I followed his look and was surprised to see him watching Donatella, not Sofia.

"Mama, it's just a girl." The young woman rolled her eyes, the smile around her lips soft. "Stop being paranoid, nobody is trying to kidnap me." She gave me an apologetic look. "My mother is overprotective. She takes it to a whole new level."

Yeah, something weird was going on, but I didn't need to know what. I just knew I had to get out of here, alive and intact.

"No probs," I muttered, sidestepping her before her crazy mother could get anywhere close to me.

Once I reached the girls, I yanked on Phoenix's hand and nudged Raven, grabbing Reina and Athena's attention.

"*Trouble*," I signed. "*We have to get out of here.*"

We ran out of there like the devil—or in this instance, a crazy dead wife—was on our heels.

Twenty minutes later, we were back in our hotel suite. The door shut and locked securely behind us, we stared at each other, our breathing still labored from running all the way back to the hotel, all the while glancing behind us to ensure we weren't being followed.

"*What happened?*" It was Phoenix who broke the tension. "*Is it because I sent the video to Marchetti from your phone?*"

My brows scrunched. Maybe I misunderstood what she signed. "*Can you repeat?*" I asked.

"*I didn't think he could get here fast enough to corner you,*" Phoenix continued signing rapidly.

When I gave her a blank look, she sighed and looked at Reina. "I think you and Isla are talking about two different things," she explained to both of us. "Okay, let's start with what happened with Isla in the bathroom."

Oh, shit! The bathroom. I never ended up making it to one, and suddenly going pee was a matter of life or death. I couldn't hold it anymore.

I rushed to the bathroom, slammed the door behind me, and pulled my panties down.

As the fountain started flowing from down under, I yelled through the door. "Keep an ear out in case those psycho bitches find us." A heartbeat of silence before the door swung open. "Hey, some privacy, please."

"We've seen you naked," Reina remarked soundly. "Seeing you pee is hardly a novelty. Now explain."

"Get out," I hissed. "Seriously, or this sunshine attitude will turn to thunder."

The door immediately shut with a grumble, and I hurriedly finished my business, flushing the toilet and washing my hands. "Okay, now you can come in."

It was probably better if we talked about this shit in the bathroom. It was easy to hear private conversations through thin hotel walls and doors.

All four of them crowded in the bathroom of our hotel suite. Phoenix and Raven hopped onto the counter while Reina and Athena leaned against the long, mirrored wall.

I sighed. I didn't like to use a sharp tone with them, but we had to maintain some boundaries. Privacy around these girls was pretty much nonexistent. After all, we'd been crammed together in boarding school dorm rooms and apartments for the better part of the last eight years. But there were certain things I preferred to do alone.

"So I went in search of a bathroom," I started, meeting their gazes in the mirror. "And I got sidetracked by a moan. I went to check it out. It was right outside the club, out the back door."

"First mistake," Raven said, popping a bubble in her chewing gum.

Ignoring her, I carried on with my story. "There was someone going down on a woman. And by the sound of it, her partner was eating her out like the world was ending. So I thought, good for her. But then the woman on her knees said something and she sounded familiar—"

"Whoa, whoa. Woman?" Reina's eyes scrunched. "I thought you said a woman was being pleasured."

"Yeah, you said someone was diving into her muff," Athena chimed in.

"Dining at the Y," Raven added, like it needed more clarification. "Someone decided to do it the French way."

It would seem my girlfriends felt the need to use every single term for "eating a pussy" they knew. Half of them didn't even make sense.

I waved my hand as I dried the other off. "Well, she was being pleasured. By. Another. Woman."

Athena grinned. "Hot."

"*Gross*," Phoenix signed.

"*Would you both please stop with the commentary?*" I signed, then continued exasperatedly. "Anyhow, like I was saying. The voice sounded familiar. So I stayed."

Athena scoffed. "You just wanted to watch them get it on."

"God grant me patience," I muttered under my breath. "The woman on her knees was Donatella, okay? Enrico's wife."

A round of gasps echoed through the bathroom. "*No!*" all four of them exclaimed at the same time.

"Yes. And she was talking about killing someone. I think she meant me. And then the two bitches saw me and I bolted."

"*They didn't come after you?*" Phoenix questioned.

"They did."

"*How did you escape?*"

"I ran into a woman. Girl. Young woman." I shook my head. "Whatever she was, but she was her daughter, and it stopped them."

"Donatella's daughter?" Reina's blonde brows furrowed.

"No, the other woman's daughter."

"What the fuck is going on here?" Raven demanded to know, her head swiveling between Phoenix and Reina, then back to me, long black hair reflecting the harsh lights of the bathroom. "I thought Enrico was a single, hot daddy. And who is this other woman?"

Oh shit, I forgot I hadn't updated the rest of the group on the Marchetti situation. "Short story is that his wife is alive and has been stalking me," I said with a shrug. "And I don't fucking know, Raven. I've never seen her before. She said she's the 'Pakhan,' whatever that's supposed to mean."

"No, it can't be," Reina muttered. "Women are rarely leaders of criminal organizations, and anyway... I know for a fact that a woman isn't the head of the Russian Bratva."

"How would you know that?" Raven, Athena, and I questioned at the same time.

Phoenix and Reina shared a glance. "Because Illias Konstantin is Pakhan."

SEVENTEEN
ENRICO

I was back in my villa in Italy, handling my local businesses. For a change, it was my legal business. The Marchetti legacy had its roots in vineyards and farming. Lemons. Oranges. Olives. Even producing and distributing exquisite chocolate based on a family recipe. I'd handled all of it, on top of the fashion empire, before I took over as the head of our organization.

Now, I spent most of my time ensuring our drug business boomed. Our weapon-smuggling routes were clear. And nobody was stealing from us.

I missed my legitimate businesses.

But the choice to take over the Marchetti empire and a seat at the Omertà table wasn't really a choice. If we'd given up our position, the family to take our spot at the table would have come after us to ensure we'd never return to claim what was ours.

So I had no choice. This was to protect my family.

Beads of sweat cascaded off my body as I finished the final sprint of my ten-mile run on the treadmill. I worked out every morning, but today I couldn't seem to stop without running an extra mile. Lifting an extra ten pounds.

The goddamned video that Isla sent me last night played on repeat in my skull. The woman looked happy and so fucking sexy, it made my balls ache. All night I fantasized about having her in every position imaginable to man—up against a wall, bent over a couch, from behind, on her hands and knees, under me, over me, in the shower. I wanted to fuck her into oblivion until she screamed and begged for me to stop, unable to handle any more.

Cazzo, why did the woman who had such a hold on me have to be almost half my age?

I cranked up the speed, running faster, my muscles screaming in protest. I'd tell myself not to obsess over the woman, but I knew it was too late. She was already a dark obsession of mine and there was no turning back.

Not that I wanted to turn back.

It was way too late for that. I needed to drink her sighs. I wanted to inhale her into my lungs and have her take up a corner in my black heart. I wanted her to light it up with her fire and be one with my darkness.

Slapping the stop button, I slowed down and let my heart rate ease into its normal rhythm. My cell phone rang just as I was stepping off the deck of my treadmill.

"*Pronto*," I answered, not bothering to look at the caller ID.

My erection was so hard, it hurt. I'd have to jerk myself off in the shower to the fantasy of Isla's moans and whimpers. *Again*, for fuck's sake. I needed that ginger-haired woman back, writhing under me as I fucked her hard.

"Donatella is in Russia." I tensed at Kingston's voice. "If I had to bet, she's there for your woman."

"*Cazzo*." I dried the sweat off my chest. "I'm going to Russia myself."

"Not a good idea, Marchetti. Konstantin will consider it poaching."

"I don't want his freeze-your-balls-off territory," I hissed, my muscles tensing. I trusted Kingston to keep Isla safe. The unhinged Nikolaevs not so much. And considering Isla was Konstantin's sister, he was out of the question to ask. I couldn't reveal my cards too soon. "I'll go."

"I strongly advise you not to."

"Donatella is *pazza*." Then just to ensure he understood the Italian word, I added, "Crazy. Off the deep end. Isla doesn't stand a chance if I don't go."

"I'll ask Alexei for a favor." Kingston's voice turned a notch darker. "Don't go in and ruin the peace we've built for the Omertà."

"I don't like the Nikolaevs knowing about Isla." She was my responsibility. My woman.

"Alexei won't share anything with Konstantin," Kingston assured. "He only has eyes for my sister—" It would seem my poker face was nonexistent when it came to Isla Evans. "—and considering Tatiana was just kidnapped by Konstantin and wedded, it's a safe bet."

Well, fuck me.

It was easy to keep up with everyone's business relationships. Personal ones, not so much. I completely forgot that his sister married Alexei Nikolaev.

I let out a sardonic breath. I wondered how long it'd take Konstantin to wait for Tatiana to be ready for him. It turned out he was done waiting. The timing might work out perfectly for me too.

"Okay, but if one thing is off, I want to know about it."

My dark mood lingered for the day, even after I learned that Isla was safe and sound and back in Konstantin's castle.

The need to storm that medieval establishment itched under my skin, urging me to start a war. The sooner Isla was under my roof, the better. She belonged under *my* protection.

I sat in my vineyard, waiting for Enzo and Amadeo to get their teenage asses into gear. When I was a little boy, the harvest usually started mid to late August. In recent years, we'd been picking grapes in October, which was what we'd be doing today to kick off the harvest. Together as a family. It was a family tradition that dated back five generations.

Manuel sat next to me at the table that sat here even when I was a little boy. He was ready to kick off the grape season too.

"What's with you?" Manuel asked. I rubbed my eyes, exhaustion weighing me down. The last time I slept well was that first night I fucked Isla. Damn Costello interrupted my sleep that morning, but it was still the best sleep I had gotten in years. "Isla's safe under Konstantin's protection."

I didn't turn my head, instead keeping my eyes locked over the horizon. If there was heaven on earth, this was it. The vineyard stretched as far as the eye could see and beyond it lay a clear, blue sea. This should have been my life. Not Omertà. Not being the head of the Marchetti family.

Yet, here I was, weighed down by responsibilities that threatened to drag me under. I'd gotten a taste of heaven and now I wanted more of it. Although I didn't really deserve it.

Unlike my brother, I was good at running both our empires. The criminal one and the legitimate one. At least until my sons were old enough to take over. A part of me didn't want this life for them, but the cycle would repeat. One of them wouldn't have a choice, just as I didn't, and the other would get to decide whether he wanted to be in the underworld, or get out completely. I feared both Enzo and Amadeo would throw themselves into the Omertà and thrive in it.

"I need Isla out of Russia so I can bring her to my home and put a ring on her finger."

"So you're going through with it?"

"I've made my decision," I snapped, my tone sharp. "Stop asking, hoping for a different answer." I had never been more certain of anything else. The only worry swarming my mind was the fucking curse, but as long as I kept her from truly loving me, it should be a nonissue. Only women who loved the Marchetti men ended up dead— gunshot, knife wound, poison. No leads nor motive.

Clearly Isla didn't love me, since she didn't have any issue walking away from me. That would keep her safe at the very least.

But even as the ideas played in my mind how to keep Isla close to me—and her heart still at bay—I knew I was lying to myself. I wanted to be her everything. The air she breathed. A shoulder for her to cry on. Her strength. Her weakness.

Bottom line, I wanted to consume her and let her consume me.

"I hope you know what you're doing," Manuel reasoned. "This could cause a war not only with Konstantin, but also with the Brazilian cartel."

"Not if she's my wife." I stood up, hearing my sons' approach. "Let's pick grapes. After dinner, I have to run to town. I'm picking up a wedding dress."

Manuel's eyebrows met his hairline. It'd be comical if I weren't in such a piss-poor mood. "You had a wedding dress made?"

"Yes. And I'm taking my mamma's wedding ring."

"Sorry, Papà," Enzo and Amadeo both uttered at the same time. "We were playing Call of Duty and couldn't die."

"Ah, *Dio mio*," I muttered. "We better hope we don't die in real life." I tilted my chin to the baskets that waited for us, signaling for them to grab them. "*Allora*, time to kick this off. May the best man win."

For the next three hours, we raced to fill our baskets with as many grapes as we could. For the first time in decades, neither my mind nor my heart was in it.

Instead, my thoughts were in Russia with the young woman who liked to push my buttons.

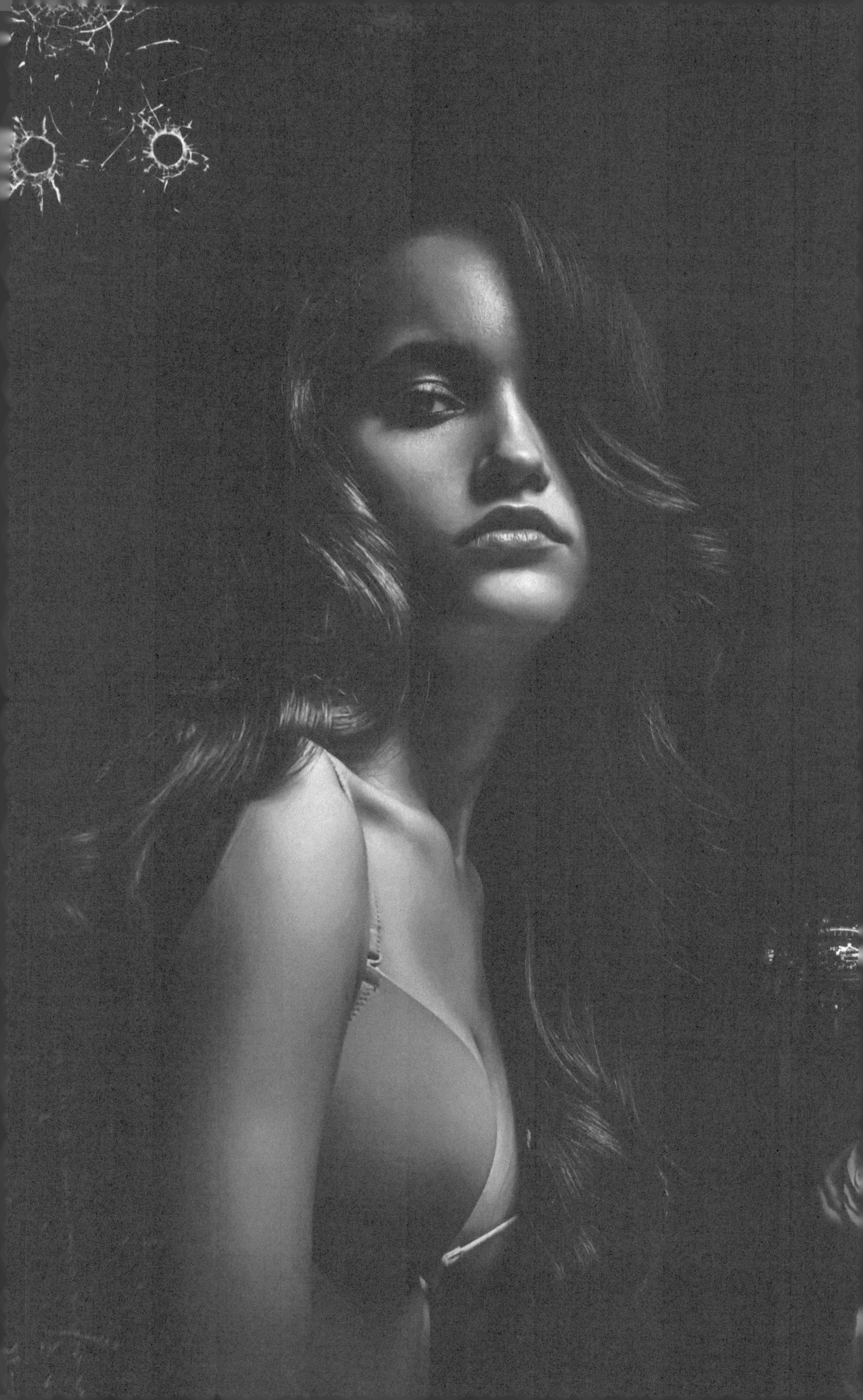

EIGHTEEN
ISLA

Illias Konstantin was the Pakhan. My brother was a criminal. The latter somehow didn't surprise me; the former shocked me. Illias wasn't just involved in shady shit, he was running it.

And still my love for him didn't waver. It turned out maybe I wasn't a good person either, because it didn't shake me as badly as it should have. I mean, it was just a title. It was no different than being CEO of some big corporation. Right?

Okay, maybe slightly different.

And then there were the messages from my hot daddy after Phoenix sent him a video of me and my friends dancing our asses off and lip-syncing to "Truth Hurts." It just so happened that those lyrics fit our situation perfectly. It was a final "fuck you" to Daddy Enrico. That was two days ago, and now I had to block his number. Because the reply I received from the man had gotten me all hot and bothered, making me more than willing to entertain him for another round of sexual fantasies.

> For your insolence, next time I see you, you'll get my cock and my hand on your ass at the same time.

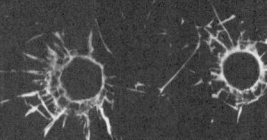

Good thing I wouldn't be seeing him again.

I let out a frustrated breath and focused on the situation at hand. I was in Illias's office. I'd already checked his sock and underwear drawer as my girlfriends suggested. There was nothing worthwhile there, and I felt extremely uncomfortable going through my brother's boxers.

So I was back in his pristine office. Reina claimed there had to be a secret compartment in here somewhere, and that nobody kept their office this spotless. He had to have a place where he hid the important stuff.

> Every man has secret compartments. Are you sure you checked every single corner?

I yanked the phone off the desk and typed back lots of angry emojis.

> I have checked every inch. I'm telling you, there isn't crap here.

My phone buzzed again. Phoenix's text message glared back at me.

> She's probably been dreaming about her Italian daddy so much she can't focus.

Another buzz. Athena's snickering message followed.

> What are you going to do if he prefers business women over artists?

Phoenix's message chimed.

> You mean smart women? We're all smart. We just prefer our artistic selves.

I could already hear them all laughing their heads off. It was the only downfall of group messaging with your best friends. Everyone always ganged up on you, then rode your ass. But I wouldn't trade it for anything.

I couldn't resist replying.

> If he likes intellectual responses, I could just
> beg the hot daddy, "Oh, my patriarchal Italian
> figure, please restrict my airflow." That'd get
> him going.

Well, that got them going. My phone buzzed like an alarm clock that couldn't be turned off.

I even got a voice recording of Athena singing in her soprano voice a made-up lyric, "Look at this foxy, foxy. Look at this silver fox, daddy go. I need his cock and rock."

I snickered, typing back while her voice kept playing in the background.

> This hot daddy is not silver. He has plenty of
> thick, dark hair.

After twenty smartass messages and silly GIFs, I sent another text. They really had to stop acting so immature.

> Let's forget the damn patriarchal daddy here
> and focus on the task at hand. PLEASE.

Phoenix's reply was instantaneous.

> Ladies, let's not be mean to Isla. She needs
> inspiration and some dick.

Beep. Beep. Beep. More messages coming through. Laughing emojis. Rolling eyes emojis.

I typed back.

> Y'all are acting like damn horny teenagers.

Reina chimed in next.

> Damn straight. It was more fun back then.

Raven's message followed.

> Your artistic ass doesn't know how to snoop.
> You might as well give it up. Let's focus our
> energy on the Italian daddy.

My brows furrowed. What did that have to do with anything?

> What the fuck are you? A businesswoman with a paintbrush? And fuck the goddamn Italian daddy.

Phoenix was next.

> Now we're talking. Give it to me, Daddy.

My mouth just about dropped. That, coming from Phoenix, was unheard of. Maybe she was horny as fuck.

Athena didn't help with her next message.

> Sign me the fuck up. I'll give some to Daddy Marchetti.

It wouldn't be complete without Raven's wiseass comment.

> Yeah, you'll give him a fucking heart attack.

God, they behaved like immature teenagers sometimes.

> Y'all are acting like horny hoes.

Well, that got the emojis going. Eggplants. Bananas. Donuts (I had no fucking idea what that meant). Smiling devil. Peaches (I knew what that meant).

Another buzz signaling yet another message, and I seriously considered just muting the chat. But it was a message from Reina.

> Forget those hoes, Isla. Let's get serious and focus. Every man has a secret compartment where he hides shit. Crawl under the desk and check every surface.

It was how I found myself on my knees underneath my brother's stupid desk, trailing my fingers along every nook and cranny. Until I felt something. My heart sped up. *This could be it,* I thought.

Gently, I applied pressure against the slight indentation, and a compartment opened with a light *bzzzz* noise.

I grabbed my phone and typed a message back.

> I found it!

My phone vibrated against the hardwood floor as messages started pouring in, but I ignored them all. My fingers trembled as I pulled out the neatly stored, suspiciously thin folder, and opened it.

It was a birth certificate. For Louisa Maria Cortes. My brows furrowed. Could it be—

A sharp gasp left me. Could this be my mother's birth certificate? My eyes skimmed over the document, memorizing names. Kian Perez Cortes Sr. Maria Cortes. I murmured their names, testing them out on my tongue. I'd have to look them up. Then I remembered. Duh, my phone. It was then, even in my frazzled state, that it occurred to me to take a picture of it. I quickly snapped a few, then put it back where I found it.

I trailed my fingers around the secret compartment, hoping to find anything else. Another document.

"There it is!" I exclaimed to the empty room, feeling another document under my fingertips.

I pulled it out and held my breath as I read the names. It was my birth certificate. Isla Louisa Cortes Konstantin, born to Louisa Maria Cortes and Sergei Illias Konstantin. I wasn't even Isla Evans, but then I wasn't exactly surprised at this point.

My heart thundered as I stared at the documents, wondering why Illias would keep something so important from me. There had to be a reason; people didn't keep secrets just for the hell of it. Trepidation flickered to life in my heart, but I refused to let it hold me back. I'd have to uncover who my mother was. Who these people were! I had the right to know.

Hoping for more answers, I checked the secret compartment. There was nothing else there.

I started opening the drawers one by one again, searching for secret compartments there. Three hours of going through every file cabinet and drawer passed.

Nothing. Zilch. Nada.

Frustration bubbled inside me.

It was as if Illias knew I'd be snooping around and cleaned out his desk. There was hardly anything in there. I didn't know much about running a business, but I would have expected at least some paperwork of significance to be in his office.

Instead, all I found was paperless bullshit. A hard drive that I couldn't hack into. A laptop I couldn't unlock.

Fuck paperless. I needed evidence on a damn piece of paper. I was old-fashioned like that.

My phone buzzed again and I remembered the group chat. Shit. I crawled under the desk to grab it and shook my head with disbelief. One hundred and fifty messages!

Clearly my friends needed lives.

Voices echoed through the castle and I froze. The guards that were here had all been sticking to the outside.

"They'll be here soon," I heard Boris say.

I froze.

For a moment, I even stopped breathing. Fuck! Wherever Boris was, my brother was. That got me moving. My fingers trembled as I rushed to put everything back to the way it was. I shoved the thin folder back into its secret compartment, then scrambled to figure out how to close it.

"Come on," I whispered, skimming my hand over the surface looking for the stupid button. My heart drummed so hard, I couldn't hear anything else aside from the adrenaline buzzing in my ears.

I kept swiping across the general area until I felt the small indent again. I pushed it and an electric buzzing sound filled the air. It sounded like a damn earthquake in the silence of the office. My eyes darted to the door, holding my breath.

Click. The compartment closed and a soft swish of air left my lungs.

Grabbing my phone and tucking it safely into the back pocket of my jeans, I let my eyes sweep across the room one last time to ensure there was no evidence of me ever being here. I tiptoed to the door, then pressed my ear to it. I couldn't hear anything. No footsteps. No voices.

Bringing my hand to the handle, I held my breath as I pushed it down and waited. Nothing happened. I peered through the small crack of the door, and seeing that the coast was clear, I squeezed through and shut it softly behind me.

I rushed through the hallways and to the front of the house where I stopped dead in my tracks. My brother stood at the door, in his arms—bridal style—a woman with blonde hair wearing a man's coat. She tipped her head back to admire the mosaics painted on our ceilings, her gaze curiously studying our home.

"Vaulted ceilings have nothing on this," I heard her say, but all I could see was my brother watching the woman in his arms with a vulnerable look in his eyes I could never remember seeing before. There was such feral longing in his gaze that for a moment, I was unable to look away.

Holy fucking shit!

My brother was in-freaking-love. There was no mistaking it. It was plain as day.

I squealed so loud, it shattered the air and startled both my brother and his woman. My eyes darted between them, lingering more so on the blonde woman, curious how she'd gotten him so smitten.

"Isla, what are you doing here?" Surprise was evident in my brother's voice as he studied me under furrowed brows. I noted he never put the woman down. "I thought you were in Paris, attending your friend's fashion show."

My cheeks flushed remembering what happened the night of the fashion show. It didn't matter that it was a few weeks back, the memories were still fresh.

"That was last week," I muttered. Or a few weeks before it. No matter, it wouldn't make a difference to Illias. It was a small white lie. Despite Illias's ownership of many shopping malls, he showed no interest in fashion, so he wouldn't be able to know I was fibbing a bit. My eyes darted to the blonde beauty in his arms. The stark difference between them was evident. The paleness of her hair and blue eyes was contrasted by my brother's dark hair and even darker eyes. "If you want me to go, I can leave though," I half-teased.

With my brother back, it'd be hard to snoop around. Not that I'd had much success so far. Except for the birth certificate that possibly belonged to my mother... and my own.

My brother's gaze softened on me, and I couldn't help a warm smile slip through. Illias was always the more serious brother. Maxim and Illias were twins, but apart from their looks, they were nothing alike. Illias was always the stronger one. He took care of Maxim, and when I came around, he took care of me.

A light pang in my chest vibrated through me. I didn't like to think about the past. It was how I kept my sadness at bay. But I missed Maxim. A lot. Even though over the last few years, I felt like he was already gone. When Maxim lost the love of his life, he'd pulled away. It pushed me closer to Illias, depending on him even more. After all, I was only in my early teens. Yet now I wondered if maybe we should have paid more attention to Maxim.

Illias's eyes narrowed on the woman. "Where are you going?"

My eyebrows shot up to my hairline. Was he freaking growling?

"Put me down," she demanded, glaring at him. I stifled a chuckle. Looked like she wouldn't be taking Illias's shit.

"No."

"We're inside. I can walk now." My eyes darted to her feet and noticed she had no shoes on, and by the looks of it, she was wearing my brother's coat.

Illias, in his usual way, ignored her and returned his attention to me. "Isla, meet Tatiana. My wife." My eyes widened in shock.

"Oh my God," I sputtered. "I'm so happy for you, brother. When did you get married? Where?" Then I narrowed my eyes. "Why wasn't I invited?"

"We got married right before my plane took off." My brother's explanation made no sense. "You would have been invited, but it was an emergency."

Disappointment washed over me.

"I could have dropped everything and come to you." My voice cracked with hurt; I couldn't help it. He was all the family I had, and for some reason, I didn't like that he left me out.

My brother pulled me into a bear hug, which turned a bit awkward since he refused to let go of his new wife. *Tatiana.* I liked the name.

"Don't worry," she said, attempting to soften the blow. "He kind of kidnapped me, then forced me to marry him, so it truly was an emergency."

I blinked in confusion as she smiled smugly. My brother just groaned.

"You kidnapped her?" I hissed, panic twisting inside me. "Oh my gosh, we're going to go to jail." Jesus, why wasn't Tatiana freaking out. I narrowed my eyes on my brother, then offered my new sister-in-law an apologetic look. "I'm so sorry. We can still fix this. Illias didn't mean it." I glared at my brother just for good measure. "It's probably because you're so... s-so... beautiful?"

She waved her hand nonchalantly, seemingly amused by my reaction, as though it was just a minor inconvenience. Maybe the world had gone mad. It had started to feel that way with that crazed, stalker woman, after all.

"Don't worry about it. My brother kidnapped Branka last summer. In the middle of her walking down the aisle to marry someone else." My eyebrows shot to my hairline. Who in the fuck was Branka? "Happens more often than you think."

Huh?

Either my brother married someone slightly crazy, or there was some serious shit about to unravel. Awkward silence followed while my eyes darted between them. She didn't seem concerned at all while my brother seemed slightly annoyed at his new wife's explanation.

Okay, maybe there were a few things I could learn from Tatiana, starting with how to get under my brother's skin like that. And even more importantly, what was my brother involved with exactly? Clearly kidnapping a woman was a breeze to him.

Reina's words rushed to my mind. Illias Konstantin was the Pakhan. The head of the Russian mafia. I studied my brother and saw what had been there all along. The darkness. The ruthlessness. But there was also such fierce protectiveness. And it all reminded me of one other man.

Enrico Marchetti.

"It's nice to meet you though," Tatiana added, smiling warmly. "I hope you won't leave because I'm here. I hate being stuck in Russia in the winter."

Well, we had at least one thing in common.

Illias pecked me on the cheek before his wife could say anything else. "We'll talk to you tomorrow, sestra." I had so many questions. How could he possibly get away with kidnapping a woman? And why did she seem so... okay with it? I opened my mouth, but before a single syllable could leave me, he cut me off. "Tomorrow," he repeated.

My eyes darted to Tatiana and she smiled mischievously. "Tomorrow," she mouthed.

"Um, oh... okay."

I remained glued to my spot, watching them disappear up the stairs, heading to Illias's wing of the house.

And all the while I couldn't shake the feeling that things were about to unravel. It remained to be seen whether for good or bad.

NINETEEN
ISLA

The smell of freshly baked pastries filled the air.

Our home was quiet, the early hour and cold morning keeping most of the guards in their respective booths around the perimeters or in the kitchen. It left me alone to roam the portrait-lined hallways with the ghosts of this castle's past.

Priceless paintings hung everywhere. Works by Aivazovsky, Repi, Malevich, Michelangelo, Monet, Da Vinci.

And then there was the family portrait. The familiar pang in my chest throbbed.

Like always, I paused by that ten-by-ten frame, probably painted by someone famous. It was the original Konstantin family. My father with his wife, and my brothers. Illias and Maxim.

There was something about it that always stirred resentment. Not toward my brothers, but at my father and my mother. Illias said when his mother died, Father lost himself and couldn't find his way back to normalcy. When I questioned him about my mother, he'd just shut down.

Shaking my head, I made my way downstairs. The moment my feet touched the last step, I heard my brother's phone ringing from the study. My brother was a dedicated workaholic.

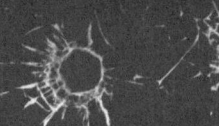

"Hello?"

"Konstantin." A shiver ran down my spine as I crept closer to the threshold, trying to make sense of what this meant and the familiar voice. "I heard you finally got married. Congratulations," the voice spoke. My brother must have had him on speaker, because I could hear him clearly.

"Somehow I have a feeling you didn't call me to congratulate me on my marriage, Marchetti."

I knew it. It was Enrico. But how did he and my brother know each other?

Glancing around, I ensured none of my brother's men lingered around before pressing my ear against the cool wooden door. I didn't want to miss a single world.

"You're right," he drawled, his deep voice cold. Indifferent. "Honestly, I'm surprised it took you this long to marry the woman. You must have her willing by now. No?"

Illias scoffed. "If this is the reason for your call, I'm hanging up."

Enrico's chuckle sounded through the speaker. "I doubt that. Especially when you hear what I have to say."

"What's that?"

A heartbeat passed before an answer came. "I know your sister."

Blood rushed through my veins. Oh my gosh, if Enrico told my brother about us, I'd die of embarrassment. I could feel my cheeks burning as images of the two of us flashed through my mind. Enrico on his knees, eating me out. Me on my hands and knees as he thrust inside me with such force I thought I'd died and gone to heaven.

I gave my head a slight shake, chasing memories away. I needed to hear where this was leading, not remember those erotic images.

"I don't know what in the fuck you're talking about." Illias's voice was deathly calm, but the undertone of the threat was unmistakable.

"Really? So Isla Evans is who? Your protégé?" Hearing my name coming from him made my heart speed up. Except, I was unsure whether it was in anger or arousal. "Let's stop playing games, shall we?" I detected a hint of annoyance. "She's your sister. She told me herself."

A growl vibrated through the room. "You've been speaking to my sister?"

"You could say that. We've gotten pretty close," Enrico replied coolly. The tips of my ears burned knowing exactly how close he'd gotten to me. Jesus, he'd buried himself so deep inside me, I hadn't known where he started and I ended.

"You stay the fuck away from Isla." My brother's voice thundered, and I could almost feel the whole castle shake with his threat. "You better not pull her into this shit, Marchetti, or I swear to God... I swear to God, I'll send this alliance we have burning to ash, and you'll find yourself at war with not just Sofia Volkov, but also with me."

My brows furrowed. Who in the fuck was Sofia Volkov?

"I have no desire for war, Konstantin," Enrico drawled. "In fact, I was thinking of a more formal alliance between your family and mine."

There was a moment of silence while I contemplated the meaning of Enrico's words. They made no sense. What alliance? I was growing more confused by the second.

"Elaborate, Marchetti."

Good, at least I wasn't the only one.

"A marriage between your sister and me," Enrico said. Wait. What? His words had me reeling. I stared at the mahogany door, willing it to explain to me what I just heard. My heart pounded against my chest as the words played over and over again in my skull.

"You're out of your fucking mind," Illias bellowed. "She's half your age, and let's not forget every fucking woman that marries a Marchetti ends up dead. Your family is cursed."

Enrico laughed on the other line. "I didn't take you for a superstitious man."

"I'm not, but fuck if I'll risk my sister to test it."

"And if she's pregnant with my child?"

Oh, he did not. He. Did. Not.

Yet, I heard it with my own ears. He gave my brother the very clear idea that he'd slept with me. This son of a bitch was playing at something. *And let's not forget his wife!*

My temper flared. My heart drummed in my ears as I had to restrain myself from bursting through the door and shouting at both men. There was no chance in fucking hell I was pregnant. Firstly, I was on birth control. And secondly, I just had my period. Thirdly, I'd murder both of them before anyone forced me into marriage.

So thank you very much, Mr. Marchetti, and kindly fuck off. He wouldn't be getting any babies from me.

"I don't even want to know what you meant by that comment," Illias hissed. "But you can bet your Italian ass I'll murder you with my bare hands when I see you next."

"You're a strategic man, Konstantin." Clearly, Enrico was used to my brother's temper because he didn't cower. "I know her heritage. Her *maternal* heritage." I froze. He knew something about my mother?

The words of his dead—or not dead—wife came rushing to the forefront of my mind. If my mother worked in one of Marchetti's brothels, that had to be how he knew about it.

Then a thought rushed to me. What if—

No, Illias wouldn't have ever allowed it. If my mother was alive, he wouldn't have ever let anyone keep her in the brothel. He wouldn't lie to me and tell me she was dead. But still, the thought remained. Or was it hope? No, it would be cruel to wish that on my mother. My brother wouldn't lie about something so important. He wouldn't have taken my mother from me, especially knowing the pain himself. He and Maxim lost their mother when they were very young too.

Goose bumps broke over my skin, and I had to fight a shudder.

"I'll let my sister decide herself whether she wants to marry an old ass like you." I had to stifle a scoff. I didn't know Enrico's exact age, but I'd bet he and my brother were close in age. So basically, Illias was calling himself an old ass.

"Leave her to me." I snickered softly. *Yes, leave me for him, brother.* I looked forward to cutting that man's balls off. "Marriage arrangements are being made everywhere it seems, and it'll make us all stronger allies."

I rolled my eyes. I had never heard anyone talk about marriage in such unappealing terms aside from… well, the Romero family.

"Who else is arranging a marriage?" Illias inquired.

"Dante Leone to Reina Romero. Her father wants to put her and her sister under the Leone protection and the wedding alliance will afford him that." My brows furrowed. This was getting increasingly confusing. Why would Enrico and my brother be discussing Reina? Why would either of them care? "It will strengthen the Leone position in Italy."

"Isla will not marry you, so you might as well give it up." My brother's dry tone traveled through the door. "But if you let Reina and Dante's wedding happen, it will cause bigger problems than a position in Italy. It will tear down the Omertà."

I gasped, my eyes widening. I wished I could peer into the room and see my brother's face. To judge by his expression what the heck was going on. I heard whispers of that organization from Reina and she hadn't said anything good about it.

A noise came from upstairs and my eyes lifted to find my new sister-in-law descending the stairs. I stumbled away from the door and quickly rushed to the side hallway, taking cover in the small alcove.

Pressing my hand to my chest where my heart beat wildly, I peeked around the corner and watched Tatiana head to the door where I just stood. I held my breath, waiting for her to enter my brother's office so I could go back to my post and eavesdrop. I watched her press her ear to the door and, to my disappointment, do exactly what I'd been doing just a few moments ago.

Shit! Shit! Shit!

I wanted to know what they were talking about. Would it be odd if I pranced over there and took up the spot next to her? I sighed. I couldn't risk her saying something to my brother. So I took the secret staircase that brought me to the first floor. I stomped my feet a few times and then went back down the way I came, finding my sister-in-law several feet away from Illias's office.

"Hey, Tatiana," I greeted her cheerfully as she whirled around and faced me. I had to bite the inside of my cheek to keep my composure. She had no idea I was doing the same exact thing just before. "You looking for the dining room?"

I kept my voice innocent, but judging by the expression on her face, she must have heard something she didn't like. She looked furious.

"Actually, I was thinking about taking a drive." She forced a smile and even went as far as unclenching her fists. "Maybe pick up something from the nearby bakery. Want to come along?"

I studied her. Surely she could smell pastries in the air, but then it wouldn't hurt to get to know her a bit better. "Sure."

"Lead the way to the garage, then," she announced.

Why did it feel like she wanted to run away?

TWENTY
ENRICO

"And you're sure you traced the signal to my home?"

I stood in my home back in Italy with Manuel and Kingston. My sons were safely tucked in the safe room—I had one of those in every home I owned—while we evaluated whether the threat was here. Or better yet, the signal. My men were searching every corner of the house—the undergrounds excluded since nobody but Manuel and I knew about them and we didn't want anyone else in on that particular secret—while we were checking the electronic devices in my office.

"Yes, Marchetti," Kingston replied dryly.

"Ignore my *nipote*. He's just cranky because the lady evaded him a second time and is now hiding in Russia."

"She's not hiding," I snapped, narrowing my eyes on both of them. "You want to be shot by your capo?"

"Bring it on." Not much ruffled Kingston.

"Don't tempt him, Kingston, or he might actually shoot us." Manuel was having too much fun with this. "Unfortunately, this nephew of mine is an excellent shot."

"Well, you can shoot us." Kingston didn't appear chastised in the least. "Or you can trust me. But if you'd like a second opinion, be my guest. You won't hurt my feelings."

The three of us stood in my office. The curtains on the large French windows were open, thanks to the fact that all the windows in my castello were bulletproof. The garden of dwarf lemon trees, vineyards, and the view of the Tyrrhenian Sea stretched as far as the eye could see. This was the only place I felt at peace, my favorite place in the world.

Right now, though, peace was impossible to find.

I went to the liquor cabinet. Manuel sat himself in one of the armchairs while Kingston typed away on his laptop. I poured myself a glass of bourbon, slammed the bottle hard on the tray, and went to sit behind my desk.

Breathing deeply and evenly, I attempted to keep a level head. But between Isla and the mole that was monitoring my estate, slipping details of my businesses to my enemies, I felt like I couldn't catch a break. These were the puzzles that irked me, and I needed to solve both.

"Maybe we should go through the staff again," Manuel suggested. "Most of the men have been part of the family for generations. Their fathers. Their grandfathers. But maybe we'll find a weak spot."

I pinched the bridge of my nose.

The pit in my stomach churned. The fact that it was taking us this long to nail down the traitor told me it wasn't some clueless soldier or brainless twat that was doing this for money. It was bigger than that. This *needed* to be resolved, especially before I brought Isla around my men.

Letting this go and leaving this traitor in the shadows could risk everything and everyone I loved.

"How many men do you have on your payroll?" Kingston asked.

A sardonic breath left me. "Thousands. This will take time." And I wanted Isla as my wife the moment she stepped foot out of Russia.

"Not necessarily," Kingston reasoned. "We can easily eliminate the individuals that don't really come around. Let's focus only on the ones that come and go from Castello Del Mare."

I turned this over in my head. Part of me wanted to start torturing every single one of my men until we found the culprit. Someone was helping Donatella and therefore putting Isla's life in danger. Whoever it was, they should die for it. They threatened my whole family—my boys, my uncle, my friends, Isla. I'd be damned if I just sat and waited.

"*Va bene*," I said carefully. "But anyone we suspect is to be brought into the torture wing."

It was about time it got used again. The last man those walls had seen was Luca DiMauro.

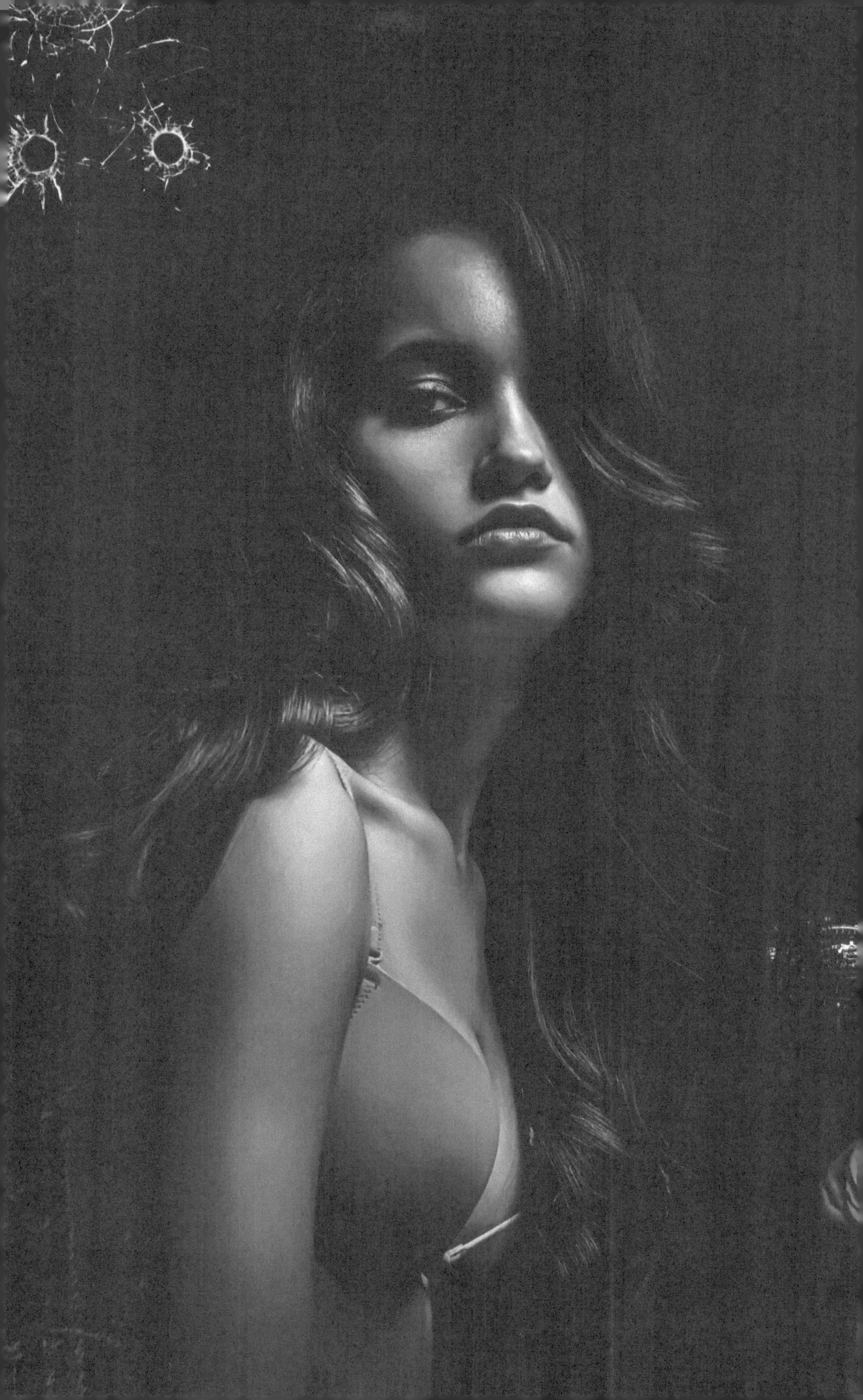

TWENTY-ONE
ISLA

It had been almost two weeks since my brother brought Tatiana to our Russian home. Illias had disappeared to take care of some "business." Now that I knew he was the Pakhan, his urgent businesses made sense. So it left Tatiana and me to get to know each other. As it turned out, we got along great... despite some displeasure she had toward my brother. The joys of marriage, I supposed. She behaved like my sister, and sometimes even like my mother.

I hadn't yet decided whether I liked that or not.

Either way, I was happy for the company. I went through my brother's office again and found no new clues. I googled the name I had found on my birth certificate but came up blank. Not a single lead.

At least the castle was no longer boring with Tatiana around. Life had spiraled into a slightly weird version of chaos. First, we were attacked in the garage by two imposter guards. She had saved me—fucking saved my life—by pushing me onto the ground. Then a simple *bang* from my brother's gun, and it was all over. It didn't seem to frazzle Tatiana at all. She acted like a badass bitch.

And all the while Reina's words rang in my ears. My brother was the Pakhan. In truth, it finally made perfect sense. Yet, I said nothing to

Illias. Not that he was around much. He came, flew out urgently. Two weeks of chaos with my sister-in-law and getting to know each other in Russia, only for her to fake my kidnapping and for the journey to return us to Paris. I was now the presumed-kidnapped Tatiana's sister-in-law—what a mouthful.

But she needed a favor to unravel her own secrets concerning her dead husband and apparently Enrico Marchetti had that information. And she did save my life, so here we were. In a charming little hotel—although I had a perfectly good apartment—both of us crammed in a little bed.

Hotel Marignan Champs-Elysées was romantic. Far too romantic for the two of us to be sharing a room.

I turned my head to find Tatiana sound asleep. Christmas lights glimmered—although it was only November—through the windows from the City of Love, casting flickers over her blonde hair. The woman looked like an angel when she slept. While I, with my red hair, looked like a female version of the devil standing on her opposite shoulder. She could probably fool most people, but I'd seen her in action. Looks could be deceiving.

Returning my attention to the dark ceiling, I stared at it, unable to sleep. I was perturbed. Worried. After hearing the conversation between my brother and Enrico two weeks ago, I wondered what Enrico's angle was. But if he thought I'd just accept it, he was sorely mistaken.

And then there was the whole revelation that my brother and Enrico knew each other, and that my brother was apparently the Pakhan—also known as a badass criminal involved in a lot of suspicious shit. I only had one murder under my belt, but according to Google, the heads of criminal organizations had many.

What kind of secrets was my brother keeping exactly? Maybe instead of trying to find out, I should just let him keep his so I could keep mine. Well, my friends' and mine. It was very likely that if Illias knew the Marchetti family, he'd know the others too.

I tucked a curly strand of hair behind my ear, my fingers trembling lightly. If Illias knew what we had done to help Reina, I feared he'd blow a gasket. There'd be a volcanic eruption with no way of stopping it. Although one thing I was certain of: Tatiana would find a way to cool my brother's temper.

I didn't even want to imagine the ways she'd calm him, actually. I snickered, turning to my side and staring at the flickering lights of Paris. The City of Love, and I always seemed to find myself in charming hotels with friends.

Reaching for my cell on the tiny nightstand, I started typing a message. After all, we couldn't just show up at Enrico's home and shoot our way in. Tatiana would be carrying a gun, but we'd agreed it would be blank.

> Hey, it's Isla. Can I see you tomorrow morning?

The moment I pressed send, I groaned. I should have done this earlier; it was past midnight. I mentally slapped myself. Who sent messages to mysterious mobsters at midnight? Clingy, needy hook-ups who wanted another night of hanky-panky, that's who.

My phone's beeping interrupted my inner monologue.

> Why?

Okay, that reply was a bit short and to the point.

> Just because?

> Your last message said you're done. Should I quote to you what you said?

For Pete's sake. Men weren't supposed to hold grudges.

> There were rows and rows of middle fingers.

> I'm not done with your dick. We could get started tonight with some phone sex. Ever done it, old man?

Oh my God, Isla! What are you doing? The plan wasn't to antagonize him. Nor to have phone sex with him while Tatiana slept like the dead next to me.

My phone rang before I could take my next breath. I glanced at the caller ID. Enrico.

Well, at least I knew what worked with him. So I'd have to use my body to get us in tomorrow.

"Hello?" I whispered. My voice came out altogether too breathy for my liking.

"You're asking for trouble, aren't you, *dolcezza*?"

I rolled my eyes in the darkness. "I've never been in trouble in my life." Such a damn lie. Reina, Phoenix, and I were in trouble all the time. We just never got caught. "So why are you calling?"

"This wild *piccolina* with a ginger mane offered phone sex. I'd be a fool to refuse."

I chuckled softly but immediately stifled it.

"What does 'piccolina' mean, anyhow?" I questioned him. "You have way too many Italian nicknames for me."

"Little one." He paused for a moment before answering. "With a big and sweet personality."

My cheeks heated. I couldn't quite decide if it was hot or corny. *Definitely hot.*

"What are you doing?" I asked, keeping my voice low.

A dark chuckle echoed through the line. "You don't want to know."

I let out a frustrated breath. Why did he always assume he knew what I wanted? He definitely didn't.

"Yes, I do."

"I'm jerking off," he grunted. My breathing stalled, the image of Enrico lying naked in bed searing my mind. I could picture his hand wrapped around that thick cock, pumping his hips. Desire, raw and carnal, clawed in my gut. I shouldn't picture him. I shouldn't want him. Yet, I couldn't stop.

"I want to see," I breathed, my skin prickling with lust. "We could FaceTime."

His response was prompt. "Only if you let me see your pussy."

Oh God, I should say no. I shouldn't think about him naked in bed, his thick, muscular thighs parted as he jerked off.

"Okay," I heard myself answer. There was no harm in FaceTime. It wasn't like he could touch me, or I could touch him and succumb to this attraction that sizzled even through our text messages.

Slipping out of the bed, I drifted into the small hotel bathroom and closed the door behind me, the tile cool on my feet. I pressed the call button, the soft ringing stopping short as Enrico answered almost instantly.

I had no idea where he set up his phone, but it gave me the most magnificent view of his naked body. He was propped against the cushions of his bed, his smooth, rigid muscles a work of art. Bracing his feet on the mattress, his muscular legs parted to give me a perfect view of his length. He worked himself hard, his hips flexing and biceps straining as he jerked himself off.

"You're so beautiful," I said, a soft sigh escaping my throat. I licked my lips, wishing I could taste him. Feel his hard body against mine. I wanted him so badly. My pussy clenched, remembering the feel of his dick, the stretch of it as he filled me. It was a good thing we were not in the same house, or I'd be tempted to seduce him. Or let him seduce me.

Our eyes locked through the small screen, the definition in his abs making my thighs quiver with desire. Jesus Christ. When it came to him, I was a wanton woman.

His movements paused. "Touch yourself, *dolcezza*. I know you're hungry for my cock."

"I am," I breathed. "So much that it aches."

I propped my phone against the mirror, hooked my fingers in my boy shorts, and slid them down my legs.

His body went still, his entire attention focused on my movements. He seemed to be holding his breath.

"Get on that counter behind you," he instructed. "I want to see your pussy. I want to watch you get off at the same time as me."

His fist wrapped around his shaft once more as he began stroking slowly from root to tip. Each pump sent a throb inside me. I was soaked... a needy, panting mess.

I hopped on the counter, and almost instantly, the coolness of the surface soothed my overheated skin. I spread my legs wide and slipped my fingers between my legs. My clit was swollen, and the brush of my fingertips against it sent a shudder through my body.

He sucked in a quick breath, his fist squeezing the head of his dick. "*Madonna*, you're fucking hot," he continued, shifting to squeeze his balls. "Such a pretty pink, glistening pussy. All mine." This felt too good. So dirty. So erotic. "My *dolcezza* likes being watched, doesn't she?"

His eyes were locked on my pussy as I watched him pump up and down, the muscles in his forearm bunching, working.

"I do," I moaned. "But only by you."

"*Madre di Dio*," he groaned, his hips punching forward. I swiped my clit again, biting my lip to keep from moaning.

"I want you inside me," I whimpered.

Enrico's expression twisted like he was in exquisite pain, and his hand picked up speed along his erection.

"Pull apart your lips and show me how wet and swollen you are." Eager to please, I parted my folds and let him see. "Taste yourself. Imagine it's my mouth on your clit, tonguing that pretty pussy." I dipped a finger in my wetness and brought it to my lips, sucking the tip inside and cleaning the arousal off.

"*Cazzo!*" Enrico barked, his body tense.

I worked my clit faster, circling and rubbing in sync with his pace, pleasure within reach. Moaning, I picked up speed. I couldn't remember ever being this turned on before. But my clit craved the friction, and I moved faster, in time with Enrico's hand. I imagined him inside me, his body heavy on me.

"It would feel so good if I were fucking you right now, no?" Fuck, that Italian accent would be the death of me.

"Yes," I panted, grasping the counter with one hand while continuing to work myself. A tingling sensation blossomed at the base of my spine, gathering and pulsing. A wave of pleasure rushed toward me, but I wanted to see him come undone first. His fist wrapped tightly over his shaft, his movements fast and rough now.

"*Cazzo*, Isla. Be a good girl and come for me." My name on his lips was my undoing. The orgasm crashed into me with the strength of a category-five hurricane.

I came all over my fingers at the same time as thick spurts shot from his cock and trickled down his six-pack abs.

We both panted, our muscles shaking and our gazes locked as the pleasure sparked through the video feed like a live wire.

"I want to taste you so badly," I admitted softly, my breathing erratic.

"Tomorrow," he promised.

I swallowed hard, knowing that after tomorrow, we'd likely cut all ties. Because I'd betray him to help Tatiana.

"Tomorrow," I repeated. I slid off the counter and reached for my boy shorts, pulling them back on. Tomorrow we'd end whatever this was, and that thought was depressing. "Good night."

"Good night, *piccolina*."

Our call ended, but my heart still raced. After washing my face with cold water in hopes of cooling off, I snuck back into bed.

Just as I was setting my phone on the nightstand, it buzzed again.

> See you in the morning. Wear a dress. Fully expect to get on my knees.

A soft gasp tore through my lips. Gosh, this man and the images he could paint in my head. He was better than any music I ever made. Maybe he was my muse?

Enrico Marchetti.

The name alone made my heart flutter. The man was clearly wrong for me on so many levels. Too old. A liar. A cheater.

All that was left was learning he was a killer, and I'd be certain I found myself a winner. And yet, here I was, craving him like the air I breathed.

I twisted around and buried my face into the pillow. I really needed a sanity check. And some sleep so I could play my part tomorrow.

I pushed all lustful thoughts from my mind and focused on the soft music in the distance of this city that never rested, letting the soft glimmer of the Eiffel Tower under the moon pull me under.

I peeked at my sister-in-law through my heavy eyelids as she slipped on her Louboutin heels. Tatiana looked gorgeous wearing a champagne-colored dress that reached her thighs. Her back was open with the crisscrossed strings connecting them. She wasn't wearing any makeup and her hair was pulled up in a slick high ponytail. She looked like a woman on a mission.

And I... I just flew by the seat of my pants while fighting sleepiness. And then there was my mane that refused to be tamed.

Usually, I was the petite one, even among my friends. But next to Tatiana, I felt even shorter than my five foot four. It was stupid, but I felt self-conscious next to her. Her confidence and her height made her stand out, and the insecure part of me almost regretted taking her to Enrico.

He'd never notice me next to her.

But then I immediately scolded myself for such pettiness. Bottom line, Enrico didn't matter. He wasn't family. My brother and Tatiana were, and when push came to shove, I'd always choose family.

I watched her reach into her purse and pull out the handgun, checking the magazine for the nonexistent ammunition. It was amazing how comfortable she was around guns. I envied it.

"Are you plotting world domination?" I murmured, still in bed while she looked ready to head out.

She rolled her eyes, but her soft smile kind of ruined it. "Not while you're in bed."

"You've got to relax." She was eager for answers, but getting to Enrico's house at six in the morning wouldn't open doors.

"I am relaxed," she retorted dryly. It was a total lie. "Did Marchetti confirm?" I smiled smugly, remembering his reply,

Fully expect to get on my knees.

That man was insatiable when it came to oral sex. I didn't know if it was normal or not, but I freaking loved it. Although I was still mad at his idea of marrying me. As-fucking-if. "What?"

I must have been daydreaming too much because Tatiana stared at me with interest.

"Nothing."

Her shoulders tensed.

"Then why the smugness?" She took two steps and put her palms on the bed, leaning over me like a mother prepared to bestow punishment. Or a smattering of kisses. My heart clenched. Not that I ever experienced those things with my mother... I'd missed out on so much. "You better tell me, or I'll tickle you to death."

I rolled my eyes. "Yeah, he confirmed."

She narrowed hers in return. "You're not telling me something."

"What?" My tone was too defensive. After all, I had nothing to hide. Except for the amazing sex I had with a man full of secrets. "It's not like you tell me everything."

We had grown surprisingly close over the last few weeks. I liked her a lot and was thrilled to call her family. Illias was an overbearing, protective brother-slash-father, but Tatiana was the perfect balance of caring and trouble. I could see us becoming friends.

"For your own good."

I blew a raspberry in frustration. "That's for me to decide."

"Did you talk to him?" she asked suspiciously. Her eyes narrowed even further on me, and I could feel heat rising up my cheeks, my blush betraying me. I nodded wordlessly. "When?" she demanded to know.

"God, if you were my sister, I'd be a nun," I muttered under my breath. "Doesn't bode well if you have a daughter." Their favorite aunty would help them out. But I kept those words to myself. I couldn't reveal all my plans on how I'd become her future children's favorite aunt, could I?

Tatiana's expression turned dreamy. I was certain she already pictured different ways she'd spoil her children and kill anyone who got anywhere near them, but the sober look returned to her eyes way too soon.

"When did you talk to him?" she repeated.

"Last night." Curse my red hair and my pale skin. If I hadn't seen the birth certificate, I would have guessed my mother was of Irish descent to have passed such a complexion down to me. Or Scottish. But Cortes sounded more Spanish. Jesus, I just wished there was a way to stop the blushing.

Tatiana's eyes widened. "Oh my gosh." She was really taking this caretaking thing to a whole new level. "Oh my gosh. Did you... Did you have phone sex with him?" My body heated up. "While I slept? In the bed next to you?"

"Well, I had to ease his worries," I mumbled. "I left him with a note that I never wanted to see him again. And now, I'm asking to see him. So—"

"So you played him," she finished for me. She sounded slightly impressed. "Are you sure we're not related?"

I let out a chuckle. "We are now." Although truth be told, how in the fuck would I know? I had my mother's name, but I had no clue where she was from. Or who she was.

"Go get ready. Make yourself gorgeous but not slutty. Kind of innocently beautiful." I gave her an eye roll. "That way when I 'hold you at gunpoint,' Marchetti will spill all the secrets in his attempt to save you."

I gave her a dubious look. I wasn't sure that Enrico would go as far as saving me. "He might be suspicious."

"Why?" I shrugged.

"He's not a dumb man."

"Well, duh. The man hides behind his luxury brands and somehow has time to run a large part of the underworld. Yeah, I'd say he's dumb. But he's blind when it comes to you."

My eyes bulged out of my head. "What makes you say that?"

She shrugged her slim shoulders. "I saw the way he looked at you in the video at the fashion show."

She referred to the video from Reina's fashion show. I shared it with her last week, wanting to show her my friends and Reina's designs. She'd spotted him in the crowd straightaway, and now I was blushing all over again thinking of the way he'd stared at me.

"Goddamn it, you're scary." I jumped out of bed. "If only we knew you—" I cut myself off and averted my eyes from her. I was scared she'd see the secrets lurking within. But the truth of it was that I really wished we'd known her when we needed help getting rid of the body. And the man.

A shudder rolled down my spine. I didn't like to think of it, never mind saying his name out loud. For Reina's sake. For all of our sakes.

I was padding toward the bathroom when my sister-in-law's voice stopped me. "Isla?"

Please don't ask questions. Please don't ask questions. The chant played over and over again in my mind.

I glanced over my shoulder to meet her eyes. "Hmmm?"

"If you're ever in trouble or need anything," she said softly, holding my gaze. "And I seriously mean anything, I'm always here. No matter what."

The scary—and amazing—part was that I was certain she meant it.

I disappeared into the bathroom, shutting the door behind me. It was so tempting to tell her. To ask for her help. We buried the body, but the knowledge of it being discovered hung over us every day.

"Tatiana?"

Her muffled voice came through the closed door. "Yes?"

"Thank you."

"I'd burn the world down for you, sestra."

I'd stake my life that she really meant those words. Literally and figuratively. She'd be a good mother to my nieces or nephews one day.

The backs of my eyes burned. Would my mother have burned the world down for me?

"Ditto," was my reply.

And I meant it.

Later that morning, we stood in front of Enrico's massive house in the heart of Paris. There was an actual iron gate surrounding it, looking every bit the mini-castle I remembered from that first night.

Tatiana was nervous. I was too, especially after that FaceTime sex last night. In the light of day, my plan didn't seem so smart. But it couldn't be changed. It happened. It was hot. And I was moving on.

Besides, how was I supposed to know the man would call me out on sending him "fuck you" emojis? Tatiana assumed I had him wrapped around my finger. She was so damn wrong.

"This is the house?" Tatiana asked, her tone incredulous. I nodded. "Who did it belong to? Marie Antoinette?"

I shrugged. "No fucking clue." History wasn't my forte. In fact, I was a lost cause when it came to pretty much anything and everything, except music. For a while, my teachers thought me dense, but they'd been too scared to say anything to my brothers.

I went over the plan we discussed again in my head. Tatiana would stick an empty gun to my back and threaten Enrico to get him to talk about her dead husband. The plan seemed kind of silly, considering Enrico and I barely knew each other. But if all else failed, I'd offer him another night of sex if he told my sister-in-law what she needed to know to move on.

It wasn't a horrible sacrifice. The man was good in the sack—my principles were skewed at this point—and his wife fucked with me for the last time. Maybe I'd even get some information on my own mother. Two-for-one kind of deal. Great plan!

Tatiana started to shake her hands and loosen her legs. Almost as if she readied for a marathon or a fight. The latter was more likely.

"Nervous?" I asked her.

"Yeah." She wasn't scared to admit her weaknesses. It was what I liked about her. She gave it to you straight. "Let's do this."

She dug into her purse for the unloaded gun. We argued for an hour about that little fact. If shit hit the fan, an unloaded gun would be useless, but she stood firm on it. She was too worried about my safety.

"Okay, I'm gonna put it against your lower back. Hopefully, his guards don't notice anything until we're inside."

"He doesn't have any guards," I mumbled under my breath. At least I hadn't seen any last time I was here.

After all, kidnappers didn't usually chitchat with their victims. Right? Fuck, I should have watched more movies on this shit.

But then I never thought I'd end up on the wrong side of the law.

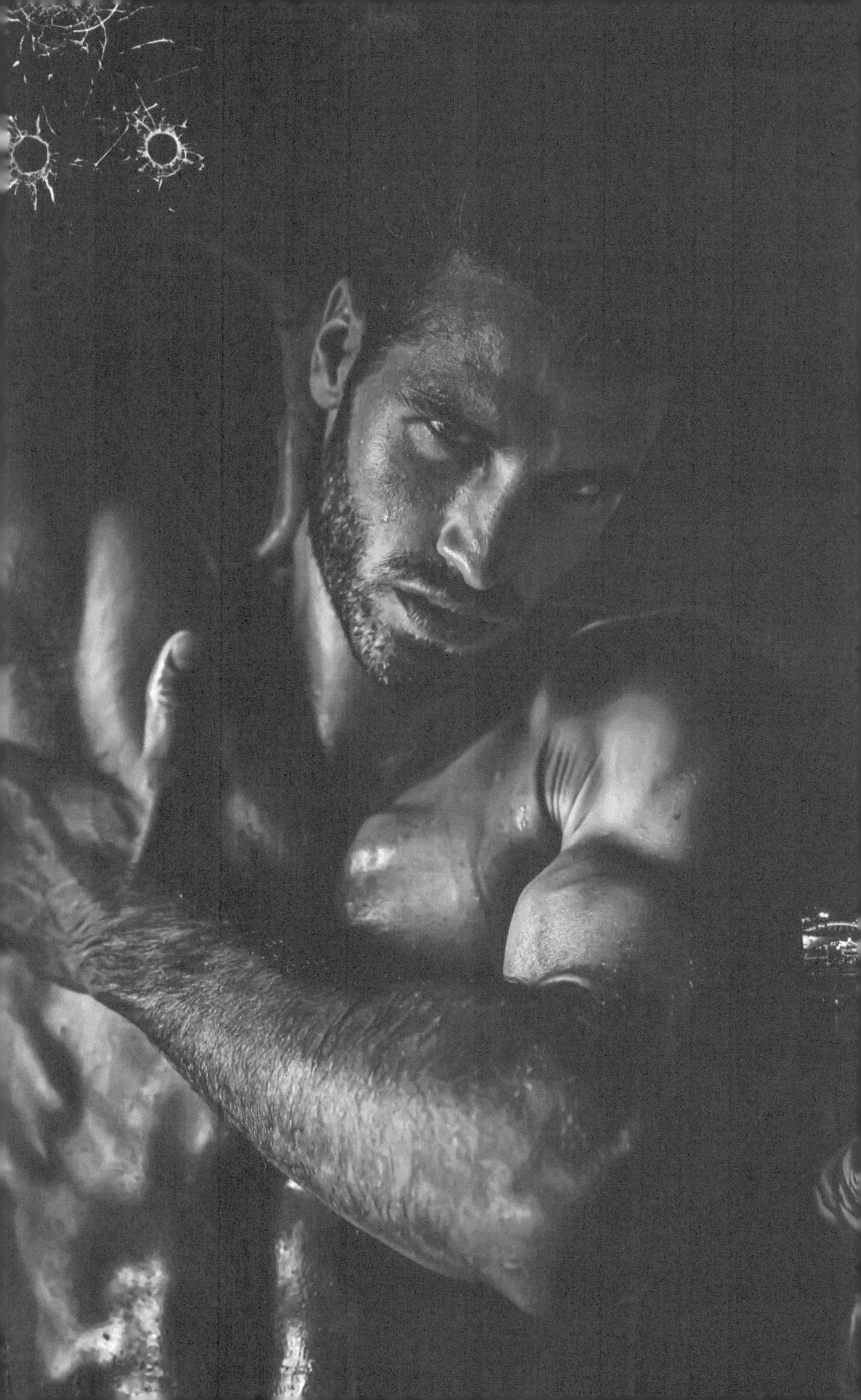

TWENTY-TWO
ENRICO

I really needed to pull my head out of my ass.

I had risen earlier than my normal five a.m. and paced around anxiously for Isla to get here, glancing at the clock like an eager schoolboy.

I shook my head, disgusted with myself. I was too old to behave like this. The truth of the matter was that Illias had every reason to be worried. Every woman who married a Marchetti over the last five generations had been killed. Well, almost every woman.

But Donatella would be dealt with. I had men looking for her, and I'd end her as soon as she was found.

The door to my study opened and Manuel strode in.

"We have guests."

My chest made a strange flip that seemed to happen every time that red-haired goddess was about, but then my cousin's words registered. *Guests*. As in, more than one?

"Who?"

"Your woman—" Shit, that sounded so fucking good. *My woman*. "—and Tatiana Nikolaev. Or rather, Konstantin."

The latter didn't sound good. It meant Illias wasn't far behind. What the fuck was Isla playing at? She never mentioned coming with her sister-in-law. Not that I asked for specifics. I was too eager to hear her voice… and then that phone sex. I seemed to be getting hornier in my old age, but only for Isla.

I pulled up my security, and sure as fuck, Isla and Tatiana stood at the corner of the street, studying my Paris home through the gate. Most people only had the immediate surroundings of their home surveilled. I took it a step further and expanded it to several blocks.

Tatiana and Isla discussed something, their mouths moving, and I decided it might be time to have surveillance outside my home include audio because I fucking wanted to know what those two minxes were talking about.

I watched Konstantin's wife shake her hands and loosen her legs as if preparing to run a marathon. It looked slightly comical in her dress, although I wasn't laughing. My eyes were locked on what Isla *wasn't* wearing.

"Didn't I tell her to wear a fucking dress?" I grumbled, slightly annoyed. She wore a pair of skinny jeans and a cropped green sweater that revealed a sliver of her midriff. She paired it with a pair of heels. Her jeans hugged her long legs and shapely hips, giving me a glimpse of what was now inaccessible. The waves of her curly red mane reached her back and framed her face. Even through the grainy video feed, I could see her emerald gaze—one that could make angels and demons alike weep.

Dio, I had to get a grip.

"*Scusi?*" Manuel gave me a blank, confused look and I waved my hand in agitation. At Isla. My uncle. At myself.

Instead of focusing on what the fuck these women were up to, I was fixated on Isla's choice of wardrobe and how it wouldn't give me easy access to her pussy. Maybe that was the problem. The young woman was too sweet and too distracting.

I watched as Tatiana reached inside her purse, pulled out a gun, and pointed it against Isla's back. My spine instantly stiffened.

"Take the boys into the safe room," I barked out, fury rushing through my veins. Manuel followed my eyes to the screen before rolling his eyes.

"They're clearly working together, but sure, I'll take the boys into the safe room. No reason to let them stand in the way of two women who are determined to get themselves killed. The amateurs should have done more recon to realize that we have cameras and can see them plotting."

I picked up my phone and barked out orders to all my guards. "Make sure you keep your eyes sharp, but don't let yourselves be seen. The two women that are currently approaching... Let them pass without them seeing you."

I hung up without waiting for the acknowledgement.

Manuel rushed out of the room to usher the boys into the safe room while I watched the two women make their way across the empty street and toward the iron gate. Pushing it open with a soft creak, they marched forward and found themselves in front of the door, then disappeared inside my home. I switched cameras and thanked all the saints that the surveillance system inside my home had audio.

I turned it on and watched as Isla made her way to the stairs. After all, she knew her way up the stairs and into my bedroom from our first night together. *And out of it,* my mind mocked. I immediately shut it up.

"Please tell me he didn't instruct you to go to his bedroom." Tatiana's voice barely registered, but it was clear she wasn't happy about her young sister-in-law having anything to do with someone like me.

Isla let out a soft groan but didn't answer as she continued ascending the stairs. My cell phone buzzed with confirmation that my boys were safe, so I made my way out of my office and into the hallway where I expected the two women to show up at any moment.

And sure as shit, there they were. Isla's attention wasn't on me, instead she shifted slightly, murmuring soft words to Tatiana.

I announced my presence. "I must say, I didn't expect two of you here."

Both women shifted and Isla stumbled forward with a soft whimper. "*Ouch.*"

I knew they were playing me, but fuck, hearing Isla's pain—that was clearly feigned—had my insides reeling. Instinctively, I took a step forward to help her, my gun out of my holster and in my hand. It was pointed at the pale blonde woman whom I spared on Konstantin's behalf a year ago.

So much had happened in the past year. We killed Adrian, Tatiana's previous husband. He had been sending incriminating videos to the members of the Omertà, threatening to bring down our organization. However, the problem was… they didn't stop once he died.

"I wouldn't," Tatiana said coolly, unfazed by the fact that I was holding a gun pointed at her. The woman had courage, I'd give her that. "Not unless you want to see Isla's guts scattered all over your white marble."

My movement stilled, the images of Isla's body on my marble floor hit me with such a volatile feeling that it stole my fucking breath away.

Jesus Christ, had I fallen that hard for a woman who could easily walk away from me? The time for those questions wasn't now.

"What do you want, Tatiana?" I suspected I knew. The woman had been restless ever since her husband's death, seeking answers.

She met my gaze head-on, keeping her shoulders straight. She was brave, but not foolish. She understood what I represented and was smart to be scared. After all, she grew up in the underworld.

"I told you I'd come after you when you killed my husband." So she remembered her accident. Good for her. "Here I am."

She was dumb to keep looking for answers about Adrian instead of thanking all the saints for her current husband. She was only alive thanks to Konstantin. He vouched for her, assuring me she didn't know what Adrian was doing to all of us. I, on the other hand, didn't like to leave loose ends for this exact reason.

I gave her a cold smile. "But your new husband is alive. In fact, he just landed in Paris. My guess is he's headed here."

"I guess that means we only have a short amount of time to get this over with, then." The woman was as stubborn as a mule. "Don't even try to move," she warned Isla, pushing the gun harder against Isla's back. I couldn't stop the growl from forming in my throat, even as Isla's eyes flashed with mischief. "Now, Marchetti, unless you want to see your blood or Isla's staining these floors, you're going to give me some answers."

God save me from crazy women. I seemed to be surrounded by them.

"Are you a cold-blooded killer?" I drawled, challenging Tatiana.

She shrugged. "Aren't all Nikolaevs?" She was dodging my question. Maybe I should call her out on her bullshit. "Kind of like you and the men you work with, huh?"

I put my gun away, for now, then slipped my hands into my pockets. I leaned casually against the wall as I studied both women. If Tatiana wanted answers, I'd give them to her. However, at the end of it all, I'd have Isla. She'd hear the story and my gut feeling warned she'd run. Well, there'd be no running for her.

"Men?" I asked, glancing around pointedly. "What men?"

Annoyance flared in her eyes as she narrowed them. "I don't give a shit about your men," she spat, glaring at me. "I want to know what happened."

"A lot of things happened," I retorted dryly. "You're going to have to be a bit more specific."

"Why did you kill him?" Compassion filled Isla's expression, and something about it bothered me. I wanted her always on my side, not caring about others. But I suspected maybe it was exactly that which attracted me to her. She had that innocent aura about her, but also a strength. "What had he done to find himself on your hit list?"

"You sure you want to know?" I finally asked, giving her one last out.

She let out a frustrated breath. "That's why I'm here."

Well, if we were going to do this, we might as well sit down. So I extended my hand, pointing to my office. "Please, enter."

"I'm not going into your bedroom," she sneered. "I'm not here to fulfill your fantasies. I'm here for answers."

A sardonic breath left me. "I'm starting to see why Konstantin is so obsessed with you."

My eyes flickered to my own obsession, then returned to Tatiana

Konstantin. The newest pain in my ass. "Last chance, Tatiana," I warned her in a cold tone. "Certain things are best left in the past."

She shot me a dark look. "Just tell me so we can be on our way."

There'd be no "we" because Isla would be staying behind. With me. "Fine, have it your way," I drawled.

TWENTY-THREE
ISLA

I held my breath, watching Enrico and Tatiana's exchange in fascination.

There were two things I noticed. Firstly, Enrico seemed completely unaffected by Tatiana's beauty—much to my giddiness. I'd mentally slapped myself several times, but it didn't bring reason back into my brain. Secondly, I had a feeling my sister-in-law and I had lost our footing and our upper hand before we even walked into Enrico's home.

I stared at Enrico, the shadows of his sharp cheekbones giving him a lethal edge.

"Tell me why he had to die." Tatiana's raspy voice ended the silence, and for some reason, my heart thundered in my chest. For her. Or maybe even for me, because the vehemence in Enrico's gaze had my insides scrambling.

He met Tatiana's eyes, the darkness in his expression sending fear rolling through me.

"He targeted our organization," he finally answered.

"What organization?"

Enrico's eyes returned to me and every fiber of me stilled as I held his darkness. The kind that terrified me.

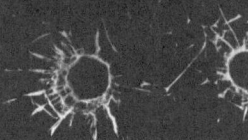

"Thorns of Omertà." My breath caught in my lungs. *No, no, no.* I knew those three words. Reina had learned about it when she was with Amon. I knew what they represented. And I knew if Enrico found out what my friends and I had done, we'd be dead. I had never fainted before, but at this moment, I feared I might. "And unknowingly he dragged you into it."

I gasped incredulously. Reina insisted they killed anyone who threatened their organization. The Thorns of Omertà were thorough. They eliminated threats and didn't stop until their entire families were killed.

Yet Tatiana lived, my mind whispered.

"Why?" Tatiana demanded to know, and every fiber of me wanted to scream at her to stop asking questions.

"He used you to pay back the Konstantins for killing his parents." Tatiana gasped, bringing her hand to her mouth. "He blamed them and the organization for losing his parents. Adrian's father was my old man's gardener. During a trip to New Orleans, my father took his gardener along. To study botany. It's where he met Adrian's mother." Tatiana seemed to get paler with each word that Enrico uttered. My heart clenched at the pain she must feel.

"Illias's mother," Tatiana echoed, her voice barely above a whisper.

This time it was Enrico's turn to be confused. His brows scrunched as he repeated, "Illias's mother?"

Tatiana waved her hand in dismissal. "Never mind."

But Enrico was unwilling to let it go. "You think Adrian and Illias's mother is one and the same?"

"Finish your story." Tatiana's demand was curt.

Enrico nodded, then continued. "Anyhow, the gardener had a kid and left my father's employment. Years later, he attempted to make a run for it with Illias's mother. She tried to leave the old Pakhan, take the twins, and go into hiding with Adrian's father. It didn't work out. They got caught and were executed on the spot."

Illias's mother was killed by our father? Two little boys seeing their mother shot dead. Why hadn't they told me?

"So Adrian made you all a target as revenge for his father's death?"

I asked Enrico because Tatiana seemed at a loss for words. Tears burned in my eyes, and I swallowed hard to keep them at bay.

Enrico nodded.

"How?" Tatiana rasped, her voice trembling.

"He dug for information that could destroy us."

"I went through the videos on that laptop," Tatiana said. I blinked in confusion, unsure what she was talking about. Tears rolled down her cheeks, her flawless skin glimmering with moisture. "He had stuff on my brothers. Other men. But nothing on you nor the Konstantins. Not even the Yakuza."

My heart drummed against my ribs. First, Thorns of Omertà. Now the Yakuza.

"It's on the chip." Enrico's answer was somewhat resigned.

"Where is the chip?" Tatiana asked.

Enrico let out a sardonic breath, his frigid facade terrifying. "We all hoped you could tell us."

"The Yakuza," Tatiana murmured. "Maybe—"

But Tatiana's voice faltered when Enrico shook his head. "If they had it, they'd come down demanding all our territories and give up on chasing you. They don't have it either."

Tatiana removed the gun from my back, sighing heavily. Her shoulders slumped as she met my gaze.

"What's on that chip?"

Enrico scoffed softly, shaking his head. "You really think I'd hand you information that could destroy my family?"

I had a suspicion I knew what could be used against the Marchetti family. It had something to do with his dead wife who was not-so-dead. But what did these people—or Tatiana's dead husband—have that could be used against my brother?

"What's on there that could destroy Illias?" I heard myself ask while the lead weight in the pit of my stomach grew heavier. My sixth sense flared in warning, and the way Tatiana's eyes widened promised the answer wouldn't bode well for me.

Tatiana shook her head, her lips moving around a soundless *No, no, no.*

Enrico's answer came as swiftly as an executioner's blade. "Among other things, video footage of Illias killing your mother."

I reeled backward. The silence stretched. Tatiana's eyes found mine, guilt in them screaming at me. Her knowledge stared clearly back at me and the realization slammed into me like a tsunami, tearing through everything in its path. My brother killed my mother. Betrayal. How many times had he told me she died in childbirth? How many lies had he told me?

"You knew," I accused, my voice hoarse. It hurt to talk, even more to breathe. The pain in my chest swelled until I felt like it'd explode.

The ache throbbed. *My brother killed my mother*. How? Why? I didn't understand anything.

"Isla—" Tatiana's voice cracked, but I couldn't feel nor hear anything beyond my anger. My fury.

"How could you not tell me?" It felt like a double betrayal. My brother's. Hers. "I thought we were—" Friends. *Sisters*.

"We are," she croaked, her pale blue eyes shimmering. I could see the regret in her eyes. Except I wasn't sure whether it was there because she was truly sorry, or because she'd been caught.

But then determination entered her expression and she straightened her shoulders. Her gaze held mine, her affection glimmering in them.

"I can't give you your story. That's for your brother to tell. But I'll give you my story." I watched her swallow a lump in her throat. "In recent months I found a video of my own mother when going through my late husband's things. I knew she killed herself. What I didn't know was that she was going to kill me too. To get back at my father for not loving her. Sasha, my crazy brother, who was only ten at the time, took me from her and saved me." My lips trembled, and I didn't trust myself to say anything. All I could hear over and over again were Enrico's words. *Illias killed your mother*. Tears streamed down Tatiana's face while pain clawed its way through my chest. For her. For me. I didn't know. "My brothers still don't know I learned that truth. And I don't want them to. They're finally happy. They've earned it, and the last thing I want to do is give my mother more power. After all she did."

I clenched my teeth, unwilling to forgive right away. I was sorry she learned the painful truth, but unlike hers, *my* mother didn't kill herself. My brother killed her. Why? I needed to know why.

I tilted my chin stubbornly. "He should have told me."

"I'm sorry." I had no doubt she was. "Let's go back to the hotel. I'm sure he's there waiting for us now; we can make him explain."

I shook my head. I couldn't see my brother right now. I knew I'd say things that I would regret later. "No, I'm going to crash at my friend's house."

"I don't think so." Enrico's voice startled me. For a moment, I forgot he was here. I turned to find him pointing a gun at me, his expression dark. My eyes widened. What the fuck?

"What are you doing?" Tatiana screeched. "Drop that gun before I shoot you."

It might turn into a full-blown war… if Tatiana actually had bullets in her gun, but luckily she didn't. The smile Enrico gave her told me he knew, and it sent ice down my spine. It was ruthless and so fucking cruel, that my heart fluttered with trepidation.

"Before you even move, she'll be dead."

Tatiana's eyes darted my way, worry swarming her blue eyes before flashing back to Enrico, only to end back on me. I didn't think Enrico would hurt me, although I wasn't willing to stake my life on it. But if I sent Tatiana away, she could go get my brother.

The irony of the situation didn't escape me. I just learned my brother killed my mother, and still I counted on him to save me.

"I—I'm fine." My nonexistent confidence was evident in my voice.

"No, you're not." Tatiana narrowed her eyes at Enrico, shooting him deadly glares. "That psycho daddy's holding you at gunpoint."

It had to be my nerves or terrible state of mind because a choked laugh escaped me, remembering how he insisted I call him daddy last time. Tatiana's comment made it sound as if I shared my experience with her. If she only knew what Daddy Enrico could do with his hands and his mouth, she might not be so quick to call him daddy.

"Funny," Enrico remarked, unamused.

I waved my hand. "I'm used to it by now." Not exactly at having the gun pointed at me, but at this push and pull with Enrico. Confusion entered my sister-in-law's eyes. "Tatiana, you go and get my brother. Okay?"

Tatiana let out a frustrated breath, her eyes on Enrico. "You put even one scratch on her and what Adrian wanted to do to you will pale in comparison to what I'll do to you."

"Really?" Amusement now colored his voice. "Considering you married Illias, you're part of our organization too. And that means, you're required to protect Omertà interests. When he married you, he signaled to everyone you're off-limits and under our protection."

"Now see, he failed to mention that." I wasn't sure how Tatiana was keeping her cool. My palms were damp, every pore in me sweating. "And I'm not much for *all for one and one for all*, you know. That shit has never been my thing, so I'm not gonna start now. Besides, if this"—she gestured between me and Enrico—"means being under your organization's protection, please take it the fuck away."

Fuck, she was such a badass. I was still mad at her, but I couldn't help but be impressed.

Enrico let out a sardonic breath. "Go to your husband, Tatiana," he drawled. "I'll deal with Isla."

Tatiana's gaze found mine again, and I tried to relay that I'd be safe. That I wasn't scared.

"I'm still mad at you," I muttered. "But I'll be okay. You go and find Illias." When she didn't move, I barked, "Tatiana! Go. Now."

I watched her leave, praying I wasn't a fool. But just like Tatiana, I had my own questions to ask, and they had everything to do with my mother.

TWENTY-FOUR
ISLA

With Tatiana gone, I gave Enrico my undivided attention. "Are you going to shoot me?" I said, tilting my chin at his gun. He secured it into his holster without a word while my nerves short-circuited. I waited for him to say something, but he remained quiet. His gaze flicked up and caught mine, heavy and emotionless. He seemed so different from the man I'd met weeks ago who took me to his bed in this very house. Now he stood in front of me, his tailored Italian suit flattering his broad frame and making him appear in his late thirties, not forty-five. Even his leather shoes screamed power. Control. It was his features that made you question his age. Taut, hard, and fierce. His angular jawline spoke of his self-assurance. A slight stubble covered his face, giving him a harsh look that matched the one in his eyes. I felt like I was seeing him in a completely different light. "What do you want, Enrico?" I finally asked again. "I'm in no mood for your bullshit now, and honestly, I'd rather not see you ever again."

I went to sidestep him when his strong fingers wrapped around my elbow. I froze, my skin searing from his touch. I raised my eyes, his presence wrapping around me and his gaze filling me with fear. He looked like a Roman god full of wrath, whose fury I wouldn't survive.

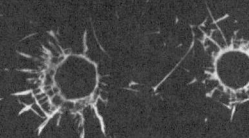

"You're not going anywhere."

My heart turned cold in my chest, but I refused to show it.

Stay calm. Breathe in. Breathe out.

"Well, I'm certainly not staying here," I snapped, my ears buzzing with so many emotions. I had no doubt he could crush me under the soles of his leather shoes, but I had reached my limit of shit for the day. "I don't know what you're playing at, Enrico, but I'm telling you, I'm done."

He took a step closer and my body warmed, betraying me. My heart fluttered and I fought the instinct to lean into him. His strong, distinctive scent invaded my lungs, and I instantly recalled memories of when I trailed my mouth over his skin. It was almost as if I could taste him. Spicy. Powerful.

Apparently, I was into self-destruction.

"Doing what, little one?"

My cheeks heated, but I rolled my eyes. "Okay, Italian. You can cut that shit out now. And the cat's out of the bag. I heard your conversation with my brother, and frankly, I'm done being left in the dark. So let's make something clear, shall we? Fuck. Off."

"Elaborate." The deep tenor of his voice set my skin alight, but the smile on his face was downright ominous.

My spine stiffened and my temper flared. "Well, first you fuck, and then you off," I said with such a sugary-sweet smile, I was surprised he didn't immediately turn diabetic. "I don't need any of your shit. With you and your supposed dead wife. Apparently, I have plenty of shit of my own."

This time his gaze sharpened. "Donatella came to see you?"

I ignored him. "I want to know about my mother," I spat out. "Is it true, what she—"

My words were cut off by another deep voice, and a man with the same dark eyes and dark hair as Enrico appeared out of nowhere.

"Shit's happening outside."

The man held a gun, and instantly, Enrico's big body sheltered me as if he expected someone to start shooting at any minute. He refused to let go of me, his hand clutching my forearm. It was ridiculous, considering he himself had just held me at gunpoint.

"Who is it, Manuel?"

Manuel shook his head. "You'll think I'm crazy, but it's a blast from the past. Adrian Morozov."

Tatiana's dead ex-husband? The crazy maniac who used her for revenge against the Konstantins… against my brothers? It couldn't be. The guy was dead.

"I have to go tell my brother," I hissed, attempting to jerk my arm out of Enrico's firm grip.

"Are you sure?" he barked, ignoring me and his entire focus on Manuel. "I saw the man executed with my own eyes."

Jesus Christ. Enrico just admitted to being part of a man's murder. I needed to get out of here. *Now.*

"Yes. I saw him on the street cameras." I rolled my eyes. If the man had street surveillance, he probably saw Tatiana and me coming toward his house, discussing the best way to point the gun at me so that it looked believable. "He snatched Tatiana Konstantin. She fought him tooth and nail, but he overpowered her. Shoved her into the trunk."

A gasp tore through my lips. Adrian, the dead ex-husband, kidnapped my sister-in-law. *What a shitshow.*

"Enrico, I have to go help her. Tell my brother." Yes, Illias wronged me. He killed my mother. But that didn't mean I'd leave him in the dark about the danger his wife was in. I didn't want anything happening to her. She made my brother happy and—

"She's pregnant."

Enrico ignored me, his focus on Manuel.

"Take guards with you and neutralize him." I was fairly positive "neutralize him" meant "kill him" although if it came down to my sister-in-law or this horrible ex of hers, the choice was a no-brainer. "Konstantin won't be far behind if I had to guess."

Enrico's fingers, still wrapped around my forearm, tugged me forward. We moved down the hallway instead of going downstairs.

"What are you doing?" I gritted. "Let me go and I'll be on my way. I want to help Tatiana."

"Even after her betrayal?" he questioned, his steps never faltering.

"She doesn't deserve to die for it." I attempted to elbow him in his ribs. Unsuccessfully. "Now let me *go*."

"No, this conversation isn't over." *Oh, yes it is.* "Leave it to your brother to save his wife. You are my responsibility."

I was about to scream at him when he abruptly stopped in front of a large steel door.

"What the fuck is this?" I hissed, my eyes widening as he punched in a code. It started to slide and I watched it swing open. "You better not put me in there or I swear to God—"

I cut myself off as my eyes adjusted to the scene before me. Two teenage boys who looked suspiciously like Enrico sat there—no, the better word was *lounged*—playing games on their phones. Their eyes flicked up and I reared back. Jesus, they appeared to be as dark as Enrico's. Maybe even darker.

I turned to Enrico, then back to the boys.

A movie I didn't recognize played on a mounted television alongside dozens of framed posters. Along another wall sat an assortment of recliners and couches and—was that a popcorn machine in the far corner? Jesus Christ, what was this? Children-in-the-attic type of situation, except replace the attic with a creepy, steel-reinforced room? Unease slithered through me.

"It's a safe room." What in the fuck was a safe room? "You'll be inside until the dust settles," Enrico ordered. I didn't move, too shocked at seeing the boys in here, locked up. Maybe this guy was crazy. And I'd hooked up with him. *Lovely.*

Such great taste in men, Isla.

Enrico said something to the boys in rushed Italian. Of course, it didn't matter if he spoke slowly. I wouldn't have been able to pick up a single word.

"*Bene, Pàpa*," both boys answered. I blinked. I thought that one meant "Okay, Dad," but what the heck did I know?

Enrico gave them a terse nod, his attention returning to me.

"Get inside, Isla," Enrico ordered. I shook my head. "Isla." His tone was full of warning.

"Don't you fu—" I cut myself off, unsure of what age it was appropriate to start using bad words in front of kids. I mentally slapped myself. Duh, never. "Don't you dare leave me in here. I swear to God—"

He didn't let me finish. He shoved me in, slapped his hand over the outside remote screen, and closed the door behind me. And damn if it didn't close as fast as lightning.

I stood, immobile, my eyes darting between the two boys and then back to the TV that seemed to be playing… an Italian soap opera. *Typical Italians.* I wouldn't have thought teenage boys would be interested. Although, in their defense, their attention was glued to the devices in their hands.

Neither one of them seemed concerned with the fact that I was standing here. As if it were a normal, everyday occurrence.

Maybe it was.

I studied them. They looked alike, although not twins. One of them looked older. They were the spitting image of their father.

"Ummm, how long have you been in here?" I finally asked.

The boys didn't even look up from their phones. "Twenty minutes or so. Maybe an hour."

Okay, at least they could speak English. Although their sense of time seemed to be off.

"Do you… do you often have to sit in this room?"

My voice came out sharp. Concerned, even. Like, what the fuck would I do if they did? Go and kill their father? It didn't sound like a bad idea, but I wasn't quite sure I wanted to add another murder to my list. I was already an accomplice to one, but that was different. What kind of friend would I be if I'd left Reina hanging when she needed my help?

One of the boys—the younger one, if I had to guess—shrugged, while the other didn't even bother to acknowledge me.

"When something bad is happening," younger Enrico Jr. answered in perfect English.

"Or when Mother's trying to kill us," the other one—older Enrico Junior—added.

I froze.

Did he say—

No, I must have misunderstood it. It had to be his accent. "Can you repeat that? I don't think I heard you correctly."

Two sets of dark eyes lifted off their phones and met mine. "Our mother tries to kill us once in a while," the older one said slowly, like he was speaking to an idiot.

"She's sick," the other said. He brought his hand to his temple and tapped it with his index finger. "*Pazza.*" When I gave him a blank stare, he added, "Crazy. She's crazy." What in the actual fuck? Their mother was trying to kill them? Then I realized he said "is," not "was," as if their mother were alive. It wasn't a language barrier—his English was perfect—and I took it as another confirmation that Enrico's wife was alive. Donatella Marchetti had been the shadow stalking me from the moment I had that incredible night with Enrico. "Are you an American?" he asked, curiosity in his dark gaze.

I stared at him. How could a kid so calmly go from "mother's trying to kill us" to "are you an American"? I was still reeling from the revelations about my own mother and could barely move past it.

"Yes, I'm an American," I murmured as their attention turned back to their phones.

Lowering myself to the floor, I pulled my knees up to my chest while trying to think of what to say. His casual tone had hit me right in the chest.

"I'm so sorry your mom tried to hurt you," I murmured, feeling this pain for them deep in my chest even though they seemed unaffected by it. Maybe my sorrow for them was ridiculous—I didn't even know them well—but no kid should feel unwanted by their mother. "Sometimes people just suck."

Their bodies froze as if they were unaccustomed to condolences and compassion. Something told me, though, that their father took care of things in this department. He might have been brutish and manipulative, but I sensed that he would be a good dad. A caring dad. After all, not too many men built safe rooms to protect their children. And for some reason, that warmed me to these boys.

"Do your parents suck?" the younger one asked.

"I never met them," I said, the wound still fresh in my chest. "But before we give each other our life stories, I need to know your names." I laughed softly. I couldn't keep referring to them as younger and older Enrico Jr. "I'm Isla Evans."

They shared a glance, communicating wordlessly. Just like their father, it was hard to read them.

"I'm Enzo Marchetti."

"And I'm Amadeo Marchetti."

I smiled at them. I had a feeling both of these boys would grow up to become dominating men just like their father. It was terrifying. However, I was certain girls would soon be falling all over themselves for them.

"Nice to meet you both." I reached over and extended my hand for a handshake. They both hesitated for a second. It was Amadeo who took it first, then Enzo followed. "You're brothers, right?" They nodded. "How old are you?"

"I'm thirteen," Amadeo answered.

"I'm fourteen," Enzo supplied. "I'm going to be head of the Marchetti family one day."

I raised my eyebrow, surprised at the offhanded comment. "Congratulations, I guess." My eyes darted to Amadeo. "Does that bother you?"

Amadeo shrugged. "Not really. I'll be the hitman for our *famiglia*." My mouth parted in shock and my eyes bulged out of my skull, causing both of them to chuckle. "Aren't you in the mafia?" Amadeo asked.

I scoffed. "Well, as a matter of fact, I just learned my brother is."

Something, I realized, that would have been helpful to know when we'd needed to figure out a way out of that mess all those years ago. But no, my girlfriends and I had to fumble through Google and Reddit for "hypothetical" ways to dispose of a body.

"Sometimes men keep women in the dark," Enzo said knowingly.

"To protect you. It's for your own good," Amadeo chimed in.

These little shits, I thought with affection. I couldn't even hold their confidence against them. They'd had to grow up in the mafia with a mother who regularly tried to kill them and a father who was... I searched for the right word. The only thing my bitter, frustrated brain could think of was *lying bastard*. Yeah, they needed all the confidence they could get.

Seeing these two boys holding each other up in support had me thinking of my own brother. I loved him and would always be grateful for everything he'd done for me growing up, but he should have told me. Warned me. It wasn't something I should have learned from anyone else. Even Tatiana knew. Shit, why did it have to hurt so much? Even more importantly, why did he do it? But I wouldn't be finding the answer to that by sitting here in this room.

"Don't hold it against your family," Enzo added. "It's our job to protect our own."

I scoffed incredulously. "Ease up, you two. Don't act all high and mighty. Girls hate that about boys."

Enzo puffed his chest. "They think they do, but girls want to be bossed around." *Okay, little Enrico*, I mocked in my head. He had it all wrong, just like his father. "Do you have a boyfriend?"

My eyebrows shot up at his question. Or maybe it was his audacity. "Why?"

He shrugged, his eyes traveling over me. "You're hot. Not beautiful, exactly, but hot." Geez, this was getting better and better. "Maybe I'll marry you."

"Okay, lover boy. Hold your horses," I croaked. Jesus, what was it with Italian men? Maybe it was part of the elementary school curriculum to teach boys about the art of seduction. Well, Enzo must have missed the class. "You're too young for me."

"I don't mind."

"I bet you don't," I muttered. "By the way, don't think I haven't noticed what you're doing."

Something flashed in Enzo's dark gaze, and I realized his eyes weren't dark brown like I'd initially thought. They were dark blue, like a midnight sky. Amadeo's were more like his father's.

"I don't know what you mean." Enzo blanched, his expression

turning nonchalant as if he didn't have a care in the world. It was his armor. I didn't know much about kids, but I'd bet he hid all his emotions somewhere deep.

"You're avoiding talking about your mother," I remarked, keeping my tone soft. "And you think flirting with me will distract me." He didn't say anything. "Am I right?"

Both boys shrugged, and for some reason, I felt so damn sorry for them. I knew what it meant to grow up without the love of a mother. And while I had my brothers, they'd both been very busy and didn't have the woman's touch that I often observed with other girls my age and their mothers.

"I'm sorry," I murmured softly. "But remember, your father loves you. Your family loves you." It was easier to comfort them than think about my own problems. They deserved the world.

"Our mother is not important," Amadeo answered.

I tilted my head, studying them both.

"Your mother's mentally unwell. I'm sure she cares about you. I'm sorry you had to experience it," I told him. "I never met my mother, but she's important to me. I don't know if she even loved me, but still, she's important to me. It doesn't make you weak to care about her."

"She doesn't care about us," Enzo said coldly. It was scary, but I could see his father in him. "We don't care about her."

"Does your father know?" I asked quietly.

Both boys shrugged. "That she's trying to kill us?" Amadeo asked. I gulped, then nodded slowly in answer. I didn't think I could find my voice. "Yes, Papà knows. He's been protecting us from her." Amadeo tilted his head, the look in his eyes pensive. He looked so much older than his thirteen years at this moment. "Papà said deep down she loves us."

"She doesn't," Enzo grumbled. "A mother who loves her children doesn't want to kill them."

I stared at them, lost for words. Two lonely boys that would soon become men, but would forever be looking for reasons why they lacked their mother's love. My heart just ached for them and didn't know how to make them feel better.

"Do either of you have girlfriends?" I asked instead, changing subjects. I didn't want to keep digging at their wounds. It wasn't fair to them.

Enzo snickered. "Aria is in love with Amadeo."

"Shut up, Enzo."

The two started bickering in Italian. It was actually quite entertaining, despite the fact I couldn't understand a single word.

I grinned and cut them off. "Who's Aria?"

"She's a baby," Amadeo snapped. "She's not in love with me."

"Oh, yeah," Enzo mocked. "She wanted to fight me to protect you."

"How old is she?" I asked curiously.

"She's seven now," Amadeo muttered like a boy scolded. "Or maybe eight. I don't know."

Enzo pushed his hand into his thick dark hair. "She was five when she tried to beat me up. Crazy girl."

I smiled. "Well, it seems to me Amadeo is a lucky guy, then. If a five-year-old wants to fight for him, just imagine what older girls will do." I gave a pointed look to Enzo. "You might want to take notes."

Enzo rolled his eyes. "Whatever."

The corners of my lips tugged up. "Okay, Enzo. Tell me how you'd make a girl fall in love with you." Amadeo snickered, but I kept my gaze on the older sibling. He gave closed-off vibes, and I was certain it was because he wanted to appear strong. "I'm waiting."

"What do I get if I tell you?" Enzo asked bravely, meeting my gaze. "A date with you?"

I bit the inside of my cheek. I imagined Enzo's courage got him in trouble a lot.

"Sure, why not," I agreed. "I'll take you to a concert."

Enzo's eyes flashed with curiosity.

"Really?" I nodded. His expression turned serious, contemplating his answer. I didn't need to know this kid well to understand he was competitive and liked to get his way. "I'd play her a sonata under her balcony."

I cocked a brow. "Really?"

"Yes. I know Dad says girls snicker at romantic stuff, but I think girls are into that stuff. He just says to buy them nice things."

I was just about to open my mouth to agree with Enzo's logic when the mechanical door started to slide open. I jumped to my feet, coming face-to-face with Enrico.

Fury swarmed me as I remembered what I was doing stuck here in the first place. "You… you…"

"Papà!" Both boys sauntered to their father and hugged him while I remained glued to the spot. I couldn't help but notice how deeply both boys seemed to care about him. Something about it made my anger toward him waver. That was, until Enrico's dark gaze met mine, and I shot him a glare for good measure.

Averting my eyes, I swept my palms down my jeans, smoothing out the nonexistent wrinkles. When I raised my eyes, all three of them were staring at me.

"Well, I'm outta here." I waved casually at the boys. "I have quite a bit of catching up to do at the orchestra."

"No."

"No what?" I hissed.

"You're not going anywhere." The simple words out of Enrico's mouth had me seeing red.

"Yes, I am," I gritted. "And next time you decide to shove me in a room without windows, I'll murder you." Then, realizing his sons were watching my every move, I quickly added, "Not really. But he'd learn his lesson."

"So do I get the date?" Enzo didn't seem worried whether I'd kill his father. Men. Boys. Italians. They were a different breed.

I smiled at him. He was persistent if nothing else. *Probably gets that from his father too*, I thought.

"You won a date, Enzo. And let me tell you, sonatas and romance will get you more female attention than buying girls pretty things. And never, *ever* lie or cheat." I narrowed my eyes on his father. "Unlike some men, it's not too late for you."

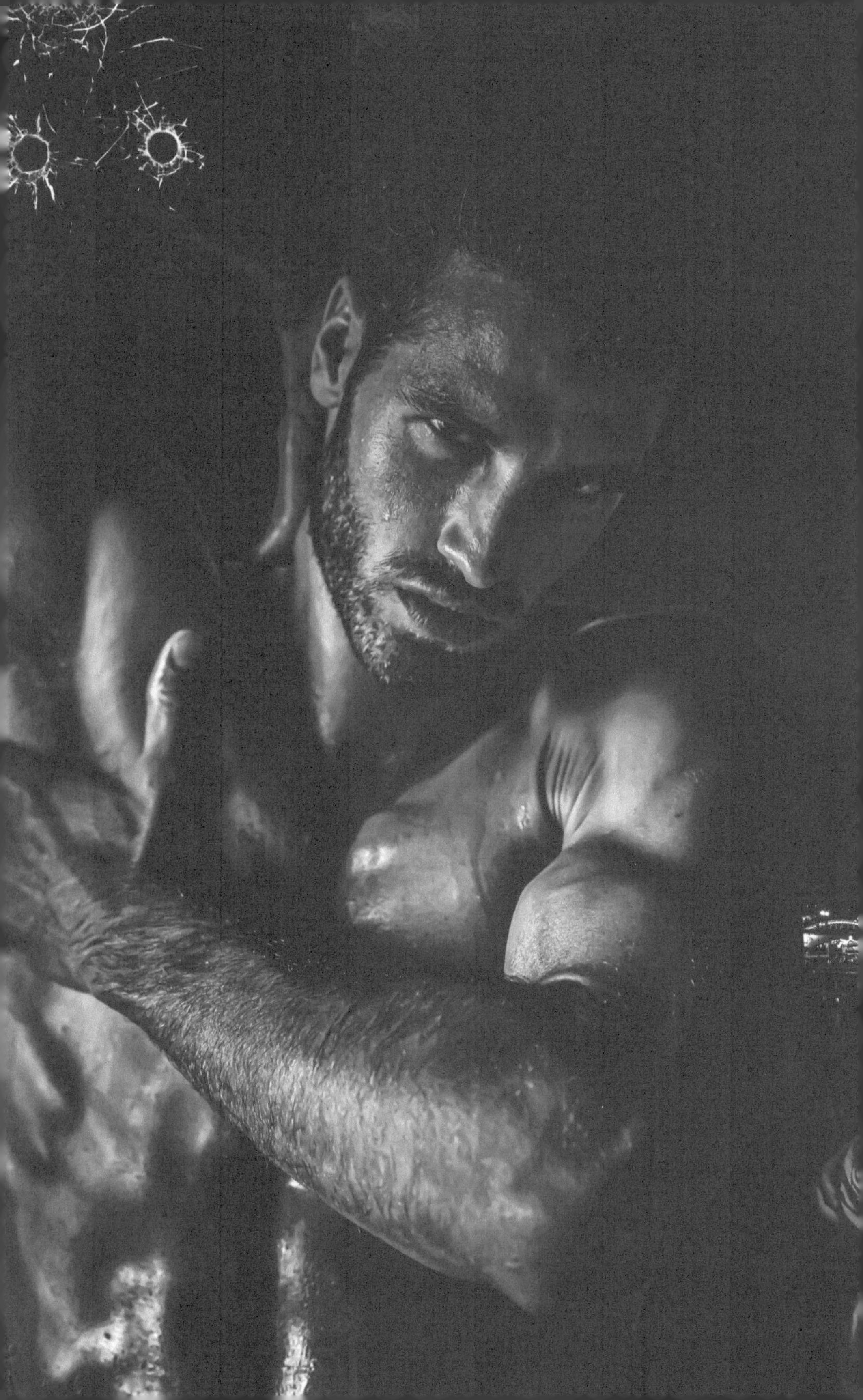

TWENTY-FIVE
ENRICO

Isla was a challenge, and I fucking thrived on those. I could feel her emerald eyes on my skin, and even though she was glaring at me, it felt like a soft caress. How such a beauty could be related to Illias Konstantin was beyond me. She was sweet, compassionate, and so fucking sensual that something primal in my gut tightened.

She was mine. The stars had aligned and made her for *me,* and by God, I intended to keep her.

Just as I predicted, Konstantin showed up, but he was preoccupied with Tatiana's kidnapping. He went after her with the information I supplied him. He asked me to keep Isla safe, and I fucking would, the only way I knew how. The window to execute my plan was small, but it was a good thing I had set everything in motion last night.

She'd be mine, for better or worse, in sickness and health. For richer or poorer. I'd have her in my bed every night and at my table every day.

My sons' curious eyes darted between my unknowing soon-to-be wife and me.

"Boys, will you give my woman and me a few moments to talk?" I asked, holding her emerald gaze.

"Ah, that's why she doesn't want to be my girlfriend," Enzo

muttered in disappointment. "She saw you first." Isla rolled her eyes, but my eldest kept his eyes on her reverently. I sincerely hoped I wouldn't have to compete with my son for my soon-to-be wife's affection. "What about that date to the concert you promised me?"

I raised my brow. If Isla thought she'd be going on a date with anyone, my son included, she was mistaken. She was mine, and I refused to share her. She could mother them to whatever extent she chose, but all her dates belonged to me.

"We'll all go as a family," I answered before she could.

"I don't know what you're doing, Enrico, but I am not your family," she snapped. "And stop putting these poor boys through havoc with your delusions. They have a mother. Who's alive, by the way."

"I'm aware," I argued calmly. I wouldn't tell her the whole truth until she was my wife. Then she'd be under the same rules as our organization and the motto of Omertà would apply to her too: Silence above all else. "But you'll be my wife. After all, we had some activity without protection last time."

"What activity?" Amadeo asked curiously. I certainly wasn't going to elaborate that I fucked this woman without a condom. I'd had a safe sex talk with my sons, and a condom was always a must.

A stain of embarrassment marred her cheeks. She opened her mouth, then closed it, only to open it again.

She forced a smile to her lips, turning her emerald gaze to the boys. "Enzo, Amadeo. It was so nice to talk to you while we were all locked up in this dreadful room. But now, would you please give me a minute so that I can talk to your father and try not to murder him?"

"I kind of want to stay," Amadeo protested, eager for some action.

Enzo's eyes narrowed to slits. "I like you, Isla, but if you kill Papà, I'll have to come after you."

His tone was serious, his expression even more so. He'd carry this family well one day.

Thankfully, Isla didn't take offense, and her own expression softened. "I won't really murder him." Her eyes shot a glare my way, but the moment they returned to Enzo and Amadeo, her emerald gaze melted to liquid. "But I *will* give him a piece of my mind, and he probably won't like it."

She was glaring at me again, storms raging beneath her delicate red brows. There was something satisfying about the knowledge that I could make someone as sweet as Isla *burn*. With desire. With anger. With passion.

"Enzo. Amadeo. Go to Manuel."

The two of them flicked another curious glance Isla's way, then scurried away. Her hands went to her hips, striking a pose full of sass and fire as she glared at me with that green gaze.

"Now, you will tell me everything you know," she demanded dryly. "Starting with my mother and what you have to say about what your very much *alive* wife—" She emphasized the last two words, and I grinned rakishly as my gaze slid down her body. "—has told me." Unable to resist, I reached out and ran a thumb over her collarbone. That creamy skin that blushed pink when she was aroused. Or upset. She tried to slap my hand away but I caught her wrist, her soft skin silky under my rough palms. "Oh, no! You don't get to touch me anymore."

We'd see about that.

"What has Donatella told you?" I asked casually.

"She told me my mother was… *is* in one of your brothels. That she's a whore."

She gulped, her bottom lip quivering. My chest squeezed painfully, but I ignored it. I couldn't afford weaknesses. It was peculiar… The sorrow of others never bothered me. My sons were the exception of course, but otherwise, I found myself indifferent to it. When it came to Isla, I hated seeing it on her face. I wanted to be her villain *and* her savior. I wanted to make her smile and be the only one to make her cry. But those would be tears of pleasure, not pain.

I inclined my head. "Do you believe her?"

"Don't play mind games with me, Enrico," she countered. "I want the truth. I deserve it."

She was right. She deserved the truth, but it was neither the time nor the place for it. I wanted her first as my wife with no chance of turning back. Once she was mine and had no opportunity—or intention—to run away from me, then I'd tell her the truth.

"You want to know the truth?" She nodded. "Then marry me, and I'll tell you everything."

I watched, fascinated, as Isla's entire demeanor changed. Her temper flared like an erupting volcano. Something dark flickered in her eyes, and I realized at that very moment there was a lot more to her than met the eye. Gone was the sunshine, smiling young woman. In its place was her wrath.

"Marry you," she repeated, sneering. "You're deranged, just like your wife. Let me tell you the reasons why I won't be marrying you." She lifted her hand to list off each item on French-manicured fingernails. "Firstly, you are *already* married. To that crazy woman that seems really out there. You should check into that shit." She had no idea I'd had Donatella in and out of institutions for the past thirteen years. "Secondly, you are a lying cheater. Thirdly, apparently you're also a criminal. A disgusting human who has brothels. Brothels! I don't want to be in the same room with you, never mind marry you."

She raised an eyebrow, challenging me. But I refused to be baited. I'd have to play this right and win my bride. With blackmail, naturally.

"I don't have any brothels, and I'd strongly advise you to reconsider your words. Unless you'd like your friends and family to pay for your disobedience. Particularly, your friend Reina."

A soft gasp left her soft pink lips and horror entered her expression before she pulled herself together and set her chin stubbornly.

"You might think you're the only criminal I know, but you're wrong. I can get a bigger and badder wolf to come after you."

I shot her a grin that usually terrified the men that worked for me. "I'm ready for it, *piccolina*. But don't cry wolf when you see your brother and friends hurt."

"You wouldn't."

"Oh, I would."

Her creamy skin flushed. "My brother will destroy you," she snapped.

"You mean the one that killed your mother?" The moment I said the words, I regretted them, but I ignored the pang in my chest that I understood was guilt. I ignored the pain that flashed in her eyes. I couldn't afford to be weak. I had to get her cooperation at all costs.

I advanced on her, the soles of my Italian leather shoes firm against the floor. Isla started to back away, but I didn't stop. Not until I came chest to chest with her, her back against the wall.

Fear flashed in her gaze, but there was something else there too. Desire. Hunger matching my own. Her pulse throbbed at the base of her throat, and it took all my self-control not to lower my mouth and suck on it.

Then, as if she remembered we were arguing, she lifted her chin. "Stop trying to intimidate me."

I sneered. "*Piccolina*, I don't need to intimidate you. You're already scared." The desire to touch her won out, and I brought my thumb to the base of her throat, trailing it softly. God, that scent of hers would drive me insane. Coconuts mixed with her arousal. It was intoxicating. "And trust me, I can make one phone call and have your friends dead, just like that. I'll start with the youngest and work my way from there."

She licked her lips, her chest rising and falling. "Are you insane?" she breathed.

"Yes," I admitted. "I'm *pazzo* for you."

And I *was* fucking crazy for her. I was prepared to start a war against her brother *and* the Brazilian cartel for her. After all, she was the unknown Bratva and cartel princess. They didn't know about her yet, but it was only a matter of time before they learned. Then they'd come for her, but as my wife, they wouldn't be able to take her away from me.

She stared at me, her eyes unreadable. They sparkled like emeralds under the sun. You could almost see the way she was weighing her options and not liking the conclusions she was reaching.

"If I marry you, you won't touch my brother or my friends." We stared at each other, her scent seeping into my lungs and threatening to overtake me. My control teetered on the edge, and my impulses urged me to bury myself inside her, right here and now.

She was heaven. I was hell. Together we were the perfect sin. How could she not see—*feel*—that?

"Marry me and they'll be safe."

Her eyes darted to my mouth before locking with mine. "You won't touch Reina regardless of what she might have done or anything we were accomplices in. Swear it!"

Her response piqued my interest. My threat with regard to Reina was merely a tactic. I knew from Kingston that the girls were protective of each other, but in particular toward the youngest member of their group. Twenty-one-year-old Reina.

"I swear it." Fuck, I'd swear to everything holy and unholy, living and non-living, to get her agreement.

"You'll keep us all safe. Promise."

I let out a sardonic breath between my teeth and ran my hand across my jaw. This was getting more and more interesting by the minute.

"I'll keep you all safe." She blew out a relieved breath, though it was just as likely a resigned one. It was hard to tell. Her complexion was slightly pale. They had to be hiding something. "I promise. Besides, if you ladies haven't done anything wrong, there should be nothing to worry about. Isn't that right?"

I watched her slim neck work as she gulped. I needed to win over her trust as well as her body, that much was obvious.

"What do you know?" Her voice trembled and so did the fingers she desperately tried to steady.

I raised an eyebrow, watching her. "I know many things. What, specifically, are you asking?"

She shook her head. "I'm not falling for that. You don't know shit, and I'm not telling you shit." Then she smiled tightly, glowering at me. At five foot four, she managed to appear taller. Especially when those emeralds flashed like lightning over a copse of trees.

I shrugged. "You'll tell me sooner or later. But know this, Isla. If you want your friends protected, you will accept my proposal. For their sake. For your family's sake. For your own."

She shook her head in exasperation.

"Who in their right mind threatens someone into marrying them?" Clearly she didn't know her brother well. The story went that he'd kidnapped Tatiana from her brother's wedding and married her on the fly—literally—by having a priest perform the ceremony on the plane.

"Now tell me what you and your friends got into. I don't want to see my bride end up in jail."

Her gaze sparkled with anger.

"If you refuse to give me answers until after I marry you, I shall do the same. *Stronzo*."

"I see you learned some Italian." Too bad she didn't start with a more useful word. "You can't keep secrets from me for long."

She snickered. "Well, watch me. *Daddy*."

My cock was now rock hard, twitching to bury itself inside her. Fuck, it had never been my kink, but suddenly I needed to hear her scream "Daddy" and beg me for it.

Instead, I slapped her ass. Hard.

Her lush mouth parted, a blush spreading over her pale skin.

"Remember to use that mouth when I'm fucking you next—" I paused when she rolled her eyes. "As my wife."

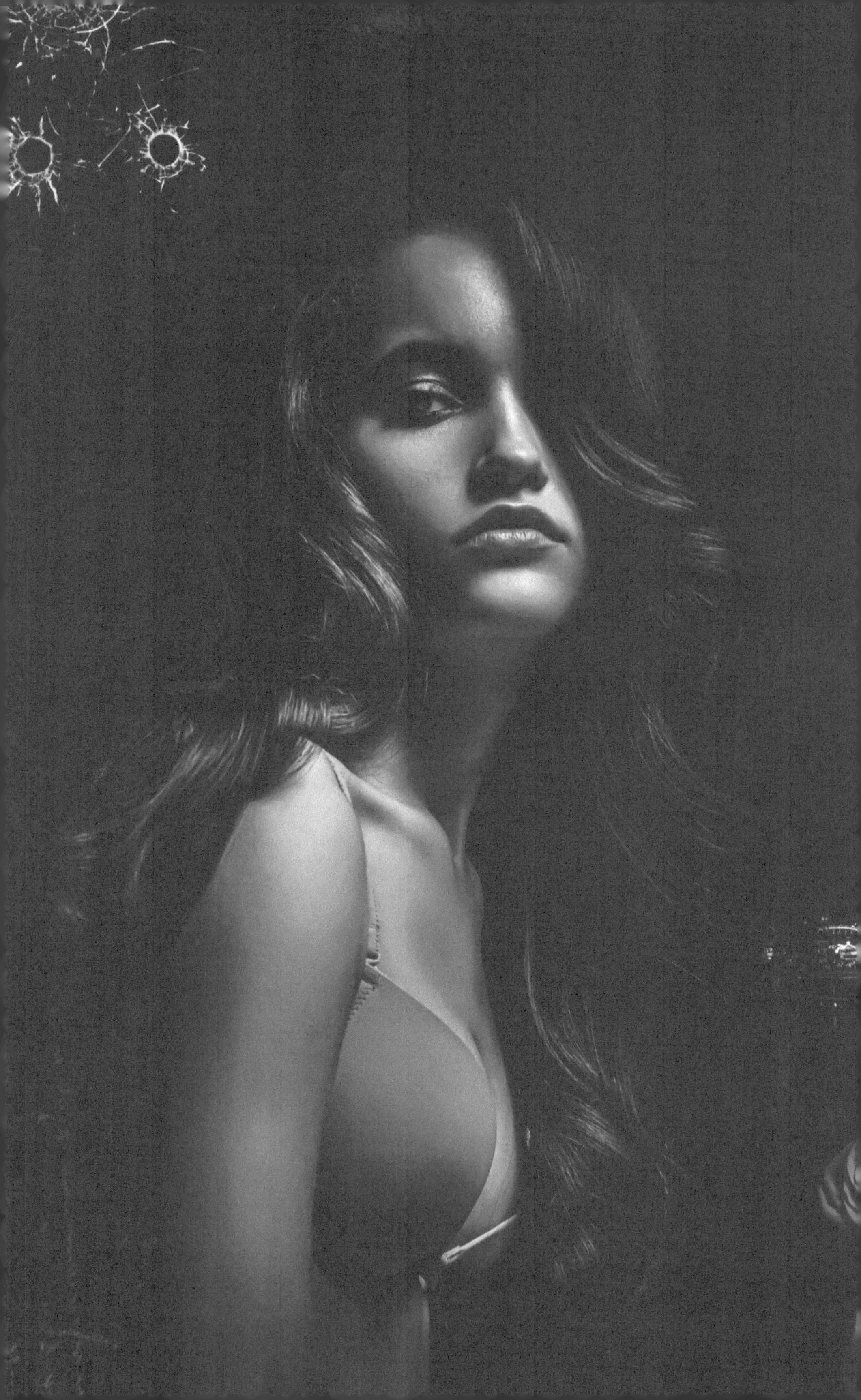

TWENTY-SIX
ISLA

My sister-in-law was kidnapped and here I stood in a wedding dress, three hours later, about to be married.

Alone. I wished my girlfriends were here with me. It would have made this bearable, and at least someone would be able to see this beautiful wedding gown, fake marriage or not.

My heart squeezed as I gazed at my reflection in the tall mirror. This wedding dress was beautiful and fit me perfectly. It told me that Enrico had planned this. He certainly hadn't gotten an exquisite dress like this off the rack in a store. I also dismissed any thoughts of it belonging to his supposedly dead wife, since she was taller than me and built differently.

Which brought me to my final point. I'd agreed to marry him, but only to keep my friends safe and to learn the truth about my mother. The fact he was married already would mean the marriage would be null and void.

Bingo. Take that, motherfucking handsome Italian daddy. Game. Set. Match.

My attention returned to my reflection. It was truly a fairy-tale wedding dress. Its sleeveless bodice hugged my frame, accentuating my breasts and the tiny curve of my waist as it flowed down my body.

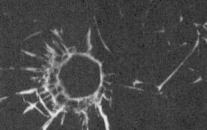

The dress sparkled against the light that poured in from the large French windows of the bedroom.

The very same bedroom he brought me to that first night.

I should have known playing with someone like this powerhouse of a man would be like playing with fire. He wasn't the type to have a fling with. He was untouchable. He was corrupt.

And the way he looked at me spoke of ownership. He was *possessive*.

I let out a heavy sigh. Why did it feel like I was preparing for my own doom?

The door to the room opened and Manuel strode in. I couldn't resist an eye roll.

"And here comes the bodyguard," I muttered under my breath.

"Uncle."

My brows scrunched. "Huh?"

His eyes narrowed ever so slightly at the corners.

"I'm not his bodyguard," he clarified. I had a feeling the man didn't like me much. Well, too bad. I didn't like any of them either. Well, except for Enzo and Amadeo. "I'm his uncle."

My eyes traveled over him. He didn't look older than Enrico. He had to be pulling my leg. But it didn't really matter—I wouldn't be around here much longer.

"Actually, newsflash." I brought my hands up to my waist and glared at him. "You're a blackmailer's accomplice."

He shrugged. "You make your bed; you lie in it."

"What in the fuck does that mean?" I spat. A muscle jumped in his jaw. "I hooked up with him. I know y'all are old and maybe slightly old-fashioned, but to 'hook up' means to have sex for one night, and then everyone goes their own way."

Manuel cocked his head and stared at me. He didn't seem impressed with my definition. "I will keep that in mind. Now, let's get to the church."

I scoffed. "How about you tell me what you know about my mother, and I won't implicate you in this blackmail?" He didn't move.

"I swear to God, Manuel, I'll send you both to fucking jail. For manslaughter, or some shit like that."

I was talking out of my ass, and by the looks of it, Manuel knew it. Well, fucking sue me. Law and business weren't my strength.

"Okay. But first we'll get you to the church."

I had never given a thought to marriage. Ever!

Yet, here I was in the Saint-Denis Basilica in Rue de la Légion D'Honneur, making my way down the aisle while the organist played Mendelssohn's traditional "Wedding March." It was a burial place for forty-three kings and thirty-two queens, and somehow Enrico managed to secure it for this farce of a ceremony. How strong were Enrico Marchetti's connections, exactly?

At the altar stood a priest who probably had no idea what cardinal sin he was committing us to—marrying an already wed man to an innocent young woman. Okay, maybe I wasn't so innocent. Enrico and Manuel stood in front of the old priest, looking at me as I made my way down the aisle. Alone.

It felt wrong. It felt... lonely. My brother should be here. My friends. Even though this was all fake, I wanted to cry. It was so stupid.

I stared at the man whose gaze never left me. I had to admit, he looked perfect in his three-piece suit. Every inch the wealthy Italian mogul. Like a dark mafia king preparing to corrupt his innocent bride.

And God help me, despite everything, I *wanted* to be corrupted. It was the only thing I could actually accept when it came to this bogus wedding ceremony. I'd get laid, then I'd be on my way as if nothing ever happened.

Great plan.

I'd be sexed out, learn all the secrets relating to my mother, and then I'd get back to my life, my music, and my friends.

My steps slowed as I approached the altar, passing the empty pews. Enzo and Amadeo sat in the far front pew, two lone figures in the church that could house at least two hundred people. All the while, I couldn't shake off my worries about my friends. About Tatiana. Even my brother. No matter how mad I was at the latter two, I wanted them safe.

Yet, instead of calling up my brother and checking on the situation, I was here. Getting married. The worry for both of them was like lead in the pit of my stomach, refusing to ease. Enrico didn't have more information either.

I let out a heavy sigh, turning my attention back to Enrico. His obsidian expression pulled me into the pit of darkness where only sin, pleasure, and carnal urges existed.

Goose bumps rose over my skin when he took my arm. A shudder erupted beneath my skin as we faced each other. The priest began to recite blessings, and much too soon, it was time to recite our sacred vows.

Even though I knew this ceremony was a hoax, the gravity of what we were doing hit me full force.

"When you're ready, you may say your vows." The priest's voice sliced through my thoughts.

His eyes found Enrico first, who didn't even hesitate and started to recite his vows in a clear, deep voice, although he kept it surprisingly low.

"I, Enzo Lucian Marchetti, take you, Isla Evans, to be my wife. I promise to be true to you in good times and in bad, in sickness and in health. I promise to honor you for the rest of my days."

I inhaled a sharp breath. *Enzo?* What the hell? Why was he using a different name, and why did it sound familiar? I had heard it before, I was certain of it. But where? My brain refused to cooperate, although that could be from all these words the priest was reciting. Jesus, was this a Catholic mass or Orthodox one? The latter went on and on until you found yourself asleep and snoring in the pew. Although the former one wasn't exciting either, there was a lot of "sit, stand, kneel," so dozing off was impossible.

The priest cleared his throat and pulled my attention from the piece of information that continued to bounce around my brain.

I swallowed, then started reciting my own vows. *Fake vows*, of course. "I, Isla Evans, take you, Enrico—" The priest cleared his throat.

"Enzo Lucian Marchetti," the priest chimed in to correct me. I didn't like this. Hearing that name again made my mind tickle with a memory that refused to come forward.

"—to be my husband. I promise to be true and faithful to you in good times and in bad, in sickness and in health. For the rest of my life."

Shit, I actually said the words. Everything about this moment felt way too real. What was I getting myself into?

The priest smiled and gave his full focus to Enrico. "Do you, Enzo Lucian Marchetti, take Isla Evans to be your lawfully wedded wife, to have and to hold, from this day forward, for better or for worse, for richer or for poorer, in sickness and in health, until death do you part?"

"I do." There wasn't an ounce of hesitation in his voice. His eyes flashed with satisfaction, probably thinking he had me trapped. Or counting on me not to call him out on this fraudulent affair. He was even using a fake name. That in itself had to nullify this whole thing. Right?

The priest's attention moved to me. "Do you, Isla Evans, take Enzo Lucian Marchetti to be your lawful husband, to have and to hold, from this day forward, for better or for worse, for richer or for poorer, in sickness and in health, until death do you part?"

I felt all eyes on me while the wheels in my mind kept turning. It was right there, if only everyone would shut up, back off and let me *think*.

"Miss Evans?" the priest urged, rushing my answer. I shifted on my feet and felt Enrico's grip tighten around my fingers.

"I do." The breathless words escaped my lips without my permission.

Manuel stepped forward with the rings, allowing the priest to bless them before handing me mine. How convenient he had everything—the dress, the rings, the priest, the church. He was a well-prepared man.

Enrico—Enzo?—I was confused on what to call him now—took

my hand and said, "I give this ring as a sign of our union and faithfulness in the name of the Father, the Son, and the Holy Spirit."

I stared in my dazed state as he placed the beautiful vintage ring with emeralds and diamonds around the band onto my finger, the cold metal sending shivers through me. The ring was a perfect fit.

When it was my turn, my hand shook so badly, it took me several tries to slip the band onto his finger.

"I now pronounce you husband and wife. You may kiss the bride."

Before I could even process the words, Enrico cupped my face in his hands and took my mouth.

Hard. Possessive.

His tongue invaded my mouth. I tried to pull away, but he refused to be deterred. He held my jaw, his mouth working me until I began kissing him back. My body softened, leaning into him, and all my reason went out the church.

It would seem I was unable to resist this man. Fraud or not. Cheater or not.

Much to my dismay.

TWENTY-SEVEN
ENRICO

I married her in the church, binding her to me for eternity.

Manuel snapped a few photos of our wedding and would ensure the world of Omertà learned she was mine. Isla looked dazed, following along, oddly complacent. It made me suspicious.

"Are you our stepmom now?" Amadeo blurted out.

She attempted a smile but failed. "How about you just call me Isla?"

Enzo grinned like the troublemaker he was. "I think I like Mom. Or *Matrigna*."

Amadeo chuckled. "*Matrigna*. But a good one."

Isla rolled her eyes. "You can call me Mom, but I won't answer. And I have no idea what 'matrigna' is."

"Stepmom in Italian," Enzo answered. "*Mia matrigna*. Or *mia mamma*."

Both boys liked her; otherwise, they wouldn't be teasing her.

Enzo told me what they talked about in the safe room. It only affirmed my decision to marry her.

In those twenty minutes or so that Isla was in the safe room with them, she gave them more attention than their own mother had since the moment they were born. It wasn't much of a comparison, but I knew Isla was nothing like Donatella. I knew she'd protect Amadeo and Enzo, as well as our future children, like the lioness she was.

"Okay, boys. No more teasing." I wrapped my hand around my young wife's waist. "You will go with Manuel. I'm taking the driver with Isla."

They grumbled and complained but followed Manuel to his car nonetheless. Once they drove away, I ushered my wife into our own car and slid in right behind her.

"Take the long way to the house," I said to my driver in Italian before shutting the partition.

I grabbed her tiny waist and lifted her, bringing her to my lap.

"Whoa," she squealed, her small palms pressing against my shoulders. "What are you doing?"

"You left me without a word." I spread my legs wide, my cock rock hard for her already. "My balls have been aching for you."

Her porcelain skin flushed pink. "I'm sure you had a line of women just ready to ease that ache in your balls."

I spanked her ass lightly, the silk of her wedding dress obstructing my access to her skin.

"I don't want those women." I pushed my hands to the nape of her neck and tightened them into fists around her fiery curls. "I want you. My wife."

She shrugged her slim shoulders, her hips swaying. "Unzip my dress, then," she murmured, watching me through hooded eyes.

"Little one, it's the wrong time to tease me."

The sound of the zipper sent a seductive echo through the car space. Her dress slid down her body and pooled around her waist. My nostrils flared as her breasts came into full view.

Dio, she was so fucking sexy.

I pulled her dress over her head and let it fall to the limousine floor with a soft ruffle. My hand roamed her hip, then inside her thighs. I reached her panties, noting the fabric was soaked. I stroked over her seam and heard her breath catch.

Every muscle in my body was rigid, fighting the urge to pin her down and thrust into her tight, hot entrance. The city streets blurred through the tinted window, but none of it mattered. Nothing did, except this woman sitting on my lap.

The need for her was so overwhelming, so animalistic, I thought I'd lose my mind. I wanted to grind into her, shoot my seed into her.

Her tits were in my face, her small waist perfect under my palms.

"I want answers," she murmured as she leaned forward, her nipples brushing against the material of my suit. I slapped her ass again and she whimpered, her thighs squeezing me as she straddled me.

"Didn't I tell you to wear a dress when you came to see me?"

Her brows pinched. "Does that really matter right now?"

"You're right. It doesn't," I agreed. Stretching out on the seat, I pulled her with me. "Sit on my face. Right now."

"What?" she said, and I slapped her ass again.

"Last warning. Your pussy needs to be on my face." I slapped her ass once more for emphasis. "Now."

She climbed over my body, removing her panties like a contortionist, and adjusted her knees until she came to straddle my head. I could smell her sweet arousal, making my mouth water. I jerked her hips down until her pussy slammed onto my face, eager to get to work. My fingers dug into her ass cheeks as her thighs pressed into the sides of my head.

"Fuck," she breathed, her palms sprawled against the limo window to brace herself for support.

I ate her like I was starving. Like it was the first meal I'd had in years. Like it was my last. She rolled her hips, whimpering as I sucked and licked her. She was so wet, her cunt swollen and needy as I laved at her. I drove her closer to the edge with my mouth, only to slow my tongue, lapping up her juices.

She let out a tiny frustrated growl as she sped up her movements, rocking back and forth, fucking herself with my face.

"More." The woman was as demanding as I was. I usually hated that trait in women, but with Isla, I fucking thrived on it. "Get me off, Enrico, or I'll just do it myself."

A dark chuckle escaped me as I swept my tongue across her

swollen clit, dragging the tip of my tongue toward her aching center and sinking it inside her sweet folds.

Her back curved, and a loud moan vibrated through the small space of the limo. Her breathing quickened as my tongue teased her center again, only to dive back inside her. I wouldn't stop sucking and licking if my life depended on it. Like an addict, I shut my eyes with reverence and ate her as shudders rolled through her soft body.

"Fuck, fuck… Oh… I'm going to—" I stopped, lifting my eyes to see her dazed and watching my every movement. I blew cool air against her swollen clit, and a visible shiver rolled down her body. She dug her fingers into my hair, holding my head against her core. "Why did you stop?"

I smirked. "Beg for it."

She blinked, confusion entering her expression. "W-what?"

"Beg me to make you come." She didn't need to know I'd make her come even if she refused to beg. Fuck, I couldn't keep away from her pussy even if I tried. "Beg me for my mouth. For my tongue. For my cock."

For a moment, I thought she'd tell me to fuck off, but her hunger for pleasure must have outweighed her reason.

"Please, Daddy. Make me come," she breathed, her pale skin turning pink. "Fuck me with your mouth. Give me your cock. Give me everything."

My cock just about exploded in my slacks hearing her moaning, raspy voice calling me daddy. I dove back into her pussy and went straight to work.

I shoved two fingers inside her roughly while at the same time I drew her clit between my lips and sucked.

Her fingers threaded in my hair, her body jerking and trembling as she came apart. I could barely breathe, smothered by her beautiful pussy. I nipped at her clit and she shuddered, slumping over me, completely spent.

Breathing hard, she moved off my face and slid down my body. I stared up at her, my cock hard in my pants. Her glimmering emeralds found my gaze. She licked her lips, her hooded eyes darting to my crotch.

"You want my cock?" She nodded eagerly, her eyes zeroed in on my bulge. "Then take me out." She grasped at my belt, began unbuckling it, and then reached for my cock, wrapping her fingers around it. I closed my eyes at the feel of her warm skin. "Put me inside of you, *dolcezza*."

She lined my tip to her entrance and began lowering down, her wet heat surrounding me. Unable to hold back, I bucked my hips as I thrust inside her. Her one hand came to rest on my chest, her other against the window.

"Holy shit," she panted. "Fuck, fuck, fuck."

I pulled out, only to thrust back inside. She was so fucking tight, she felt like heaven.

"*Cazzo, tu mi fai sentire così bene.*"

Her green gaze glazed with lust found mine. "What does that mean?"

"It means you make me feel so good."

"God, you make me feel good, too, with that big dick."

Cazzo, she could make me come with just that sassy mouth of hers. I'd fill it with my cock later, but for now, I needed to feel her pussy strangling me. I thrust up while dragging her hips down, impaling her fully. I had to close my eyes and grit my teeth, it felt so goddamn good.

"Fuck, Daddy," she gasped.

My balls instantly tightened, lust shooting straight to my groin like a lightning bolt. I grabbed her by the back of the neck and pulled her head down to where my mouth reached the shell of her ear. "Is your pussy ready for me? Because I've been holding back."

"Oh, fuck," she whispered, her hips rocking. "I'm ready."

"Good girl," I crooned, my voice rough. I wrapped her long curls around my fist and pulled hard, her mouth finding mine. "Now, ride Daddy's cock."

I held her head close to me, my other hand on her hip guiding her movements up and down. Her tits bounced against my chest, her hips rolled, my dick sliding in and out of her drenched pussy.

"*Mia moglie.*" I bit her neck, marring her perfect skin. "*Mia piccola puttanella.*"

Her eyes fluttered shut, her pussy strangling my dick as she rolled her hips. I let go of her hair and dug my fingers into her soft flesh. I bucked my hips upward, piercing her. Hard. Rough. Her muscles trembled. Her pussy tightened, and I knew she was close to coming.

I had never connected with a woman like I did with Isla. She fucked freely, enjoyed pleasure with her entire being, and held nothing back. It was as if she were made for me. Every curve of her body molded into my body like we were made from the same flesh.

Reaching down, I found her clit with my thumb and brushed it lightly, teasing her.

"Yes, yes," she panted, sliding her hands into her hair as she leaned back, never stopping to rock herself against my cock. "Please. Please give it to me."

"Say '*Ti prego*' and open your eyes," I ordered. "I'll give you what you want."

"*Ti prego*," she breathed.

With my other hand, I grabbed her breast, squeezing it hard. She moaned, her pussy constricting around my hard length. I circled and rubbed her clit with my thumb, and I felt her walls clamping down, milking my cock. She came hard, moaning "Daddy," and fuck, nothing had ever felt so right.

My balls tightened, and our eyes locked as her body shuddered uncontrollably. My cock swelled inside her, the orgasm rushing through me as cum shot out of me and into her warm, welcoming pussy.

The world had ceased to exist for a moment as my climax dragged, my cock twitching inside her. It was better than ever before. It always felt different with her. And always would.

She collapsed on top of me, our breathing harsh.

All my secrets were about to unravel.

Cazzo, this woman. She'd be my undoing.

TWENTY-EIGHT
ISLA

My heart threatened to explode in my chest as I slid off my husband.

Jesus, I never thought I'd be married, never mind to someone who clearly operated within the criminal boundaries of the underworld.

It's temporary, my mind whispered. But something about the way my husband looked at me told me the exact opposite. God, what had I done? For some reason, I couldn't find regret in each hard beat of my heart as I watched Enrico clean me up.

I was too overwhelmed to say anything as he assisted me with my dress. He zipped it back up, his mouth coming down to press where my neck and shoulder met.

"Do you like the dress?" The rumble of his voice sent a vibration through me, winding me up. After learning all these disturbing details, I should have been repulsed by him. But I wasn't, and that's what bothered me most of all.

"I do," I admitted. "Very much." I turned my head to meet his gaze. "How long have you been planning this?"

I might lose my head every time he fucked me, but that didn't mean I'd pretend all was okay and bury my head in the sand.

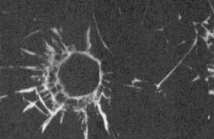

"A few weeks." He didn't even stop to consider this might be disturbing for me to hear.

"Why?"

"Because I wanted you."

I released a heavy exhale while the hole in my chest grew until it threatened to consume all the warmth from the orgasm. "You had me. I would have probably slept with you again. So tell me something real."

Something about this lust—about *him*—terrified me. I feared it'd leave me feeling cold and alone at the end of it all.

Several emotions passed over his expression. Admiration? Dissatisfaction at my challenging him? I wasn't certain.

"I want to protect you." The sincerity in his voice caught me by surprise.

"From what? Your wife?"

His jaw tightened. "*You* are my wife. Or did you forget already?"

I had to stifle the scoff. I didn't know what he was playing at, but there had to be a reason he was doing all this. If he wasn't going to tell me, I'd find out on my own.

"Why did the priest call you Enzo Lucian Marchetti?"

His shoulders visibly tensed. "That's my name. My full name."

It was at that very moment everything clicked into place. I had read the name before. In the obituary. *His brother's obituary*. From what I remembered, the article told the story of how he and Donatella had died on the same day.

My brows scrunched as I felt my mind turning over every possible explanation. If his wife was alive, maybe his brother was too. Or—

I rubbed my forehead, the beginnings of a headache settling in my temples. Today was just too much. Starting with the fake prisoner situation with Tatiana to this sham of a union. Yes, I'd gotten laid, and it was… not terrible. Not terrible at all. Somehow, though, the good didn't outweigh the bad.

"Who are you?" I asked, my voice weak.

"Your husband."

Wrapping my arms around myself, I scooted away. I'd married a stranger. Suspicion that I realized now had always been there started to creep up my spine. This man might not be Enrico Marchetti at all.

It was almost three in the afternoon when the car came to a stop in front of the now familiar mansion in the middle of Paris. It felt fitting that we'd end up where it all started.

I held my husband's gaze as I heard the driver's door open and close before our own door opened shortly thereafter.

With agility, he slid out of the car and extended his hand. "Shall we, *mia moglie*?"

Hesitantly, I put my hand into his outstretched palm and he helped me out of the car. Once I stood next to him, my hand enclosed in his warm one, I felt ice-cold fear mix with dread, both emotions slithering through my veins.

If my suspicions were confirmed and this man was who I believed him to be, my plans of getting out of this marriage on a technicality were not looking promising.

"Have you heard any news about my sister-in-law?" I asked, deciding to focus on something easier than the Marchetti mystery.

"No." Although it felt like days since Tatiana's kidnapping, it had only happened this morning. "Don't worry. You and your brother are safe."

"And Tatiana?"

He let out a sardonic breath. "Trust me, your brother won't let anything happen to his wife."

He was right. Illias was a force to be reckoned with; he'd move heaven and hell to keep her safe.

My stomach hollowed with nerves as we made our way inside his home. I guess it was my home now too. Enrico's—*Enzo's*—hand found its place on my lower back as he led me inside the white marble walkway.

He opened the door and motioned for me to enter. My steps were hesitant as I made my way back inside the home Tatiana and I entered only this morning with a plan to expose all the secrets. In hindsight, I could admit it was ridiculous.

"We'll have an early dinner," Enrico remarked.

"When are we going to talk?" I demanded to know.

"Later." Warning rang in his voice, and I had enough common sense not to push him. Not now. But I fully intended to. Later.

He moved into a room I hadn't been in before. A lounge, by the looks of it. He stopped in front of a liquor cabinet and poured himself a drink, downing it in one go. I stood in the middle of the room, unsure what to do. This was new territory for me.

I licked my lips, suddenly feeling thirsty.

"Can I have some of that, or is the liquor only reserved for you?" I was his wife, after all. The least he could do was show some gentlemanly qualities. "It's been a rough day for me too."

Enrico's eyes bore into me. He poured himself another glass of cognac, and he downed the drink. My lips parted in indignation, but before I could say anything, he closed the distance between us and cupped the back of my head. He pressed his lips to mine. I grasped his bicep while he devoured me, the taste of cognac swirling from his mouth to mine, setting me aflame. This man was intoxicating.

When he pulled back, I was dazed, my fingers clutching his vest like my life depended on it.

"There you are." Manuel's voice came from behind me and I whirled around to find him and Enrico's sons standing there. Manuel's eyes were unreadable, but the boys grinned like they'd just gotten a front-row seat to a porno.

Embarrassment washed over me.

"We have a surprise for you, *Matrigna*."

I groaned. "I told you stop calling me—"

"Surprise!"

The air left my lungs as I stared frozen at the smiling faces. My friends were here. Reina, Phoenix, Raven, Athena, all dressed in matching pink dresses.

"How... What are you...?"

I glanced at my husband who'd come to stand next to me. He wasn't smiling. His face was a cold mask, but something in his dark gaze warmed my heart. His hand came around my hip and he bent his head, his mouth by my ear as he whispered, "I'm sorry it was just us in the church. This is for you. Surprise, *amore mio*."

Emotion swelled inside me and something in my chest cracked, warmth pouring through the creases. How could someone who had threatened my sister-in-law and all but forced me to marry him be so fucking sweet?

I pecked him on the cheek, and without another word, I took off toward my girls. A huge smile graced my face as I reached them, squeezing them all into a circle. We crashed in a messy hug, laughing. You'd think we hadn't seen each other in months, not just a few weeks.

"Fuck, I'm suffocating," Raven mumbled, laughter coloring her voice.

"Holy shit," Reina breathed. "I can't believe you are *married*."

"I knew you were obsessed with daddy dick." I choked hearing Raven's words.

"There are kids here," I said, giving her a pointed look.

"Oops."

I eased back to see their faces, signing and talking at the same time. *"I'm so happy you're here. It's been a hell of a day."*

Phoenix shook her head, her eyes darting behind me as she signed without speaking. *"I'll say. Did he force you to marry him?"*

I answered wordlessly. *"Kind of, with a tiny bit of blackmail."*

All the girls widened their eyes, their gazes traveling to Enrico, then Manuel, to the boys, then back to Enrico.

"At least he's hot," Athena signed. *"Getting laid will be fun."*

Raven chuckled. *"Someone's gotta take one for the team."*

"Are you a stepmom now?" Phoenix asked.

I glared at her and signed, my hand movements slightly erratic. *"Don't say that word."*

The girls snickered, throwing their heads back and laughing, when the clearing of a throat interrupted us.

"I want to know what you're saying too," Enzo demanded, his expression slightly darkening.

"They're probably saying how hot we are," Amadeo said, his wolfish grin wide.

The girls laughed, shaking their heads.

"Ladies, you better be careful," I warned, smiling. "Enzo and Amadeo here are heartbreakers. They'll seduce you and then leave you."

"Not right away," Enzo muttered.

Athena and Raven burst into full-blown laughter. "Wow, lover boy," Raven teased. "Too bad you're like ten years too young."

"We don't mind cougars," Amadeo announced, smiling like the world was at his feet.

The girls got into a rowdy discussion with the boys while Manuel observed.

I felt Enrico slip a hand onto my hip, the touch possessive and claiming. My insides quivered, already craving the feeling of his warm body on mine. I had never wanted to be consumed so badly. Owned.

"How about a celebration dinner, and we can continue the discussion of cougars," Enrico suggested.

Reina interpreted for Phoenix.

"Or we can talk about sugar daddies," Athena deadpanned, her eyes sparkling.

Laughing, we all headed toward the dining room.

TWENTY-NINE
ENRICO

I knew Isla had spirit.
    It was something I spotted the moment I'd laid eyes on her. She sparkled. She smiled. She was happy. At least, at this very moment she was.

Bouquets of red and white roses were scattered over the center of the table. The dining room had been transformed for the wedding dinner. The crystals in the chandelier glimmered, throwing a soft glow around the room. Candles set off a romantic mood in the atmosphere, making the space feel cozy and intimate.

Except every so often, I'd catch Isla sigh as she glanced down at her phone. She worried for her brother and her sister-in-law. I had been checking on the situation too. There was nothing new to report, but if I knew Konstantin, he would protect his wife at the cost of the entire world.

My gaze found my own wife. My beautiful bride, through blackmail or not.

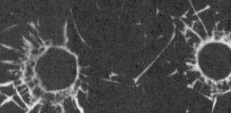

I'd burn down the entire world for her. I'd destroy empires, including my own if it meant keeping her. How was it possible to go from not caring about anyone but my sons to caring for someone so deeply? It was different with Enzo and Amadeo. They needed me. But this woman didn't, yet I couldn't let her go. The truth of the matter was that her brother could protect her. After all, he had kept her a secret from the Omertà for the past twenty-three years. Our one night together exposed her to the underworld.

I grabbed a glass vase, straightened up, and extended my hand to my young bride.

She eyed the vase and my hand curiously. "What?"

"It's time to break the glass," Manuel announced. "For *buona fortuna*."

By the expression on Isla's face, and her friends', they had no idea what he said. Honestly, I was surprised the Romero girls weren't aware of the Italian term signifying good fortune. Their family must have really kept them sheltered.

"For good luck," I clarified. "The number of broken pieces will represent the number of years we'll be happily married."

Isla snickered softly, her little button nose scrunching. "Well, by all means. You're gonna need all the luck you can get."

She took my hand, stood up, and together we made our way to the corner of the room.

"I hope you know, I won't be cleaning this up," Isla warned.

I could hear Manuel's chuckle, and I wanted to wring his neck. "It's your wedding day. You're not expected to clean nor cook today."

She rolled her eyes. "Or ever."

We both held the vase and I counted. "One, two, three. Now."

We dropped the glass and watched it shatter all over the marble flooring into hundreds of tiny little pieces.

"Well, shit. It seems you'll be stuck with my nephew for quite some time," Manuel remarked.

I thought I heard Isla say, "We'll see."

We made it back to our seats and she kicked off her heels. The moment dinner service began, Isla's attention was back on her friends.

Manuel sat next to me while my sons abandoned their seats to sit between the girls. Isla was right. They were actively trying to charm them all. Even my wife wasn't spared.

It had been a long time since I felt this light. Even this happy. At this very moment, I felt at peace. Like the world had been turning only to get to this moment.

Isla laughed and talked with her girlfriends, all of them using American Sign Language for Phoenix's benefit. Enzo and Amadeo chimed in often and my wife or Reina would take turns signing what they were saying. I gathered it was because those two were the most proficient.

"How does it feel to be a married man?" Manuel asked offhandedly, switching to Italian. None of the girls spoke the language. Each time Enzo or Amadeo said something in their native language, the girls pulled up their Google Translate app and had them speak into it.

"Good. You should give it a try."

Manuel shook his head.

"I saw what it did to my brother. Your brother. Our fathers. I don't need that headache." For a long time, I thought the same. Until I met her. Now, I'd burn hell itself if it meant keeping Isla with me. "Have you told her?"

"No," I muttered.

"Will you?"

I didn't want to tell her. Any of it. But she already suspected something.

"Where in the fuck does one even start?"

He let out a sigh. "Maybe at the beginning."

My head tilted to the side to glare at him.

"Sometimes you really act like an old man." He chuckled, leaning back into his chair. Then, because he liked to be the comedian in the family, he rubbed his non-existent belly and his chin. "Now you're just acting like some deranged Santa Claus."

He waved his hand, dismissing my insults. "I'd be the hottest Santa Claus that ever walked this earth."

I rolled my eyes. "You wish."

"I see your young wife's already rubbing off on you," Manuel noted. "Such disrespect for your elders."

"Better watch it, *vecchio*," I mused, switching back to English. "Or I might find you an even younger wife."

It didn't sound like a bad idea at all.

THIRTY
ISLA

I tried to keep my friends around for as long as I could. Not because I feared the wedding night, but because I feared what I'd learn. Each time they readied to leave, I'd pull them down and start another conversation. Until my husband caught on and put an end to it with a single dark expression.

With a heavy heart, I said good night to them and waved at the door until they disappeared from my view. Reina kept glancing back at me with a worried expression, and I forced a somewhat reassuring smile.

The words she signed in ASL so only we could understand kept playing in my mind. *Don't tell him anything about the body. He'll seek revenge or tell the Leone brothers. They're bound by the Omertà oath.*

"He swore he'll protect us all," I signed back.

"*Don't trust them,*" Reina signed. "*Never fully trust them.*"

After all, she trusted blindly and look where it got her. I couldn't blame her for her mistrust, so I nodded. I'd be careful with our secret because it wasn't only one of us who would pay for that death. All of us would. The thorns of death wrapped around my lungs, plunging its spikes into me and pulling me into darkness. That day was a hard one to forget.

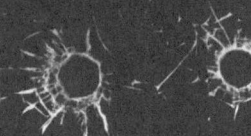

"Enzo, Amadeo, it's time for bed," Enrico said, interrupting my thoughts.

My muscles tightened. I was going to try and pull them into conversation and delay the inevitable. I was eager for more sex, but suddenly, I was terrified of learning the truth.

"Hopefully you won't make the boys sleep in the safe room," I snickered. "They should watch that movie *Flowers in the Attic* so they know how this shit goes."

The temperature around me instantly plummeted.

"Isla, you don't want to test the limits of my patience right now. Don't think I don't know what the fuck you were doing."

The sharpness of his tone pierced my chest. My brother had never used such a tone with me, and truthfully, I hadn't really done anything drastic to deserve it from my husband.

Unless he understood ASL, my mind whispered.

I shook my head. There was no way he understood it. So I bravely squared my shoulders, and feigned innocence.

"I'm not sure what you're talking about," I said, blinking rapidly. Phoenix always said it was hard to resist me when I fluttered my eyelids.

He looked over my head to his family watching us in fascination. It would seem Enrico wasn't accustomed to being challenged. Well, welcome to your new reality, my dear husband.

"Go now," he barked. He waited until they were out of sight before burning that gaze into me.

"Are you looking to be punished?"

I gasped in mock horror, bringing my hand to my chest. "Who? Moi?"

Damn, I should have been an actress.

However, by the looks of it, he wasn't impressed. So maybe an acting career wasn't a smart choice. He yanked my hand, and I nearly stumbled as he started dragging me up the stairs.

"Slow the fuck down," I hissed. "I mean, I know you want to drag me to bed since I'm so damn irresistible, but you shouldn't forget about chivalry."

That seemed to entertain him—at least a bit—as his steps slowed. "You're right, *amore*. I do want to get you to bed. I've been waiting hours for you to wrap dinner up. I've been eager to get my wife to bed and fuck her senseless."

"Ahhh, so this is you when you're sexually frustrated," I remarked. "Duly noted." Why did I keep poking at the bear? "Well, you'll have to get on my schedule for any sexual favors. I prefer to have sex only when I'm in the mood." I feigned a yawn. "I'm afraid tonight is not the night."

What was wrong with me? Maybe he was right and I was a glutton for punishment.

The corners of his lips curved up. "You're my wife. I will fuck you whenever I want until you're screaming my name and losing that attitude of yours."

Heat flooded every single cell in my body and my thighs quivered. "That sounds like quite the task, Daddy. Hope you can keep up."

Jesus, I must have wanted to get fucked more than I thought I did!

"Not to worry, little one," he purred. "You'll be begging me to stop before the sun comes up tomorrow."

"And if it doesn't? What if it's a cloudy day?" My voice was too breathless. I didn't like it. I should sound insulted, instead I sounded horny. Maybe that was better than learning the truth that in my gut I knew already.

"It will be a gloriously long day for both of us, then," he said, his tone dark and full of sinful promises. "Because I will be buried deep in your tight, greedy cunt."

Well then. There was that plan.

We made our way up the grandiose marble staircase, and I couldn't help but note how different the emotions dancing through my veins were. The first night I came here, excitement and adrenaline rushed through me, anticipating a wild night.

Tonight, I climbed the stairs—still turned on—but with dread brewing in the pit of my belly. It warned that I had made one giant mistake. I didn't account for Enrico telling the truth when he claimed he wasn't married.

Why oh why didn't I believe him?

He had caught me in his thorns, and by the dark possession that glimmered in his eyes, I feared he wouldn't let me go. He watched me like I was his and belonged in his corrupt empire, locked in a gilded cage.

I hadn't realized that with each step, my feet got heavier and my movements slower. My husband came to a stop halfway up the staircase that led to his—*our*—bedroom and threw me over his shoulder like some Viking.

A squeal escaped me at the sudden movement.

"What are you doing?" I screamed, my fists pounding on his sculpted back. "Put me down!"

He didn't even bother answering. Not unless you counted the hard slap on my ass as an answer. I yelped, mortified that his sons and Manuel might have heard it. I dug my nails into his jacket, even went as far as attempting to bite him.

"You can't possibly be mad at me for talking to my friends during the wedding dinner that *you* invited them to," I hissed.

He carried me up the steps and down the hall as if I weighed nothing, before kicking open the door to the bedroom. He threw me down on the bed, my ass bouncing off the mattress like a ragdoll.

Then as if he had not a care in the world, he strode back to the door and slammed it shut.

"What in the fuck is your problem?" I grumbled, pissed off. "First you give me little choice but to marry you, and now you're pissed off about who knows what. Are you hormonal or something?"

He'd turned my life upside down in the matter of a single month. *Oh my gosh, it's our one-month anniversary.* The corny side of me beamed. I had to immediately kill that side of me, because this was very far from any kind of anniversary bliss.

"Do you know what today is?" His deep voice sent goose bumps rolling over my skin. He yanked his jacket free and threw it onto the lounge chair. My eyes followed the movement as flames ignited through me. It was the very same chair that we *thoroughly* used that first night. He must have read my thoughts because a smug smirk played around his lips. "Want to get bent over that chair again?"

Yes. "No."

He shrugged. "On your hands and knees, then." Jesus, this conversation was giving me whiplash. "Back to my question. Do you know what today is?"

I peered at him from under my lashes. Why did it feel like a trick question? "The day we got married?" I answered with my own question.

"Our one-month anniversary." *Looked like it wasn't just me with a corny side.* Without pausing to catch my reaction to his words, he continued removing his tie, his strong fingers gripping it. He took a step, like a jaguar eyeing its prey.

I lifted my chin and pursed my lips. "And you're mad because"—I waggled my eyebrows cockily—"I gave you the best sex of your life?"

He chuckled darkly. "I've had a lot of women in my life." To my own horror, a growl vibrated in my throat. I had to learn to control some of my impulses around this man. "Not to worry, *dolcezza*, none of them hold a candle to you. I knew you were the one the moment you blew me that kiss, and once the first tune sounded from your violin, it was game over for me."

He stalked toward me, his eyes burning with something I wasn't sure I wanted to be the object of. Oh, who was I trying to kid. The sight of him liquified my insides in anticipation. The hot buzz beneath my skin flared through me, heating me from the inside out and vibrating with the need for a release that I'd learned only he could give me.

He reached for me, and I held my breath as I watched him, my heart beating out of my chest. He slowly lowered the zipper of my dress. I hadn't even realized I'd lifted my butt to give him better access until he had it off, tossing it on the floor, the white silk a puddle by the bed.

He sat next to me, his fingers trailing up my leg so slowly that shivers broke out on my skin.

"What secrets are you keeping?" he purred so sweetly that I was tempted to open my mouth.

"Tell me your secrets first," I breathed, my legs parting slightly as his hand came to rest between my thighs.

His jaw tightened and a shadow crossed his face.

"I'm going to learn all your secrets, wife. Sooner or later."

I smiled, showing him my teeth. I hoped it was a menacing grin and not the cute one that my girlfriends always teased me about. "And I will learn all of yours, husband. Be warned."

I held his darkening gaze with determination. I wouldn't shrink away. Not from him. Not from anyone.

"Maybe you do crave punishment."

I rolled my eyes. "Bring. It. On." *With your dick.* Because anything with his cock would be pleasure before it ever became pain. I refused to cower in front of anyone. It only gave them ammunition to stomp all over you, and I knew my husband thrived on a challenge. Well, so did I!

A dark chuckle filled the electrified space between us as his hand ventured deeper between my thighs. He brushed his fingers over my soaked panties and a soft moan slipped through my lips without my permission.

"I think you crave the idea of being owned," he remarked darkly.

"Maybe, but don't forget, I'll own you too." His fingers slipped beneath my panties and my head fell back.

My hips arched into his touch. "You said we'd talk."

"We are talking." His finger slid inside my folds, and I gasped at how good it felt. "There'll be a lot more talking. Your moans, my grunts." He pulled out his finger, added one more, and thrust in deep again. Another moan echoed through the room as if to prove his point.

Then without warning, he pulled out his fingers and his hand bunched around my panties, only to rip them off.

"Neanderthal," I murmured.

He didn't seem offended. He leaned forward, his mouth brushing against my cheek and his hot breath tickling the side of my face. "Get on your hands and knees, facing the headboard." The firm tenor of his voice sent shockwaves rippling through me while my thighs quivered with arousal. My nipples peaked into sensitive buds, throbbing and pulsing in rhythm with my core. "Now."

I scrambled to obey, my brain too slow to catch up. It wasn't until I was in position that I realized he was still mostly dressed. I arched my back—hoping it looked seductive—and glanced over my shoulder as both of his palms came to rest on my ass cheeks.

"Aren't you going to take your clothes off?" My thighs clenched together at the images in my mind of his naked body. Good God! This couldn't be... healthy. Could it?

He reached a hand around me to pinch my hard nipple, twisting it between his thumb and forefinger.

"You're so demanding, *mia moglie*."

"Huh?"

"Wife. *Mia moglie* means my wife."

I released a broken moan when he pinched my sensitive nipple again. "I believe in... equality." My voice sounded distorted to my own ears from the buzzing in them. "We should both be naked."

He stood behind me like a god promising pleasure and punishment. Fuck, was it sick that I wanted both? My inner thighs were coated with slick desire. I should be running and screaming from this ruthless man, yet all I could muster strength for was arousal.

He slapped my ass, hard. Then he leaned in, his chest against my back as he whispered into my ear, "Now, let me demonstrate what the term 'toss your salad' means to my young wife."

He sank his teeth into the side of my neck, and I was desperate to feel his hands everywhere. My sex throbbed with an ache that only he could relieve.

He pulled away from me, but before I could complain about the loss of heat, I felt his fingers on my ass first, and then his tongue. My body bucked, but his hand held me in place, preventing me from shifting away from his hungry mouth.

"Ohh... fuck..."

My voice broke as my legs shook and my stomach flipped. I'd never let anyone close to my back entrance before, but the moment I felt his tongue there, the deep contraction in my belly told me I'd like it. I felt my arousal drench my pussy as he smeared it up to my ass.

With each touch of his tongue, my pussy pulsed with a need so violent I thought I'd burst into flames. The need for release clawed through me, begging to be set free.

"Please… Oh… God… Enrico…" I sobbed, my body a throbbing mess.

He instantly stopped. "My name," he demanded. "In the bedroom, you'll scream my name."

I blinked in confusion, then met his gaze over my shoulder. "E-Enrico?"

"Daddy." His fingers ghosted around my neck, but fear didn't choke me enough to run from him. Or to even want him to stop touching me, kissing me. He grabbed a fistful of my hair and yanked me back by it. "No more Enrico when we're in the bedroom."

There was my confirmation. My fingers curled into the blankets. I was so needy for more of what he was offering, I'd call him the fucking devil if it meant we'd go through with this.

"Why not Enzo?" I croaked, although it didn't really matter, did it? He wasn't Enrico.

"It's best you don't get used to calling me Enzo. It's too risky." I wanted to ask why. I had so many questions, but his fingers dug into my scalp, his grip becoming merciless, and I forgot them all. "Say it. I want to hear *it* on your lips."

The part of me that always loved to push the boundaries pouted at him. I licked my lips, fluttering my eyelids seductively. "Okay, Daddy."

He released the grip on my hair and started unbuttoning his vest. I could see the outline of his erection through his trousers, and my pussy pulsed in anticipation. His vest hit the floor and he moved on to his cufflinks.

As he unfastened them, his eyes were on me the entire time. I wiggled my ass, hardly able to breathe as I waited for him. His shirt came off shortly after and my mouth watered at seeing all his glorious muscles on display.

That tanned skin. Those firm, sculpted abs. He was all man with rough palms and barely leashed power. I needed to feel him lose it.

"Are you going to fuck me now, Daddy?" I wanted that thick cock so badly, I'd say and do anything to get it. "Or are you going to spank me first?"

Darkness flashed in his gaze, pulling me into those obsidian pits. He unbuckled his belt slowly, the leather swishing through the air as he pulled it free from the loops of his trousers. He held on to the belt as he toed off his shoes and socks, then unfastened his pants. He stepped out of his trousers, leaving him standing gloriously naked.

Clearly the man didn't believe in boxers.

"Have you ever been spanked before?" His voice was so full of carnal promises, I could hardly breathe. The sweet seduction in the tone of his voice and that Italian accent were enough to make me see stars.

"No."

"Would you like to?" I squirmed under his intense scrutiny. What the fuck was wrong with me? The man all but forced this marriage on me. Held secrets involving my mother. There were so many lies surrounding him that he'd suffocate us all. And here I was, contemplating the thought of him spanking me.

"Yes, but don't use the belt," I murmured against my better judgment. The way his nostrils flared intoxicated me. He snatched my jaw, holding it tightly, then kissed me hard, brutally and demandingly.

Like a flower to the sun, I yielded, eager for more of him. Something about his touch and his possession had awakened a part of me I didn't know existed.

"Count to five, *dolcezza*," he purred, clearly satisfied with my answer. "We'll start slow. *Va bene*?" His mouth came to my left ass cheek and he pressed a kiss on it, biting gently. "*Va bene*?" he repeated.

"I don't know Italian," I reminded him.

He kissed my right ass cheek. "You count to five. Okay?"

I briefly closed my eyes, trying not to picture what he was seeing. My ass in the air, drenched with my arousal. But then I remembered how he'd kissed my dark hole a few minutes earlier with fervor, and I allowed myself to relax.

"Okay."

He inhaled deeply.

"*Cazzo*, you smell so fucking good." A shudder rolled through my spine hearing his thick accent. His rough palm petted me gently, and something in my chest shifted. He put his one knee on the mattress, between my legs. "Are you ready?"

I nodded.

The first slap reverberated in the air and my ass cheek caught on fire. I sucked in a breath. *Fuck!* He quickly brought his hand to the burning flesh and rubbed it gently. "Shhh, it will bring you pleasure. *Te lo prometto.*" Then, remembering I didn't understand Italian, he added, "I promise." His strong hands held me, keeping my ass in the air. "Count, *dolcezza*."

"One," I panted. Another slap. "Two." My body reeled forward and my clit throbbed in response as my slickness ran down my inner thighs. He rubbed the sensitive flesh, then switched to the other side. Another slap. "Three," I moaned.

The pain from the slaps turned into heat. I pushed back, rubbing like a cat against his muscular thigh, seeking friction.

"Such a good girl." His hand rubbed my skin, soothing the fire. The contrast between his roughness, control, and tenderness was my undoing. I wanted more of it.

"Don't stop."

He spanked me again and again. He etched himself inside me with each slap and I fucking thrived on it. My knees went weak as sensation exploded on my skin with each of his ministrations, and I would have collapsed to the bed if he hadn't been holding me up. My skin sang with pleasure, every inch of me throbbing with the need to feel him inside me.

"Please, fuck me. I need to come," I whimpered. I was an incoherent mess, my skin sensitive. I pushed my hips back into his pelvis, causing his tip to skim to the entrance to my ass. We both froze, the temptation right there. I turned my head to find his fingers gripping his cock, the burning look in his eyes matching the fire licking my skin.

"*Tu sei mia,*" he growled. "You're mine now. My wife. My toy. My everything."

My resistance perished. "Yes, yes… yes." The needy edge to my voice was evident. My voice was breathy—sultry. "Just fuck me already," I sobbed.

In the next moment, I felt his hard length at my hot entrance. I waited, the throbbing on my ass matching the one between my thighs.

He leaned over until his lips met the shell of my ear. "I like hearing you beg."

He reached his thumb around and found the swollen nub of my clit. He flicked it once and my back arched into him.

"Please… please." I panted, ready to go up in flames. "I'm begging you, Daddy, give me your cock."

Before I could take my next breath, he thrust inside me until he was fully seated, my walls stretching around his length. He grunted. I moaned. My fingers clutched the bedding, and I turned my head, seeking his mouth.

His lips found mine and he kissed me hard.

He released my mouth too soon. "Ready, *dolcezza*?"

"I was born ready."

Then he started moving. He fucked me like he was punishing me and rewarding me at the same time. His hips hit my sensitive, raw flesh with each thrust, his flesh slapping against mine making obscene noises, urging me further into my pleasure.

His fingers dug into my hips while he drove deep, pounding hard and rough. Unforgiving. And God help me, I loved it. Fuck vanilla sex, this was so fucking good. Give it to me dirty and rough.

The bed rocked as he worked himself in and out of my body. His grunts were erotic. The words in Italian that he uttered were even more so.

The bed rocked. The mattress protested. My screams urged.

Each ruthless thrust knocked the breath out of my lungs. He grunted with every slam, his cock sheathed deep inside me. I started to think each touch by this man would get me more addicted to him and soon—very soon—I'd be putty in his hands.

My husband grabbed a fistful of my hair as he hit that sensitive spot over and over again until tears burned in my eyes.

"Let me hear you, *dolcezza*. Every sound you make is music. All fucking mine."

When the first tear rolled down my face, he released my hair and wiped it—almost reverently—with his finger. He brought his index finger against my lips, and I opened them eagerly, letting him slide it inside as I sucked greedily.

He kept working himself in and out of my body, mirroring the rhythm of his fingers pushing in and out of my mouth.

His finger slipped from my mouth down to my legs in search of my clit. He pinched the swollen nub at the same time that he slapped my burning ass, and the world exploded.

Sparks shot through my veins. My body convulsed, and every single cell in my body shut down while the pleasure coursed through me. My ears buzzed and my brain blanked as I let myself bask in the intensity of my orgasm.

My husband kept thrusting through my clenching sex until his body went rigid and he finished with a roar, hot liquid spurting inside my channel.

Enrico pulled out of my folds and I slumped on the bed, weak but sated in the afterglow of the best orgasm of my life.

Still high on languid post-coital bliss, I startled when I felt strong arms pick me up.

"Let's clean you up."

THIRTY-ONE
ENRICO

After I cleaned her up, we stretched out on the bed, although tension rolled through her. She tried to mask it by closing her eyes.

It was selfish of me, but I never wanted to let her go. As I held her in my arms, I felt at peace for the first time in a very long time. From now on, she'd be in my home, in my bed. I'd give her anything she wanted—anything but her freedom. This marriage was for life and to hell with it all.

Isla seemed to always have something to say, but she remained silent, her cheek pressed against my chest. The tension between us—sexual and emotional—had been our dance since the day we crossed paths. With each touch, she became more engraved in the marrow of my bones, but I seemed to be out of her system immediately after we fucked.

My chest tightened in frustration.

"Are you clean?" she asked, never opening her eyes. "Considering you're not using condoms anymore."

It had never been my style to fuck a woman without a condom, but with her, I didn't want to fuck her any other way. I didn't want anything separating us.

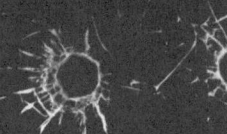

"I'm clean." I stroked her hip, her soft skin silky under my fingers. "And a husband doesn't need a condom with his wife."

She scoffed softly, her breath brushing against my chest.

"Aren't you going to ask me if I'm clean?" She shifted, raising her head to look at me.

I kissed the crown of her head. "You're clean." She glared at me and I let out a sigh. "What's the matter?"

She pushed away from me and I already hated the distance. "Well, where do I even start?"

"How about at the beginning?" I said, repeating Manuel's words from earlier in the evening.

She sighed. "Fine, let's start there. Who are you, really?"

"Your husband." Pulling her back to me, I kissed her. I just couldn't resist. I kept kissing her, my hands roaming her naked body until she writhed against me. When I pulled away, her gaze was hazy and unfocused. "Next question."

She blinked her eyes up at me. "Why did the priest call you Enzo Lucian?"

"My Christian name."

She blew raspberries. "I despise you."

That was probably better than loving me. It'd keep her alive. I didn't need her to love me. *Liar*, a voice whispered, mocking me.

"Despise me all you want." I pulled her up my torso. Her legs parted, her knees bracing on either side of me. My hand found her clit and circled it, her arousal smearing on my chest. A moan sounded between us and my cock instantly responded, ready to thrust into her hot entrance again. As if she read my thoughts, a shudder rolled down her body and her pupils dilated. "But your cunt is mine, and it loves my cock."

"You are crude," she let out in a small voice as her arousal coated my fingers.

I cupped her pussy harshly. "Whose pussy is this?"

She rocked her hips, grinding herself against my hand. Fuck, seeing her so greedy, needing more of me—just like I needed more of her—was such a turn-on. It made my balls ache.

I slid her down my body and, without warning, lifted her slightly to line my cock up at her entrance. I looked to where we were connected, then gripped her hips tightly enough to bruise. Tension radiated from me, every muscle in my body pulled taut. Then I slammed her down my length and drove deep into her wet heat.

Her back arched and I slapped her ass. "Whose pussy is this?" I growled again. When she stayed silent, I started pounding into her, my rhythm wild and untethered. I slapped her ass again, hard, and she gasped. "Whose pussy is this?"

She watched me through half-lidded eyes. "Yours."

I rose until we were chest to chest and bounced her on my erection. Over and over, not allowing her any reprieve. Her moans and whimpers were better than the sounds she made with her violin. She was fucking consuming me.

"Oh, God, oh… God."

I slapped her ass. "Your husband. Not God."

"Yes, yes," she whimpered. "More, Enrico."

Cazzo, it got me so fucking hard when she called me Daddy. But when she said *paparino*, I was ready to spurt deep inside her cunt. I groaned at how tight she felt. Her face was flushed from pleasure. I slid my fingers between her ass cheeks and found her hole. I pushed the tip of my finger inside as I thrust up into her. And that did it.

Her orgasm ripped through her, her whole body shuddering. Her walls tightened around my dick and her nails dug into my shoulders as she shattered around me.

My orgasm rushed over me next, following her right over the edge and stealing my breath as cum shot out of my cock and into her warm, welcoming cunt. I drove into her harder, like a madman seeking sanity. Like a sinner seeking salvation, and she was the only one who could give it to me.

We climaxed together, both of us shuddering and muttering incoherent sounds. Hers, a mix of Russian and English. Mine, a string of filthy Italian words. I pulled her against my chest, wrapping my arms around her, and stroked her back as she tried to catch her breath.

Sweat cooled our skin, her forehead coming to rest against my shoulder. I kissed her hair, its coconut smell the best scent on this earth. It reminded me of the beach in front of my home in Italy. Of carefree summers when I was a little boy, running up and down the shore.

I slid out of her tight folds, then lay back, pulling her with me. My hand traveled further south, cupping her ass.

"You must have an obsession with ass," she muttered into my chest.

"Only your ass."

I moved my fingers between her legs, where my cum mixed with her juices. I teased her entrance lightly. She bit my shoulder as her hips ground against my finger, her muffled whimpers vibrating against my skin as I pushed my cum back into her pussy.

Cazzo, I was obsessed with more than just the woman's ass.

Literally dragging my hands away from her pussy, I brought them up to her back. We remained silent, my hands traveling down her back. Her silky skin soothed, the best kind of therapy for the chaos inside me.

A soft snore sounded against my chest and I shifted to find my wife's face. Her long red lashes fanned her cheeks, her expression serene and her breathing even. The sweetest expression I'd ever seen, and suddenly, I wanted to keep it that way. My thoughts strayed to the image of our future, with little girls running around that looked like their mamma and had me wrapped around their little fingers.

Just like this woman did. Fuck, I was whipped. My throat tightened. Fuck! It was even worse. I loved this woman.

Fear filled my mouth with a bitter taste.

I could not allow this woman to die, the curse on my family be damned. She was mine. I'd make her love me and keep her with me until my dying breath.

This time around, a Marchetti man would die before the woman he loved did.

THIRTY-TWO
ISLA

The morning light blinded me even before I opened my eyelids.

Ignoring the day and responsibilities—I wasn't even sure at this point what they were—I rolled to my side, burying my head under the pillow. A stinging pain exploded on my ass and my body was sore in places it had never been sore before.

Jesus Christ, was it possible to die from too much sex?

My core tingled, as if Enrico—Enzo Lucian, or whatever his name —were still inside me. Like he still drove into me with feral power, punishing and rewarding me at the same time.

A rough palm rubbed my ass, and I recognized the touch, causing hot blood to rush through my veins. In such a short period, I had come to crave his presence. The control and ruthlessness he emanated, as well as the carnal and feral power with which he fucked me.

God help me!

I wanted my husband's savage brutality in the bedroom.

He squeezed my ass, the stinging flesh sending tingles through my entire body. "I know you're awake."

"Go away," I muttered, my body craving him even now, despite the soreness.

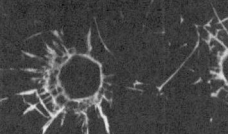

Slap. Pain exploded across my ass. "Never tell your husband to go away."

My eyes shot open, and I glared at him. "Ouch."

Enrico sat on the edge of the bed, his hand never leaving my body. He was already dressed in his signature black suit, his jacket open, giving me a glimpse of his vest. Why did he look so goddamn hot in a suit? Although, not even that elegant three-piece suit could hide his hard muscles nor disguise his brutality.

"Get up, shower, and get dressed."

"Marriage sucks," I muttered, facing away from him.

He pulled me back so I'd face him, and I pursed my lips in annoyance. "What did you say?"

I smiled sweetly. "You heard me. Or has your hearing diminished with your old age?"

Fuck, that was a good comeback. One point for Isla.

He narrowed his eyes.

"Do you fancy a mouth fuck?" My thighs clenched and fire ignited through every cell of my body. Oh my freaking God! Someone needed to pour ice water over me and cool me off. "Because it seems to me you're craving punishment again. And the only thing that will diminish my hearing, *piccolina*, are your screams while I fuck you."

He smacked my ass to emphasize his words, but before I could yelp, his fingers started kneading the flesh, soothing the burn. "Now, do you want me to fuck your mouth, or will you behave?"

Hmmm.

Immediately, I mentally slapped myself to get some sanity back. "I'll take a rain check on letting you fuck my mouth," I muttered. Got to leave my options open, right? He had gone down on me, but I had yet to taste him. I'd hold on to all the power I could in this *marriage*.

"Excellent," he said, clearly not wanting my mouth on his dick. Challenge accepted. I'd make him crave it. He wrapped his strong arms around me and picked me up Neanderthal-style, throwing me over his shoulder and carrying me effortlessly into the bathroom.

"God, what is it with you manhandling me like I'm a sack of potatoes?" I muttered, smacking his back which resulted in him smacking my ass. "Jesus, stop touching my ass. I know you're obsessed with it—it's a cute ass—but come the fuck on. It's sensitive from—"

I stopped myself, images from last night bouncing through my mind and making my pussy clench. Lovely. I had turned into a sex maniac.

Then as if he thought the same, his free hand came up to my ass and he rubbed it gently. Affectionately.

"I already told you, *dolcezza*, I love your ass."

The palpitations of my heart caught me by surprise. The smart part of me knew he was saying he loved my ass and probably wanted to fuck it, but the romantic side of me took it to mean "he loves *me*."

At this rate, I'd need a head doctor by the end of the week. I lifted my head and caught a glimpse of us in the mirror. Me, butt naked and disheveled. Him, suited up and looking every bit the hot Italian mobster I was learning he was.

He gently lowered me, letting me slide down his body, the friction of his clothes against my bare skin making me come alive. His dark, shimmering gaze found mine and held on for seconds that seemed to stretch into hours. He watched me with unnerving silence—desire and need reflecting my own in his obsidian depths. But there was something else there.

Worry.

I couldn't shake the feeling that something was wrong.

"Is everything okay?" I heard myself ask. "Are your kids okay?"

"Yes, our boys are okay."

It was terrifying how effortlessly he pulled me into his life and included me as if I was always meant to be. I liked Enzo and Amadeo, but to think of them as our kids… Yeah, it was a bit of a stretch. They were, like, a decade younger than me.

Before I could say something, he sidestepped me and turned on the shower.

"We're leaving soon. Get ready."

He turned to leave but I caught his sleeve, gripping it tightly and refusing to let him go.

"Where are we going?" He didn't move or say anything, almost like he was debating whether or not to tell me anything. "Enrico, if you keep me in the dark, I swear to you I'll set your entire world on fire."

He raised a brow, then brought his other hand to his sleeve and slowly peeled my gripping fingers from his expensive suit, studying me intently as if determining whether I was sane.

Too late, stud, I thought to myself.

Then, he surprised me. "If that will make you happy, Isla, I'll let you burn down my entire world. But you'll still remain my wife. I refuse to let you go."

His words sent an unfamiliar tingle down my spine. It wasn't arousal or lust. It was something else, but I couldn't quite figure out what.

"Are you always this possessive?" I muttered, although there was no bite to my words.

"No."

I didn't believe him. The man was a control freak. Ruthless. I was fairly sure it was his savage and obsessive ways that captivated me. Maybe there was darkness inside me, just like my father. Just like my brother. Then I remembered Tatiana, and shame filled me.

"Have you heard anything from my brother about Tatiana?" Something flickered in his eyes and I zeroed in on it. That was it. It was that look that I wasn't able to pinpoint. Dread filled me. "Oh my gosh, something happened. Didn't it?" Slowly, panic bubbled inside me, rising to the surface. I took Enrico's hand into mine and squeezed. "Something happened. I can see it in your eyes." He reached a hand to my face and I stiffened. "D-did he die?" He shook his head. "Did she?"

My voice cracked. I hadn't known Tatiana for long, but I knew if something happened to her, it'd destroy my brother. Despite learning Illias killed my mother, I wouldn't wish that upon him. I was mad, but I didn't hate him.

"She's alive." The breath I'd been holding swooshed out of my lungs. "But she's in the hospital." Before I could open my mouth and demand he take me to her, he said, "We're going to Russia so you can be there for your brother and her."

Tears burned in the back of my eyes. "We?"

My lip trembled and my heart squeezed. I didn't expect him to want to go and make sure my brother and his wife were okay. I didn't think he cared, even though he clearly knew my brother.

"Yes, *we*, Isla." He cupped my cheek, something feral and possessive in his gaze. "Wherever you go, I go. Wherever I go, you go. We are one now. If you cry, I cry. If you smile, I smile. If you rage, I rage."

There it was again. The palpitations of my heart.

"Why Russia? She was just here in Paris with me."

He shrugged. "She made it back to Russia." I knew he wouldn't expand. "And you're not going alone. I'm not risking losing my bride on the first day of my marriage."

I rolled my eyes. He knew me too well while I was left in the dark about him. How could I trust him when he was keeping secrets? Although, I was tempted to tell him I actually kept my word.

"I don't trust you," I murmured, keeping my guard up. "You forced me to marry you. You're keeping secrets from me and leaving me in the dark. I cannot trust you."

Was I convincing him or myself?

He must have read something on my face, because he pushed his fingers through his hair, tugging on the thick strands.

"I'll earn your trust," he vowed. "But I won't apologize for arranging this marriage. You were made for me and we both know it." I shook my head, ignoring the sinking feeling of disappointment. The tightness in my chest sent warning flares again. "When I believe you're ready to hear the secrets, I'll share them with you."

That was where he was wrong. That wasn't only his call to make, and whether he liked it or not, I'd unravel those secrets and drag them all into the light.

Husband or not.

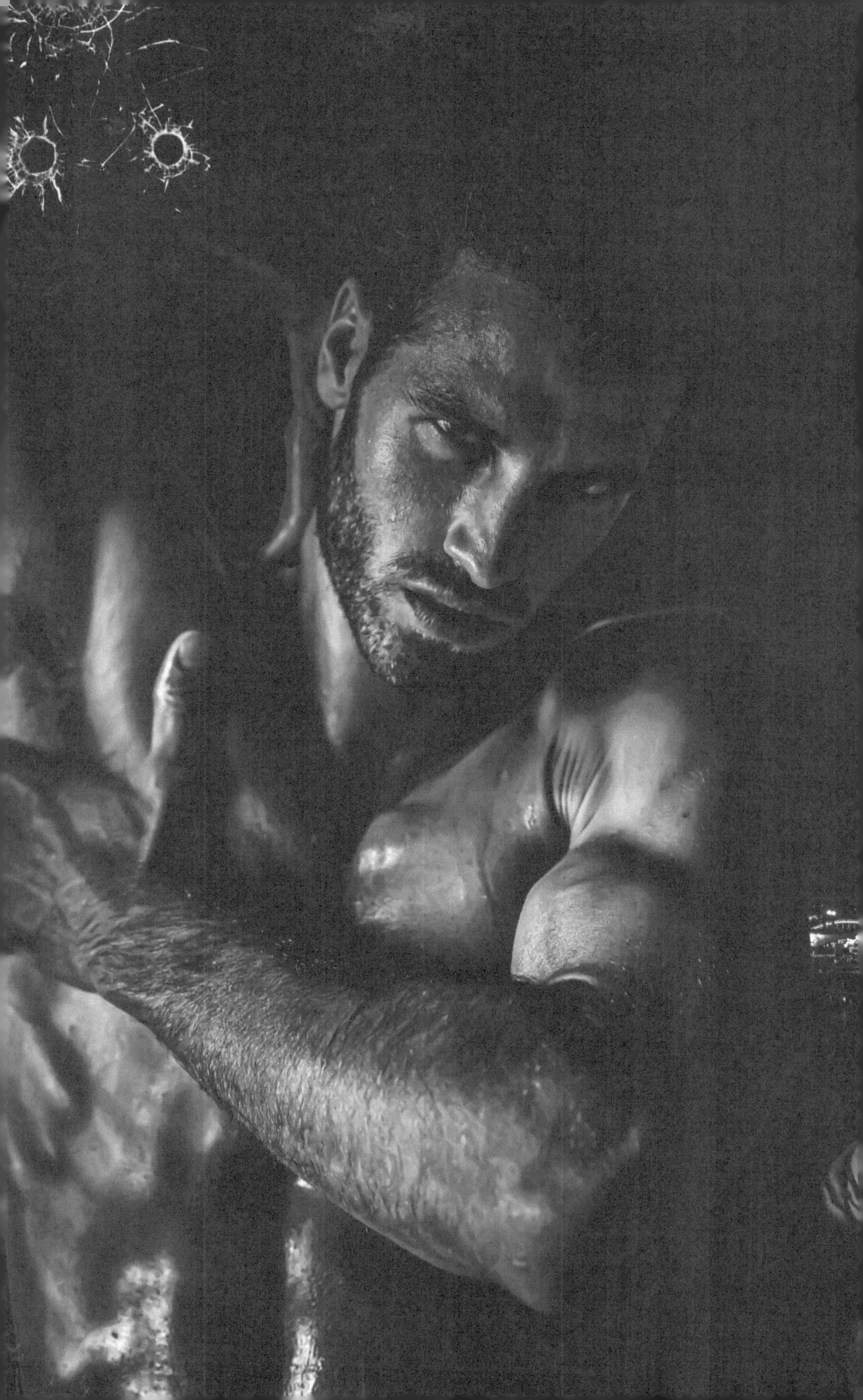

THIRTY-THREE
ENRICO

When Kingston called me with the news, I knew I'd have to let Isla go to her sister-in-law and be there for her brother.

She'd regret it otherwise.

But fuck if I'd let her go alone. Kingston tried his hardest to convince me no Marchetti should step foot in Russia, especially with Sofia Volkov making her moves, but I ignored him. He knew I'd go, so I wasn't sure why he wasted his breath.

I couldn't demand that Kingston accompany us. I knew his limits and Russia was it. So I did the next best thing. I called up Kian and his crew and had them meet us in Moscow.

Kingston wasn't off base when he said going into Russia was like walking into Sofia Volkov's den. But I had to do it. For Isla. We'd start this marriage off the right way, and if her brother needed her, that's where she'd go.

Kian and his men would provide us with protection. Of course, Manuel would come along. He was the only man I trusted explicitly. Kingston came in close second.

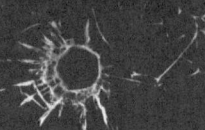

"Are you certain pulling in her Brazilian family so soon is wise right now?" Manuel studied me, concerned. The same unease I felt reflected in his eyes.

We were seated in the office, waiting for my sons and wife to get ready. Sleeping in was something they had in common already.

"Kian Cortes is *not* his fucked-up brother." If the head of the Brazilian cartel was her only living relative from her mother's side, I'd hide her from him at all cost. But Kian was a different story. He was an honorable man, and everyone knew he disagreed with his brother. It was the reason he branched off and kept his distance from his family. "We have threats coming at us from all angles. If something should happen to you or me, Isla will need all the protection she can get."

"Do you think that protection will extend to the boys too?" Manuel remarked thoughtfully.

I tilted my head pensively. "Only if Isla accepts them. Kian has no allegiances to the Marchetti line, aside from his niece. If she demands protection for them, I have no doubt that Kian will protect them."

Manuel let out a sardonic breath. "The girl might not know it yet, but she has already accepted them." *Cazzo*, the thought of Isla being a part of my boys' lives made my chest tighten. It made my feelings for her skyrocket. "You might be right, *nipote*. Connecting her with Kian Cortes is a smart move. She'll have his and Konstantin's power behind her if shit hits the fan."

The door swung open and my sons stormed through, ceasing all conversation.

"Papà, is it true?" Enzo demanded to know, his voice getting deeper by the day. Amadeo wasn't far behind. They were growing up way too fast. "We're going to a hostile country?"

"*Allora*, boys. Firstly, Russia is Isla's home country. That's where she was born."

My eldest's cheeks reddened a bit. He liked Isla. He didn't like her Russian connection. "She's American. She told us that herself."

Amadeo smacked his older brother on his back. "Idiot, she lied to us."

"She didn't lie," I corrected my youngest. "She is American. She grew up in California. She went to school there, but she was born in

Russia. Her brother is the Pakhan and both of you will show respect. *Capisce?*"

The two shared glances. "So she's a mafia princess?" Enzo asked.

"Damn, Papà. You scored big," Amadeo chimed in, grinning like a shark. I was fairly certain my youngest got my brother's impulsiveness too. Enzo and Amadeo seemed to alternate traits depending on the occasion. "It's going to be impossible to top that. But we'll try. Maybe we'll tap some royal ass."

Dio mio! I'd have to start seriously talking to them about protection so we didn't end up with tons of little baby Marchetti bastards before I managed to even get my own wife pregnant.

"Neither of you will be tapping any ass." I kept my expression stern and my tone scolding. "We're going to Russia. Isla's sister-in-law is in the hospital. Her brother needs her, and she will need us. Can you do that for her?"

Their expressions sobered and they nodded in unison. "*Sì, Papà.*"

Enzo shifted on his feet uncomfortably, hesitating before speaking his next words. He didn't like to show his emotions.

"When we were in the safe room, she comforted us about Donatella trying to kill us," he stated, his voice pitching. It had been a while now since both of them began referring to her as *Donatella* rather than *Mother*. "She said sometimes people suck, but it's not our fault."

I nodded. "È vero." *It's true.* "You are good boys and make me proud. Donatella is lost. In her mind and her hate."

They agreed. I fucking hated that they had to know their mother wanted them dead. I tried so fucking hard to shelter them from her mental illness. But when she'd almost gotten to them when they were seven and eight, I had to come clean. I couldn't leave them blind and vulnerable to their mother.

"Isla's too soft," Amadeo stated matter-of-factly. "It's dangerous. Donatella will take advantage of that."

I agreed with my son. Isla was soft, but I also sensed strength and courage. She certainly had no qualms standing up to me, and that gave me hope. There were some women who were oblivious to the dangers lurking. My gut told me Isla wasn't one of them.

"It's our job to keep an eye on her," I said. "We are a family, and we take care of each other. Sì?"

Soft footsteps sounded behind me and the four of us shared glances with the unspoken agreement.

Isla appeared at the door, dressed in jeans that hugged her curves and a purple cashmere sweater that hung off her shoulder and offered a glimpse at the outline of her breasts. On her feet were plain black flats. Practical for the long journey ahead.

Madonna, she was breathtaking. Like a fallen angel ready to seduce the devil. She could parade naked, in the most breathtaking dress, or in rags, and she'd steal my breath away every time.

"Did you know your closet is bursting with women's clothes, all of them with the tags still attached and in their garment bags?" she remarked. She waved at the boys and gave a non-committal nod to Manuel. "Either you have tons of female guests who have no clothes, or you planned my kidnapping."

I let out a sardonic breath. She really liked to push my buttons. "It's not kidnapping if you came into my home of your own free will."

While I waited for her to leave Russia, I stocked up on clothes for her in all my homes that I usually frequented. I couldn't wait to see her reaction to her closet in Italy.

She let out a sardonic breath. "For a visit."

"Potato. Potahto."

She cocked her eyebrow. "Wow, I'm impressed. I didn't know Italians knew English expressions."

"You'd be surprised by what I know." I smirked knowingly, and her cheeks reddened.

Apparently, she decided to ignore me, turning her attention to my sons instead. "Hey, boys, I like your mini-Enrico suits. Wouldn't you be more comfortable traveling in jeans, though?"

Enzo shrugged. "Real men wear suits. And real women wear dresses that show off their legs."

Madonna santa. I'd have to talk to Enzo about throwing those kinds of remarks at my wife.

"Enzo, that's not how you speak to a lady," I snapped. "Especially not your stepmom."

Isla raised her palm and narrowed her eyes on Enzo who was about to say something.

"Okay. Let's set some ground rules," she started sternly, and my dick stiffened in my pants. For crying out loud. This woman could recite the Bible and I'd get a hard-on. "You need to get to know a girl, not her legs. Let's crawl before we start walking."

All four of us gave her a blank stare. Who in the fuck was talking about crawling? Although, I wouldn't mind my wife crawling to me, naked, wearing nothing but heels.

A clearing of a throat pulled my head out of my fantasy. Everyone was staring at me.

"What?" I barked, annoyed that I was so easily distracted. Usually I was laser-focused. "Don't you forget, I'm capo here. So cut the shit."

"Calm down, *nipote*. Nobody was challenging you. Your wife asked you a question."

Cazzo, I didn't hear her say anything after crawling.

"Repeat your question, *piccolina*."

Her gaze flashed with that green fire I loved so much, but this time, I kept my bodily response in check.

"Stop calling me that," she stated, her voice bleeding with annoyance. "I asked you whether we are *all* going to Russia?"

When I nodded, she continued. "Okay. Then we need a game plan. First, stop shoving this mother thing on your sons and me. We just met and need to get acquainted. *Capisce*?" Manuel choked out a laugh, and when my gaze found him, he wiped a hand across his mouth in a poor attempt to hide his amusement. "Second, Illias will kill you and your family if he learns of the marriage, so we will keep that on the down-low."

My gaze darkened, conveying my refusal to hide our marriage—and the fact she was mine—from anyone, let alone her brother.

"No." She was mine, and I needed the world to know. "Besides, I didn't know you cared enough to protect me."

She shot me a glare, her hands coming to her hips as she widened her stance. "Yes. While I'm okay to let you two go at each other's throats and let the best man win, I'm not okay getting Enzo and Amadeo caught in the crossfire."

I paused. Fuck, Manuel was right. She'd already warmed to them and was already thinking about their safety. No wonder it was so fucking easy to love her. My uncle's eyes snapped to me and he cleared his throat, warning me that my feelings were painting my features no doubt. Of course, Isla took that wrong and shot him a guilty but unapologetic look.

"I'm sorry, Manuel, but you're a big boy and on Enrico's side. So you're on your own."

Enzo and Amadeo burst into a full-blown laugh. The kind that I hadn't heard in a long time.

"She likes us more than you, Papà, and you, Zio Manuel." Amadeo really liked to poke the bear. If I wasn't so fucking thrilled at the idea she had their safety at heart, I might have growled at him.

"Anything else, *piccolina*?" I asked her, keeping my voice even.

"Yes. Illias is going to be distraught over Tatiana. So no upsetting him. This might be your territory, but Russia is mine."

There she was! The Russian mafia princess that I sensed all along.

"*D'accordo*," I heard myself say. "For now, we'll do it your way. When we get to Italy, we'll do it mine."

THIRTY-FOUR
ISLA

"This is ridiculous."

Enrico and I argued in the parking garage of the hospital, both of us locked in the bulletproof Land Rover. He refused to let me go upstairs alone; I refused to go with him.

Five of Enrico's men were in the two cars behind us. Apparently, another security detail was coming later. Manuel and the boys were back at the hotel with their own security. Enrico's obsession with security superseded Konstantin's tenfold.

"It is ridiculous," he agreed. "But it wouldn't be if we just walked up together."

"You agreed we wouldn't break the news of this marriage to my brother here."

"And I intend to stick to that, but I didn't agree to let you roam the hospital alone."

I let out a frustrated growl. "If we go together, it's no better. He'll lose his shit if he sees you with me."

Enrico's jaw tightened, and I heard his molars grind. "This is non-negotiable. I'm going with you or you're not going at all." I opened my mouth to protest when he cut me off. "Knowing your brother, he's probably tied to Tatiana's bed. I'll walk you to her hospital room and remain right outside."

I took a deep breath and exhaled slowly. My temper protested at his controlling asshole ways, but I recognized stubbornness when I saw it. I'd seen the same look plenty of times on my brothers' faces growing up. He wasn't going to let up.

"Fine," I muttered, reaching for the door handle. "I honestly don't know why I ever found your ass attractive. You don't even keep your promises."

One second I was pulling on the door handle, the next a hand grabbed me by my nape and pulled me back.

"Don't push me, Isla." Enrico's dark eyes glimmered like the pits of hell. "This might be your home, and your brother might be the Pakhan, but there are still threats lurking. I won't fucking lose you to them. Regardless of your bratty attitude, *piccolina*."

Did he just—

He just called me a brat.

I closed the distance and bit his lip. *Hard*. Fuck, even when I was mad at him, he tasted good. The slight taste of copper touched my lips. "I am not a brat," I mumbled, our lips brushing. "You are an asshole. It's like you're *trying* to start a war with my brother."

His mouth crashed against my aching lips for a bruising kiss. He plunged his tongue inside and twirled it against mine, drawing a moan from me. I sucked on his tongue greedily, my thighs quivering with need.

Good God. This lust and attraction between us had to extinguish eventually. Right? I didn't understand it. For some reason, it grew instead of faded.

He pulled away. Too quickly.

I blinked my eyes, disoriented, while he looked completely composed. Bastard.

"If that is what it takes to keep you, Isla, I will go to war." His voice was cold, sending a chilling feeling of dread down my spine. "I'll end every goddamned business alliance my father and grandfather built to keep you with me. You *will* give me everything. Your all."

Was that deranged or romantic? Fuck if I knew. My heart skipped a beat and my chest tightened. I didn't know whether it was anger, hate or… something else.

"Who are you?" I asked, my voice barely a whisper. "How can you ask me to give you everything, when you've given me nothing?"

It wasn't until I said those words that I realized what held me back. He wanted to strip me naked while remaining fully clothed. It'd leave me vulnerable, but he'd still have his shield.

I was young. Maybe even naive, in some cases. But I knew it should be a two-way street. We studied each other intently, each measuring the other. Or maybe both of us readied for a battle of wills. It was hard to read this man. He kept his thoughts and emotions locked in a vault.

I held my breath while I waited for him to say something. Anything. When he didn't, my stomach sank with disappointment.

"I'm going upstairs to be with my brother," I said, finally breaking the silence. "Come or don't, I don't care, but keep out of Tatiana's room."

He raised a brow at my sarcastic tone, but he didn't comment on it. Instead, we both exited the car, his bodyguards rushing forward. I didn't wait for my husband to join me as I neared the entrance of the hospital, but he caught up to me just the same.

His hand came to rest on my lower back as he pulled me closer to him.

"I'm sorry, *piccolina*," he murmured into my ear. "After the hospital, we'll talk."

My heart shuddered in my chest, and I turned my head to meet his gaze. He'd said this exact thing before and didn't follow through.

As if he could read my mind, he added, "*Te lo prometto*. On my brother's grave. On my parents' grave."

With that promise, I took his hand off my back and held it the rest of the way to Tatiana's room.

Enrico kept his word.

He remained in the hallway as I entered Tatiana's room, even though I knew it killed him. He gave me a reassuring smile, but his hands were fisted so tightly, his knuckles turned white.

"If you need me, text me," I murmured, rising on my tippy-toes and pressing a kiss on his lips. "It'll buzz in my butt pocket."

His lips curved into a smile, molding against mine. "You know I love your butt."

"I do."

Another kiss. "Make sure you come out, *dolcezza*. Or I'll level this hospital to the ground until I find you."

I rolled my eyes. "Italians are so intense." Although I started to think it was just him. This man. "I'll come back to you. Always."

His eyes flashed like black diamonds. I didn't know why I uttered those words, but I realized I meant them. I didn't know how things had shifted so quickly. Maybe it was the sex, maybe it was that crazy obsession that I saw lurking in his gaze, or maybe it was that simple apology a few minutes ago. Nobody had to tell me this man never apologized, but he did for me because he knew I needed it.

"*Va bene.* Go to your brother," he said. "I'll be here."

I nodded and turned to face the door where my sister-in-law looked to be fighting for her life, my brother by her side. I hadn't talked to him nor seen him since I left the castle with Tatiana. Gosh, now it seemed like it was ages ago when it was only a few days ago.

So many things had changed. I'd learned my brother killed my mother. I'd gotten married. Tatiana had been hurt. All in the span of a few days.

I started to push the door open and noticed my wedding ring on my left hand. I managed to remove it discreetly and tuck it into my pocket, before opening the door and stepping inside, praying that Enrico didn't see me do that. The crazy Italian wouldn't be happy but tough shit.

Everyone's eyes were instantly on me, some of them reaching for their guns, clearly visible under their suit jackets. So many pale blue eyes matching Tatiana's. They had to be the brothers she mentioned.

Jesus, they were huge. Tall and built like MMA fighters.

My steps faltered and I almost retreated, when a familiar voice stopped me.

"Isla." My eyes snapped to Illias. He looked like shit. Dark circles under his eyes. Bloodied clothes. And the scruff of a beard marred his cheeks and jaw.

The sound of the machine monitoring the pulse matched my own heartbeat. *Beep. Beep. Beep.*

Illias jumped up and rushed to me as I quickly shut the door, keeping Enrico out of sight.

"I came to check on Tatiana."

Bigger than God. That's how I'd always thought of my big brother. I loved him, I really did, but I couldn't help my instinct flaring and taking a step back when he approached me. "Don't."

"What's the matter?"

"I know what you did," I rasped, my heart drumming hard. It threatened to crack my ribs.

Recognition flashed in his eyes and his shoulders slumped. "I wondered how long it'd take. Who told you?"

That's right. Tatiana was kidnapped when I learned and didn't have time to tell him. Fuck, I didn't want to make him upset. I didn't like seeing this larger-than-life man tired and broken. I knew I should pretend I didn't know the truth, but I couldn't.

I squared my shoulders. This wasn't about me. It was about Tatiana. I'd be here for my brother, but it didn't mean I'd pretend everything was okay.

"It doesn't matter who told me. I know and I don't forgive you, Illias," I said, keeping my voice even, although my hands trembled. "All my life, I've been asking you about her and you lied. Over and over again. We won't talk about it now." I tilted my chin toward the bed where Tatiana's body lay unmoving, her face too pale. "I'm here for her." Hurt flashed in my big brother's coal-black gaze. "And for you," I added, my voice softening. "I love you and I want you to be happy. But I won't just pretend I don't know you killed my mother." My voice cracked with emotions I tried to keep at bay. I wouldn't cry now while Tatiana was fighting for her life. "When all this is over, and

Tatiana is safe and healthy, I want answers. And you're going to give them to me. Understood?"

Tension slithered through the air. It seemed everyone stopped breathing and their eyes were locked on us. Everyone's but Tatiana's.

"Where is my little sister?" Illias murmured softly, something resembling pride flashing in his eyes. But I had to be wrong. I couldn't —no, I *refused* to believe he killed my mother to be vindictive. That wasn't who he was. But somewhere along the line I'd started to wonder who Illias Konstantin really was. And I was done being treated like I couldn't handle the truth.

"She grew the fuck up," I said quietly. "And it happened almost overnight. Now, tell me, how is Tatiana? Are the babies—" I swallowed hard. I didn't want to ask the painful question. "Is she going to be okay?"

"She's stable," he rasped, his voice breaking. "By some miracle, so are the babies."

I smiled, taking his hand in mine and squeezing it. "She's strong. She'll pull through. If for nothing else than for the babies."

My eyes flickered to the other side of the room to the three large figures with light blue eyes and pale, yellow hair. The same shade as Tatiana's.

"Those are some genes," I muttered under my breath, staring at them. The tattoos covering their skin were enough to frighten a man, never mind a woman. Yet, here I was, feet firmly planted. Maybe I was more Konstantin than Evans. *Or Cortes,* I couldn't help but think.

Well, now you're a Marchetti, my mind whispered. At this rate, I'd end up with an identity crisis.

"Hello," I greeted them. It was rude to stare, but I couldn't peel my eyes off them.

My brother followed my gaze, then shook his head, almost as if he forgot they were here.

"They're Tatiana's brothers," he said, confirming my suspicions. "Vasili Nikolaev." My eyes flickered to his large hand, tattoos on every one of his fingers screaming danger.

"Nice to meet you, Mr. N—"

"Vasili." He cut me off. "Just Vasili. After all, we're family now."

Uh-oh.

"Alexei." The man nodded, and I swore the temperature in the room plunged a few degrees. No wonder Tatiana claimed her brothers were scarier than Illias. "And Sasha. The latter is always in trouble, so you're to keep away from him."

"Why does that make me want to go talk to him?" I grumbled.

Sasha grinned. "Because you have more sense than your brother."

I let out a strangled laugh. I'd stake my life on Sasha being the slightly unhinged member of this family.

"Are you all, like, MMA fighters or something?" A blank look. I took that to mean no. "Mobsters, then, huh?"

"Isla, I don't want you around that kind of life," Illias growled. "Sooner or later, everyone ends up dead."

I kept my eyes on Tatiana's brother as I answered. "Everyone ends up dead eventually, brother. Or should I call you Pakhan, since that's what you are."

I sensed tension rolling off my big brother in waves that could have resulted in a tsunami. I ignored it. He'd have to stop sheltering me. Once he learned I married Enrico Marchetti, he'd realize I was in this life and he couldn't judge me for it.

"Fuck, did Tatiana tell you?"

"Nope."

A growl vibrated. "Marchetti. That fucking bastard. If he laid a finger on you—"

I raised my palm and stopped him.

"Wrong again." Although the man had put a lot more than a finger on me. "Like I said, later. Now what can I do to help?"

All the men looked at me confused. "With the mafia?" Sasha asked suspiciously.

I rolled my eyes. "With Tatiana."

A round of relieved breaths circled the room, and I couldn't help another eye roll.

"The knife was plunged in her abdomen." I gasped, my eyes flickering to Tatiana's flat stomach. It was a miracle that she was still pregnant, then. "Dr. Sergei said we just have to wait," Illias muttered, returning back to his chair and taking Tatiana's hand in his.

"Shouldn't you shower or maybe change your clothes?" The moment I said those words, I wanted to kick myself. If he left this room, he'd see Enrico. We didn't need conflict right now.

"When she wakes up."

He was either lying to himself or me, because every person in this room knew he'd remain by her side until he took her home.

THIRTY-FIVE
ENRICO

I waited in front of the hospital room for hours in one of those cursed chairs. I'd wait days if need be.

Except, I fucking hated hospitals, and not just because of the uncomfortable furniture they provided for visitors. While Isla was on the other side of the wall with her family, I had plenty of time to remember my family, and the source of my hatred of these sterile spaces.

My mother died in one.

Mamma was laughing, her dark eyes twinkling with delight. The breeze swept through her hair, blowing it around her like a dark halo. The sounds of the waves rode the wind.

Father and brother were building a stone castle that flooded with each wave. Their laughter carried through the breeze. It was a perfect day.

No sooner had the thought left me than a loud bang echoed through the air.

My gaze darted left and right, looking for the source of the noise. When my eyes returned to my mother, I took note of her white dress that was now stained red. Her face that glowed with happiness barely a moment ago now portrayed sheer horror.

Her knees touched the sand and I found myself next to her, my own knees hitting the rocks. I caught my mother's head before it hit the ground.

"Mamma." My voice cracked. The voice didn't sound like my own. It was full of anguish. Terror. My mamma's blood stained my hands, soaking through my fingers and dripping onto the ground.

Then the haunting sound pierced the air. I felt it deep down in my soul. It was full of agony. Full of pain, mirroring what I felt in my soul.

It was my father's. Our day started on the beach and ended in the hospital.

The day turned out not so perfect after all.

My grandmother died in the hospital too. My father was gunned down in an alley, coming out of a club we owned. And my brother... Well, he died on my front lawn.

I pulled myself out of the memory to focus on the present.

I ignored the tightness in my chest as I vigorously typed on my cell phone. I checked on Manuel and my sons. They were safe. I touched base with Kian who agreed to meet me in the lobby at St. Regis Nikolskaya hotel. We'd booked all the suites on the top two floors to ensure maximum security.

The door to Tatiana's room opened and relief washed over me as I watched Isla slink out. Jumping to my feet, I met her halfway. Our bodyguards were on their feet too, lingering in the back.

"How is she?"

Isla's hand slipped in mine and she craned her neck, those beautiful, shimmering greens locking with my gaze.

"She still hasn't woken up," she murmured. "I feel useless just sitting there. Illias is a mess."

I squeezed her hand in comfort. "I can understand that. My father was a mess when my mother fought for her life."

"She was attacked too?" I nodded. "I'm sorry, Enrico. That must have been hard on your family."

This was the part Amadeo called too soft, but he was wrong. Isla had the right mixture of compassion and strength. Stubbornness and meekness. Konstantin might have sheltered her and protected her, but that was part of her DNA.

"It was, *piccolina*," I admitted. "But that was a long time ago. Do you want to stay longer, or should we go back to the hotel?"

"Let's go back to the hotel, but I'd like to come back tomorrow if that's okay. I just know she'll pull through, and I want to be here for it."

"Then we'll be here for it."

I scanned the surroundings as we made our way toward the exit sign and took the stairs to the garage. Two of my men were in front of us and two were in the back. She slipped her hand into mine, her palm small in mine but so fucking right. My chest warmed and I gently squeezed her hand.

She was starting to trust me. Would the truth turn her away from me?

Ten minutes later, I drove us out of the parking garage, my guards tailing us.

I kept Isla's hand in mine, and when I had to shift the gear, I'd put her hand on my thigh. The fact she'd leave it there and wait for me to take it again made so many emotions bounce around in my chest.

Cazzo, I had it bad for my wife. And the deeper I fell, the stronger the fear of seeing another person I loved die in front of my eyes grew.

"Isla, what I'm about to tell you has to stay between us," I started. I felt her hand tense on my thigh and her nails dig into my flesh.

"It's about time you trust me."

I let out a heavy sigh. Fuck, I wasn't ready to tell her that her mother was dragged into one of my father's brothels. I didn't want to lose her. I needed her love before I could dump that on her. I craved it. But the fear of seeing her die—just like every woman who had ever loved a Marchetti man—was buried deep inside my heart and in the marrow of my bones.

"I'll start with my story." I gripped the steering wheel and the rubberized grip of it creaked in protest. "When we get to the hotel, I'll share what I know of yours." Some of it, at least.

"It will stay between us, then," she vowed, looking at me seriously. "I promise."

"Fuck, where do I even start?" I muttered.

"Wherever you want. Or if it helps, I can ask questions," she offered. There was that softness again. She wasn't dumb, and after hearing the priest refer to me by my birth name, I knew she suspected it. Heck, she knew it, but she needed my confirmation.

"Fourteen years ago, when Enzo was just a baby and his brother was still growing in his mother's belly, my brother died." God, it seemed like centuries ago, yet also only yesterday. "My older brother."

Her gulp sounded loud in the small space.

"Enrico Marchetti died." There was my smart wife. "So that means you're really the dead brother."

"Yes, Enzo Lucian Marchetti."

I tensed, waiting for her to yank her hand back. She never did.

"That's why you said you weren't married."

A sardonic breath pulled on my chest. It was a peculiar and unexpected thing to focus on. "Donatella was my brother's wife. They despised each other."

"And the boys?"

"Enrico called it a hate fuck," I muttered. "Donatella called it rape. Fuck if I know, but the boys are innocent in all this."

She squeezed my hand. "They are. And we won't let anything happen to them." No fucking wonder I fell for her. How could I not? "I'm assuming they don't know?"

They didn't. I could never bring myself to tell them something like that. Not after they experienced their mother's hate and rejection. For Pete's sake, she'd been trying to murder them since they were born.

"They are *my* sons." My voice came out sharper than I intended it to. "I'll never let Donatella have them. I had to have her restrained while pregnant with Amadeo so she wouldn't hurt the baby. I didn't know until my brother was dead that he did the same while she was pregnant with Enzo."

"Jesus Christ."

"I don't know what happened between Donatella and my brother. I was close to him when we were growing up, but when he took over our papà's seat in the Omertà, our paths didn't cross as much. I ran the legitimate side of the Marchetti business. My brother ran all the Omertà businesses. I knew what he did, but I kept to my side. Except that Enrico kept pulling me into his shit. He was impulsive. I was strategic. But Enrico was smart, and we both knew if something was to happen to him before Enzo and Amadeo became men, our enemies would come knocking on our door. They'd wipe out our entire family for our seat at the table."

Her delicate eyebrows scrunched. "What table?"

"As one of the five Italian families in the Omertà. Greed and power are compelling motivators." Isla remained silent, listening intently. "My brother and I had a clause put in place when little Enzo was born after our papà died. If Enrico died, I'd assume his identity."

"But why? Why couldn't you have just taken over as his brother?"

"Because I rejected my blood and oath in front of all the Omertà members to have any part of that world while my father was still alive. The responsibility would have fallen to baby Enzo who was just approaching his first birthday."

"So you became him." Her whisper was barely audible. "Couldn't you have rejected it for all your family and for Enzo?" She knew the answer, but it was a lot to take in. "I can't believe nobody recognized you."

"People often couldn't tell us apart. The only thing that really set us apart were our tempers."

"But not even Donatella?" Her raspy voice shook. "She didn't realize you're not her husband?"

I shook my head. "My brother and Donatella didn't share rooms. Barely even talked. She was on medication and drugs. Sometimes she couldn't even recognize her own husband. It was easy to fool her, plus her mental instability was always there. She has been in and out of psych wards for the duration of their marriage. Later we learned, for most of her life."

"This is like a soap opera," she muttered. "My head is spinning." It was understandable. "I just cannot grasp how you pulled it off."

I shrugged. "It wasn't all that hard. We claimed Enzo's body was in that car. It helped that Enrico had been driving my car, although that was what ultimately cost him his life. My car wasn't bulletproof. His was."

This talking in the car wasn't bad at all. No wonder people raved that it was therapeutic. Fuck if I didn't want to pour my soul out. But only to her—my wife.

I switched lanes, recognizing the exit to our hotel.

"What about Donatella's death?" she murmured, still staring at me with disbelief. "How did you pull off convincing people she was dead?"

"She was supposed to be in the car with my brother. He was coming back with her from the psych ward, but being the fucking lunatic she is, she jumped out of the moving car. According to my uncle who was tailing my brother's vehicle, not a moment too soon because in the next instance, they were ambushed by the Callahans." When she gave me a blank look, I clarified. "The Irish from New York." I took a deep breath, then exhaled. It took me a long time to learn that it was Luca DiMauro's father who set them up. "He died on my front lawn. Before our *soldati*—" She frowned at the vocabulary and I clarified, "Before our soldiers could see which one of us was dead, I had my brother's body in the car and set fire to it. We told everyone Donatella was in it too."

"Wow, Enrico. This is a lot." Then she shook her head. "Am I supposed to call you Enrico? My head is spinning."

I brought her hand up and brushed my lips over her knuckles. "It's best if we stick to Enrico. But in the bedroom—"

She sighed, but her eyes glimmered with that mischief that I saw the first night when she blew me a kiss.

"I guess I'll just have to call you Daddy."

A strangled laugh escaped me, tension slowly draining out of me. Instead of feeling relief, though, I got rock hard. Clearly my dick loved it when she called me daddy. Good Lord.

"I like that, *dolcezza*. I like it very much."

She sat straighter and leaned over, pressing a kiss to my cheek. "I guess we'll have to show them all not to fuck with us, huh?"

My lips pulled into a grin. "That's right. Nobody fucks with us. Especially not with my queen."

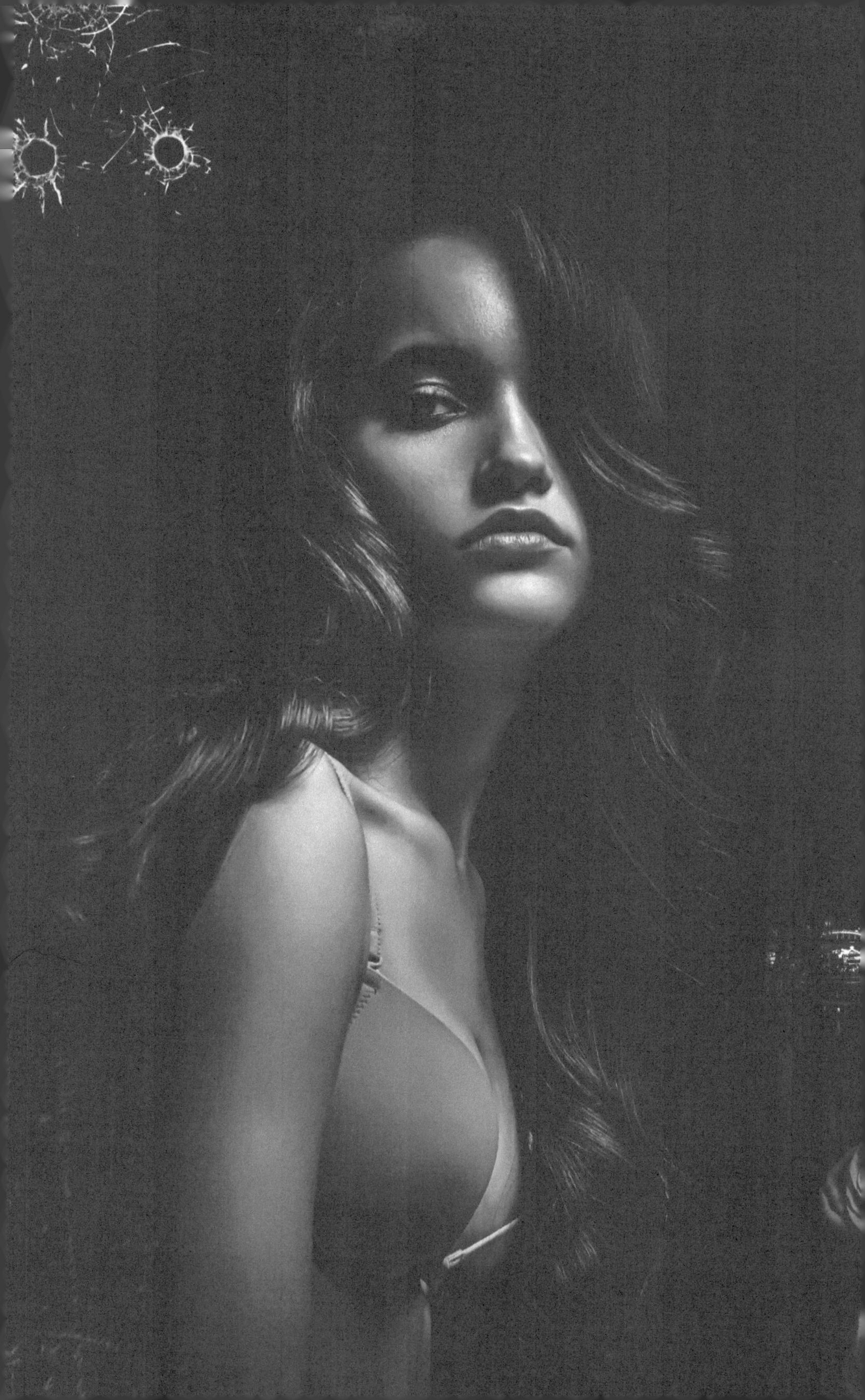

THIRTY-SIX
ISLA

I mulled over all the information Enrico shared for the rest of the ride.

Admittedly, I hadn't expected such an explanation. Not sure what I expected, but this wasn't it.

"How old are you?" I blurted out. If he wasn't his older brother, he was younger.

"Forty-three."

"Oh."

Enrico let out an amused breath. "Yes, I'm still much older than you." I nodded in agreement. He wasn't quite double my age, so I guess it was an improvement. His hand landed on my inner thigh, squeezing lightly. "I'm still your husband when your cunt strangles my dick. When your ass rubs against my cock, inviting me inside even though you refuse to say the words."

My cheeks reddened at the explicit images those words painted in my head. Gosh, this chemistry between us sizzled and buzzed with a current so strong, the small spark threatened to explode.

I caught his hand that was inching closer to my hot entrance. Even through my jeans, his touch burned. I caught it, tangling my fingers with his strong ones.

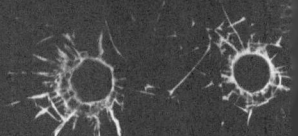

"Thank you for telling me." Surprise flashed in his eyes. "It's not insignificant, and your willingness to share it means everything. Not to be left in the dark and be blindsided." My shoulders tensed and I swallowed. "Like learning that my brother killed my mother."

His surprise changed into guilt. After all, it was Enrico who dragged those words out into the open.

"That wasn't the right way for you to find out." Leaving our fingers interlaced, he shifted my arm onto his muscular thigh and kept it there.

"You're right," I agreed. "My brother should have told me himself one of the million times I asked him." Enrico's jaw tightened. "I know he's not bad or cruel... so why would he do it?" A vein in my husband's neck throbbed. "Do you know?"

He flicked a look my way. "I don't, *piccolina*. But I agree with you. Konstantin isn't unnecessarily cruel."

We came to a stop, and I realized we were back at the hotel. Swiftly, he jumped out of the car and came around to open my door, beating the valet to it. The valet who ogled me as if I were naked.

Enrico threw him the keys. "I got my wife. You park the car."

Surprise flickered on the valet's face. It was the first time he glanced my husband's way and he reeled back, seeing his dark expression. "Yes, sir."

The valet didn't spare me another look.

I slipped my hand into Enrico's—for the third time today—and relished in the simple act. It felt natural, almost as if we'd been doing it for years.

We entered the hotel when a voice called out to Enrico.

Both of us turned our heads as one to find a tall man standing there. A good-looking, fifty-something-year-old man.

"Ah, Cortes. Thank you for coming."

The man approached us. His silver-gray beard had Athena's soprano voice singing the words, "Look at this foxy, foxy, silver fox daddy go," in my head.

My flats were silent against the marble floor. Ambient lights were everywhere—presumably in preparation for the holidays. The lobby buzzed with life. But the man's eyes couldn't care less what decorated the fancy lobby. Everything might be glittering, but his eyes were locked on me.

I thought I saw recognition flickering in them, but I had to be mistaken. I had never met this man before. Trepidation buzzed to life in the center of my heart. I couldn't quite understand why, but something about this man had me on edge.

It only hit me when we all came to a stop. *Cortes.* This man had the same last name as my mother, and the same name as Louisa Maria Cortes's father. I refused to believe it was a coincidence.

"*Piccolina*, are you alright?" Enrico's voice sounded distant. Distorted, far away. Like I was at the bottom of the sea. "Isla, look at me."

Swallowing a lump in my throat, I met my husband's gaze. "Yeah, I'm fine. Why?"

He bent down, his mouth brushing against my earlobe and sending goose bumps across my skin. "Your fingernails are digging into my hand."

I lowered my eyes and found my knuckles white, my fingernails buried in his flesh.

"Sorry," I muttered, forcing my grip loose. "I'm so sorry."

He studied me for a moment before returning his attention to the man whose eyes were locked on me.

"Kian, this is my wife. Isla." Enrico's voice was formal. Almost dark. "Isla, this is our head of security here in Russia. Kian Cortes. He will ensure your safety at all costs."

Tension seeped through my veins, my muscles knotted. "Who are you?" I needed to know who he was in relation to my mother. "And who are you to Louisa Maria Cortes?"

The man suddenly smiled warmly, his eyes never wavering from me. "I am... was... her brother."

My eyes darted between the men. "So you are my—"

"Uncle." He shook his head, disbelief clear in his eyes. "You are the spitting image of my baby sister; I can hardly believe it. I thought she—" His voice cracked and he cleared his throat. "When Marchetti called me earlier and provided details on this assignment, I didn't dare believe it."

My breath caught in my lungs. Enrico knew he was my uncle and called him. He was following through with his promise. My heart picked up speed at this gesture. Enrico pulled me closer to him, bringing his hand down my back and settling it on my hip.

"I'll be better at keeping promises, *amore*," he whispered into my ear. "*Te lo prometto*."

Emotion swamped me. I studied my husband, his broad shoulders stretching the fine fabric of his suit. Emotions bloomed. Fragile and new, but strong.

"Thank you," I rasped. I wanted to show him exactly how grateful I was, but I needed to talk to this man first. My uncle. It was incredible to even think it.

I turned my attention to Kian who waited patiently. We didn't look alike. I was short; he was tall.

"Is your hair red?" I blurted out. "Or was it?"

He shook his head, sliding his hands into his pockets. "Louisa was the only one who had red hair."

I inhaled a shuddering breath.

"Illias, my brother, says the same thing." Contempt flashed in Kian's eyes. It pulsed through every pore of him, hot and heavy. I took a step closer to Kian, straightening up and fixing him with a look. "You won't hurt him. He's my brother. The only one I have left."

A sardonic breath left him. "You are your mother's daughter in appearance, but I see you have Konstantin's spine." While I debated whether he meant it as a compliment or an insult, the corners of his mouth lifted. "That's probably good."

I had so many questions. I wanted to know everything, but at the same time, I feared the truth.

"I have a meeting room reserved for us," Enrico chimed in. "Let's discuss this in private."

The guests rushed all around while we made our way to the back of the lobby and into a lounge. The moment the door clicked behind me, questions began to pour out.

"I want to know everything," I burst out, unable to hold back anymore.

Uncle Kian—how odd to think of him that way—extended his hand, motioning for us to sit down. Enrico and I took one sofa, while Kian lowered himself onto the chair with utter confidence. He studied me, and it was then that I saw it. His darkness. His ghosts.

Silence stretched. History haunted us. But somehow it left me in the dark. Only Enrico and Kian knew what was coming.

"I'm waiting," I reminded him, patience never being my strong suit.

Kian didn't seem offended by my tone. Instead, he appeared rather amused.

"Your mother never spoke back." He wasn't chastising me. He didn't even seem displeased. But there was a lethal presence about him that was undeniable. "It ended up being her undoing."

"What do you mean?"

His gaze darted to my husband and anger shot through me. "This concerns me and my mother's history, so don't look at Enrico."

My husband's hand came to rest around me, his fingers tracing the crook of my neck. The touch was comforting. Soft. He seemed unperturbed by my sharp tone, his posture relaxed and his touch feeding my own assurance.

Kian let out an incredulous chuckle. "Very well, Isla. I'm just wondering what you already know."

"Nothing." My tone portrayed exasperation and frustration. "I know nothing, but I want to know everything."

"But you knew who I was," Kian reasoned.

I scoffed softly. "Because I snooped through Illias's desk like a damn criminal and found my and my mother's birth certificates." From the corner of my eye, I caught Enrico's smile. I waved my hand nonchalantly. "Yeah, yeah. My brother and my husband are criminals too. I'm new at it." Then I zeroed my attention at Kian. "Are you a criminal? I looked up my mother's name, but came up empty, unsurprisingly. Same thing happened when I typed in her parents' names."

"Your grandfather was the head of the Brazilian cartel." Kian's words felt like a bomb dropping, but he didn't even miss a beat as he continued. "When he died, it passed on to my oldest brother."

"I have another uncle?" The words escaped me in a rush.

This time Enrico tensed, and I felt it with every fiber of my body. "You're never to go around him."

I cocked my eyebrow at his demand. "Why?"

"Because it was my brother who helped our father sell your mother," Kian answered, and my head whipped in his direction. My uncle's face remained stoic, unchanging, but his gaze turned cold and dark.

Gulping in a deep breath, I found myself asking, "Sold?"

Kian's jaw clenched. His darkness cloaked the room, dangerous and all-consuming. It was so thick, I could smell it. Taste it, even. Kian's body seemed to swell, anger coming off him in waves.

"Yes, sold. To a Marchetti brothel."

And there it was. There it fucking was. In the corner of my mind, I noted Enrico's body language, his hand stilling on the nape of my neck.

Donatella Marchetti was crazy, but she was sane enough to throw that fact in my face. She'd known I was in the dark. Yet again. I sat stiffly while my blood boiled. I fought the urge to throw something across the room. To scream bloody murder.

"Sold?" I repeated, my voice distorted from the buzzing in my ears. "I don't understand."

Kian flicked a glance to Enrico, then back to me. "My old man and Enrico's father had a business arrangement. When our family was responsible for a Marchetti shipment being lost, my sister was handed over to settle the debt." Kian's jaw clenched, his expression turning thunderous. "She was only sixteen."

A gasp tore from my lungs. Sixteen. So fucking young. "Why didn't you stop it?"

"I wasn't in the country at that time," he gritted. "When I learned about it, I went after her. But I was too late. I searched brothel after brothel, only to learn she had died. I never knew about you. If I had—" He didn't finish the sentence. Instead, he pushed his hand through his silver hair. My heart ached, each breath piercing my chest at the knowledge that my mother must have suffered. The truth had finally unraveled, and it was ugly. It was dark. It threatened to pull me under. "Your brothers... were they good to you?"

Kian's jaw clenched and suddenly I knew that this man would be just as protective as Illias. I appreciated it, but I didn't want to be smothered with it.

"Very." I leaned over and took his hand into mine. "I couldn't have asked for a better life. Illias was always there for me." I let out a dry laugh. "Even when I didn't want him to be. He was there like a shadow, chasing all the ghosts away."

That seemed to appease Kian and he gave me a dazzling smile that made him appear so much younger.

"It makes me happy to hear that," he murmured softly. "It'd make your mom very happy." My chest twisted as I thought about the woman I had never met. Would she be proud of me?

"Back to your other Cortes cousins, Isla. You have to stay away from the rest of the Cortes family. My brother in particular. It's best to let them continue thinking you don't exist."

I exhaled a shuddering breath, a single tear rolling down my cheek. Enrico pulled me closer to him, and despite the role his own father played in my mother's downfall, I couldn't find my fury. It had all started with my grandfather who'd sold his own daughter.

"Okay," I rasped.

"Do you mean it, *dolcezza*?" Enrico questioned. "I can't have you in danger. Kian's a good man, but his brother isn't. A decent father doesn't send his daughter to a brothel to pay off his debt. We arrange marriages. We make alliances, but never use our women for something so lowly."

Gulping in a deep breath, I nodded my agreement. If my other uncle and grandfather had no qualms hurting my mother, they certainly wouldn't feel any attachment to me.

Enrico's fingers resumed massaging my shoulders, touching me, almost as if he needed the comfort as much as I did.

"If you ever need help or want to get out of this life"—Kian didn't bother looking at Enrico, but judging by my husband's low growl, he knew what he intended to say—"just say the word and I'll come for you. No matter where. No matter when. I'll go up against everyone to keep you safe if I have to."

I leaned back into Enrico's touch, either to comfort him or ensure he didn't lunge at my newfound uncle.

"Thank you. I appreciate it." Enrico's fingers resumed tracing my skin. "But I'm safe right where I am."

And I meant it. If I needed rescuing, I wouldn't be a damsel in distress. I'd fight tooth and nail and reach out to my new alliances. But first and foremost, I'd depend on myself.

"How did your mother die?" Kian's question sliced through the air.

My spine snapped straight and tension seeped into my bones. Instinctively, I knew if I told Kian that my brother had killed his baby sister, he would go after him. I didn't forgive Illias, but I couldn't condemn my brother to death. When Tatiana was alive and well, I'd drag the truth out of him. If it was the last thing I did.

"Childbirth," I said instead.

After all, one took care of his or her family. Maybe I was more Konstantin than Cortes.

THIRTY-SEVEN
ENRICO

Two hours later, we arrived at one of Konstantin's restaurants. Isla had a surprise for the boys and refused to stay inside the safety of the hotel. I was quickly coming to the realization that I was incapable of refusing any of my wife's wishes.

She had exchanged her jeans for a beautiful strapless black top and tulle skirt, Christian Louboutin heels, and a vintage purse. She looked incredible, of course, but I thought she was just as gorgeous in jeans and a T-shirt.

While we waited for the hostess who was bustling around the busy restaurant, I kept my eyes on her as she whispered softly back and forth with the boys. Kian stood on the other side of her, his eyes often coming back to my wife. It was unsurprising that he recognized her the moment he spotted her. From the photos I'd seen, the physical traits between Isla and Louisa Maria Cortes were strong. They could have been twins.

"Did it go well?" Manuel questioned, speaking in Italian.

It certainly *went*, although I wasn't sure if it went well or not. Isla had barely uttered anything of significance since learning the truth about her mother from Kian. I waited—anticipated—for her to explode from the confirmation that her mother ended up in one of my family's brothels.

Instead, she hadn't commented on it.

We returned to our room, the boys already dressed and waiting for us. Isla had promised them a night out, and they were ready. I was so fucking tempted to send them back to their room. I needed to know what was going on in that brilliant head of hers.

"As well as it could," I answered in the same language.

"Kian is already protective," Manuel remarked, sticking to our native language. "I'm surprised he didn't try to give her a way out of this life."

"He did." My tone was dry. In truth, I was still surprised she refused her uncle. It remained to be seen whether it was to bestow her own vengeance on me or to embrace our life together.

She was part of the Marchetti family, whether she liked it or not. I meant what I said on our drive from the hospital. Nobody fucked with my family. And nobody would fuck with my wife. Family or not. Friend or foe. She was mine to cherish. To fuck. To love.

Granted, it started out rocky. *Cazzo*, I wished she were pregnant with my baby. That would secure her commitment, if nothing else.

"Oh my gosh." The hostess's eyes widened as she watched my wife and I stiffened, ready to reach for my gun. "Is that really you? Illias's little sister?"

"Hello, Mrs. Pavlov. Nice to see you again."

The former pulled her into a hug. "I never thought I'd see you again. You have grown up."

Isla chuckled. "Not much taller I'm afraid."

"But still beautiful."

Isla tilted her chin to me. "This is my…" I waited, holding my breath. Fuck, if she called me her friend, I didn't think I'd be able to keep my cool. She cleared her throat and continued, "My husband. Enrico."

"Nice to meet you."

Isla continued. "His uncle, Manuel. My uncle, Kian. And these are our boys." Fuck, was it possible to fall in love with my wife even more? Apparently so. "Enzo and Amadeo." Her eyes flickered to all of us. "Everyone, this is Mrs. Pavlov."

Everyone murmured their acknowledgements while the hostess clapped her hands excitedly. "You are married?" Isla nodded. "Wait until I tell my husband. He swore you'd be married to that violin."

"The violin refused to utter 'I do,' so the priest called it an invalid union," Isla joked.

Enzo and Amadeo found it funny, cackling and snickering.

The hostess led us to the table, glancing over her shoulder at Isla and beaming. "So nice to see you again, Isla. I still remember your brother bringing you over for dessert when you were a little girl." She stopped at the table, set apart from the rest of the restaurant. "And now you have your own family. And you're the best violinist the world has seen."

Isla chuckled softly. "Surely not the best the world has seen."

A stern expression entered the hostess's expression. "The best," she claimed, determined. "Don't bother with modesty." Isla rolled her eyes, but couldn't keep the smile off her face. "When it's dessert time, should I bring your favorite?"

My wife grinned. "If there are some extra, yes, please. Some for the boys too. I want them to give it a try." Isla flicked a glance at Enzo and Amadeo. "Unless they're scared."

Both boys rolled their eyes. "We are not scared, but Italian desserts are first class. Russian... not so much."

I pulled a chair out for my wife and she took her seat, her eyes sparkling like emeralds. "We shall see." She looked to me for confirmation and I nodded. She leaned over to Enzo and Amadeo, whispering conspiratorially. "By the way, we have a surprise for you two."

"Tell us. *Adesso*," Enzo demanded. Now.

"Women hate to be bossed around." Amadeo jabbed his shoulder into his older brother. "Say *per favore*. Please."

Enzo glared at his younger brother. "Girls like to be bossed around."

"Maybe girls, but not women," Kian remarked dryly. "And my niece is not yours to boss around."

Enzo let out a heavy sigh. "I honestly don't understand what is going on."

"Do you want your surprise or not?" Isla demanded, diverting his attention from her newfound relative. I hadn't had a chance to talk to both of them about Isla's connection to the Brazilian cartel and caution them to keep it between us.

"Tell us," Amadeo answered for his brother. "*Per favore*, Isla."

Isla smiled, clapping her hands enthusiastically. "After dinner, we're going to the opera house."

The horror on the boys' faces was comical. "Opera?" Enzo asked, his expression clearly stating he'd rather drown in icy, polar-bear-infested waters than listen to the opera.

Isla burst into laughter. "A concert is playing at the opera. Don't worry, I won't make you listen to a soprano singing opera. Not unless Athena's singing."

"Thank fuck."

"Enzo," both Isla and I warned at the same time. My wife's gaze found mine for a flicker of a second, then returned to our son. "No cursing. If I can't curse, then you can't either."

Okay, that wasn't exactly the reprimand I expected, but I went along with it.

"I'll take a rain check," Manuel chimed in. "I dated an opera singer once. It brings back memories."

"Zio Manuel has had a lot of girlfriends," Enzo remarked seriously.

"That's good to know," Isla noted. "How about you, Uncle Kian? Did you have a lot of girlfriends?"

I winced at her question. Kian was notorious for his privacy. Everyone in the underworld knew it.

"No."

"You never married?"

"No."

Isla rolled her eyes. "Okay, then. Not talkative. Do you want to come along with us to the opera?"

"I'm with Manuel, I'll pass." He shared a glance with me, then added, "I have Darius and Astor assigned to you."

"*Bene.*" Those two were efficient and blended into the shadows perfectly. Without thinking, I brought my hand up and stroked my knuckles along the soft skin of her forearm. Everywhere I touched this woman, she was soft. She didn't pull away, so I took that as a good sign.

"Are they my cousins?" Isla asked curiously, staring at where I was touching her. It was always complicated yet so simple with her. She'd either show you all her emotions, or she'd rein them in. I looked forward to understanding both sides of her.

"No," Kian answered. "And you won't even know they're around."

She returned her attention to the boys. "So what do you say? Is it a date?" Enzo and Amadeo murmured their agreement, clearly having different ideas of what a date looked like. "Wonderful. It can be a tradition. My brother used to take me there for our dates too."

"Clearly, he doesn't understand fun," Amadeo muttered under his breath, but we all ignored his comment.

The dinner was surprisingly pleasant. I had to admit it was one of the best Russian dishes I'd had in my life and, admittedly, I wasn't much into Russian cuisine. The boys were perfect gentlemen and commended Isla on her choice of dishes.

"What about you, Kian?" She turned to her uncle. "Is Russian cuisine better than Brazilian?"

Kian smiled and it hit me that in all the times I'd heard from him or seen him, I had never seen him smile. Until today.

"Brazilian cuisine is influenced by multiple cultures. It's very diverse. You'd like it."

Isla grinned, then glanced at the boys as if asking them, *What do you think?*

"Italian food is the best," Enzo claimed. You couldn't take the Italian out of him even if you beat it out of him. It made me so fucking proud.

"How about for the next family outing, I take you all to an authentic Brazilian restaurant?" Kian recommended. "But not in Russia."

"Then where? Italy?"

Kian chuckled. "No, not Italy. And not Brazil. Not until your other uncle is out of the picture." *Translation: not until I kill him.* "There is a really good Brazilian restaurant in Washington, D.C., and another in New York. We can pick one of those two."

"New York." Isla's answer was immediate. I cocked an eyebrow and she shrugged. "What? Illias always kept me out of the Big Apple. I want to go."

Amadeo scoffed. "You mean you never sneaked behind your brother's back? I would have—"

My wife narrowed her eyes on him, and his words trailed off. I couldn't help but grin.

"I was the perfect kid, never did anything behind his back."

"Somehow I find that hard to believe," Manuel muttered before realizing he'd said the words out loud—and in English. Isla fixed her stare on him, challenging him. "Ma dai." *Come on.* "You and your friends... trouble written all over you."

Isla's cheeks flushed. "We were saints."

"For a day, perhaps," Manuel retorted dryly.

"Don't listen to your uncle, boys." She decidedly ignored Manuel. "Just ask my brother. The girls and I were never caught doing anything bad."

Laughter broke out over the table. "There is the key word," Kian mused. "You were never caught."

Isla blinked her eyes innocently, but she didn't answer. Instead, a coy smile played around her lips, and I knew the children we'd have one day—as well as Enzo and Amadeo—would give us a run for our money.

But my wife and I would be two steps ahead of them.

THIRTY-EIGHT
ISLA

Dinner was a pleasant affair.

Between learning who and what my mother was and the fact she was placed in one of the brothels owned by the corrupt Marchetti empire, my thoughts were swirling with dread.

It wasn't an easy pill to swallow. It lingered in the corner of my mind, conjuring so many emotions—both good and bad.

What if I wasn't a Konstantin? How could they possibly know who my father was if she was working in a brothel? I had so many questions for my brother and for my husband. And once I got my answers, I'd set some ground rules.

I was sick and tired of being the last to know details about my own life.

I watched Enzo and Amadeo give the Russian dessert a try. Ptichye moloko was referred to as the Russian "Raffaello" coconut candy and melted in your mouth. It was a simple yet perfect milk-based soufflé coated in chocolate. It was a special treat Illias and Maxim used to get me as a little girl. The latter would often sneak me an extra portion while Illias grumbled that it was a delicacy and should be savored, not gorged on.

Maxim and I ignored him.

"So?" I asked them all. "What do you think?"

Of course, it was Enzo who answered. "It's not as good as Raffaello—" *That little Italian prick*, I thought fondly. He shrugged nonchalantly. "—but I like it. It's okay."

He reached for another cube of it.

"If it's only okay, why are you grabbing another portion?" Amadeo complained with a full mouth. "Leave it for someone else."

"I'm saving you from gaining weight," Enzo snapped back as he shoved a piece into his mouth.

"How about I save you all from gaining weight?" I smacked his hand as he reached for his third helping. "And I eat it all."

Enrico chuckled. "It's no wonder you're so sweet."

He looked at me like he wanted to eat me, and I could feel all my questions and boundaries crumbling. Those dark eyes that flickered with lust. That sexy Italian voice.

I rolled my eyes. At him. At myself.

I'd checked my phone several times throughout dinner. The status of Tatiana's health was unchanged. Despite Illias's warning, I'd exchanged numbers with Sasha Nikolaev. He said he'd keep me in the loop. His brother Alexei was a bit too terrifying and his other brother Vasili was too broody. It left me with the unhinged brother. At least, that was how I perceived them.

God, I really hoped Tatiana would pull through. She had to—for my brother's sake and the babies'.

Finishing our dessert, we made it out of the restaurant. Enrico behind me, we hung back as Enzo and Amadeo entered our waiting car. Suddenly, I caught a movement from the corner of my eye. I turned my head and my eyes widened.

White hair styled perfectly in a delicate chignon. Diamonds around her neck, glittering, and her frail body wrapped in a fur coat. But it was the eyes, empty and cold, that somehow still burned. Just like her crazy bitch girlfriend. She stood at the corner of the street, and I wondered whether Donatella was around too.

A sliver of fear trickled down my spine as her lips moved. It was only then I noticed the guy next to her. I recognized him from my run-in at the bar all those weeks ago as her daughter's bodyguard. They both turned around.

"What is it?" The three men—Enrico, Kian, and Manuel—asked the question at the same time, following my gaze across the street.

"That woman in the fur coat," I murmured. "I've seen her before."

"What woman?" The dark note of Enrico's voice didn't escape me.

"She was with—" I cut myself off, my eyes darting to the boys. I didn't want them to know that their mother was stalking me. I wanted to protect them. So I shook my head. "I'll tell you later."

Enrico shared a look with Kian and Manuel. Kian bent his head and kissed my cheek. "I'm going to check it out."

I swallowed. I might have just met him, but I didn't want anything happening to him. "Just be careful. I think… I think she's not all there."

He nodded. "Do you know her name?"

I paused for a moment as I tried to remember, then shook my head. So much had happened since that night. "Hmmm." I thought back to those few words I heard her utter back in the club. "Sofia. I don't think she's Russian. She barked orders in English, even though she was in a Russian club."

"*Cazzo*, I hope it's not her." It was Enrico who spoke.

"Who?" When Enrico remained quiet, I glared at him, anger boiling in my blood. "You better not start this shit again, Enrico," I warned, my voice quiet. "Or there'll be hell to pay."

He held my gaze, his teeth grinding.

"I'm going to chase the lead," Kian called, cutting off our staring contest. "You two work this shit out. But I agree with my niece. It's better she's aware of the danger than blind to it."

Fucking finally! The first man who didn't act like women were incapable of taking care of themselves. He took off on a run, his eyes darting to two blond men in the distance and—holy shit. They had to be Greek gods. Holy macaroni!

Acting on instinct, I reached for my phone and was about to snap a picture of them to send to my girlfriends when Enrico stopped me.

"What are you doing?"

I blinked. "Taking a picture?"

His brows scrunched as he glanced around. "Of what?"

I smiled sheepishly. "Those two hotties." A growl vibrated around me and I felt it in my bones. "It's for my girlfriends."

"Not a troublemaker, huh?" Manuel drawled, tilting his chin to the car. "You two get in before I have to shove you in."

"Well, just because I'm married, doesn't mean I'm blind," I muttered under my breath as I slid into the seat next to Amadeo. "Besides, you're acting all macho and refusing to keep my brain busy."

Enrico took a seat next to me, his muscular thigh resting against mine, causing my libido to instantly respond. As if he knew the effect he had on me, his mouth hitched, stealing my breath from my lungs. God, I was a wanton, greedy woman when it came to my husband.

At least he's mine, I thought. *Mine.* The word slammed into me like a freight train. I realized suddenly that I had chosen Enrico and wanted to keep him as mine forever. *You've fallen for the man*, I thought, feeling my heart expand in size.

Good Lord. I had fallen in love with my husband. How did that happen?

"Sofia Volkov," Enrico deadpanned, refusing to acknowledge my earlier statement while I struggled with the idea that I had fallen in love. "She believes herself to be the Pakhan. *Pazza* doesn't even come close to describing Sofia Volkov's brand of crazy."

The Greek gods forgotten and my love placed on hold, I tilted my head, considering his words. "That's her, then." I took my husband's hand. "It's the same woman from the club."

His eyebrows rose. "The same club from where you sent that video, shaking your ass and singing those foul lyrics?"

I grinned. "Yes, but Phoenix sent it. She had my phone."

"Can we see the video, Papà?" Amadeo asked.

I snickered softly. "In your dreams, buddy. You're underage."

"Oh, now we have to see it," Enzo drawled, his eyes shining with a challenge. He reminded me so much of my husband at that moment. He might not be their biological father, but there was no mistaking they were his sons.

Enrico ignored them both, his attention on me. "Why are you so sure it was her?"

I let out an exasperated breath. "Because someone called her Sofia and then Pakhan a few moments later." He reached for his phone and started typing. Quick. Efficient. With a look that promised retribution and swift execution. "What are you doing?"

"That's Papà's pissed-off face," Enzo explained.

"Well, that's good to know. I shall take note."

Enrico raised his head and pinned his dark gaze on me. "Do you know how dangerous that woman is?" he hissed, the vein in his throat pulsing. "She could have taken you. Hurt you." Enrico's voice cracked, and regret instantly washed over me.

I grabbed his hand. "We escaped her. I didn't know who she was. I wouldn't have even spared her a second glance if I hadn't seen—" I swallowed, flicking a glance to the boys. "I don't think she knows who I am."

"We'll talk later."

Three hours later, we were back at the hotel. The boys were in their suite. Enrico was in the shower. And I was sitting on the edge of the bed in my lingerie.

Whoever packed my clothes must have had a wonderful sense of humor, because it was the only thing I had to sleep in. The ridiculous babydoll gown barely covered my ass, and that was saying something considering its matching pair of panties was a thong.

"How the fuck am I supposed to have a serious conversation wearing this?" I muttered under my breath, staring at my reflection in the mirror.

I stood up and padded across the floor to Enrico's suitcase. "Aha."

Reaching for the hem of my babydoll, I pulled it over my head and slid his shirt on.

I found my reflection in the mirror and nodded in satisfaction. It came down to my knees, but at least my ass wasn't on full display.

"I like it." Enrico's voice startled me and our eyes met in the mirror. He was naked except for the towel around his waist, his big body glistening from the shower.

An ache pulsed between my thighs and I gulped. Loudly. A shiver worked its way over my skin, leaving goose bumps in its wake. I could feel the dampness between my legs, the throbbing urging me to go to him and demand he relieve this need.

I mentally slapped myself. I'd covered my ass, but failed to ensure Enrico was covered too. So now I was gawking at his temping body while my mouth salivated. *Wonderful*.

"Put some clothes on," I demanded, my voice breathless.

The smile appeared on his handsome face, making him look younger than his forty-three years. "I have something on," he drawled, his deep voice doing things to me.

I averted my eyes. I was stronger than my body's response. We'd talk, and then if he was good, we'd fuck.

Yes, good plan.

"How long have you known about my mother?" Might as well cut straight to the chase.

I didn't have to look at him to know he'd grown tense. The temperature in the room lowered by a few degrees, and I held my breath as I waited.

"I learned after I left your apartment, the day you made me those god-awful cucumber sandwiches."

When I looked at him, I saw the truth in his gaze. He was no longer smiling, regret evident on his face.

I swallowed. "Why didn't you tell me?"

He walked over to me, stopping barely a foot away. His scent washed over me—strong and masculine—and my body shuddered with the familiarity of it. Lust surged through me, but I refused to cave.

For this to work, it had to be a partnership. An equal one.

All these men had to stop leaving me in the dark. It was fucked up that Donatella knew about my mother's past and I didn't.

"I wanted us to be married first to keep from losing you." His admission had me doing a double take. Judging by the serious expression on his face, he wasn't joking.

"Why didn't you tell me right after the wedding?"

Enrico's gaze darkened. "Fuck, Isla. You really don't know?"

Hope—or something like it—flickered in my chest. "I want you to tell me."

"Because I want your love, not your hate." He cupped my cheeks, his fingers firm as he bent his tall frame, pressing a kiss to the tip of my nose. "I didn't even fucking know I was falling for you until it was too late. I fucking dread losing you. To your brother. To your uncle. It seems you're able to leave me without a second thought while all I think about is you. On my dick. In my home. In my bed."

He was falling for me, my heart sang. I clearly had to re-evaluate my priorities.

"I don't want secrets between us." His thumb rubbed my lower lip and my lips parted of their own will. He pushed the pad of his finger inside and I gently bit him. He slid his finger from my lips. "I shouldn't be blindsided by Donatella telling me about my mother in a Marchetti brothel." His whole posture tensed and anger rolled from him in waves. "It is no different than Illias keeping secrets from me. I'm done with that shit."

"How does Donatella know about your mother?"

I shrugged. "I don't know, but that's what she said."

"When?"

"It was a day or two after you came into my apartment." He let out a string of Italian curses while I stared at him confused. "Everything has been happening all at once. So many secrets unraveled, and I couldn't keep up. It wasn't that I forgot." Enrico's expression turned pensive as if he was pondering something. "What are you thinking?"

His gaze met mine.

"I only learned about your mother after I left you that day in the apartment," he grumbled. "Meaning the traitor is among my close inner circle. Only a handful of people had access to that information."

I swallowed. "It couldn't be Manuel, right?"

He shook his head. "No. He has been with me through thick and thin. He is the only Italian who knows my true identity. He doesn't need this information to hurt me." That was a good point. "Kingston wouldn't care enough about it to use it."

"Then who?"

Frustration was clear on his face. "I don't know, but I will find out."

My tongue darted out and licked his thumb. "So do we have an agreement?"

His eyes turned into dark pools. "No more keeping you in the dark."

I nodded. "No lying. No more protecting me from the truth, even if it might hurt." I could see his macho protective streak flare up, but I ignored it. "If we do this, we do it together, Enrico. I'm all in, but only if we are equal partners."

He let out an incredulous breath. "I'm really starting to see the Konstantin in you." A pang of fear pierced my chest and he honed in on it right away. "What is it?" I chewed on my bottom lip, feeling stupid to even voice my concern. "Isla, if we do this as partners, it goes both ways."

Of course he'd call me out on it.

I sighed. "I was thinking about the brothel thing." My voice was a soft murmur.

"I don't have any of them. I ended all that the moment I took over."

It was a relief to hear it. At least he was a criminal with morals. It was all I could ask for.

"If my mother was—" God, I couldn't even say the word. "How do I know that Illias and I share a father?"

My husband held my gaze, understanding flashing in his expression. "The old Konstantin would have been pretty sure you were his to take your mother. I didn't know him, but from all I've heard, he wasn't a soft-hearted bastard that would ever concern himself with a problem unless it had a direct link to him." I still wasn't convinced and Enrico could see it on my face. "We'll drag it out of your brother."

A strangled laugh escaped me. "That sounds like a threat. I don't want him getting hurt."

He grinned, mischievously. "Okay, partner. Then we won't hurt him. We can drug him."

"Not that either," I scolded him softly. "So we have a deal?" He nodded without hesitation. "We do this together. No more secrets." The latter wasn't exactly fair since I had a secret the size of a poorly dug grave I was keeping from him, so I quickly added, "No more secrets that relate to us and our family."

It didn't take a genius to know he picked up I was hiding something. Although to his credit, he didn't call me out on it.

"It's a deal, *piccolina*."

"Thank you," I murmured, rising onto my tiptoes and brushing my lips against his.

It was all the encouragement he needed. His mouth took mine in a bruising kiss. We kissed like two starved souls. Like two humans who'd finally found each other after a lifetime of searching. He kissed me with abandon, his tongue dancing with mine. I let him devour me whole, feasting on my moans and whimpers.

My husband kissed me with a desperation matching my own, robbing me of all thoughts. My fingers dug into his chest, clawing at him like he was my lifeline. Maybe he was.

But then I remembered. I had to tell him. I pulled away from him, breathing heavily.

"I'm falling for you too," I admitted, my breathing heavy. "I didn't know. I didn't recognize the signs. You might be obsessive, but so am I. You are mine and only mine. Give me that, and I'll be only yours."

Besides, my heart had already left my chest and joined his. It was singing at the lingering touches and gentle words, swelling with happiness at the closeness between us.

"You have me, *dolcezza*." He didn't even hesitate, and my heart warmed with so many raw emotions. Yanking the towel from his waist, I flicked it across the room. "I'm yours and only yours."

That was all I wanted—and needed—to hear.

So I did the one thing I had never done. I lowered myself down on my knees.

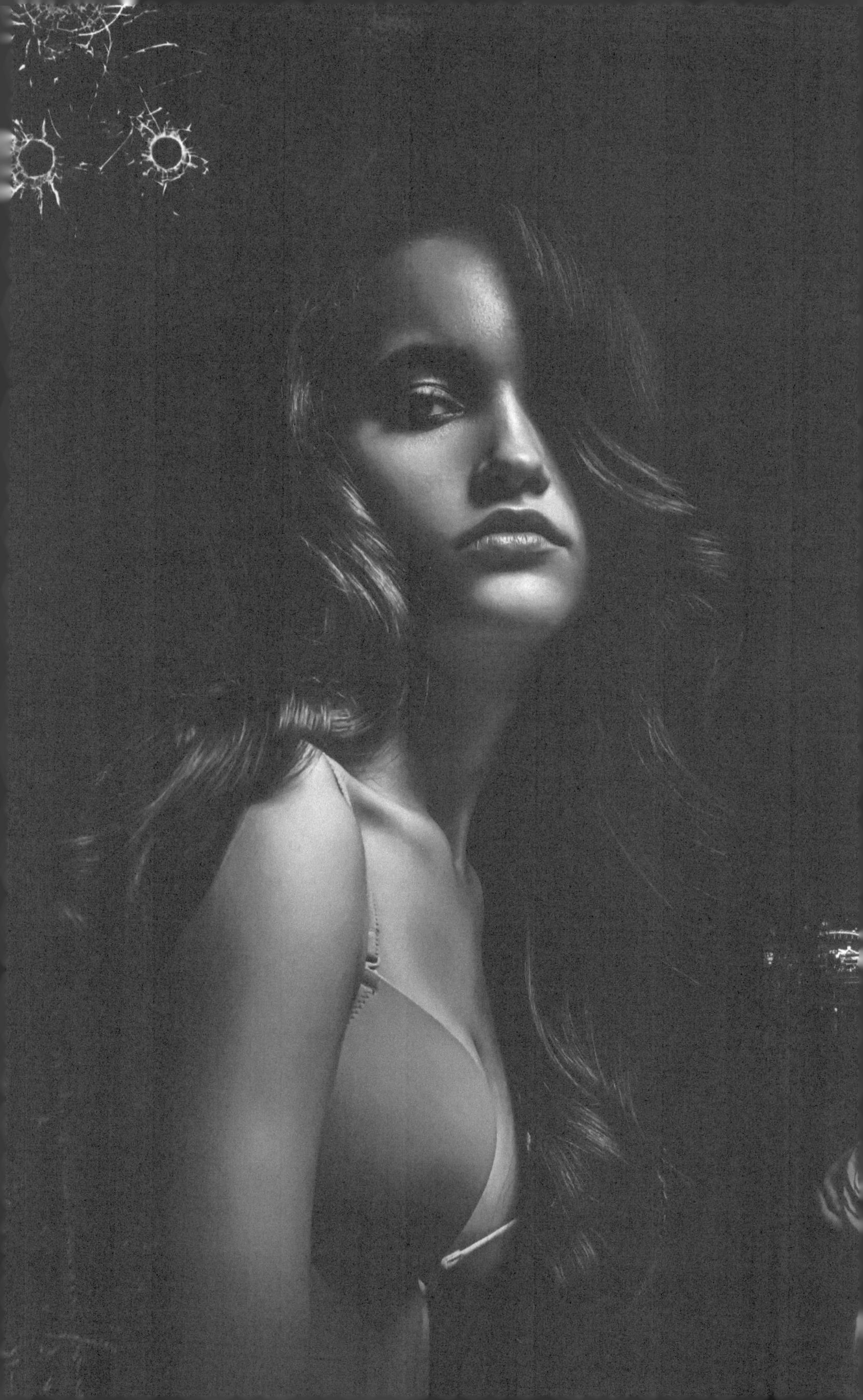

THIRTY-NINE
ISLA

"I want to suck your cock," I murmured, meeting his gaze that burned hotter than the flames in hell. "I've never done it before, so you might have to guide me."

"*Cazzo, piccolina.* You'll make me come before your lips even touch me."

The words melted my insides and my thighs clenched, desperate with an ache only he could ease.

This felt unexpectedly powerful.

"I want to see your tits while you suck my cock."

His hand came to grip the collar of his shirt I wore, and in one swift move, he ripped it off, buttons flying all over the room. The shirt slid off my shoulders and fell on the floor, letting my breasts spring free. His chest rose and fell rapidly as I let my fingers trail over his length.

God, I wanted to make him feel good. I wanted to give him everything and take everything from him at the same time.

I glided my hand over the smooth length, up and down, jacking him off. Enrico's gaze darkened, pulling me into his darkness that was now a part of me too. I clutched his thick, hard cock, my mouth watering as I glimpsed pre-cum glistening at the tip.

"I love your cock," I murmured softly.

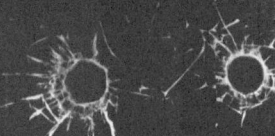

"Show me how much. Put it in your mouth. Now."

I leaned over, licked the pre-cum from the tip, and sucked him into my mouth.

A deep groan slipped from his lips and a weird sense of empowerment surged through me. My thighs clenched as my own arousal throbbed in my aching pussy. The warm, salty taste of him glided across my tongue, and my eyes fluttered shut as a moan vibrated in my throat.

Enrico sunk his strong, lean fingers into my hair and tugged me back by it.

"Keep your eyes on me, *dolcezza*." His voice was a rough grunt. I loved his bossy tone. His dominance. "Good girl." My clit pulsed as he praised me. "Now remove your hands from me."

My brows scrunched in confusion. I might not have given a blow job before, but I was fairly sure one was supposed to touch the dick. His grip in my hair tightened. "Now, *dolcezza*, or I'll deep-throat you before you're ready."

Shit, why did that turn me on even more?

I dropped my hands to my lap and let him take control. He started to thrust in and out of my mouth, deeper and harder.

"That's it," he praised. "Your mouth is heaven. *Cristo santo*, I want to ruin you." I whimpered, arousal trickling down my inner thighs. He pulled his cock out, only to thrust it to the back of my throat. My gag reflex kicked in and my palms came to his sculpted thighs.

"You're doing so good." His expression was soft, reverence shining in his eyes as he watched my mouth. "I won't choke you. Let me in. All the way."

His hands held me in place as he pulled out, only to thrust back in. "You're my good girl," he grunted, thrusting in and out of my mouth. "*Mia moglie. Tu sei perfetta.*"

I had no fucking idea what it meant, but the prideful tone was my undoing. I wanted to please him. I wanted to make him feel good.

He drew back, only to drive back in. He hit the back of my throat and tears burned in my eyes, rolling down my cheeks one by one. He moaned. He grunted.

My lungs burned. He pulled his shaft out, and I took a deep breath in.

"You okay?" I nodded. He smeared my tears over my cheeks. "Want to stop?"

"Don't you fucking dare."

It was all the permission he needed. He pounded in again with a merciless thrust, pushing all the way in. He powered in and out of my mouth with a mad rhythm, slowly losing control.

I gagged. I moaned. My nails dug into his thighs, but thankfully, he seemed to have forgotten his command to keep my hands off him.

"I want to spray you with my cum," he grunted as he used my mouth like it was his toy. "Mark your skin. So everyone knows you're mine."

I nodded my head, but the gesture was barely there. He pulled out, allowing me a sliver of air before he rammed back inside.

"Look at your nipples," he grunted. "You like this."

Another barely there nod.

My thighs tightened. Drool dripped down my chin.

He fucked my mouth like he was punishing me. Rewarding me. Ramming in and out, shoving in deeper on a grunt until I could feel he was close. He murmured words in Italian, moaning. He kept going on and on, stealing my breath.

"Open your mouth wider," he grunted, and I instantly obeyed. His grip on my hair was almost painful, but I took it. Because this was for him. "Mine." Thrust. "Mine."

I moaned and he came with a roar, all over my lips, tongue, and throat. I swallowed as much as possible, his cum dripping down my chin. He slipped his cock out of my mouth, his fingers still tangled in my hair. I panted, staying in a kneeling position. The aching between my legs was unbearable. My breasts were heavy and craving his touch.

His thumb swept over my chin, scooping up cum and smearing it over my lips. My tongue eagerly darted out, sucking his finger clean.

"Whose mouth is this?"

"Yours."

He released my hair and helped me up to my feet.

"Good girl." He leaned over and licked my bottom lip, then bit down on it gently. "Now I'm going to reward you."

A shudder rolled through me, my whole body buzzing in anticipation.

"Bring it on, husband."

FORTY
ENRICO

Two hours later, our bodies drenched in sweat, I held my wife in my arms. She stretched out on the bed, cuddling into me while her breathing slowly returned to normal.

I kissed the crown of her head, letting her coconut scent wrap all around me.

She sighed, almost dreamily. "For being in your forties, you have the stamina of a twenty-year-old."

I slapped her ass. "Just trying to keep up with my wife."

She pushed away slightly to look at me. "Keep up with me? I'm trying to keep up with you. I fear if we continue this, I might have a heart attack by the time I'm thirty. You are in great shape. I hate exercise." She tilted her head before adding, "Well, except sex with you. Although I don't think that qualifies as exercise."

I chuckled. "It does. So we'll have a lot of sex."

She rolled her eyes, but it had no merit to it. Her cheek coming to rest against my chest, she put her palm right underneath my heart that drummed just for her. I had avoided attachments for years, and this one snuck up on me.

But now that I had her, I feared losing her. Like my father lost my mother. Like my grandfather lost my grandmother.

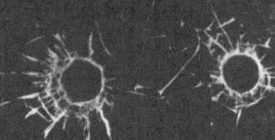

I traced my fingers over her slim shoulder, her soft curls brushing my knuckles.

"Tell me what you saw in the club," I murmured. "The night you saw Sofia Volkov."

She let out a heavy sigh. "I was heading to the bathroom when I heard a noise. My curiosity got the best of me and I saw these two women. One was servicing the other. I was about to retreat when both of them snapped their attention to me, and I realized the one on her knees was Donatella."

I tensed. I couldn't have possibly heard her right.

"Donatella with Sofia?" She nodded, and I took her shoulders between my palms. "Are you sure?"

Blowing out an exasperated breath, she said, "Yes, I'm sure. Donatella was eating Sofia's... you know what. It's not something you forget seeing."

"*Puttana*."

She rolled her eyes. "Well, to each their own. You can't fault her for who she wants to go down on."

I groaned. "I don't give a shit who Donatella goes down on. But her working with Sofia Volkov is bad. Really, really bad."

She sighed. "Yeah, her working with anyone is bad." She shifted so her body covered mine, her breasts pressing against my chest and her thighs straddling me. Of course, my cock instantly hardened. At this rate, we'd never finish this conversation. "Anyhow, I took off and they came after me, but then I ran into this young woman. It made both Sofia and Donatella pause. I think she was Sofia's daughter."

I shook my head. "No, it can't be. Her only daughter is dead and she wouldn't be young at this point."

She shrugged. "Well, I'm telling you what the young woman told me. She apologized for her mother, saying she's paranoid."

"*Dio mio*," I murmured. "This might be our break. If she has a daughter, Sofia is vulnerable."

Isla's delicate red brows furrowed. "I don't think you should use her kid against her."

"We won't hurt her, but maybe we can use her to end her mother."

When it looked like Isla would protest again, I quieted her with my mouth by pressing a kiss on her lips. "Sofia has ruined numerous lives. She has to be stopped."

"I agree, but don't hurt her kid."

"*Te lo prometto*," I promised.

She shifted, grinding her pussy against my hard shaft, and I let out a strangled groan. "Isla, unless you want to get fucked hard again, I suggest you stop moving."

My wife gave me a sweet smile. "You said sex will be my exercise. I need to be in top shape."

In one swift move, I rolled her onto her back and drove into her with ease, her tight heat welcoming as I filled her to the hilt. She moaned, wrapping her slim legs around me. I groaned. *Cazzo*, she felt like home.

"Oh, yes..." She arched off the bed, the soles of her feet digging into the backs of my thighs.

"At this rate, we'll have a baby by next year," I grunted as I slowly pulled out, only to power back into her body with deep, long thrusts.

"Wait," she breathed, her eyes locking with mine. "What did you say?"

My hands roamed her body. Squeezing. Grabbing. Needed this connection with her like it was my oxygen. "I want to have children with you."

She wrapped her arms around my neck. "No."

I stilled. "No?"

"I'm not having a baby while crazy Donatella roams this earth, trying to kill me."

"I'd protect you and the baby."

She shook her head. "Non-negotiable. Besides, I'm on birth control." She tapped her shoulder. "I have another year."

I let out a string of Italian curses. "A fucking year?"

She started grinding herself against me, moaning softly. "Yes." She watched me through hooded eyelids, her eyes glistening like emeralds. "Once the Donatella threat is gone, we can talk about babies and removal of my implant. Not a moment sooner."

"*Va bene*. It's a deal."

Then I took my time powering into her body, rolling my hips and letting her feel every stroke, every touch. Her lips remained parted, her moans getting louder with each brutal thrust into her body. My hands were hungry for her, touching her all over. Grabbing her, feeling her.

I kissed her with the same rhythm of my thrusts, sucking on her tongue.

"Oh... Oh... God..." She panted, holding on to me, her channel strangling my cock as she fell apart, crying out for me.

Her soft moans and clenching pussy had me orgasming soon after. Hard. She drew out my pleasure, milking my cock. I buried my head into her hair, my groans reverberating as spurts of my cum dripped all over her warm, welcoming pussy.

She held on to me as my thrusts turned shallow. "I love you."

Her words sent a jolt through me. It was like a dream come true. "For you, Isla, I'd start a thousand wars." I kissed her lips greedily. "And negotiate a million peace treaties. Just to hear those words again."

She nibbled on my lip. "You can have them for free. The words and my love." Her grip tightened around my neck and she sought out my eyes. "But if you fuck with another woman, I'll cut your dick off and shove it up your ass."

I chuckled. "It's a deal, then. I love you, *dolcezza*. Always and forever. And by God, by the end of this year, we'll be trying for a baby."

She grinned. "I'll remove my implant the moment she's out of our lives."

Now all I had to do was finish Donatella for good.

FORTY-ONE
ISLA

Beep. Beep. Beep.
The next day I was back in Tatiana's hospital room, listening to the sound of her heart rate monitor. It was strange how soothing it was because it meant she was alive and breathing. And all the while my husband waited for me outside.

My brother hadn't moved from his spot, and even when the doctor came to check on her, he refused to stray too far. It was like he needed his strength and only Tatiana could give it to him.

The doctor had repeated the words "*the babies are healthy and safe*" numerous times, but I worried that if Tatiana didn't pull through, my brother wouldn't either. I'd take care of my nieces and nephews—I suspected the Nikolaev family would too—but it'd turn into another vicious cycle. Two more children growing up without parents simply wouldn't do.

"I can't believe she's having twins," Sasha blurted out of nowhere, his big frame looking comically large in the single chair in the corner.

Dr. Sergei—the man on my brother's payroll—performed another sonogram, mainly to assure the four men in the room. The Nikolaev brothers refused to leave until their baby sister was awake, and something about their tight-knit family reminded me of my own relationship with my brothers. Well, with Illias, since Maxim was dead.

"Not that shocking," I muttered, my soul aching for Maxim. "After all, my brothers were twins. Unless you've forgotten."

"We didn't forget," Sasha growled. "He tried to kill my wife."

My brother's battered face flashed in my mind and the bullet in his skull shot rage through me.

"He needed help," I snapped at him. "Not a bullet in his skull." If Maxim had threatened Sasha's wife, I suspected it was the Nikolaev family who ended him. They weren't the kind to take any threat lightly. "Which one of you did it?" How could Illias put up with these men being here? More importantly, why would he be okay with it? Family was everything to my brother. Yet, he wasn't avenging Maxim. "Maybe you'd like a bullet in your little brain?" I challenged.

Okay, that was not the best way to talk to your brother-in-law, but I couldn't help it. Sasha, the unhinged brother, glared at me, his expression darkening. Well, fuck him. I could hold my own and he didn't scare me. I thought I heard Vasili hiss something under his breath at Sasha, but my ears buzzed loudly with adrenaline.

It was Dr. Sergei who broke the tension.

"Twins are usually from the mother's side. But as you can see, it's possible to have surprises."

"Maybe we'll get to beat those Morrellis who breed like rabbits after all," Sasha remarked. I had no idea what he meant and I didn't ask. I honestly didn't care.

"Don't you have a wife to go back to?" Illias snapped at Sasha. "You know, the one you kidnapped."

"She's at the hotel. I'm not leaving until Tatiana wakes up."

My brother's shoulders slumped. Maybe he was relieved, or maybe he'd just given up. Either way, silence followed, and with each *beep* of the machine, my own worry grew. With increased connection to the underworld, I worried that the dead body we chopped up years ago would come back to haunt us.

Agitation itched underneath my skin at feeling so inadequate. Obviously, the men in this room had committed crimes. But they knew what they were doing. My girlfriends and I didn't. Google wasn't a good guide when it came to covering up a murder. Reina insisted if it came up, she'd be the one to take the blame, but that didn't sit well with me either. She had suffered enough.

The beeping sound went off and everyone's heads snapped in the doctor's direction.

"Ooops, too far," Dr. Sergei grumbled, and a round of relieved breaths immediately followed.

I must have lost my mind because I heard myself blurt out, "When a body is chopped up into pieces, can you identify its DNA?"

I kept my tone conversational, although every fiber in me twisted. My fingers itched to play with the wedding band on my finger, but I'd hidden it once again in my pocket so Illias wouldn't ask questions. He'd never known me to be the jewelry type of girl. In fact, I'd rarely worn it.

"I don't know if that's an appropriate question," Dr. Sergei said, his accompanying look slightly reprimanding. Well, it wasn't his life that was hanging in the balance here. "I will give you some privacy." He addressed Illias next. "No changes. Babies are good. Mother's vitals are good. Now we just wait for your wife to wake up."

He made a beeline for the door, leaving me with everyone's attention. Okay, sure, it would seem totally out of left field for anyone else sitting in this hospital room, but how could I explain that this question loomed over me every single day? If my brother and in-laws refused to share information, I'd have to figure out another way to find out. Not doing anything and having those chopped-up pieces haunt us for the rest of our lives was unacceptable.

Alexei was staring at me, mouth parted. My brother merely shook his head and resumed stroking Tatiana's hand.

It was Vasili, pale eyes boring into me and making me feel entirely too seen, who ended up answering my question and becoming my favorite Nikolaev brother. "I'm not a DNA expert"—bullshit, this man knew what he was doing—"but chopping up a body won't remove his or her identity. Not unless you burned it to ashes."

I studied him pensively, quite disappointed with myself for not thinking of that. "Burn the body, huh?" His brothers confirmed, nodding their heads. "Hmm, that's good to know."

"Just make sure there's nothing left of it," Sasha chimed in. "Burn it to ashes, then get rid of the ash."

My brother snapped at the Nikolaev siblings, but I ignored them all, tuning out their words. They were like old women, bickering back and forth.

"She needs to know," Sasha said, defending himself. "After all, she is a Konstantin."

I let out a sardonic breath. "Killing is in our blood, isn't it, brother?"

Sasha had no idea how true those words were. I reached for my phone and typed a cryptic message to my girlfriends.

"We shall burn it to ash and dispose of it."

I knew I wouldn't need to elaborate—they would know exactly what I was referring to.

FORTY-TWO
ISLA

Two days later, we were in a secluded landing area at an airport outside Moscow. We were going home to Italy. At least everyone else kept calling it home. It remained to be seen what it would be for me.

A gilded cage. Or a happy home. The former, I'd escape. The latter, I'd embrace.

"You're going to like Italy," Enzo claimed enthusiastically.

"You'll have to taste our desserts," Amadeo said. "*Gelato*." I knew that meant ice cream thanks to Rosetta Stone. Amadeo and Enzo helped me download the app and set it up for me. It was most helpful, but much to my suspicion, it didn't have any Italian curse words. "Cannoli. Tiramisù. Panna cotta."

I let out a strangled laugh. "I'm going to turn into a boat with all those desserts."

My husband flicked his gaze my way, smirking. "We'll work out more."

My cheeks heated, knowing exactly what he meant. If we "worked out" more than we already were, we'd never leave our bedroom. I'd never believed sex addiction was a thing until now. Luckily, it appeared both of us were affected by it. Thank God!

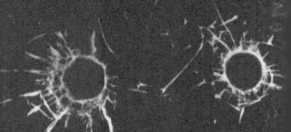

"Andiamo." *Let's go.* Enrico playfully slapped my ass and the sting reminded me of the way he fucked me last night. Bent over the bed, my face smashed against the pillow and my ass up in the air for him to spank. My thighs quivered and my arousal soaked my panties in response, ready for a repeat. At this rate, all my underwear would be ruined. "The plane is waiting for us."

"Does that plane have a bedroom?" I muttered under my breath so only Enrico would hear me.

The way his eyes darkened told me he liked the idea. "It does, *amore mio.*" He bent his head and whispered into my ear, "Does your pussy want my cock as we ascend or descend, *dolcezza*? Your choice."

My eyes glazed over. I loved his endearments. Every single one of them. But *dolcezza* was still my favorite. It was the first one he'd called me by. "My choice, huh? You're the best boyfriend—" He cleared his throat, his expression turning slightly darker, and I immediately corrected myself. "Best *husband* I've ever had."

"As far as I know, I'm the only husband you've ever had," he retorted dryly, biting my earlobe to punish. All he accomplished was to turn me on even more. "The only husband you will *ever* have, *moglie.*" The man loved to call me wife. "Remember that."

I smiled sweetly while my insides quivered with so many emotions. I never thought I'd marry, especially not this young. But I had to admit, marriage had so many perks. Lots and lots of sex. Sexy Italian. Sweet and filthy words. Life was fucking good.

"I'm the only wife you've had," I reminded him back. "And the only wife you'll ever have. Remember that, *marito.*" I proudly uttered the word I'd learned earlier today. Husband. His eyes flashed with satisfaction, burning hot. I tilted my head to drown in those dark, shimmering depths.

"I fucking love when you speak Italian." Then he nudged me up the plane stairs as if he couldn't wait to get me inside. "I'm going to reward you the moment the plane takes off."

A strangled laugh vibrated in my throat. The man was insatiable. But then, so was I.

Enrico's plane was ready to take off, the engine noise traveling through the air. Giulio, Manuel, and the boys carried the luggage while I climbed the stairs to the cabin with my husband's hand on the small of my back.

He glanced over his shoulder and said something in Italian. Manuel snickered but Enzo and Amadeo looked my way, frowning and nodding. They seemed almost worried.

The moment we entered, he shuffled us to the back of the cabin.

"Enrico," I protested, albeit weakly. "The boys are here. We can't—"

"I told them you're feeling sick."

My cheeks heated. No fucking wonder Manuel snickered. But before I could ponder on it any more, we were in the back of the plane and the door was shutting behind us.

My husband whirled me around as he caressed my cheek with his calloused hand, watching me with doting satisfaction. I pleased him a lot, I realized. And something about that had my heart fluttering, like the fragile wings of a butterfly.

"Take your clothes off."

His commanding tone sent shudders through me. This man was turning out to be everything I didn't know I wanted or needed. He was more than I ever thought. I didn't know how it happened, but he'd become an essential part of me.

It was terrifying and exciting. Thrilling and mind-numbing.

Holding his gaze, I started shedding my clothes. My shoes. My dress. All of it, until I stood naked in front of him.

His eyes raked my naked body, lust burning in them.

"Your turn," I rasped. He didn't have to be told twice. He discarded his suit jacket before unbuttoning his shirt. He pushed his trousers off his hips, then toed out of his shoes and socks. My thighs clenched at seeing that magnificent body.

"You really don't believe in boxers."

His lip curled in a look so fierce and dominating that my knees shook.

"I don't need them with my wife." He took my left hand and brushed his thumb over the wedding ring that marked me as his. "I want to cover your breasts in my cum. See your skin glisten. Mark you with my teeth so everyone in the whole world knows you're mine."

Oh shit, why did that sound so fucking good? He reached out and pinched one of my nipples.

"Do it, then."

His erection swelled in response. The view was magnificent. Almost obscene. Definitely erotic.

"Get on the bed," he rasped, and I quickly obeyed while he reached for the little cabinet next to it. He reached inside and took out a bottle of lube.

Wait, what?

I instantly shifted onto my elbows. "Who have you used that with?"

Enrico paused, his mouth hitching as he tossed it onto the bed. "It's brand new. I had it brought in here while we waited for Tatiana's condition to improve."

I instantly relaxed and curved my lips into a seductive smile. "So you've been planning this all along?"

"I have to keep up with my young, naughty wife." I scoffed, but he wasn't deterred. "I read your book."

My brows scrunched. "What book?"

"The filthy romance you have on your Kindle."

I almost choked, heat traveling through every inch of my body. "You've snooped through my Kindle?"

He shrugged, completely unconcerned with my right to privacy. "It was wide open."

"It's not *my* book."

The look he gave me said he didn't believe me. It didn't matter. It was the book Athena wrote, and since she considered me a sexpert now—because I had a hot Italian daddy for a husband—she begged me to read her sex scenes.

"Come here." He pointed to the edge of the bed where he stood. "We're going to act it out nonetheless. Anything and everything filthy my wife dreams of, we're going to do. So when you read those books, you'll think only of me."

Gosh, he was possessive. It didn't matter though. Because I was on board. In fact, I might ask Athena to send me all her filthy sex scenes from now on. I'd leave my Kindle wide open if that's what it took.

I rolled to my hands and knees, then crawled to him, fixing my gaze with his dark one. He followed my movements like a predator, eager to devour me. Once in front of him, I closed the distance, pressing my lips to his.

"I can smell your arousal, my filthy *piccolina*."

"And I can feel your hard cock pushing against my belly, my filthy Italian daddy." Then as if to prove my point, I wrapped my small hand around his hard length. It always surprised me to see him so big. It made my insides clench, needing to feel him inside me.

This insane attraction never ceased to amaze me.

He kissed me hard, brutal and demanding, making my body soften for him. Deep down, I loved his dominance. His control. But only to a certain extent. And only in the bedroom.

He pushed me, and my back hit the mattress. He was on me in the next breath, spreading my legs wide and bringing his mouth to me, eating me like a starved man dying for sustenance. My hands grabbed on to his thick dark hair, arching my hips and rocking against his mouth.

I throbbed with the need to come. The wet heat of his mouth set my entire body on fire. I moaned. I cried. I squirmed against his firm hold. Mindless lust danced through my veins, and I lowered one hand to my thigh, locking my fingers with his.

Sparks burned hotter, threatening to turn me to ash. I panted, my muscles pulling tight as pleasure built and built. Then suddenly, the pressure exploded.

I came so hard, my ears rang. I struggled to breathe, a languid sensation pulling on every fiber of me.

My eyes fluttered open to find him pressing a soft kiss to the tip of my nose. "I'll never get tired of hearing your moans. Until my last breath."

My heart trembled. My soul sang. Fuck, I wasn't falling for this man. I was already in love with him. So fucking in love.

"I want more," I murmured. "Mark me with your cum."

"*Madonna*, woman. You'll make me come like a teenage boy," he rasped.

He grabbed the bottle of lube and crawled over me until his knees straddled me and his cock rested between my breasts. Popping the cap, he poured the cool liquid over my breasts, and without needing prompting, I rubbed it in, making them slippery for him.

After all, that was what happened in the book.

I made a show of it, rubbing it slowly, pinching my nipples and holding his gaze.

"Can I put some on your cock too?" I offered.

"Sì." His voice was guttural. Rough. His eyes were as dark as coals. I squirted a tiny bit of lube into my palm and coated his erection.

"Is this good?"

He nodded. "Press your tits together. Tightly."

I squeezed my boobs around his cock and his head fell back, a groan falling from his lips. It was mesmerizing to watch him. So damn erotic that I thought I'd orgasm again, right here and now. He returned his stare to me, fixated on my chest as my breasts squeezed his cock. His hips started to move, his sculpted stomach muscles flexing.

I pinched my nipples, gasping as the electricity shot through my veins. My pussy throbbed and I rolled my head back as bliss washed over me. All the while his hips kept thrusting between my boobs.

"Look at me when I fuck your tits," he ordered, and I instantly obeyed.

The fire in his eyes burned brighter as flames licked over my skin. He reached for my clit, stroking it. Wet and slippery sounds mixed with my desperate whimpers made the scene we were reenacting downright filthy.

Then, *slap*. He slapped my pussy lightly and fire exploded through me. My eyes rolled in the back of my head and my back arched off the bed. My body sang with pleasure and a second orgasm slammed through me with violent and brutal destruction.

He followed right behind me with a roar, spraying hot jets of cum all over my boobs, my neck, and my chin. He scooped some of it up with his finger and smeared it over my lips.

My tongue darted out, licking his finger. "Yummy."

The feral look in his eyes ripped my soul from me, and I watched in silence as he coated my skin with his cum. It felt like being marked.

As his.

But then, I already was.

An hour later, after he cleaned me up and helped me get dressed, we made our way back into the main cabin and took our seats.

"You know we don't need seat belts while in the air," I pointed out softly.

He ignored me as he fastened me in and then sat down and did the same.

The boys were asleep on the couch while Manuel read a paper, and I tried my best not to look his way. My skin burned, imagining what obscene noises he could've potentially heard.

The flight attendant greeted us with a blinding smile and a tray of fresh fruit and cheeses. Drinks too. I accepted a glass of sparkling water and murmured my thanks as I let my eyes roam the plane.

Illias had a private plane, so I was used to luxury, but Enrico's plane was in a class of its own. The caramel plush seats were custom-made. The furniture was spotless and shiny. The seats and couches were comfortable and luxurious. There was even a section that was made into a dining area with a table and upholstered chairs around it.

My husband's mouth came to my forehead, pressing a soft kiss on it. "Get some rest, *piccolina*. You must be tired."

I nodded. "I am."

Enrico fiddled with the seat settings until both of our chairs fell back in a comfortable reclined position.

"You're an insatiable man," I murmured sleepily, scooting closer to him and placing my head on his chest.

He chuckled. "And I've met my match with you." It was true.

His strong, soothing heartbeat had my eyelids drooping, but sleep wouldn't find me. Instead, I just let him think I was sleeping while I relaxed in his embrace.

My breathing must have evened out enough for Enrico and Manuel to think I was asleep, because Manuel started talking.

"*Che palle*," Manuel said in a faint voice. "You've got to get focused again, Enrico."

"I've yet to lose it," Enrico deadpanned in a flat tone. "Any updates from Kingston? Has he been able to get a trace on Donatella?"

"No trace of Donatella, but he seems to think she's in Russia."

Duh, she'd be in Russia if she was Sofia Volkov's girlfriend.

"That makes sense," Enrico said pensively.

"Why would it make sense?" Manuel's tone clearly indicated he thought Enrico was wrong. "Donatella doesn't have any ties to Russia."

Wrong, buddy. "She does now." Manuel waited for Enrico to continue. "Donatella and Sofia are in a *relationship*." He emphasized the last word.

"*Che?*"

"It seems Donatella plays for the other team now," Enrico explained. "But none of that matters." I was dying to see the expression on Manuel's face. "We find Donatella, we'll find Sofia. And vice versa. Also, I learned Sofia Volkov has another daughter. Isla ran into her in a Moscow club. Have Kingston hack into the club's surveillance. I want information on her. Why didn't we know she has another daughter?"

I had to fight the urge to open my eyes and curse at my husband. Didn't I tell him not to go after her?

"She couldn't possibly have another daughter. She only had the one, Winter Volkov, and she married the old Brennan and died in childbirth." I had no fucking idea who those people were. "After all, it was the reason Sofia started on this warpath against everyone in the underworld."

"And seized the power for herself," Enrico pointed out. "Maybe this secret daughter is the reason for it."

"Where did you hear about this?" Manuel questioned. Enrico's fingers played with a strand of my hair, twisting it over and over again.

"Isla ran into Sofia and Donatella in a compromising position when she was in Moscow with her friends. That's where she saw Sofia's daughter." Silence followed and I held my breath, tempted to peek through my lashes. "Isn't that right, *piccolina*?"

Damn him.

I slowly opened my eyes to find both men watching me, so I shifted into a sitting position. "What gave me away?" I asked, annoyed.

"You snore when you sleep," Enrico said.

I gave a dignified scoff. "I do not snore."

Enrico chuckled. "It's an adorable snore. Soft and cute."

I scrunched my nose. "I do not snore," I repeated.

"Of course you don't, *amore*." Clearly, he was just placating me now. "Now tell us about Sofia's daughter."

I set my chin stubbornly. "I thought we agreed you wouldn't pull her into this."

"She'll give us leverage."

I folded my arms over my chest. "You won't get any help from me to do that."

"Isla, now is not the time to be stubborn."

"You promised, remember?" I reminded him before I deepened my voice. "*Te lo prometto*." I imitated his voice and accent. "A man is only as good as his word."

"I keep my promises, *moglie*." His tone turned icy and his expression thunderous. "You would be wise to remember I'm the head of the Marchetti family and the safety of *our* family comes before any fucking stranger."

My jaw fell open as anger flared to life in my chest like a match had been struck.

"Let me guess," I gritted. "Because your life is so much more important than hers."

"I didn't say that."

But something about all of this didn't sit well with me. If he could use this information against Sofia Volkov, could he use what Reina had done against *her* too? I'd be damned if I ever gave myself the chance to find out.

The words that the Nikolaev men uttered to me earlier in the hospital buzzed in my ears on repeat.

Burn the body and discard the ashes if you want to erase all traces of a dead body.

I gagged at the idea of digging up a dismembered body. But we'd have to do it if we were to ensure nothing could pin that murder on Reina. Because I didn't trust my husband to do it.

I opened my mouth to say something when the pilot's voice came through the speakers.

"We have started our descent. Please buckle up."

I reached over and nudged Enzo awake. He swatted his hand through the air.

"Wake up and put your seat belts on."

He didn't move, so I shoved him harder. He peered at me through one eyelid. "*Ma dai,* Isla. Go back to sleep."

I shook my head. Would any member of the Marchetti family ever listen to me?

"Sit up straight and get that seat belt on. Now!" I said in a stern voice, agitation clear.

Both brothers shot up into a sitting position. They blinked their eyes, sleepiness still in their expression. "What the fu—" Amadeo never finished the statement, noting his father's eyes narrowed with warning.

When neither Enzo nor Amadeo moved to put their seat belt on, I repeated, "Boys, put your seat belts on."

They stared at me confused. "Why?"

I blinked, then glanced at my husband who just sat back in his seat, watching the whole exchange like it was a movie. Why did he put a seat belt on me and let them fly without securing their seat belts?

"For safety," I muttered. "Now be good and put them on. Or I'll have to ground you."

I froze. Then brought my hand to my forehead. Gosh, I sounded like Reina now, scolding them. That wouldn't do at all.

I sighed. "Please just put them on."

To my surprise, they both did as I asked without another word.

Enrico leaned over and whispered, "Our conversation isn't over."

I dug my fingers into the plush leather, my heart racing. I turned to look at him, tilting my chin. "I'm not sure there is much more to say. If you can't keep your promise to me, how can I trust you to keep any of your other promises?"

His jaw clenched. I knew he didn't like to be questioned. Well, too bad. He said we'd be making decisions together, and this wasn't it.

"Whatever," I muttered, turning to look the other way. He shot his hand out and grabbed my jaw, ensuring I stayed facing him.

"No, not whatever." His tone was dark, warning. "I promised we wouldn't hurt her. But we will find a way to get to her mother, and we might have to do it through her. We don't have the luxury of not doing so."

"Why? Who is she, aside from someone delusional?"

Two heartbeats passed. "She's the woman who can easily make *all* our secrets known."

I froze, finally understanding what he meant. "I thought you said only two people—" I cleared my throat, flicking a glance at the boys. Neither one of them were paying any attention to us. "—know about it."

"That's correct, but with this new *relationship* you witnessed," he said, referring to Donatella, "we can't risk her drawing any conclusions."

Okay, when he put it that way, it made sense. Except, the lead in the pit of my stomach refused to ease. He might be doing the right thing for his family, but not for that young woman.

When push came to shove, would he do the right thing for my friends and me? Or would he sacrifice us for his family too?

"Are you alright?"

My attention snapped to Enrico. "Yeah, why?"

"You went white as a sheet."

My lips parted, and the worst words came out. "Did you know if you burn a body, you can't trace DNA?"

Thick silence grew so deafening as I once again had everyone staring at me. Tension licked at my skin and my blood froze. Oh. My. God. How did that shit come out of my mouth, *again*?

"Are you going to burn a body?" Enzo asked, curiosity in his eyes.

I scoffed, weakly. "No, of course not."

And all the while, I mulled over details of a plan that *had* to work.

The Marchetti estate was nothing like I imagined. I was dazed.

The car ride followed twisting and turning roads with huge mountains in the distance until we came to a long driveway that was lined on both sides with vineyards stretching for miles. Workers were out, picking fruit and working the fields, their crates overflowing with produce.

At the end of the winding road was a gate with guards, and the moment they saw the car approaching, they beckoned us through. Beyond it, the land spread out to a wide-open space where an honest-to-God castle stood.

"Welcome to our home," Enrico drawled, leaning back against the car's leather seats, legs wide apart and his entire demeanor relaxed. "Castello Del Mare."

Once we came to a stop, the door opened and Enrico jumped out, extending his hand.

The moment I stepped out of the car, I let my eyes travel over the horizon. Rows and rows of lemon and olive trees. And beyond it all, a clear blue sea.

"Oh my gosh," I breathed. "This is…"

The smell of the sea, lemons, figs, and grapes all drifted through the air. The soft, rhythmic sound of the waves made the most beautiful melody as they crashed against the shore. The kind of symphony that made you feel invincible. I wanted to capture it with the strings of my violin.

Enzo and Amadeo got out of the car and dashed into the house.

"What do you say?" Enrico cupped my face, pressing his mouth to mine. "Could you live here, *amore mio*?"

The sun was flickering its rays over the horizon. The salty air from the ocean. The tangy, rich smell of earth, sea, and fruit... I knew I'd love it here.

"This is heaven on earth," I said, beaming. "There's just one thing missing."

Heat blazed in his gaze with an intensity that flicked a switch inside me, making me ache for him. But it wasn't only the lust in his eyes that had me burning. It was the softness and adoration in his obsidian depths causing me to melt.

"Whatever it is." He pressed a kiss to my forehead. "I'll make it happen."

"My violin."

I couldn't wait to play the violin with the sound of waves crashing against the shore.

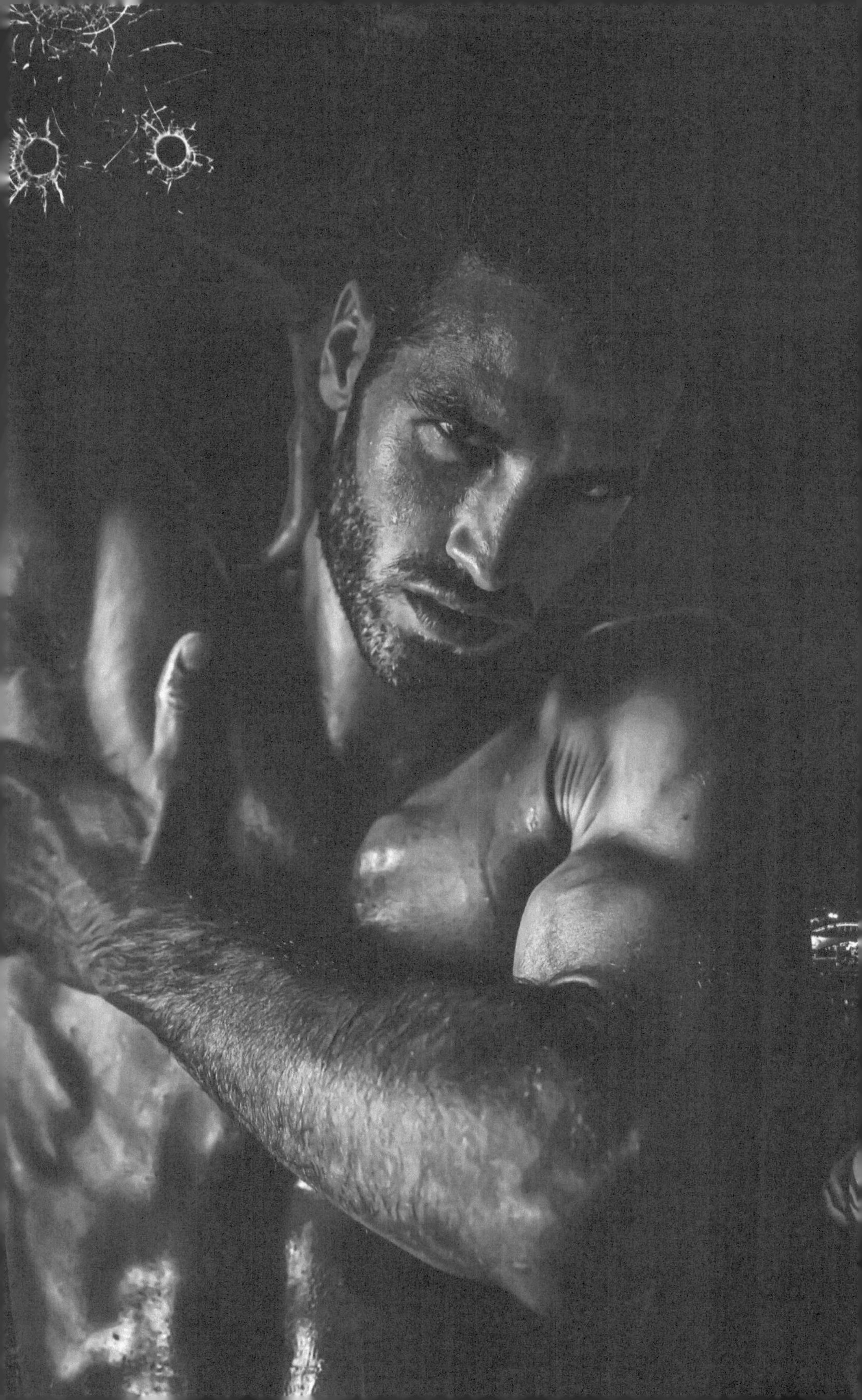

FORTY-THREE
ISLA/ ENRICO

The next morning, I left our luxurious bedroom and went in search of the kitchen. It wasn't hard to find it. I just followed the sound of chatter and laughter and the smell of food. The soothing sound of the waves traveled through the air and could be heard even from inside, making you feel like you were in paradise.

I entered the spacious, modern kitchen and found it bustling with life. Enrico was there. Manuel. A few other men I hadn't seen before. Enzo and Amadeo. And an older woman with silver-gray hair.

She spotted me and her eyes lit up with delight.

"*Ciao, bella.*"

She rushed my way, her feet surprisingly soft against the tile as she approached me and pulled me into a hug.

"Umm… ciao."

The woman was even shorter than me, and my height was definitely not something to be envied. I flickered a look over her head to my husband and boys.

Enzo and Amadeo grinned. "That's Zia Ludovica."

"The best cook in all of Italy," Manuel added.

Enrico said a few words in Italian and I realized he was translating, because Zia Ludovica gushed and waved her hand.

"*Caffè, bella?*"

I nodded. "*Sì. Grazie.*"

She ushered me to sit next to Enrico, putting my hand on his and patting it affectionately.

"Zia likes to feed everyone," Enrico explained. "She's my mother's sister and lived in South America for a long time."

"Until he brought me here when his wife died," Zia said in very broken English as she made the sign of the cross. Manuel's eye roll didn't escape me. It was subtle, but it was clear he didn't like any reference to Donatella. It made me like him all the more. "Now *mangia, mangia.*"

I knew that meant eat, so I smiled. "Good thing I like to eat."

Enzo snickered softly. "If you eat the way Zia wants you to eat, you won't fit through any door in a month."

He and Amadeo shot to their feet and bent over, reaching for their backpacks. "Are you two going to school?"

"*Sì.*"

I stood up. "I can take you." They both laughed, like I just uttered a joke. I frowned. "What?"

"We're not babies."

I shrugged. "I know. But it gives me a chance to see the area and your school. Besides, I always wanted someone to walk me to school."

"It's too far to walk," Amadeo remarked reasonably.

I shrugged. "Okay, then we drive you to school. It was different for me not living at home and going to school. The boarding school had some perks, but that wasn't one of them." Both of them hesitated, their eyes darting to their father and then back to me. I looked over to Enrico. "Is… is that okay?"

Enrico's hand came to the small of my back. "*Allora,* we'll drive them to school."

"Is that okay with you?" I asked the boys.

"Just don't walk us inside," Amadeo remarked. "It will make us look weak."

I rolled my eyes, but before I could comment, Enzo beat me to it. "Unless you're going to pretend to be our girlfriend."

I scoffed. "In your dreams, buddy."

Shoving one croissant into my mouth and grabbing another one, I said in a muffled voice, "Ready." I glanced at Zia and smiled. "Grazie for…" I raised the croissant still in my hand. "They are delicious."

Her wrinkled face lit up and she hurried to the elaborate coffee machine, pouring me a travel mug. *"Per la strada."*

The scent wafted my way and I closed my eyes, inhaling deeply. "Ahhh, coffee."

My husband's lips lowered to my ear. "Careful or you'll make me jealous of that coffee."

I peeked at him through my eyelashes. "Nobody can replace my coffee."

He slapped my ass. "We'll see. Let's go take the kids to school."

We made our way out of the castello where an armored SUV waited for us. I noticed the security Enrico had here was beefed up. In Paris, it seemed less noticeable, or maybe he didn't need security there.

"Is Manuel coming?" I asked, noticing different guards. One of them wore a baseball hat pulled far down over his forehead, making it hard to see his face.

"No, he has other things to take care of." It seemed odd since he was always around when the entire family was together. But I didn't question it. Instead, I nudged the boys into the car, then slid into the back seat with Enrico right behind me.

"Can we open the windows?" The moment I blurted the question, I groaned at my stupidity. The point of the armored SUV was to keep from getting shot, not to open the windows and let anyone take an aim. "Never mind," I muttered before anyone could respond.

"You'll get used to it," Enzo said, something in his gaze telling me he understood.

I leaned back into the seat. I didn't think I'd ever get used to having the need to hide behind the walls of Enrico's castello. Or driving in an armored car.

"What grades are you two in?" I asked instead, focusing on them. "I'm guessing I should know."

"High school," they answered at the same time. "American ninth and tenth grade," Amadeo finished.

"Are you thinking about college already?" Their blank expressions told me they weren't. "You should. The college years are something that everyone should live through at least once."

Enrico's sardonic breath pulled my attention. "Do you know someone who's done it twice?"

I shrugged. "I've heard of a few people who did it twice, yes. They had such a good time the first time around, they wanted to repeat it."

"Or maybe they flunked, so they had to go back," he challenged.

I rolled my eyes. "Whatever. I'm just saying, it's a good experience." I narrowed my eyes on my husband. "Did you not go to college?"

"University, yes."

"See," I exclaimed. "Don't tell me they weren't the best years of your life."

Enrico shrugged. "They were okay."

My mouth dropped. "Just okay?"

His gaze found mine. "I'm almost scared to ask what you did during your college years to be so passionate about it."

I grinned smugly. "You should be." Ignoring the curiosity and challenge that flashed in Enrico's eyes, I returned my attention to my stepsons. "If you tell me what you enjoy, we can set up some tours of campuses. It's still too early, but it'd give you a taste of what it's all about."

For the rest of the fifteen-minute ride, we made a list of universities in Italy, Europe, and in the States that seemed to be a good fit. The next three years would be busy.

The car came to a stop and a guard opened the door. He'd be the one staying, shadowing them all day, then bringing them home.

Enzo went to exit the car first. "Ciao, Isla."

Before I realized what he was doing, he pecked my cheek. Amadeo was right behind him and did the same.

I blinked my eyes in confusion, then darted to meet my husband's gaze. "What was that about?"

"They like you," he murmured, pulling me closer to him. So close that I was almost on his lap. "You accepted them, so they are accepting you."

I blinked. "Just like that."

"Just like that, *amore*."

Suddenly being a stepmom sounded a whole lot more enticing.

The car started moving again, and I sighed against him, inhaling that masculine, citrusy scent. "You smell like your gardens," I murmured. "Lemons and the sea, *so fucking good*."

His chest vibrated. "Women smell like gardens. Not men."

I shrugged. "Maybe like earth, then. I don't know. All I know is I like it."

He pressed his lips against my temple. "I love your scent. Coconuts and sweets, my *dolcezza*." I stifled a yawn. All the excitement over the last few days had caught up. "I have a surprise for you," he said. "Unless you want to go home and rest?"

That instantly perked me up.

"I'm not tired. I want my surprise." He grinned, shedding at least five years off his appearance. I couldn't resist bringing my palm to his face. "You look so much younger when you smile. You should do it more."

He turned his face and kissed the center of my palm. "With you I smile more than ever."

Enrico

When Giulio finally pulled over, I threw open the door and got out.

I extended my hand and Isla peered at me through her thick, long lashes. "Is this where my surprise is?"

My men rushed around me to ensure I wasn't an open target. This was a spontaneous stop and nobody knew where I was taking Isla, though, so I wasn't worried about a surprise attack.

Her fingers met mine. "We'll get some gelato first. And then we'll get your surprise."

She blinked. "Gelato at nine in the morning?"

I nodded. "It's never too early for gelato."

Pulling her closer to me, I threw my arm around her waist as we strolled to the nearby shop. There were a few customers drinking coffee, but other than that, it was empty. The owner was in the process of bringing freshly made tubs out, so we waited for all flavors to be out before Isla settled on "tutti frutti" flavor.

"Hmmm, this is the best ice cream," she exclaimed the moment the spoon touched her tongue. "I think I've died and gone to gelato heaven."

The owner beamed at her praise. Isla was smiling and laughing, telling the owner she wanted to taste them all. He was more than happy to let her. She chuckled and licked her lips, squealing with delight.

"Any time you want ice cream, I make a fresh batch and send it to you," the owner said.

Isla's eyes found mine, glimmering like the greenest forests. It was nice to see her relaxed. Content.

Her happiness sank into my bones and it was like medicine for my soul.

"We can book him for weekly deliveries," I recommended.

"Oh, yes, yes," she eagerly agreed. "Can we have it daily?"

"You got it, *amore*."

She squealed with delight, her small frame bouncing up and down. "You are the best husband. I don't care what anyone says."

I chuckled. "Give me their names and I'll have them handled."

She waved her spoon in the air. "No matter. Because everyone is wrong."

I flicked my amused gaze at the owner and told him in Italian to arrange deliveries with my staff. If my wife wanted daily ice cream delivery, by God she'd get it.

With my hand in hers, we made our way out of the shop and onto the sidewalk. Rome in late November was the best. It didn't have tourists scurrying around to see all the sights, and the locals were busy carrying on with their lives. It felt like it was just my wife and me in the world.

We walked down the sidewalk, and I watched her licking gelato off her lips, giving me way too many ideas that were inappropriate for a public place. She scooped up another spoonful and fed it to me.

"You sure you want to share?" I teased her. In truth, I didn't have much of a sweet tooth, but there was no way in hell I'd ever reject anything she was offering.

"With you, always." Fuck, when she was sweet like that, all I wanted to do was take her home and bury myself inside her. Hear her whimpers and, even more, her words of love.

By the time we arrived at our destination, the ice cream was gone and our sweet tooths were sated. For now.

"This is where we're going," I told her casually as she tossed her empty cup into a nearby trash can.

She turned to look at the store display full of instruments. It was Rome's most famous instrument shop, with musicians from all over the world flocking to it for its exquisite handiwork.

"A music store?" she asked, her delicate brows scrunching. "What are we doing here?"

"*Andiamo.*" *Let's go.* I opened the door and nudged her inside. "Don't ask too many questions."

Her hand found mine again and our fingers interlocked. For the briefest moment, her steps faltered and she inhaled a deep breath, her eyes fluttering shut. "God, I love the smell of old stores and instruments. It's the best aphrodisiac."

She gave me a secret smile and I knew exactly what my wife was thinking. It was the same thing I was thinking. "I'm your best aphrodisiac, *dolcezza*," I reminded her, pressing my mouth on her soft lips. She tasted like her ice cream. "Don't you forget that," I said as I playfully slapped her ass.

"*Signore* Marchetti."

The store owner had both of us glancing at him. The old man—

gray hair, gray beard, and spectacles on his nose—smiled, his small eyes darting between us.

"Signore Paganini, thank you for seeing us so early," I greeted him.

Isla's eyes landed curiously on the store owner. "Paganini. As in… Niccolò Paganini?"

The old man grinned. "That was my great-great grandfather."

"No!"

"Sì, he was."

Isla clapped her hands. "And you?" she questioned, taking two steps to get closer to him. "What do you play? Or do you compose?"

Signore Paganini chuckled goodheartedly. "I only listen. I'm afraid that gene skipped me."

My wife's face fell, disappointment washing over her. "What a bummer."

The old man's face twisted in confusion, and I explained in Italian that it was just an expression.

"No matter," Signore Paganini exclaimed. "I've heard you play. And I have just the thing for you."

The old man scurried away, and we waited while my blood pumped with adrenaline. I couldn't wait to see the expression on her face when she saw it. Signore Paganini was back in no time with a case.

"*Per te.*"

When she gave me a confused look, I translated. "For you, *amore*. Your wedding gift."

She shook her head. "But I didn't get you anything."

"You did," I assured her. "More than you'll ever know. Now make me an even happier man and open your gift."

Slowly, Isla took the case and placed it on the nearby table. Her fingers trembled slightly as she opened it, and a gasp filled the air. Her mouth opened and closed several times before words came out.

"I don't understand," she breathed.

"It's a violin that used to belong to Niccolò Paganini," I told her softly. "I know how much you love your violins and this was the fastest way to get you one."

"And I'm grateful. I really am. But I can't go without my own violin," she muttered. "It's a part of me, and it'd be like replacing one of my limbs."

It made sense. Everything I'd heard about musicians told me this was the case.

"We're still going to get this one, but I'll have your other violin brought in."

Her eyes darted from me to Signore Paganini, then back to me. "But... but... it's too much. I couldn't." She found Signore Paganini's gaze. "This belongs to your family. I can't take something so meaningful."

Signore Paganini grinned. "Your husband bought it, it's yours." Her eyes widened and her head whipped in my direction.

"Why?" she breathed, shaking her head in disbelief. "I have plenty of instruments. And this one... I couldn't. It's too much."

"It's my gift, *amore*. You won't refuse me. Will you?"

Signore Paganini must have been worried I'd ask for my two million back if she refused it, because he chimed in. "I wouldn't sell it to just anyone, Signora Marchetti. In your beautiful hands, the instrument will make music again."

Her delicate fingers traced the wooden grains of the violin. She wanted it, I could tell, but something was holding her back. I motioned for Signore Paganini to give us a minute, and he disappeared in the back.

"What's the matter?" I asked her, coming up behind her and wrapping my hands around her waist. I kept an eye on the glass display across us to ensure no threat came from behind. Certain habits were hard to kill. "Don't you like it?"

"I love it," she murmured. "I just don't feel comfortable receiving such an expensive gift without having one to give you in return," she admitted softly.

I leaned closer, my mouth nibbling on her earlobe. "You've given me more than I can ever repay, *piccolina*." She jutted her ass, brushing against my pelvis. "But if you insist, you can give me my gift tonight. In our bedroom."

I watched in fascination as a blush crept up her neck, turning her porcelain skin into a shade of pink. She turned her face sideways, her lips finding mine.

"Let me guess, *marito*," she murmured, her lips moving against mine. Fuck, I loved when she called me husband. "You want to play with my ass."

My cock immediately responded, turning rock hard and pushing against her ass. "Only if you're up for it," I grunted, painfully aroused.

She leaned back, her small frame pushing against my front. She was watching me with so much trust in her eyes that it had my heart twisting in my chest. I'd rather cut my dick off than break that trust or see any resentment in her gaze.

"Pick up the violin, *amore*, and tell me how it feels."

She picked it up reverently, as if she was scared it'd break, and placed it on her shoulder. The awed expression on her face and the shimmering of her eyes was addictive to stare at. It reminded me of how she looked when she came around my dick.

"Gosh, it's just so perfect," she gushed. "I'm scared to even touch it."

"You will play it, no?" Signore Paganini encouraged, coming back to join us at the perfect time.

Isla nodded, picked up the bow, and the moment the first note left the string, my chest shook with the beauty of it. Paganini must have felt the same, because he watched her with a mesmerized expression.

My wife was right. When she held a violin, she was at peace. I saw it that day at the Philharmonie de Paris, but up close, it was even more mesmerizing. Almost heart-wrenching.

The last note left the strings, and it was as if she'd woken up. Paganini discreetly wiped a tear from his cheek, and I realized I was the luckiest man alive.

"So you like it?" I asked her, although I already knew the answer.

"I love it." She turned to face me, rose on her toes, and pressed her lips on mine. "And I love you. Thank you so much."

"*Prego, amore mio.*" My nose brushed against hers lightly. "I'm going to need to hear your words of love at least twenty-four times a day."

She frowned. "That's oddly specific. Why that many?"

"Once for every hour of the day."

She grinned, glowing. "It's a deal. Now let's go home."

When I brought her home, she dragged me to the cliffs and played her new violin as the waves crashed against the shoreline.

It was the happiest I'd ever felt.

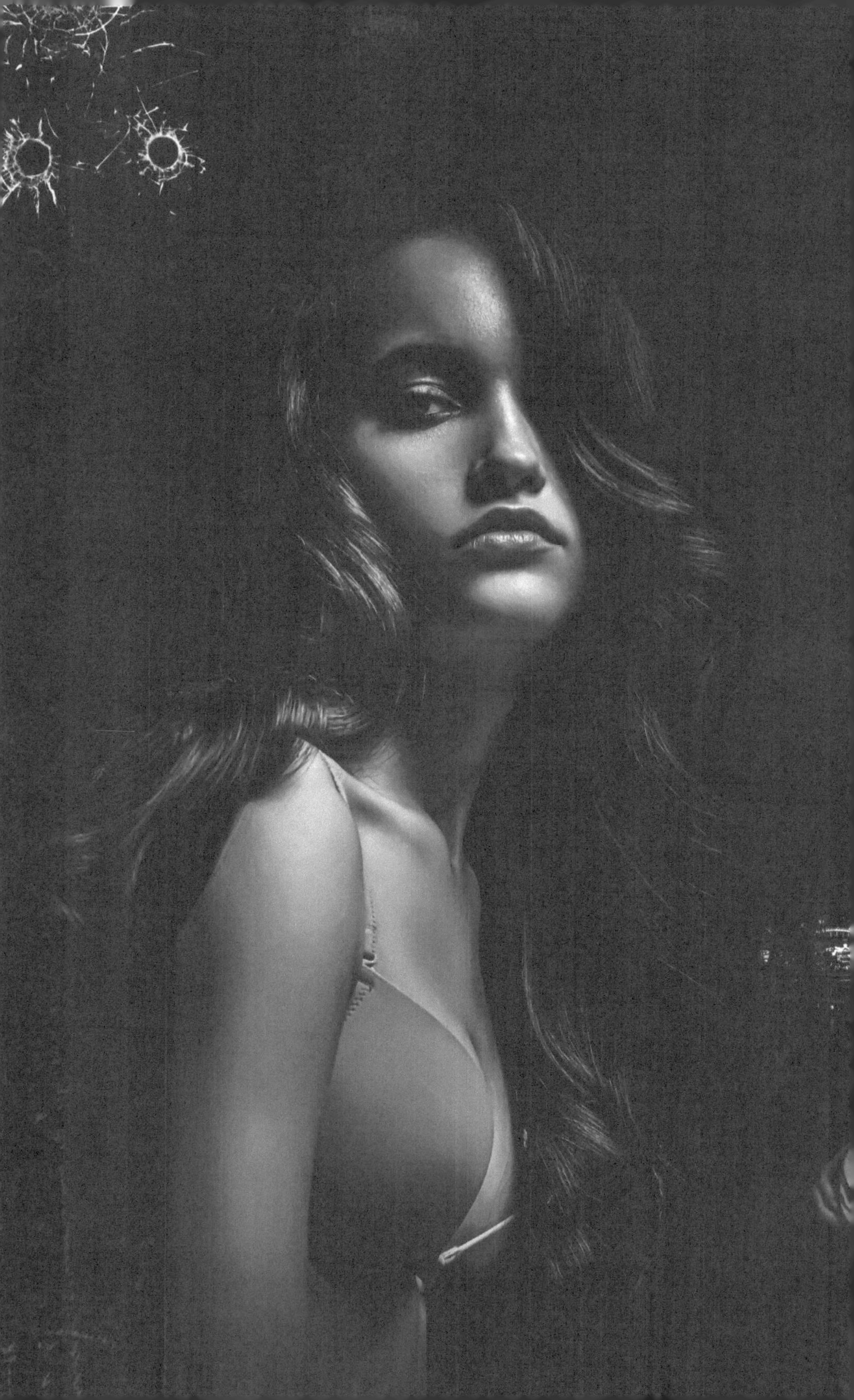

FORTY-FOUR
ISLA

It was all well and good to offer him my ass while we were in the music store, but now that the night had descended, nerves danced through me.

Dressed in a short skirt that barely covered said ass, knee-high stockings, and a white blouse I'd wrapped high around my waist to expose my flat belly, I was dressed to please my husband. I had done my hair up in high pigtails and donned high heels on my feet.

Where might I have found such a scandalous outfit? Well, it wasn't easy. I'd had to text Enzo to steal one from one of his girlfriends from school. When he questioned me about what I needed it for, I told him it was for charity. Not exactly the highlight of my stepmotherhood.

So here I was, looking like a very slutty high schooler.

I paced around the room, waiting for Enrico to come up to our bedroom. The French doors that led to the balcony were open, the breeze carrying the sound of the waves.

Reaching for my phone, I slid it open to find another message from Illias, along with a bunch from my girlfriends. My heart twisted, as it always did lately, when I thought of my brother. I wanted to understand. I wanted to forgive. Yet, without answers, I found myself unable to move forward.

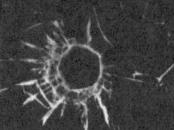

My finger hovered over his name and I slid the message open.

> Isla, please come home. Tatiana is here. We're family.

The message was sent six hours ago.

> At least let me know you're okay.

There were ten more just like it. The last one felt like a sword's edge in my soul.

> I'm sorry I didn't tell you, but please trust me. I did it for you too. Yes, selfishly, I didn't want to lose you, but I also didn't want you haunted by the past. Like Maxim was. Like I am.

It was a message that said too much and not enough. My brother had kept these secrets to protect me, but in the process, he'd hurt me even more.

I typed a quick message.

> I love you. I'm safe. You'll always be my brother. Give me time to come to terms.

It was all I had right now.

The door to the bedroom opened and my husband strode in all businesslike before stopping abruptly. His expression flickered with something dark and thrilling, his gaze lazily traveling down my body and back up, meeting my eyes.

"What's the occasion, *dolcezza*?" The rasp of his voice and the look in his eyes sent shudders down my spine.

"Presenting my ass…?" I breathed, my heart hammering against my chest. I had to be crazy. I had yet to meet a woman who loved having her ass fucked. Athena even refused to write about it in her smutty novels, since she had no personal experience with it. "But if I don't like it, we end ass play right away," I added.

A woman needed an escape plan.

He shut the door behind him and prowled across the room, his steps closing the distance.

"It's a deal." Reaching out, he stroked my jaw with his knuckles. "Where did you get such an outfit, *moglie*?"

I smiled smugly.

"I have my ways." I took his hand and brought it down to the sliver of flesh that my knee-high tights left exposed. "Want to see my panties?"

"I'd rather see you without them," he grunted, his fingers already trailing up and up until he reached my folds. I had no panties under my ridiculously short skirt.

"Wish granted," I whispered, my thighs quivering with need.

His other hand came to my hair and he clutched it in his fist, pulling it and tilting my head back. "How did I get so lucky?"

"You blackmailed me," I reminded him. "Now take off your clothes. If we are doing this, I want to at least admire your naked body."

He chuckled and took one step back, removing his vest. His shirt. I brought my palm up, my fingers trailing down his sculpted chest. He kicked off his shoes and socks, dropped his pants, and it hit me. *He's undressing like an eager schoolboy.* His eagerness made me feel powerful, emboldened.

Once naked, he stroked his thick length and my brain short-circuited.

"Can I taste you for a bit?" I asked.

He took five steps back, watching me like he was about to devour me. Destroy me. Only to put me back together.

"Only if you crawl to me." My mouth gaped and his dark chuckle filled the room. My breaths came out short, my core clenching with arousal and excitement. "After you take off your skirt and shirt."

My hands were already obeying before my brain registered what I was doing. What the heck was happening to me?

I was about to kick off my heels when his voice stopped me. "Keep your heels and stockings on, bad girl."

Holding his gaze, I shimmied out of the skirt, letting it fall soundlessly to the floor. Then I did the same with my shirt. Like the lack of panties, I also was braless. Goose bumps broke over my skin as another breeze swept through the window, cooling my heated skin.

I sank to my knees and slowly, like a cat stalking its prey, I began to crawl. The cold hardwood floor sent shivers through me. This was degrading. Humiliating. And for whatever reason, I had never been more turned on.

I caught the sight of myself in the full-length mirror and paused. In nothing but my knee-high stockings, heels, and pigtails, the scene looked every bit as filthy as I'd hoped it would.

My breathing grew choppy and wetness trickled down my inner thighs as I started crawling again. I had never been so aroused. By the time I reached my husband, arousal dripped down both legs, permeating the air.

"Good girl," he praised when I stopped at his feet and looked up.

He fisted my hair with one hand and I licked my lips in anticipation as his cock sprung out, thick and hard, ready for me. I opened my mouth. The swollen head dripped with pre-cum, and the moment it hit my tongue, I hummed my approval.

Eagerly, I sucked him into my mouth, taking him as deep into my throat as I could.

"*Cazzo!*" he shouted, his head falling back and his eyes closing in bliss.

I licked him and sucked his erection like my life depended on it. His grunts and moans were music to my ears. His grip on my pigtails tightened to the point of pain as he pushed his cock deeper until it hit the back of my throat.

I moaned. His thighs trembled. Then he pulled out.

"On the mattress. Hands and knees."

It was ridiculous how fast I obeyed him. I didn't give a shit, I was starving for more pleasure.

He went to the nightstand and pulled out an oblong object.

"What's that?"

"Lube. Touch yourself," he grunted. "Rub your clit and tell me how it feels."

I slid my hand between my legs and stroked myself.

"Good," I moaned. "So, so good." My eyelids shuttered as I watched his hands—strong and veiny—open the lube and squirt some of it out. My insides clenched, imagining those fingers, now glistening, inside me.

I moaned, rolling my hips. His nostrils flared, telling me he liked what he was seeing.

He crawled on the bed, coming up behind me. "Open your legs."

I obeyed, never ceasing circling my clit. Whimpers and sounds of wet flesh, my wet pussy and his hard, lubed cock, were like an erotic orchestra, making notes with our moans and grunts.

He grabbed the lube again, slicking it up his cock, and in the next breath, I felt the tip of him teasing my back entrance, circling. Then there was pressure and the head of it pushed inside.

I hissed. He grunted.

He stroked my back, petting me. Whispering Italian words I didn't understand. "You're doing so good, *amore*. Relax." I tried, I really did, but my body refused. "Want me to stop?"

Something about his care, his worry, had me determined to give him all the pleasure. I wanted to be his world. Own his every touch. Every glance. I wanted it all.

"Isla, do you want me to stop?" he repeated, his voice a raspy grunt.

"No."

He pushed in deeper until the burn began to subside, and then he was even deeper. I felt so full. It felt dirty. So good. It was too much. Not enough.

My chest heaved. I licked my lips, turned on like never before. Enrico began to move, slowly, rocking back and forth. Then he reached around me, replacing my finger with his as he stroked my clit. My whole body burned and tingled.

"Oh, God... Oh, God," I panted, my breathing labored like I was running a marathon. Sweat broke over my skin as the pressure built.

His palm smoothed the skin on my back, down my ass, back to my back. "*Madre di Dio*, you feel so good. You were made for me. Every inch of you. Even your ass."

God, his filthy mouth. His dirty deeds. It seemed I liked them all. "More," I demanded.

He straightened and grabbed my hips with both hands, then drove deeper. I gasped. Then he thrust in, driving himself all the way in, his hips molding to my ass cheeks.

"Is this good, baby?"

I nodded, unable to find the words. My body sang. My pussy clenched, feeling empty. As if he could read my mind, he reached around with one hand while leaving the other on my hip and drove his fingers inside my entrance.

My head fell back, and then he started fucking me in earnest. Slaps of flesh against flesh echoed, the erotic sounds filling the quiet space in tandem with the roughness of the ocean beyond the cliffs.

The thrust of his cock in my ass and his fingers in my pussy synchronized, I could do nothing but take it. Let him take charge as his grunts mixed with my gasps. He pulled out slowly, only to plunge deeper. To fill me up.

"I can feel your pussy clenching around my fingers," he grunted. "Tell me who this ass belongs to."

"You."

"And this pussy?" I moaned, not answering him fast enough apparently, because he removed his fingers and slapped my core. The tingling built in such a way I could feel it down to my toes. "And this pussy, *amore*? Who does it belong to?"

"You!"

"Good girl. Now play with your clit and make yourself come."

He didn't have to tell me twice. My hand shot between my legs and I circled the sensitive nub as Enrico thrust inside my ass, spanking me again and again. Heat spread. Everywhere I touched felt slick with arousal, slippery.

It was all too much. I came hard, my shout echoing in the room as I shuddered. The orgasm washed through me like a storm against the shoreline. He wrapped my pigtails around one fist and pulled, using it to jerk me back onto his cock and ride me, all the while I clenched around him. His thrusts became uncoordinated, jerky. His grunts became rougher. Then he was coming inside me, his length twitching as I thrashed.

When it was over, we couldn't move. We both lay there panting, holding on like we were each other's life raft.

He brought his mouth to my nape, kissing me, murmuring soft words that I couldn't grasp but still made me warm inside.

After a few long moments, he kissed my spine and slipped out. I winced, suddenly thinking that him fucking my ass was a much more appealing affair than I'd let myself imagine.

My husband swept me up in his arms and pressed his mouth on mine. When he spoke, his voice was tender and soft. "Let's clean you up and soak in the bathtub. That will help with any soreness."

As he carried me bridal-style into the bathroom, I dropped my head onto his shoulder, trusting him to take care of me.

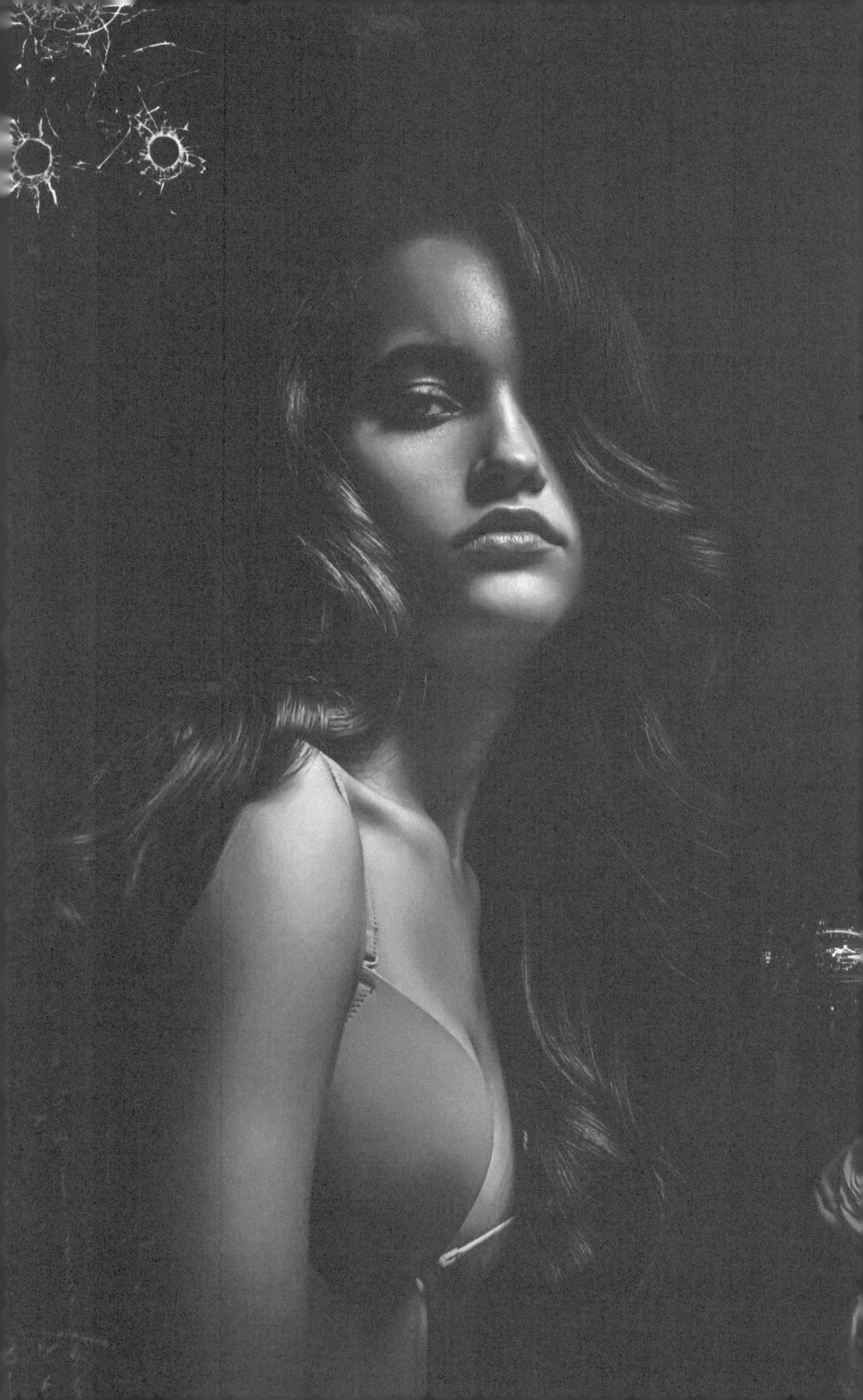

FORTY-FIVE
ISLA

A week had gone by since we arrived in Italy. I'd fallen into a routine with my husband and his family. *Our family*. From the outside looking in, we'd seem like a perfectly normal family. Large. Loving. Even fun. Although buried somewhere in all of it was also ruthlessness.

It was the last week of November, and despite winter fast approaching, the weather was fairly nice, staying anywhere between the low and mid sixties. The sun shone brightly and the forecast promised many more days like this.

"If I knew the weather here was so warm in winter, I'd have moved to Italy a long time ago." Enzo and Amadeo were giving me a tour of Enrico's yacht. The boat was amazing, luxury features everywhere you looked. I glanced over my shoulder. "You think your dad'll let me use the boat for parties?"

They shared a glance, then smiled mischievously. "If he says no, we'll help you take it," Enzo said, his tone full of trouble.

I grinned. "Perfect." I pulled the phone out of my jeans pocket and snapped a photo of the lower deck of the yacht, then typed a quick message to my besties.

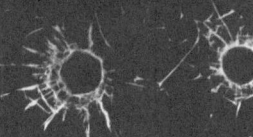

> Next party, this is going to be us. On this dingy little boat.

Replies were instant. In the form of GIFs. Emojis. And words that were inappropriate for teenagers' ears.

"But we'll only help you steal the boat if you invite us to your party," Amadeo added, pulling my attention away from all the buzzing texts.

"You got it. But a warning, you two will be the only men."

I swore their chests puffed out, and they stood even taller. It seemed like they'd grown taller in the few weeks I'd known them. Soon, they would overtake me.

"Is there anything else to see?" I asked them. They'd shown me all the bedrooms and their private en suites, the living areas, the dining room, and the general direction of Enrico's office.

They both shrugged. "The pool on the upper deck." I had to stifle a gasp. Geez, this thing had to be a super-*super* yacht.

"Well then, let's see that and get some sunshine."

The pool deck was empty aside from the three of us and a few staff. It made me wonder where everyone was. There were a lot more crew members when we first came aboard. The moment we left the shoreline, Enrico had gotten a call. Twenty minutes later, a helicopter landed and whoever came aboard rushed into the *ufficio* with him.

"Do you often come out here?" I questioned them as we all sat on the lounge chairs, and I tilted my face to the sun.

"Not often. Papà works all the time."

"Maybe we can convince him to work less."

"Maybe." Enzo didn't seem convinced.

"Or maybe the three of us can come if Papà's working," Amadeo suggested.

"On the rare occasions he can't come along perhaps," I agreed. "But we'll try to do more stuff together."

"I wish our mother was like you." Amadeo's words hit me right in the chest. Loneliness laced his words, and I felt it as if it were my own.

I thought about what to say, how to offer comfort, and the only thing I could come up with was the truth. My own story.

"I've never met my mother," I said, my voice low. "But I always wondered about her. My brother told me she died giving birth to me. It makes me sad. To think my birth meant her death." I took a deep breath, then slowly exhaled. "My brother is a good man. A good brother. He's always taken care of me. But I learned that he—" My voice cracked and my throat squeezed, but I forced myself to go on. These boys had to know they weren't alone in dealing with hard things. "I learned he killed my mother. I don't know why, but I know in my heart he's a good man."

I turned my head to meet the boys' gazes. "Maybe something happened that caused him to snap. I don't know, and I might never know. I haven't forgiven him, but I still love him and I know he loves me. Maybe your mom loves you, but her insanity—or whatever made *her* snap—has her acting from a place that has nothing to do with either of you."

Silence descended and stretched. A comfortable one. Maybe even a tad bit sad. The truth was in the unspoken. It took a while before one of us found words to speak.

"No, Isla. Our mother hates us. She's tried to kill us more than once." The even tone of Amadeo's voice just about broke my heart.

I shifted in my seat and took each of their hands into mine. "It's her loss if she does. Your papà loves you and so do I. We're family and we stick together."

"Does your brother still care for you?" Enzo asked.

I nodded. "He does. I've gotten about two dozen messages from him demanding we talk and for me to come back home."

"But you are home," Amadeo protested.

I smiled. "He doesn't know I married your dad yet. And I know Illias and I have to talk, but part of me is mad that he's kept me in the dark."

"Will you forgive him?" Enzo watched me, his shoulders tense. "Your brother."

"Depends on what information he's withholding," I answered truthfully. "I'll love him forever, but that doesn't mean I can forgive him. At least not until I learn the full story."

If only I'd known then.

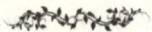

An hour later, I got tired of jumping up each time I heard a faint noise, so I went in search of my husband who, it turned out, was a full-blown workaholic. Unlike me who had left my maestros hanging.

I really hoped they'd forgive me. I had never disappeared like this before, but then I'd never been blackmailed into marriage before either. Nor was I ever wedded blissfully and coerced with lots and lots of sex.

Anyhow, all of it was beside the point.

As I approached *il ufficio,* I heard my husband's booming voice. He sounded upset. Maybe even mad, and for a moment, I stood there, unsure if I should interrupt or just go back to the upper deck.

"Nobody ever escapes you, Ghost." Enrico's voice was laced with frustration. "Kingston. Damn it, I'm used to calling you Ghost. Regardless, now you're telling me Donatella is back in Italy. How in the fuck am I supposed to take that?"

Donatella was in Italy? Shit, that didn't bode well for the boys nor me.

"Any way you fucking want." Kingston—whoever that was—didn't seem frazzled at all. "You asked me to handle Donatella. You never said she'd gotten into bed with Sofia."

"Why in the fuck should it matter?" he roared. "Just fucking end her. Both of them."

A sardonic breath vibrated through the door. "Every goddamn organization in the underworld wants Sofia Volkov dead, but you think I'll magically be able to end her?"

"That's more words than I wanted to hear," Enrico growled.

"*Nipote,* you have to calm down." Manuel's voice was full of reason. "We've strengthened security. Neither one of them will get close."

"Are you willing to stake your life on it?" Enrico was raging.

"Because I'm not. We still don't have the mole. He could be on this boat for all we know."

A mole? Shit, Enrico had a mole in his organization. That meant danger for all of us. Why hadn't he said anything? Maybe Illias—

I stopped myself. For decades my brother was the one I ran to when I had a problem. It was time I handled my problems and my family on my own. Without running to my big brother.

I knocked on the door, then made my way into Enrico's office. If there was ever a mobile office to desire, it was his. Luxurious furniture and floor-to-ceiling glass on three sides with nothing but the blue sea stretching for miles.

My eyes darted to the stranger—Ghost or Kingston, whatever he was called—and self-preservation had me taking a step back. I was met with a tall man whose dark eyes held an almost haunting chill in their depths. Dark hair. Olive skin and harsh expression. Peekaboo tattoos.

Enrico rose to his feet. "Isla, what's the matter?"

My eyes locked on his friend as I answered my husband. "Are we going to have dinner together?"

There was something unsettling about the stranger's gaze. Something broken or cruel that lurked in his eyes that reminded me of something, but I couldn't pinpoint what.

"Yes, I'll try. Can you have them set an extra plate, please?" I nodded. "This is my friend, Kingston."

My brows scrunched. Kingston, not Ghost? Maybe it was a code name.

"Kingston," I repeated. Then I remembered my manners and outstretched my hand. "Nice to meet you."

A second stretched before he accepted it, and I stared at his inked fingers in fascination. He'd be handsome if there wasn't something so unsettling about him.

"Pleasure is all mine."

His voice was deep, the hint of an accent lacing his words. But I couldn't quite place it. "Are you... Russian?"

His expression darkened to fury matching only the darkest depths of the ocean. I took a step back, unsure what I'd done or said to offend him.

Enrico was by my side in the blink of an eye. "*Amore mio*, Kingston is American."

The warning glare Enrico shot Kingston didn't escape me.

"Oh." Kingston's accent definitely wasn't American, but I didn't want to push it. I didn't really care, but clearly, Kingston cared. My husband's hand wrapped around my waist, tugging me closer. "Sorry about that," I apologized. "I grew up in California."

Kingston didn't answer; instead, he pierced me with a gaze that would have made me cower not so long ago.

"When is dinner?" Manuel asked, interrupting the stare-down.

I shrugged. "How should I know?" Manuel actually rolled his eyes. "What?" I challenged. "Do I strike you as a woman who hangs out in the kitchen?"

In our little apartment, my girlfriends and I hung out in the kitchen. We'd sip wine and make food, but none of us were great at cooking.

"You should try it sometimes," he grumbled dryly.

"So should you," I retorted. "Maybe you can start today."

Enrico let out an amused breath. "Don't taunt Manuel, baby. Go tell the staff to set an extra plate. We'll be right out."

Flicking another look at Kingston, I nodded. "See you at dinner, then. We're on the upper deck."

I made my way to the kitchen to pass on the message, then back onto the upper deck where Enzo and Amadeo sat in the same spot I'd left them in. Both of them had sunglasses on, looking very much like future Italian playboys.

Lowering onto my lounge chair, I leaned back, crossed my legs, and turned my head their way.

"Do you know who Ghost is?" I asked casually.

"He's the killer for the Omertà," Enzo answered. "And the best tracker."

"Nobody can escape him," Amadeo added.

Nobody but Donatella and Sofia apparently.

FORTY-SIX
ENRICO

The sun was just falling over the vineyards outside my office windows. The sight was magnificent, but it never quite pleased me as much as it had since Isla moved in. Life was better with her. Views were more beautiful with her. The home was fuller with her.

The only thing amiss was Donatella on the loose and Isla's brother's booming, raging voice threatening to blow up the speaker.

"You married my sister?" Illias's voice roared over the line, and there was no chance that the entire first floor hadn't heard him.

"I did."

There was no sense in denying it. It was better for him to know she was mine now. Honestly, I was surprised it took this long to get wind of the news. In fact, I had to push it his way through the grapevine. That was how much Illias was wrapped up in his own wife.

"I'm going to fucking kill you, Marchetti. You're a dead man," he bellowed. He was being way overdramatic.

"It shouldn't be a surprise to you," I drawled, leaning back in the chair. Manuel kept throwing worried glances my way. Of course, he didn't want me to antagonize the Pakhan. "I usually get what I want."

"She's my sister."

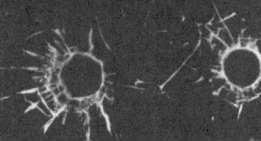

"And now she's also my wife."

"I'm going to kill you with my bare hands. You forced Isla into your fucked-up, cursed family. There's no way she would ever want to be with you." The pang in my chest was uncomfortable. I didn't fucking like his words at all. He was lucky he was on the other side of the world, or I'd have shot him. "Put her on the phone now," he demanded.

My ears buzzed with my own fury, but I refused to let it take me over. Instead, I remembered the words she told me back in Russia, over a week ago now. *I'm falling for you too. I love you.* I would keep her safe and with me until my dying breath, because the alternative was unbearable.

"Remind me, Konstantin. How did you marry your wife?" I switched tactics. The fucker didn't have a leg to stand on. Not after he kidnapped his own bride.

"That's not the same!" he barked.

"You're right," I agreed. "It's not the same. You kidnapped your bride. I simply had a conversation with mine, and then she walked down the aisle of her own free will. Even put the dress on by herself."

With a little persuasion, I added silently. But he didn't need to know that.

"Are you out of your fucking mind?" I really wished the fucker would just accept it. His baby sister was mine now. My wife. My life. And I'd never let him take her from me. "All the women that marry into your family get murdered." He must have slammed his fist against his desk because a rattling sound came through the speaker. "I'm coming for her, Marchetti. And you will give her an annulment."

"The fuck I am." It was my turn to slam my fist against the table. "Try and take her from me, and I'll come for everything *you* love."

I ended the call, my blood burning hotter and searing the word *mine* into my chest.

I didn't give a shit if he knew how much his sister meant to me, or how far I'd go to keep her with me. She was my weakness. I'd go all the fucking way.

"That wasn't wise." Manuel spoke for the first time since the phone rang.

I gritted my teeth. "I don't give a fuck."

Manuel frowned at me. "Konstantin *will* start a war." He pinched his nose, suddenly looking as tired as I felt. "We cannot go to war over this. We have too much shit on our plate already."

He was right, but it didn't matter to me. If I lost her, all the years of sacrifices and living in the underworld were for naught. I deserved her.

"I will go to war over *her*. None of this… all the fucking sacrifices were for nothing if I can't have her."

The sheer terror at the possibility of losing her had my chest twisting in agony.

Manuel studied me, his expression somber. "Then think about the Omertà," he said. "The five Italian families. The kings. We're expanding alliances with the Greeks, the Irish. Will they stand by you against Konstantin? Or will we all fall apart?"

"They will do whatever the fuck I tell them to."

Agosti, Romero, and Dante Leone might. Amon would turn his back, now that Reina was promised to his brother. The DiMauro family would sooner stab me than help. The Callahans would take DiMauro's side. Still, the odds weren't terrible.

Manuel pushed his hand through his hair. "God save me from a Marchetti man obsessed with a woman." He shook his head. "Ever since you met her, worrying for you has become my full-time job."

"Once Donatella is eliminated, you can take a long vacation. Maybe you'll fall in love and then I can antagonize you."

He flipped me the middle finger. "It'll never happen."

I grinned. "Never say never." Then I turned serious. "Have we gone through all the men and their backgrounds?"

Manuel leaned back in his chair and pinched the bridge of his nose. "We have. Twice. I can't find any connections to anyone outside our family."

My teeth ground. "There has to be one."

"Agreed, but for the fucking life of me, I cannot find it."

Frustration clawed and dug at my chest. "We're too close to it. Have we asked Kingston to check them all?"

He nodded. "I handed him the list this morning. He's making his way through it. Let's hope he has better luck than us."

"He will."

He had to. Everything depended on uncovering the identity of the mole.

FORTY-SEVEN
ISLA

Tension grew in the air, even in the castle. It didn't escape me that Enrico had tightened security yet again. He doubled the guards. He stopped the boys from going to school. They weren't happy at all, and I couldn't blame them.

It made me wonder whether my life would have been like this—a constant threat—if Konstantin hadn't sent me away to boarding school.

My phone rang and I flicked a glance at the screen. Surprise washed over me upon seeing my sister-in-law's name.

Without thinking, I answered. "Hello, Tatiana."

A relieved sigh traveled through the line. "I was worried you wouldn't answer." I remained quiet, wondering why it never crossed my mind not to answer her. I was mad at her, wasn't I? But I wasn't. She stood by her husband, as she should, and I couldn't fault her for it. Yes, she'd kept a big secret from me, but it wasn't her place to tell me my mother's story.

"I'll always answer your call," I finally said.

"But not your brother's?" There was a hint of sadness in her voice that stabbed my heart. "He loves you."

I let out a heavy sigh. "And I love him. But I cannot just pretend he didn't kill my mother."

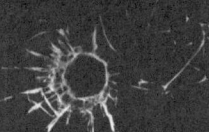

"What if I told you he did it for a good reason?"

I shook my head. "You take his side. And that's okay. But I won't accept that as an explanation."

She sighed. "I didn't think you would."

It was better if we changed subjects. "How are you feeling? How are the twins cooking?"

She chuckled. "They're not even born and already they're exhausting me."

"Ah, the joys of motherhood."

Silence followed and I waited, tension spreading. "So I hear you're a stepmom now."

And there it was.

"Yes, I guess I am."

"How's that going?"

I rubbed my forehead, unsure if I was ready to have this conversation. "Enzo and Amadeo are good kids. I like them, and they've accepted me just as I have them."

"And the sugar daddy? *Paparino?*"

A choked laugh escaped me. Leave it to Tatiana to break the tension with something like that.

"*Paparino?*" I cackled. "Where in the hell did you hear that term?"

Her chuckle traveled through the line. "I looked it up, but for God's sake, don't tell your brother. He'd lose his shit."

I grinned. "Now there's an incentive to tell him."

"You're the worst," she scolded.

"And you had me so worried when you were in the hospital," I told her, and all amusement suddenly drained away. "I was so fucking worried. For you. For my brother. For the babies."

"I know, I'm sorry."

My chest tightened remembering how she lay in the hospital bed, Illias beside himself. "Did you find all the answers?"

"I did," she croaked.

"Did it bring you peace?" *Will it bring me peace?*

She let out a heavy breath. "Having your brother beside me and the babies inside my belly brought me peace," she admitted. "There are certain things I wish I didn't know, but then I also know that it would have driven me insane wondering for the rest of my life."

"So you understand." It certainly sounded as if she did.

"I understand. I just don't think it'll give you the answers you need."

"I need the truth," I snapped, my tone sharp. "My father plucked my mother from a brothel. How do I even know if Illias is my brother?"

A sharp gasp came through the line. Maybe she didn't think I knew as much as I did.

"He's your brother," she claimed. "You are his sister that he raised. He loves you, and blood ties or none, he'll always love you. Why do you think he's on his way to Italy?"

I tensed. "What?"

"You know him," she said exasperatedly. "He's convinced Marchetti forced you to marry him."

He kind of did, but that didn't really matter right now.

"When did he leave?" For fuck's sake, my brother could be downstairs, murdering my husband, and I wouldn't even know it.

"We left an hour ago." I had to tell Enrico.

"*We*? He's bringing you with him?" It seemed very unlikely.

"We're on the plane now," she muttered. "He's sleeping in the back, so I snuck away to give you fair warning."

"Thank you," I breathed. I really wished Illias would have been the one to call me and ask me whether it was okay to barge into my marriage. "I owe you."

"No, you don't. Family doesn't owe family."

I smiled. "Family," I murmured. "I like the sound of that."

"Me too."

"How did he find out, by the way?" I knew the girls wouldn't have shared the news with him.

"Your husband wanted to ensure Illias understood you were his now."

I let out an incredulous laugh. Somehow it didn't surprise me at all.

I fell asleep waiting for Enrico. He had a shipment emergency to deal with. Or something like that.

When I woke past midnight, I made my way downstairs, following the trickle of light in the dark castello. I found Enrico sitting in his armchair, a glass in his hand and a cognac bottle next to him. His brows drawn together, he stared out the open window into the darkness. He mustn't have heard me walk in.

My husband's jacket and tie were thrown over the armrest of the chair, but he still wore his vest. The top buttons of his shirt and his cuffs were undone, giving me a view of his strong forearms.

I watched him for a few heartbeats, mesmerized by the ways my life had changed. Two months ago, I was living in the flat with my girlfriends, guarding a secret and living for the brief moments on stage. And now... everything seemed to be trumped by this force of a man and our kids. Yes, *our* kids. They had inched their way into my heart and become part of me. Just like my best friends were.

I missed them and couldn't wait to see them again. Group chats were fun, but it wasn't the same as having them in the room with me. Reina was navigating the Leone brothers with delicate hands. Phoenix had gotten quieter in our group chats. Raven was... well, the same. And Athena threw herself wholeheartedly into writing her smut.

"Are you avoiding me?" I said as I stepped fully into the room.

His eyes found me. "I'm not."

There was worry etched in the lines of his face and I hated it. I wished the Donatella threat was behind us and this mole was discovered. So we could finally live. Focus on us and our family.

I shut the door with a soft click and felt Enrico watching me as I strode toward him.

"You're worrying too much."

He shook his head. "There's much to worry about."

"Like my brother coming?" I stopped in front of him. He looked weary, but his surprise at the knowledge that Illias was coming was evident.

"How do you know?" His tone was sharp, the suspicion in his gaze real. Too real. "Did you call him to come and get you?"

I shook my head. Usually, I'd give him hell for having so little faith in me, but he looked too worried. Was it at the possibility that I'd leave him?

"Tatiana called me and gave me a heads-up," I told him. "I'm staying. Unless you don't want me here."

He put down the glass on the table with a soft thud. His palms came up to grip my ass cheeks, my boy shorts barely covering the curve of my buttocks. His fingers dug into my soft flesh.

"I'll always want you, *dolcezza*."

A soft smile curved my lips. "Good, 'cause you're stuck with me now."

A rumbled chuckle filled the space between us. "Not exactly a hardship."

I grinned. "You say that now, just wait until all hell breaks loose."

I knelt down between his legs and worked on his belt buckle, the clang sending shivers through me. Then I pulled his zipper down, the sound sending a seductive echo through the room.

I rubbed my cheek against his already hard length as anticipation danced down my spine. I wrapped my hand around his shaft and licked him, from base to tip.

He let out a grunt, watching me through hooded eyes—dark and hazy. Desire was pulling me under and I found myself not wanting to come up for air.

My gaze found his glass on the side table and I reached for it. I slipped an ice cube into my mouth, sucking on it and swirling it around before letting it slide back into the glass.

I took his hard length back into my mouth, my cold lips drawing a rasp from my husband. "*Ahh, cazzo*."

His head fell back, but not for long. He tilted it back down so he could watch me. I laved at him with my tongue, breathy noises escaping me.

Heat bloomed in my stomach, moving lower in a wave that had me clenching my thighs together. I took him deeper into my mouth, inch by inch, using my tongue to tease his crown. Taking my time; savoring his taste. Then I took him deeper into my mouth, bringing my half-lidded, lust-filled gaze up to his.

His hands came to my face, holding it as he slowly slid deeper. My eyes watered. I couldn't breathe when he reached the back of my throat, but I remained still, letting him fuck my mouth.

I wanted him to use me. I wanted to give him everything he needed. Because I loved him. I loved the sounds he made when he was close, the low grunts and sharp breaths. His fingers found my hair and gripped it, like he was worried I'd stop.

His muscular thighs quivered under the expensive fabric of his Armani pants.

"You will swallow every drop." I blinked my acknowledgement, loving the possessive gleam in his eyes a second before he came.

"Yes, baby," he rasped, tensing as he came with a small shudder, his eyes falling shut.

I swallowed and licked my lips, my skin growing hot when his eyes found me again. I kept his length in my mouth as he twitched with the last aftershocks of his orgasm, stroking his balls lightly and only gently sucking. My own lust was heavy between my legs, but I ignored it. This was for him.

He cupped my cheek and brought our faces together. When he pressed his mouth to mine, our tongues slid together. I dug my fingers into his hair, kissing him deeper as a moan bubbled in my throat.

"How is it that you married me, and suddenly, I'm on my knees for you?" I teased, nipping his lip. "At least before I said 'I do' you were the one kneeling."

He chuckled. Deep and full. I loved the sound of him laughing. It filled me with as much warmth as his kisses did.

"I'll have to compensate for it, huh?" I didn't answer, instead I just kissed him again. Wet. Hot. Needing him like I needed air to breathe.

In one swift move, he brought me up to straddle him. His hand slid between my legs, pushing two fingers inside me. "You're soaked," he murmured against my lips.

He slipped his fingers in and out of me, spreading my arousal.

"My turn," he rasped.

I moaned with anticipation, grinding against his hand, when the ringing of a phone cut through the air.

He stilled, palpable tension shooting through him which in turn sent an alert through me. He pulled away and the ache between my legs protested, but I ignored it. Instead, I watched him reach for his cell phone I hadn't noticed and answer the call.

"Sì."

Rushed Italian words came from the other line. Urgent. By the dark expression on Enrico's face, something bad was going down. Enrico was quiet for a while before frustration lit in his eyes.

"I'm coming."

He hung up, and silence swept into the room.

"It couldn't be Illias," I murmured, slightly disappointed he was leaving.

He ran a hand across my cheek. "It's not." I waited as he ran a hand across my cheek and kissed me again. "Sofia Volkov has been spotted. They have her cornered. I have to go."

Still on his lap, I kissed him hard, savoring every lick and press of our lips. It turned gentle. Soft. As if it were our last kiss.

He stood up—my legs still wrapped around him—and he set me down in the chair he'd just occupied.

"Stay in the castello until I'm back."

I nodded and watched him walk out the door, not realizing he'd left us in the jaws of the wolf.

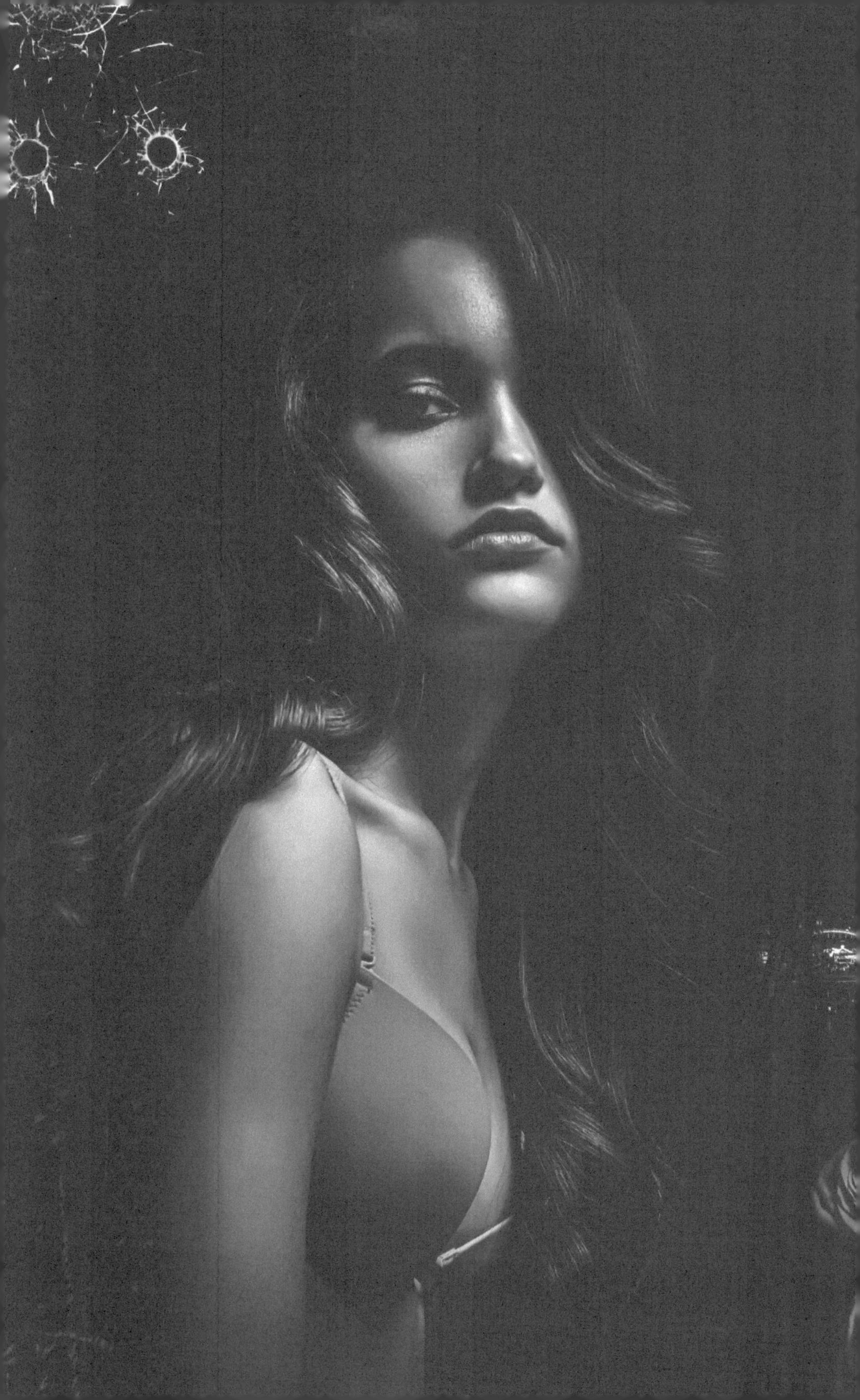

FORTY-EIGHT
ISLA

With Enrico gone, I made my way back to our bedroom. But sleep refused to find me. I stared at the ceiling, wide awake, hoping Enrico would be back by sunrise. I didn't think I was paranoid, but I swore I kept hearing hushed voices, and it was starting to freak me out.

A loud thump had me jumping upright, glancing around. I held my breath as I listened, but only silence followed. The heavy weight in the pit of my stomach warned me something was amiss.

Yet, I couldn't sit still and wait. Not knowing whether Enzo and Amadeo were sound asleep in their rooms, I slipped out of bed and decided to go check it out. Maybe Enrico was back home and the voices I was hearing belonged to him and Manuel. I slipped on the robe that would cover more of my body than these silky pajamas and made my way out of the bedroom.

A clock somewhere struck three and had me startling against the wall, cutting my breath off. My hand on my chest, I tried to ease my heartbeat. Just then, I thought I heard a voice. Or maybe it was a laugh. Low. Suppressed. Unnatural.

It sent cold shivers down my skin, almost as if someone had touched me.

"Who's there?" I whisper-cried out.

A moan. A gurgle.

My sixth sense flared and I rushed to Enzo's and Amadeo's rooms that were in the opposite wing of this castello. As I ran, keeping my footsteps silent, I cursed for not having them closer. Something wasn't right, and they were too far away.

Ignoring my fear, I rushed to their bedrooms. I shot open the door and rushed to Enzo's bed. I shook him hard. "Wake up," I hissed.

He groaned and I covered his mouth. His eyes shot open and our gazes met. "Shhh," I murmured. "Someone is here. Get up."

He blinked a few times, then immediately jumped out of bed. We ran to the adjoining door of Amadeo's bedroom.

Bang.

I fell to my haunches and shook Amadeo frantically, panic growing inside me by the second. His eyes shot open. "*Ma che cazzo.*"

I placed a finger to his mouth. "I think someone's in the house," I whispered. "Let's go."

Sleep clearing from his eyes, he swiftly jumped out of the bed and grabbed his phone. His expression turned blank, yet I knew deep down he feared it was his mother here to finish the job. My chest clenched tightly, making it hard to breathe.

"Lead the way, Enzo," I whispered. "I'll be right behind you."

Enzo and Amadeo shared a glance. "You should be in the front," Enzo reasoned.

"I can't remember where the safe room is," I lied. He was crazy if he thought I'd let him be my guard. I crept to the door and checked both ways. The hallway was clear. "Now stop wasting time. I'm right behind you."

Trembling with anxiety, the three of us staggered down the hallway. The guards were nowhere to be found. Until we reached the end of the hallway, by the top of the stairs, where a bleeding body lay. I clutched both boys.

"Let me check if the coast is clear," I rasped. Both of them shook their heads, but I ignored them, shoving them behind me. My hands shook as I staggered toward the body. I kneeled down, checking for a pulse. There wasn't one.

Glancing around, I watched each dark corner while holding my breath.

We crept downstairs, both of the boys at my back, and kept our bare feet quiet against the marble. Enzo steered me toward the back of the house.

"Safe room," he mouthed.

I nodded, following his gaze. It was on the other side of the hallway. So close but so far away.

"Go open the door," I whispered. Enzo and Amadeo made their way to it when I spotted the light under the living room door. I heard hushed voices.

The door opened and I froze. I stared into the eyes of the man I had seen back in Russia, guarding Sofia Volkov's daughter. Yet, he was here now. How could that be? How did he get in the house?

I took a step back. Dark, menacing eyes followed my every move, the side of his mouth twisting into a snarl.

Without thinking, I turned around and bolted. It was too late. A hand grabbed my arm and I jutted my elbow into his ribs. He didn't even move. So I kicked him. He grunted and I stumbled back, desperate to escape, to protect the boys.

Donatella appeared behind him, her unhinged eyes meeting mine. My breaths became erratic. My heart pounded painfully. Oxygen left my lungs.

"Hello, whore. Have you met my cousin Giulio?" She threw her head back and laughed at my surprise. "Don't worry, you won't be the only one surprised."

Without another thought, I dashed toward the safe room. It was too late, though, and I knew it. I could feel it in the ice that traveled through my veins and bit at my heart.

My muscles burned. I wasn't a runner. In fact, I hated any kind of physical exercise, aside from sex. I heard thumps behind me and in front of me, closing in. Amadeo's and Enzo's dark heads appeared in front of me.

Amadeo glanced over his shoulder. "Don't look back. Just run."

My lungs burned. They made headway, getting farther and farther away from me. Enzo slapped his hand on the keypad and the door swung open.

Before I could make it even three steps, I was slammed forward. Acting on instinct, I kicked and jabbed my elbow into the heavy body behind me. Fingers gripped my hair and slammed my head against the floor. A ringing echoed in my ears.

I ignored it as my stomach roiled. A metallic taste filled my mouth.

"Shut the door!" I screamed at the top of my lungs. I thrashed and kicked, fighting him with every ounce of strength I had.

Enzo didn't move. Amadeo didn't either. Both of them held their breaths, waiting.

"No, you can make it," Enzo shouted.

He was wrong. Feeling Giulio's breath at the nape of my neck, I threw my head back. I saw stars.

"Shut the fucking door, Enzo. Now!" The word was barely out of my mouth when a big, rough hand yanked me up by my hair and pulled me farther away from them. My scalp burned, pain shot through every inch of me, and tears gathered in my eyes. Donatella sidestepped me, making her way to the boys. "Please, Enzo. Shut the door."

It was Amadeo who finally slammed the button and the door slid shut before Donatella could get to them.

I kept struggling against Giulio, but it was no use. He pulled my arms behind my back and secured them with a zip tie before throwing me over his shoulder.

FORTY-NINE
ENRICO

I knew something was wrong the moment I saw Manuel's face. We'd been in this damn warehouse for hours, torturing the last man standing that supposedly worked for Sofia Volkov. If he did, he didn't know crap.

"Kingston found the mole," he said. My gut cramped. A bad feeling filled me.

"Who?"

A heartbeat passed. "Giulio. He's Donatella's fucking cousin."

A red mist coated my brain. Fear unlike any I had felt before shot through my veins.

"Isla," I choked out. "The boys."

A phone rang at that moment. It wasn't mine. I had left mine in the car. It was Manuel's. He glanced at it and stiffened.

"Sì?" he answered. Silence followed. "*Stai bene? Tuo fratello?*"

He hung up. "The castello was attacked. She's gone."

Every muscle in me tightened. Raw rage shot through me, tearing me apart from the inside. It was how it must have felt to have a knife shoved inside you. Two simple words "She's gone," and they destroyed me more than any gun or knife ever could.

"The boys?" My voice wasn't my own.

"In the safe room. That was Enzo who called."

Emotions I had buried deep within me for decades rose to the surface. Faces of my murdered mother and brother. Stories of a murdered grandmother. Five generations *and counting*.

"How in the fuck did this happen!" I screamed. "Get me the fuck home."

I returned my attention to the guy in front of me. He didn't know anything because he was fucking bait. And we fell for it. I pulled out my gun, put it to his skull, and pulled the fucking trigger.

The ride back home was tense. It felt longer than a flight around the world. Nobody spoke.

Once home, I pulled out the surveillance footage. I watched her struggling against Donatella and Giulio. Watched them as they put their hands on *my wife*.

"Fuck!" I bellowed, my fist flying through the air and punching the wall. The stone barely budged, but the pain in my knuckles burned. "Fuuuuuck!"

I couldn't think, the anger so swift and violent it stole my fucking breath away. With a roar, I swiped all the electronics off the desk, pushing them onto the floor where they cracked and smashed to pieces. From the corner of my eye I saw my sons entering the room, but I was too busy flipping the desk over with both hands and hurling the chair across the room. The glass frames shattered.

My eyes landed on the chair where she'd straddled me when I got the call and I lunged for it, throwing it against the door.

I was hell-bent on destroying everything in my path.

The woman I loved was taken. My wife. My love. *My life.*

I shouldn't have left her. I should have protected her. I shoved my hand in my hair, pulling tightly on the strands. I felt like I was coming apart at the seams. I had to get her back, or there'd be nothing but pieces left.

The office door opened and Manuel and I drew our guns. Then I reached for my sons and shoved them behind me.

Konstantin stood at the door with his right-hand man, Boris.

"Where in the *fuck* is my sister?"

Manuel lowered his gun, but I kept mine trained on my bride's brother. I wanted to lash out. Rage. Destroy.

Yet, I knew none of it would ease this pain. Because I was to blame. I had put her on Donatella's radar. I had failed to identify the mole. I had failed her.

Please, Dio mio. Don't take her from me. Please, take me and let her live.

Losing Isla would break me. I knew it. Donatella knew it. The world knew it.

"Papà, is that Isla's brother?" Enzo broke the silence, drawing Konstantin's gaze to him.

The haze slowly began to clear, urging me to think once again. I straightened my cuffs, my hands trembling. The image of my wife mere hours ago in this same office played in my mind.

"*Sì, figlio mio.*"

"Where is my sister?" he repeated.

"She was taken," Manuel answered vaguely.

"Giulio, our guard, is a traitor," Amadeo hissed. "He and—" His words faltered, knowing he could never share that his mother was alive. "He took her."

"He and who?" her brother growled. "Tell me now or I swear to God, I'll burn this fucking place to the ground."

I checked my watch, then flicked a glance to Manuel. "We'll need Kingston. Kian too. Hack into city surveillance. Follow whatever car they arrived in."

Manuel glanced at the smashed laptop and the equipment all over the floor, but to his credit he didn't say anything, he simply called one of our IT guys and had them bring him brand-new gear.

"Enzo, Amadeo," I muttered, rubbing my eyes with my fingers. "You two go into the safe room until we figure out how the enemy gained entry to the grounds."

"But—"

"No buts." I kept my voice firm. "I can't worry about your safety and your mother's."

I froze and so did they. It was the first time I'd called Isla their mother to their face.

"Alright, Papà," Amadeo spoke.

"But if we can help, you'll tell us," Enzo added.

Once I tucked them in the safe room, I returned to the office where Konstantin stood, his expression grim.

"I'm getting my sister out and taking her home. With me."

I let out a deep breath, my blood boiling but not letting it fire me up.

"Konstantin, we've worked together for a long time, and out of respect for those years, I won't kill you." The fact that I needed his help sucked, but I'd do anything to save my wife. "You're not taking my wife away from me," I told him. "But I'll accept your help, and if you bring her back, my empire is yours."

In the underworld, we were only as good as our strength and power, and our honor. He knew I'd keep my word.

"I don't want your empire," he answered. "If Isla wants to stay with you, I'll agree. Now tell me what you need."

I'd get my wife back, even if it started a war.

FIFTY
ISLA

I could hear voices. Distorted. Barely audible. Like I was underwater. Was I at the bottom of the sea?

I darted my tongue over my bottom lip, but the movement took considerable effort. My tongue stuck to the roof of my dry mouth. It was too hard to swallow. My pupils moved behind my eyelids, but I couldn't find the strength to open them.

Blinking my eyes—once, twice—the world finally came into focus. The foggy haze dissipated. I started to register my surroundings. A bare room. A faint light pouring through the window.

My head was pounding. My muscles ached.

I went to move but couldn't, and panic settled in my bones. I started to kick, the chair I was bound to rocking back and forth. The nausea hit hard, making me retch. The noise registered only then, rattling every time I moved. I tried to move again, shackles biting into my wrists.

Taking a deep breath in and lowering my gaze, I attempted to lift my chained arm. I couldn't. I was shackled to the chair, the chains digging into my ribs. The throbbing intensified.

Each whip of my head caused light-headedness.

"Oh goody. Sleeping beauty is awake." I turned my head, my eyes widening when I made out a camera sitting on a tripod behind me. Even worse was the woman behind it.

Donatella.

Fear wrapped around my throat and an acrid taste lingered on my tongue. She planned on recording my death.

"I wouldn't call her a beauty." I startled at the voice coming from my left and my eyes nearly jumped out of my head. That woman from the club... Sofia Volkov... joined in. Her tone was flat, her eyes stone cold. "At least not for long." My head shook violently. What did she mean by that? "Your brother and Marchetti will be destroyed with this one. Two birds with one stone."

Donatella cackled like the lunatic she was; although I started to think her partner wasn't far off. "Told you she'd be worth killing."

Tears pooled at the corners of my eyes. Not for me, but for him. My husband. For Enzo and Amadeo.

I stared between the two madwomen. What was this place? How long was I out?

My breathing picked up and my heart thundered so hard it throbbed. *Thump. Thump. Thump.*

I felt like I was on the verge of passing out. The buzzing in my ears intensified.

I forced my breaths to even out. I needed to think. Keep my wits about me.

"Donatella, you shouldn't do this." I wasn't ready to die. I had so many things to do, to live for. So many things I'd left unsaid with my husband. "Think of your sons."

It was hard to speak. My tongue was heavy and so were my limbs—probably due to the drugs I was sure they'd given me. Not that I could move either way, considering I was chained to the goddamn *chair*.

"Nothing to think about," she said as she casually sauntered over to me, opening the cap from a water bottle and splashing it against my face. "I've always wanted them dead. But now, we'll keep my eldest son alive. Once I kill my husband"—I had to rein in my features, *the stupid bitch didn't even notice that he wasn't her husband*—"we'll take over the Marchetti business and make it into something better."

Jesus, the woman was delusional. And what did she mean "my eldest son"? What was she planning to do with Amadeo? But then I caught myself. She wouldn't have a chance to do anything to either one of them. They weren't her sons. She didn't raise them. All she did was hurt them.

"Donatella, don't tell her too many of our plans," Sofia said in a cold voice. Her cold eyes met mine and she continued, "And to be clear, she means your husband. We'll end him."

I blinked in confusion. That almost sounded as if she knew that Enrico wasn't Enrico?

The former seemed unfazed. "It's not like she's getting out of this alive."

"How do you two know each other?" I breathed, hoping to buy some time. Honestly, I didn't give a fuck how they met or even less how they'd ended up in a relationship.

It was Sofia who answered. "I checked myself into a clinic years ago. Imagine my surprise when I ran into the late Donatella Marchetti."

I rolled my eyes. "Well, at least you knew your marbles were not all there and tried to get yourself some help. Should have stayed there, really."

One second I was glaring at her and the next my head whipped back, my cheek exploding in pain. I swore I saw stars for the second time that night—night? Week? I had no idea. I registered a metallic taste flooding my mouth. For an old woman, she was surprisingly strong.

I had to get out of here. If there was a way to go, it couldn't be with two fucking lunatics in a cold, dark room.

Ignoring Sofia, I returned my attention to her weaker half. "Why are you doing this, Donatella?" Her gaze made me feel sick to my stomach. "This bitch is just using you. You're blind if you can't see that."

She lunged at me, her hand connecting with my cheek again. The chains rattled and my head whipped to the side.

"Because the Marchettis stole from my family," she screeched like the madwoman she was.

"Stole what?" I asked, my lip throbbing and warm liquid trickling down my chin. *Blood.* "And what does that have to do with me?"

She stood in front of me, the whiff of her strong perfume making me nauseous. "They stole my family's business." I scrunched my eyebrows. Her explanation made no sense. The Marchettis' businesses had been around for a long time. "Five generations ago."

"Five generations," I repeated dumbfoundedly. "How?"

"They stole my family's business fifty years ago. Brothels. Drugs. All of it. We'd thrived. We were the most powerful family in Europe. But then the Marchettis pushed us out, like the sneaky, backstabbing assholes they were and still are. They stole our businesses and forced my family line to work for them. Five Italian families at the table now and not one of them ours. It's a disgrace."

I blinked. "Fifty years ago?"

"Haven't you been listening?" she screamed, and I reeled back. Except, there was nowhere to go.

"Your family has been holding a grudge for fifty years," I said, the concept sounding ludicrous. Maybe her whole family was crazy. "Don't you think it's time to let it go?"

"Giulio and I are owed a seat at the table."

"What table?" She waved her hand like I was too dumb to understand. "What fucking table?" I hissed.

"The Omertà's table."

People were really obsessed with power. "And what would you do once at that table?" I questioned.

That must have caught her by surprise, because her eyes darted to Sofia. I couldn't hold my scoff back as realization dawned on me. It was Sofia Volkov who was orchestrating it all.

"Donatella's family suffered," Sofia declared, her voice so fucking annoying. I sincerely doubted she cared about Donatella or her family. "Killing every woman who wed into the family wasn't enough. We'll take their entire empire from them, and Donatella's son will help us."

Fury swarmed me, suffocating me. I kicked against my restraints, the chair lifting off the ground only to drop again. "You won't touch Enzo. He'll never fucking listen to you. He hates your crazy fucking ass. For everything you have done to him and Amadeo."

That earned me another slap across my cheek. Then a punch.

Sofia's heels clicked on the concrete floor as she made her way over. She moved like a snake, her dead eyes freezing my soul.

She glanced over her shoulder. "Giulio, turn the camera on."

Click.

Sofia produced a knife—a butcher knife—and handed it to Donatella. An unhealthy, dark glimmer shone in both of their eyes and suddenly fear gripped my throat, choking me. With a flat glare, Sofia watched as Donatella sliced through my skin. My shoulder burned as hot blood trickled down.

I bit my lip, refusing to let her hear my cries. I refused to give her any sound at all.

Another gash followed. The blade dragged across my shoulders. Down my bicep. She had to feel my birth control implant there. Her blade stilled over it, her eyes lighting up with unhealthy excitement.

"What did you find?" Sofia asked, her voice sending chills to my soul.

"Little slut has a birth control implant." Donatella pushed the blade into my flesh, and I bit into my lip. *Slash. Slash.* "If only her mother was that smart. It's probably why Illias shot her."

The back of my eyes burned. My breaths came out choppy and hot liquid soon covered my entire arm.

"Want to see the video?" Sofia asked casually as if she were offering me choices of blockbusters. "Tatiana's ex-husband shared a few recordings with me. I learned something interesting from every one of those videos."

"Fuck. You." I wouldn't play into her hand. She could go to hell and rot there.

She chuckled. "What? Don't you want to know who your husband really is?" I pressed my lips together, refusing to answer. The lump in my throat grew. "But then, I can tell by the expression on your face you already know." And so did Sofia. She knew my husband's secret. She turned to Donatella. "Slice her up."

Then the pain started. It dragged on and on, and I found a corner in my mind to retreat to.

I wouldn't cry. I wouldn't cry. I refused to fucking cry.

FIFTY-ONE
ENRICO

Two fucking days.

I hadn't eaten. I hadn't showered. I hadn't even slept. Time dragged on, and my heart shattered each time it beat without her.

My mind kept envisioning every scenario. What they were doing to her. Would they break her spirit? Her mind? Her strength that I loved so much?

"The underground tunnels," Manuel said, drawing Illias's, Kian's, and my attention. "That's how they snuck into the house undetected."

The dining room had been turned into a surveillance room. My office wasn't big enough and we had been scouting the city inch by inch for any sign where Donatella might be hiding her.

I stood up from my chair, the legs of it scraping against the hardwood.

"Impossible."

Manuel handed me the footage and I watched, holding my breath. It clawed at my chest, demanding I punish someone, anyone. Kingston was here too, hacking all the networks around Italy. I needed him to find Isla.

Just as Manuel claimed, Donatella and Giulio had snuck into the house via underground tunnels that only the Marchetti men knew about. *Unless my brother shared it with Donatella*. He wouldn't have been so stupid. Would he have?

"I want that tunnel filled," I barked.

Manuel issued the order as my own phone vibrated in my hand. *Unknown number*. I stopped breathing, the dread in the pit of my stomach expanding.

I slid the message open and my heart stopped. I fucking froze.

My wife was chained to a chair, her body bruised and bloodied. Tears streamed down her face as Donatella sliced her, laughing at the camera with each slash she bestowed. The terror in Isla's gaze gutted me, but she didn't let out a sound.

Her lip was split open.

"Where in the fuck are they?" I roared. "It shouldn't be this hard to track them down. I want Giulio's and Donatella's heads on spikes." My hands trembled, my eyes locked on the frozen screen showing my wife's bloodied state. "We need to find her."

Konstantin snatched the phone from my grip. His jaw clenched as he watched the video, Kian's dark expression not far off.

"I've got something," Kingston announced.

I was in his face in the blink of an eye. It wasn't smart. Kingston hated anyone too close to him, but I was too much of a fucking mess to worry about his feelings.

"What? Where?"

He pointed to the computer monitor. "Here."

I stared at the blinking red dot. "That's one of my warehouses."

"That's the source of the message you just got." He zoomed in, the image turning to a live feed and small red dots moving around the building. "That's a heat sensor. There are bodies in it. Unless they're your men."

"I'm going."

Manuel's hand came to my shoulder. "No. If you go in there, you could be walking into a trap."

I shook his hand off. "I don't give a shit. I'm going."

Konstantin spoke next. "We do this right, or you might end up dead. Then my wife and Isla will have my balls." I was too tired to ask what in the fuck that meant. "We have to coordinate."

I shoved my hands in my hair for what felt like the hundredth time. I was surprised there was anything left on my scalp. All I knew was that I was falling apart. I had to get her back. I had to rip Donatella's skin from her bones. Cut Giulio up piece by piece and feed them to the fucking sharks while he watched until there was nothing left of him.

I took a deep breath in and exhaled. "Okay, let's coordinate."

Manuel shared a look with Kingston before returning his gaze to me and Konstantin. "*Nipote*. Konstantin." The pitying look he gave me set my teeth on edge. "You have to prepare for the worst. She—"

"She'll make it," I roared. "She's strong."

The sheer terror at the thought of any other possibility caused my heart to stop beating.

The ride from my compound to the warehouse in Rome was too long. I wanted to use helicopters, but they'd hear us coming from miles away, so we had them on standby in case we needed them. The images from the video kept playing in my mind. In that state, she wouldn't be able to run.

I shook my head. I couldn't think about that. I needed to get my head straight and in the game so I could get my wife out. I needed her alive. The minutes passed agonizingly slowly.

My stomach was in knots. My brain was on an endless loop of what-ifs. I was terrified of the possibility of not getting to Isla in time.

"Almost there," Konstantin said, and I finally focused back on the road ahead of us.

"We are a few miles outside the radius," Kian added, studying the satellite map on his screen. He hadn't said much since he arrived, but I knew he was reliving the loss of his sister. Except, I couldn't find the words to comfort him. Instead, I was in my own hell, fighting off my own nightmare.

There wasn't a highway around. We were on a deserted side road. The car slowed to a stop and the engine shut off.

"We get out here and go the rest of the way on foot," Manuel stated.

We all got out and then we moved in. It took us fifteen minutes on foot to make our way through the trees that surrounded my warehouse. This place was isolated for the sole purpose of smuggling my shipments. Never in a million years would I have thought it'd be used to bring my wife here. To torture her.

Silently, we accessed the location. Kingston, who was still at my castello, was watching over my sons while guiding us via satellite. We could have gone in guns blazing, but then we would have risked casualties, Isla included. Instead, we scoped out the location, and once it was clear, I nodded.

It was time. "How are we getting in?" Konstantin asked.

I held up a grenade. *Blow the door, storm the building.* "On three."

And then it began.

FIFTY-TWO
ISLA

My pajamas were soaked in blood, stuck to my skin. It was mostly dry, but each movement still caused immeasurable pain.

I felt dizzy. I hadn't eaten anything in days. I couldn't remember the last time I had a drop of water. My lips were chapped. Every inch of me ached. My mind drifted more than once, unable to cope anymore.

Not with the videos of my brother executing my mother. Not with my husband shoving his dead brother into the car and setting it on fire. Thankfully, Donatella never realized it was the older brother, the real Enrico Marchetti, who was burned to ash. But Sofia knew. She didn't explicitly say it, but she definitely knew it.

"Your sister-in-law interfered with my plans," Sofia deadpanned in a cold voice. "Now you'll pay for it."

I had to keep them talking. I knew my husband and brother would come for me. I just had to hang on a bit longer.

"How did Enrico miss the connection between you and Giulio?" I asked Donatella. If I knew my husband, he would have been very thorough researching his bodyguard.

She cackled. "Giulio is four times removed from an illegitimate daughter from one of my great-great-great-uncles. The only reason he survived is because nobody knew about his mother." She glared at me. "The Marchetti family all but ended our bloodline," she snarled.

"And yet, here you are," I remarked dryly, tasting blood on my tongue. "Unfortunately."

"We're like weeds. Strong and indestructible." The comparison was lousy. All you needed was some weed killer.

"I'll be sure to get some Roundup," I muttered under my breath, feeling lightheaded.

The look in her eyes told me she didn't know what that was, but I was too busy holding on to consciousness. But then someone's phone buzzed, and the next moment, Sofia muttered something to her partner and headed for the door.

"Where are you going?" Donatella demanded to know, her voice high-pitched. It sounded to me like she'd grown dependent on the woman. *Pathetic*.

"Just outside," Sofia answered without looking back. "Handle her."

And she was gone, her heels clicking against the marble. *Click. Click. Click.*

"I n-need to use the bathroom," I rasped. They'd let me use a bucket a few times, but I doubted I'd be allowed now. I could tell Donatella was skittish here by herself.

"Piss yourself."

That fucking bitch. I wanted to lunge at her and claw her eyeballs out of her skull. "I—I have to take a shit."

She let out a string of curses in Italian, then walked over to the table and snatched the keys to my chains. She unlocked them and they fell onto the concrete with a rattle I felt in my teeth.

"Giulio, take her to the bathroom. She stinks like a pig."

I gritted my teeth, swallowing the words I wanted to spit out. Giulio yanked me off the seat and I heard a pop in my shoulder. Pain shot through me, darkening my vision until I thought I'd pass out.

He dragged me into the bare, dirty bathroom and shoved me inside. "Two minutes."

My knees hit the concrete floor, and I racked my brain trying to think of a plan. I didn't have to use the bathroom, obviously. Idiots would have known that, since I hadn't been fed anything in days.

My gaze traveled over the concrete bathroom, looking for anything I could use as a weapon. Anything I could use to fight back. I couldn't let them shackle me again.

I rose to my feet, my legs quivering. I felt weak, exhausted, and knew there wasn't much more my body could take. I gripped the yellowish counter as I pulled myself up.

Desperately, I searched through the items. Soap. Toilet paper. Broken glass.

"Broken glass," I whispered soundlessly.

I snatched it, gripping it in my palm and feeling warm liquid already beginning to drip. I ignored the pain as I made my way to the door on wobbly legs; my bare feet bloodied and silent against the concrete floor. The bathroom door was left cracked open, and I peeked through. Giulio and Donatella were replaying the video of me being tortured and laughing. Fucking laughing.

Rage had me seeing red, strengthening my resolve.

I lunged, the tip of the broken glass piercing through Donatella's eyeball. I tackled her onto the floor, stabbing her over and over again. Giulio tried to yank me away from her, but it was too late. I'd taken both of her eyes. Her blood soaked my palms as her howls echoed. Her face was unrecognizable, a pulpy mess where her eyes once were. The adrenaline pumping through my veins was what spurred my attack. After hours, weeks, and days of her stalking and tormenting me, relief ejected from me like a geyser.

Suddenly, I was lifted off Donatella's butchered body. I tried to wrestle myself free, kicking and screaming, but my strength was faltering.

My back hit the cold, dirty floor and stole my breath. The shredding sound of my bloodied clothes filled the room. It ripped at my skin, my cuts burning. *Oh God, was he going to rape me on top of everything else they'd done to me?*

I screamed as an explosion sounded somewhere, but I didn't know whether it meant something better or worse was coming.

The door swung open, but before I could see what new nightmare was coming, Giulio gripped my hair and yanked my head up only to slam it against the concrete.

And I was pulled into the darkness.

FIFTY-THREE
MANUEL

Bang.

And then silence. Such deafening silence that told you nothing would ever be the same.

Enrico's bullet pierced through Giulio's skull. But that wasn't what had all of us frozen in our footsteps.

It was Isla's small, battered body on the ground, next to the body of a mutilated Donatella. My blood ran cold at the sight. Isla's bloodied clothes were ripped, sitting on the dirty ground. Dozens of horrible wounds marred her flesh, some crusted over, others weeping. Blood pooled around her. I couldn't find a piece of skin that wasn't affected.

Enrico found himself on his knees, cradling her broken body to his chest. His pained howl shredded my soul. It was the reason I'd never wanted to wed. I would never want to leave myself vulnerable to love.

I watched my nephew break before my eyes.

I had never seen him like this. Not when his brother died. Not when his mother died. And not when his father died.

Yet now, I watched him shatter into a thousand pieces.

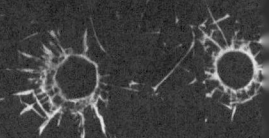

He was the boss of the Marchetti family. He changed the rules of the Omertà, made every family equal, but it was he who started changing the organization with his vision. He was ruthless, but he was always fair.

In my entire life, I had never seen my nephew cry. But right now, he cried as he held his wife in his arms. He rocked her back and forth, his arms tight around her.

I stood frozen, just a few feet away from them. My eyes shifted to Isla and my chest tightened painfully. She looked so weak, so small.

Illias rushed past me, falling down to his knees by his sister. "Isla," he croaked. "Oh my fucking God. Isla, open your eyes." All the while, Enrico kept rocking her, holding her tightly. "Enrico, give her to me."

"Get away from my wife," he hissed, refusing to move.

"Nephew," I called out to him. We could be ambushed at any minute. Boris, Illias's right-hand man, and Kian were searching for signs of Sofia. How that bitch always managed to slither her way out, I had no idea. "We have to go."

Illias shed his jacket, then wrapped it around his sister's bruised body as much as he could with Enrico in the way. A soft, pained whimper sounded, but her eyes never opened.

"Enrico, we need to get her to the hospital," Illias said, his fingers trembling as he leaned forward, moving her hair away from her face. Jesus Christ, what did they do to her? My stomach clenched at the sight as her brother placed his finger on the side of her neck. He let out a shuddering breath and raised his head. Tears glistened in his eyes. "Her pulse is steady but slow." His hand tightened on Enrico's shoulder. There was only one way to snap him out of his daze.

"Enrico, she'll live, but we have to get her to the hospital. Now," I said quietly.

Kian returned at that moment. "No sign of Sofia. We have to get going. A chopper is waiting to take Isla."

Enrico's head snapped up, his eyes meeting mine. My heart might have stopped for a second at the feral look in them. I remembered the day of his brother's funeral. He'd stood emotionless, knowing his life had changed forever. Overnight, he became his brother. He became a father. He became the head of the Italian mafia. He'd been able to bear the unimaginable.

Yet now, I feared he'd be truly lost if Isla didn't make it. I could feel his pain deep in my soul as if it were my own.

"Isla is not safe here," Illias muttered quietly.

That finally got Enrico moving. A collective sigh filled the space. My nephew shifted Isla in his arms and slowly rose to his feet. He kept her pressed against his chest, her usually vibrant red hair matted and dull. Bloodied. Illias stood up too.

Enrico looked down at his wife again and his expression softened. "I... I can't lose her," he choked, pulling her fragile body into his chest.

"You won't," I rasped.

"Isla is strong. She's always been a survivor ever since—" Illias's voice cracked and he swallowed hard. "Our priority is to get her to safety."

Taking a deep breath, Enrico nodded and his fingers brushed softly against her cheek. He handled her with a gentleness that I had never thought him capable of.

"Let's go," he said. Illias and I nodded and quickly started our way out of there.

"I'll go ahead and ensure the coast is clear," Illias said, pulling out the gun from his holster. "Manuel, you take his back."

"I got him."

With Enrico and Isla between us, we made our way out of the warehouse. It wasn't until we climbed in the helicopter and were lifted into the air that we all released a heavy breath. Enrico sat in the back seat with Isla on his lap. He kept the jacket protectively around her. Illias and I sat opposite him.

My eyes flicked to my nephew who was more like a brother to me, seeing him push his wife's hair off her forehead with trembling fingers.

"She's going to be okay," Illias said through my headset, glancing at his sister, his fists clenching by his side.

I hoped he was right.

She kept Enrico sane. She gave him a reason to carry on.

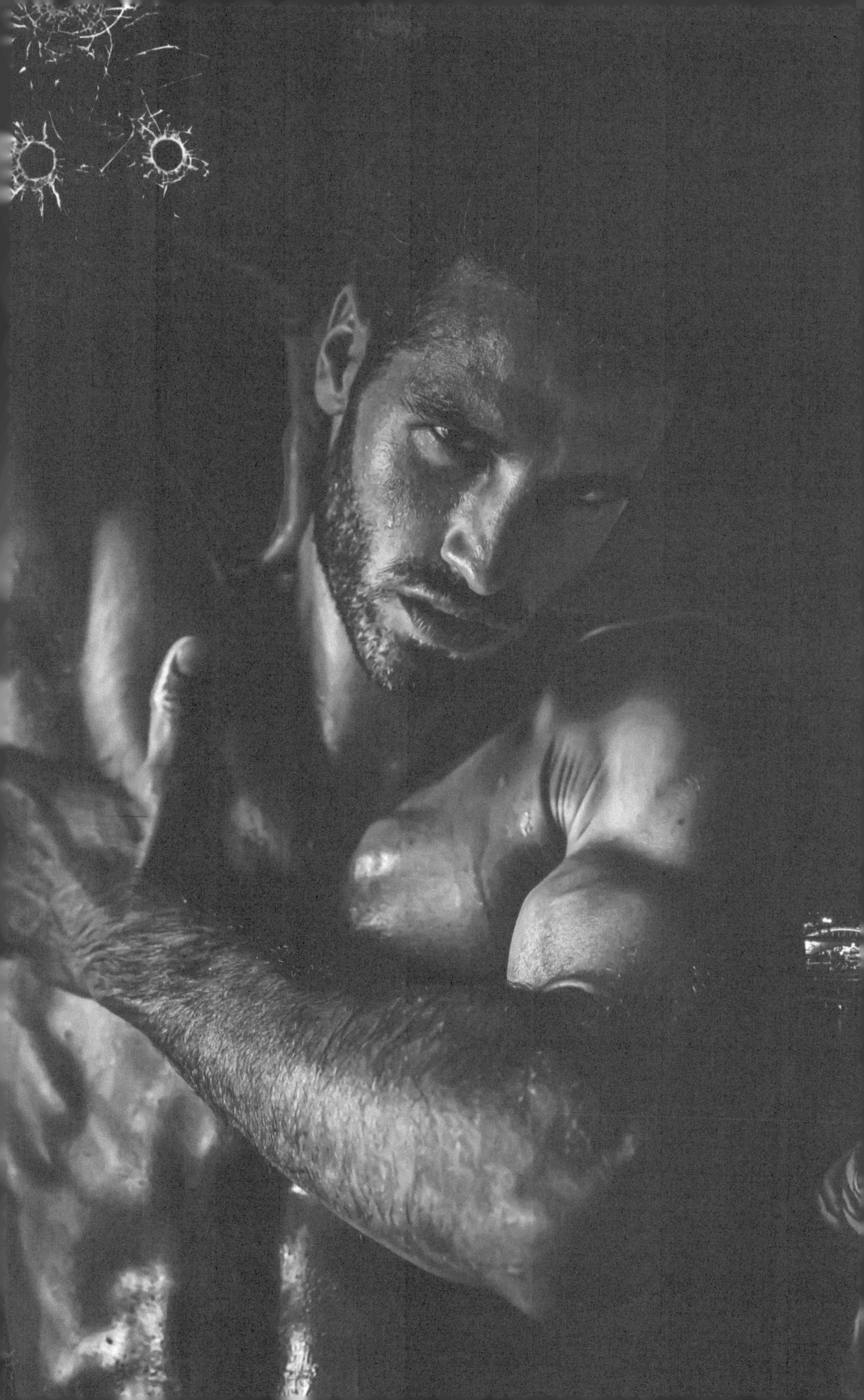

FIFTY-FOUR
ENRICO

It had been a whole day. I'd brought the hospital to my home; I didn't trust anyone to watch over her. I wouldn't let her out of my sight.

My knees were weak, my soul even weaker. Everything about the past few days had me reeling, giving me déjà vu of my mother's death. Of when she'd taken her last breath.

I refused to let my wife take her last breath. Not before I took my own.

Anger suffocated me—at the traitor, at destiny… at the world. But I shoved it somewhere deep. I couldn't let myself spiral out of control. I needed to be here for Isla. I needed to take care of her.

The doctor indicated a mild concussion. He'd run a myriad of scans to ensure she didn't have any internal bleeding. She was clear, but her body was battered. Her flesh was riddled with cuts, all of which had to be scrubbed clean to ensure no infection formed. I didn't know how she pulled through, but she did. Illias was right. My wife was fucking strong.

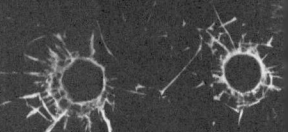

A pained whimper sounded, and I jumped up from my chair and closed the small distance between us. I cradled her in my arms, probably smothering her, but I couldn't help it. I needed to comfort her as much as I needed her comfort. And her breathing, her chest rising against mine, was the only thing that mattered.

Her body spasmed, fresh blood dribbling down the corner of her lip from where she'd bitten down hard to stifle her screams. I'd seen the videos, and they turned my blood to ice. A weaker man might have broken. But not my Isla. She refused to give them her voice. Her screams. It was probably why they hadn't moved to the next step of torture. Donatella had a fucking fascination with screams. She was determined to get a rise out of my wife, but she didn't know Isla the way I did.

"It's okay, *piccolina*," I whispered, my voice shaking. "I'm here. Just hang on to me."

It seemed to work when I talked to her. So I kept whispering plans for our future. For our family. For travels we'd do together. Anything and fucking everything. I was a goddamn sap.

The door opened with a soft rustle behind me, and I didn't need to turn around to know it was either Illias or Kian. Manuel couldn't stomach seeing Isla, nor me, like this. Enzo and Amadeo only came when they knew no one would be here but me.

"How is she?" Kian broke the silence that stretched next to the *beep, beep, beep*ing of the machine. The doctor kept trying to convince me Isla's heart was strong. That she would make it.

"No change." The voice wasn't my own. Fuck, my body and thoughts weren't my own. It was as if they drifted, right along with Isla somewhere in this universe, refusing to wake up.

"You should take a shower." Illias spoke. "When she wakes up, she'll need your strength."

"Fuck off, Konstantin." If he thought I'd leave her even for a minute, he was crazy.

His hand came up to my shoulder, squeezing. "Trust me, Marchetti. She'll not want to see you like this. The bathroom is right there. Take a quick shower. Fuck, leave the door open if you must. Kian and I will watch over her."

"She won't be moved," Kian said, his voice somber. "I give you my word. And if she stirs, we'll fetch you."

That was what finally got me moving. When I found my reflection in the mirror, I realized why they insisted on a shower. Blood still stained my clothes. My stubble was turning into a full beard.

Turning on the shower, I quickly shed my clothes and jumped in it. I was washing off the soap when the bathroom door swung open.

"Fuck, Marchetti, get your ass in here."

It took me two seconds to wrap a towel around me and get to Isla's bedside. She was convulsing on the bed, whimpering. The white bandages on her arms started to turn red. Kian and her brother tried to hold her still, but the more they tried, the worse she shook.

Shoving them out of the way, I took her small body and cradled her.

"*Piccolina*," I murmured, pulling her closer to my chest. She instantly stilled. When she turned her head and pressed her face to my chest, I thought I heard my heart crack. "It's okay. You're safe."

"Is it you?" They were the first words she had spoken since the rescue. Her voice was raspy.

"It's me," I confirmed, my voice coming out strangled. "Sleep and get better."

"Don't leave."

Tears stung my eyes. My fingers trembled as I pushed her ginger curls away from her forehead.

"Never. I'm never leaving you."

A week had gone by.

We were lyng in our bed, in our bedroom, fresh from a shower, our bodies still damp from it. She didn't seem to mind and I certainly didn't. It wrapped me up into her scent like a cocoon, making me feel alive again. Except, she kept hiding her body from me, wearing baggy clothes that covered most of her skin.

She was slowly coming back to herself. To me. She smelled like my woman. Like coconuts and the beach. Except for the ghosts that seemed to lurk in her expression whenever I caught her lost in thought.

The waves crashed against the shoreline and seagulls squawked over the horizon, the sound finally lulling her to sleep, her mouth pressed in a thin line and her head against my chest. My strong, beautiful wife.

I could see her renewed strength in the color of her cheeks. In the fading of her bruises. In the healing of her cuts. But her mind still suffered. She had nightmares. She clung to me as she fought her demons, and it gutted me that I failed her at that too. I wanted to keep her safe from the darkness in this world. Yet I felt helpless as she thrashed in my arms.

All I could do was whisper soft words to her. Anything to help ease her fears.

A soft knock rang out before the door opened. My sons' dark heads appeared, and I motioned them in. They visited Isla every day. Sometimes they'd catch her awake and other times, like now, she was asleep.

"Is she better, Papà?" Enzo's voice was full of anguish. He felt like he'd failed her. He blamed himself for not waiting for her to make it to the safe room.

"She is," I told him softly. "She asked about you two earlier."

Amadeo's eyes lit up. "*Davvero?*"

I nodded. "Sì."

"She doesn't hate us?" Amadeo asked, the vulnerable expression on his face matching his voice.

I opened my mouth to answer when Isla's soft voice responded instead. "Never. I could *never* hate you."

All three of us looked down at her, her cheek pressed against my chest. She shifted and I hurried to help her, hating seeing any sign of pain on her face.

"Thanks," she murmured, giving me a smile that could bring me to my knees.

"Of course, *amore*."

Her eyes found Enzo and Amadeo, her small hand—still slightly bruised—reaching for them. Both of them took care not to hurt her.

"We left you to them. You must hate us."

She shook her head.

"I will never hate you," she repeated, her voice surprisingly firm considering her state. "You did exactly what I told you to do and that made me so proud. If they'd gotten you too, I wouldn't have made it."

"But—" Enzo's face twisted with agony. Forever the protector. Both of my boys were.

"But nothing," she scolded him softly. "You listened. That's all a mother can ask for."

All of us froze, and I watched my sons' necks bob and their dark eyes glimmer with tears they tried so hard to hold back.

"You still want to be our mother?" Amadeo whispered, his lip trembling slightly. "Even though Donatella hurt you?"

Isla's eyes narrowed on him, but her lips curved into a soft smile. "I am your mother and you are my boys. I don't care that she gave you life. It takes a lot more than that to be a mother." Amadeo wiped his face with the back of his hand, desperate to hide his tears. "Now give me a hug or you'll see what a mad Russian-American-Italian does."

She patted a spot next to us and our sons didn't hesitate. My wife would forever have the Marchetti men wrapped around her finger.

"Thank you," I mouthed.

"*Siempre.*" I didn't bother correcting her that she'd reverted to Spanish. All that mattered was that she was coming back. To all of us.

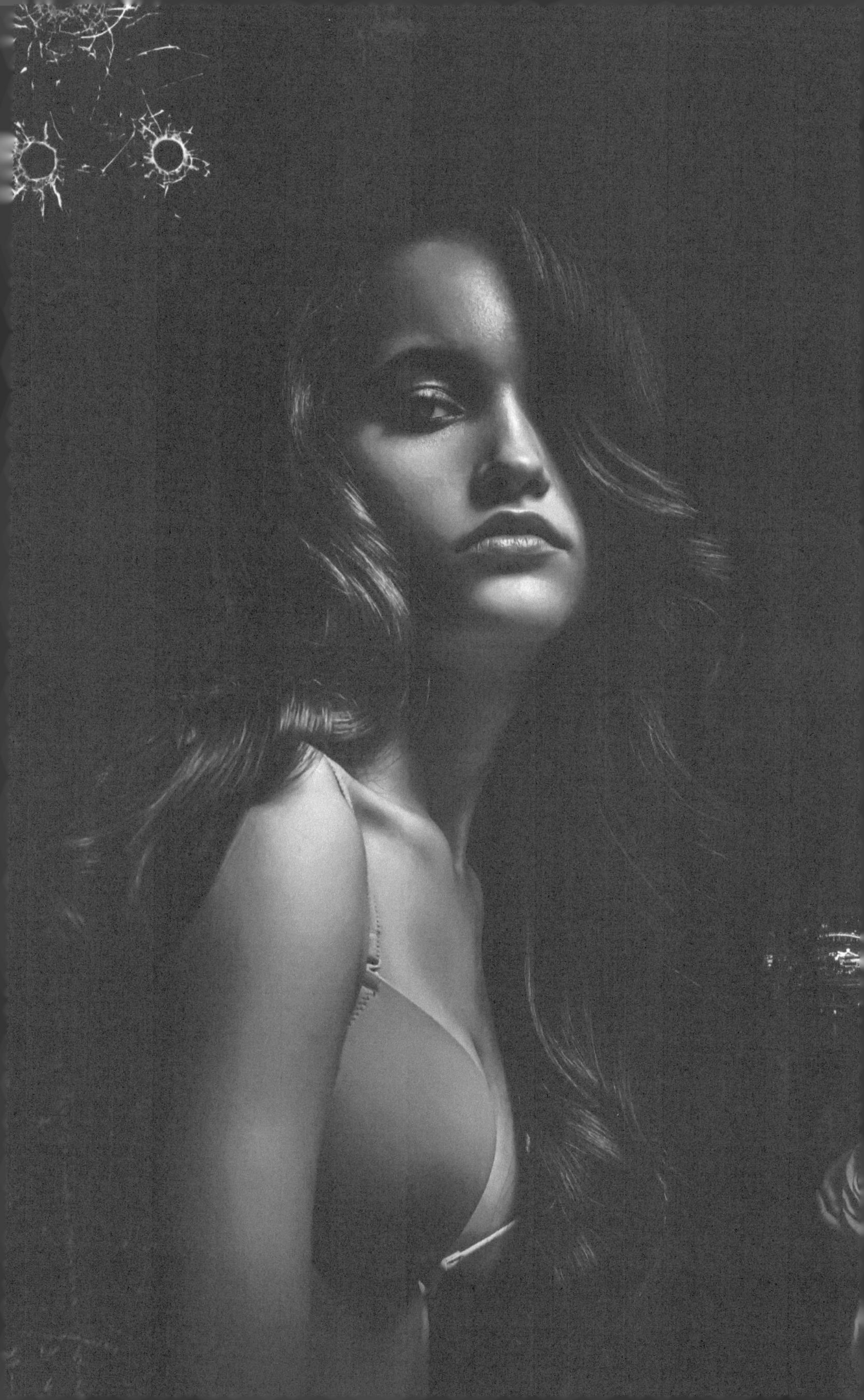

FIFTY-FIVE
ISLA

Two weeks had gone by, and each time the doctor came to visit, Enrico hovered. He refused to leave as the doctor examined me. He was making the poor man nervous, but he didn't seem to care. The doctor slipped on a pair of latex gloves and started poking and prodding. When he came to my bicep, his brow furrowed.

"Is everything okay?" Enrico asked, the alert in his voice making the doctor jump.

"It's healing properly," the doc answered vaguely.

"But?"

His bushy eyebrows and concerned gaze met mine. "An implant won't be possible anymore. Not here."

"Oh."

Enrico's spine went rigid but he remained quiet. "Do you need to be—"

The doctor struggled with words, his face turning deathly pale. Then it hit me. He thought I'd been raped.

"Nobody touched me," I murmured. "Not that way."

"*Bene*." The doctor wiped his forehead with a shaking hand. "If you need birth control, let me know."

I swallowed and shook my head. The thought of feeling a surgical knife or anything shoved into me had me reeling. There was a shot or pills I could take instead, but I hadn't forgotten about the conversation with Enrico.

When Donatella is dead.

The bitch was dead. It wasn't that I wanted to start working on getting pregnant. I had other more important things to worry about. Like moving on. Getting my head screwed on straight. Extinguishing the nightmares that plagued me.

Once the doctor was gone, I turned to look at Enrico. There was one person that I had avoided talking to. One family member who lingered, waiting for me to be ready, and he was there from the beginning.

I slowly shifted out of the bed, the cuts on my body still hurting. I had yet to find the courage to look at myself in the mirror. I'd take it slowly. One step at a time.

I made my way to the large window where the breathtaking view stretched for miles, but my gaze was locked on the tall dark form with the blonde woman. My brother and Tatiana.

"Enrico?"

"Yes, *amore*."

I turned to look at the man who'd pulled me out of the darkness every single day in the past weeks. It was his voice, his scent that kept me holding on to the light. Yes, I hated that bitch Donatella, but I didn't want to be consumed by it. I wanted to move on.

"It was Donatella's family," I said weakly. "They were killing the Marchettis' wives. For revenge. Your family—our family—isn't cursed."

Surprise flashed in his eyes. "How do you know?"

"Donatella admitted to it," I rasped. "I'm not even sure if she was as crazy as much as she was consumed by revenge. Mad with it." I inhaled a deep breath, then continued, "And I think Sofia knows or suspects your true identity. I didn't confirm it," I murmured, shaking my head. "I didn't tell her anything."

His forehead came to rest against mine. "Donatella's gone now.

Don't worry about Sofia. We'll catch her, and then she'll pay for her sins. I just want you and our family safe."

I let out a sigh. I couldn't agree more, but our family included my brother, and it was high time I cleared those waters.

"I want to talk to my brother," I murmured. "Alone." His shoulders tensed. He knew it was impossible for him to stay glued to my side. Manuel had visited me. He looked like shit. He needed help—needed Enrico back—but he didn't want to ask that of my husband, knowing he'd sacrificed a lot already. "You could check on Manuel."

Enrico lifted his head. "He's fine."

"I know, but he needs your help. Maybe Enzo can help with some of it too." He tilted his head pensively. "I can help too. I have more than plenty of time on my hands."

He shook his head. "You and the mafia don't go hand in hand."

I rolled my eyes. "That's kind of sexist," I protested. Although in my case I didn't disagree. "But I meant I could help with your legitimate businesses. Your fashion houses. After all, I know an up-and-coming fashion designer," I said, reminding him of Reina.

"You don't say," he muttered. "She and your friends just about blew up my phone."

"Sorry." They'd been blowing up my phone, too, and it was a good distraction. I assured them I was fine—physically and mentally—and I was safe now. Of course, my girls being my girls made sure to insist I got better so I could give them a rundown of the freaky shit I was doing with my husband. While I had nothing to report yet, I knew we'd get back to our physical connection soon. It was too soon though, and I wasn't ready to see my body, let alone have Enrico see it.

My husband crossed the room in five long strides and pulled me into a hug, pressing his lips on my forehead. "Don't be. I like that they care about you. We'll have them over in a few weeks and you girls can use my yacht. Sì?"

I smiled. "That'll be nice. At least we don't have to steal the yacht."

He chuckled. "The boys told me they'd help you. Somehow I'm not surprised."

"They know who runs this show."

His eyes darted over my head. "You are my show, Isla. My world. Without you, all of this would be a burden. With you, it's a life worth living."

Twenty minutes later, the door opened and my brother entered the room like a force of nature.

The look on his face when he'd executed my mother in the video that Donatella had made me watch—over and over again—haunted me. It wasn't cruel or ruthless. It was full of anguish. Pain.

"You look better, sestra."

He didn't approach and something about the guarded expression in his eyes tore at me. I loved him. I didn't know what had made him kill my mother, but I knew he loved me. He cared about me.

"You look tired," I murmured. "Is Tatiana's pregnancy exhausting you or is it me?"

He pushed his hand through his dark hair. "Both."

I smiled, taking a seat next to the window. "Will you sit?"

"Is it okay if I come closer to you?"

"Always." My voice cracked. He was across the room in the blink of an eye. "Illias, I don't want us to drift apart."

"But?"

"But as your sister, I need to know why. I need to know how you can be so sure we are siblings." My fingers twisted together in my lap. "If my mother was—" I was still unable to say the word. "I need answers. I don't want you to shield me from anything you think I can't handle. I want it all. Good, bad, sad, happy."

He took my hands into his big ones and held them in his warm palms. "I can't help it. My first instinct is to protect you."

I let out a sardonic breath. "Try, please."

He nodded. "I will, but no promises. I don't like to see you hurt."

He'd have to get used to it. I had a feeling life in the underworld was full of pain, but as long as I had my family, I'd be able to bear it all.

"Tell me about my mother," I murmured. "How do you know we're siblings if she was—"

God, I couldn't say the word. I couldn't even think it.

"Simple," he answered, still gripping my hands. "I don't care if you're my biological sister or not. You are my family. It didn't matter to me. You were born under my roof. I helped your mother during her pregnancy and during labor. You *are* my sister and nobody will ever take that from us, so help me God. Certainly not any fucking DNA."

I wouldn't have understood that a month or two ago. But now I did. Only because of Enrico and the boys.

"Fair enough," I murmured, surprising him judging by his expression. "And why... why did you kill her?"

That same expression I saw in the video flashed in his dark eyes before he quickly masked it. "That I cannot tell you."

"Cannot or will not?"

"Isla—"

"No, Illias," I protested, yanking my hands from him. "I need to know."

"Please don't ask it of me. Every fiber of me screams to protect you, and you're asking me to hurt you."

My shoulders slumped. I suspected it. I feared it even. I didn't want to think about it, yet how could I not, when the evidence was right in front of me?

"She didn't want me," I muttered, resigned. "D-did she try to kill me?" He didn't have to say anything. The answer was written all over his face. But the tiny flicker of hope refused to be extinguished. I needed to hear those words spoken out loud. "Please, Illias. Tell me everything. My mind is conjuring the worst possible scenarios."

He squeezed my fingers tightly. It was evidence of his own discomfort. "I'll tell you everything and anything else, but I cannot tell you this." My gut twisted. "Just know that if her circumstances had been different, she would have loved you. She was battered, tortured, and went through who knows what before Father brought her home. She wasn't in the right frame of mind. Not for herself and not for you."

"What happened to Father?" I asked softly, pausing the topic of my mother. My mind was racing left and right, wanting to know how it was all connected. "He killed your mom."

A dark expression passed my brother's face. "I killed him." Somehow it didn't surprise me. "He was about to hurt your mother again and I'd had enough. She was pregnant with you, and something about that made me snap. I couldn't allow him to rape her anymore. So I ended him."

I let out a heavy sigh. There were so many secrets in our family. "He didn't care whether I lived or died," I murmured.

"Maybe, but your mother would have if she hadn't been so mentally and physically abused. I could see it in her eyes. In your eyes. She would have loved you if life hadn't beaten her so badly."

Would have, but didn't. "Who named me?" I heard myself ask. Mothers that love their children name them. Enrico named Amadeo when he was born because Donatella refused to acknowledge him.

A heartbeat of silence. Judging by the dark expression on his face, he was about to lie to me, but then decided against it. "I did. I held you when you were born. I saw your first smile. Your first steps. Your first tooth. You are as much my child as you are my baby sister. I might not have given you life, but I raised you."

"You're wrong, Illias," I croaked. Illias's gaze found mine. "You did give me life."

My mother wouldn't have burned down the world for me. She would have burned the world down with me in it. It turned out the answer hurt worse than I could have imagined. Her life was cut short, but somewhere deep down I knew she would have loved me if she had been given the chance. Just like Illias said.

Then Tatiana's words flitted to my mind. She had found a reason to move on and so would I.

My family. My girlfriends. My husband. Those were my reasons.

FIFTY-SIX
ISLA

Four Weeks Later

I woke up cradled against a warm chest, strong arms wrapped tightly around me.

Blinking hard against the sunlight, I listened to my husband's heartbeat and found comfort in it. He made me feel safe, cherished, and loved. Despite the fact that I'd been keeping him at arm's length, not yet ready to be intimate with him.

He'd just hold me at night and whisper words in Italian that soothed.

Inhaling his scent into my lungs, I stirred softly. Careful not to wake him, I shifted away from him and off the bed. For a moment, I lingered by the bedpost, watching him sleep. His chest was bare, his olive skin beautiful and untainted. Even while he slept, he was a force of a man. His brows furrowed, almost as if he worried even in his sleep.

Keeping my footsteps soft, I made my way into the bathroom. He needed as much rest as he could get. He'd stayed awake so many nights, taking care of me.

I entered the luxurious bathroom, the Italian tile cool under my feet. The room was bright from the floor-to-ceiling window framing the sea. The beauty of it didn't move me. It only taunted.

The large shower still had Enrico's discarded clothes from earlier—or was it yesterday—when he helped me bathe. He'd been so patient, so understanding.

Maybe he didn't want me anymore. I wouldn't want *me* anymore.

I caught my reflection in the mirror for the first time since the rescue. I had avoided mirrors for weeks, unwilling to see the marks left by Donatella, Sofia, and Giulio.

My face was the same and so were my eyes. But the dark circles beneath them and the paleness of my skin spoke of haunted dreams. For a moment, I stood immobile as my lungs squeezed in my chest. I had to face my demons, but was I brave enough?

Slowly, as if in a daze, I took my husband's shirt off, leaving me in my underwear. I discarded it onto the counter while I stared at my scars, pink and ugly. They looked worse under the sunlight streaming in.

My heart faltered, staring at the marks on my arms and my belly. A shiver worked its way up my spine and tears burned in my eyes. It was vain, but I couldn't help it.

A soft noise caught my attention and I found Enrico leaning against the doorway, wearing nothing but his pajama pants. So beautiful. So strong. So far away.

He pushed off the door and slowly, as if approaching a skittish animal, he closed the distance between us.

"What are you looking at?"

"Nothing."

Enrico came up behind me, and instinctively, I reached for a towel, piece of clothing—anything to cover the ugliness of it.

The moment my fingers reached the cloth, Enrico ripped it from my grip.

"No." His gaze met mine in the mirror. "You do not hide from me."

I blinked desperately, tears threatening to spill. I held them back, needing my strength now more than ever. I averted my eyes from the reflection showing his perfect body next to my scarred one. My heart drummed against my ribs, each one more painful than the last.

Illias said I was brave—strong like him—but I didn't feel like it right now. I mourned my body, the way it used to be but no longer was. I mourned my soul, because it was heavy. So fucking heavy that it was hard to breathe.

"What are you looking at, *amore mio*?" he repeated.

I swallowed. "I'm ugly."

He stepped closer to my back, his chest brushing against me. His warmth heated my cold heart. He was the reason I held on. Yet, nothing was the same. I had returned damaged, hiding in the darkness of my mind.

"Isla, look at me," my husband demanded. I turned my head to do so, but he stopped me. "No, in the mirror." I followed his command to see his perfect body next to my imperfect one. "What do you see?"

I swallowed the lump in my throat that threatened to choke me. "I see you. You're so beautiful. So perfect. And I'm—"

My voice cracked, unable to utter another word.

He shook his head. "No, *dolcezza*." He kissed the crown of my head. "*You* are beautiful. My survivor." One hand lay across my stomach, his palm calming my frantic heartbeat. "My strong wife who fought to come back to me." His voice cracked on the last word and his hand trembled as he wrapped it around my waist. "You are beautiful, *mia moglie*. My wife. My lover. My reason. Without you, I'm nothing. With you, I'm everything."

A single tear lingered on my eyelashes, fighting to get free while I struggled to breathe.

"But look how ugly I am."

"You are bruised. Scarred. It only makes you more beautiful." I caught his stare in the mirror. "You are the strongest woman I know, and I wouldn't have you any other way."

A choked sob escaped me. "I don't feel strong."

"Do you trust me?" I nodded. "Then trust me when I say you are strong. The strongest Marchetti woman who has ever lived." He slowly turned me so I was standing in front of him, then he lowered down to his knees. My eyes locked on the man kneeling before me. "Do you remember our first night?"

"Yes," I croaked, my heart hammering in my chest.

"I thought you were the most beautiful woman I had ever seen." His palms trailed my hips and my thighs, then parted my legs. "I was wrong." I stiffened, but before I could break down, he continued, "Today, you're even more beautiful. Because I see your strength in your eyes. In every scar. In every breath you take. Don't ever doubt it."

My heart shuddered with need and love. God, I loved him so much that it terrified me. It made me feel vulnerable and strong at the same time. I didn't understand it.

"When will you touch me?" I breathed.

He let out a heavy sigh. "I thought you'd never ask, *dolcezza*."

His fingers teased my seam and the familiar lust brewed in the pit of my stomach. "Watch yourself in the mirror," he ordered as he turned me to the side and pulled my panties down my legs. Then his finger dipped inside me and my eyes fluttered shut. A tear finally rolled freely down my cheek, my heart beat in sync with his. My lips parted, oxygen too hard to come by.

"I was a shell of a man before you, Isla," he murmured against my core. "I love you, *amore mio*."

"I love you too," I whimpered, my bottom lip trembling. "This is the first time you've gotten down on your knees since we got married," I remarked, my smile wobbly.

"I'll always kneel for my queen." I squeezed my eyes shut as he thrust his finger in and out, the heat building inside me. "Open your beautiful eyes for me. Watch us."

I peeled my eyes open, watching him as he leaned closer and flicked his tongue against my core.

My thighs quivered. My skin flushed. My eyes glimmered.

All for him.

"Enzo." He froze, unused to me calling him by his birth name. His gaze met mine, his darkness meeting my own. "I want *you* inside me."

He rose to his full height, discarding his pajama pants. His hands reached around me, his fingers digging into my ass. I hooked my legs around him, and he thrust to the hilt inside me.

I held on to him as he moved in and out of me like a possessed man. Like he owned me. Like he needed me the way I needed him.

"I need you like the sun needs the moon." He thrust in again. Hard. "Like the sea needs the shore." He fucked me harder and faster, his moves animalistic. "Like my lungs need air." *Thrust.*

It took no time for both of us to fall over the edge.

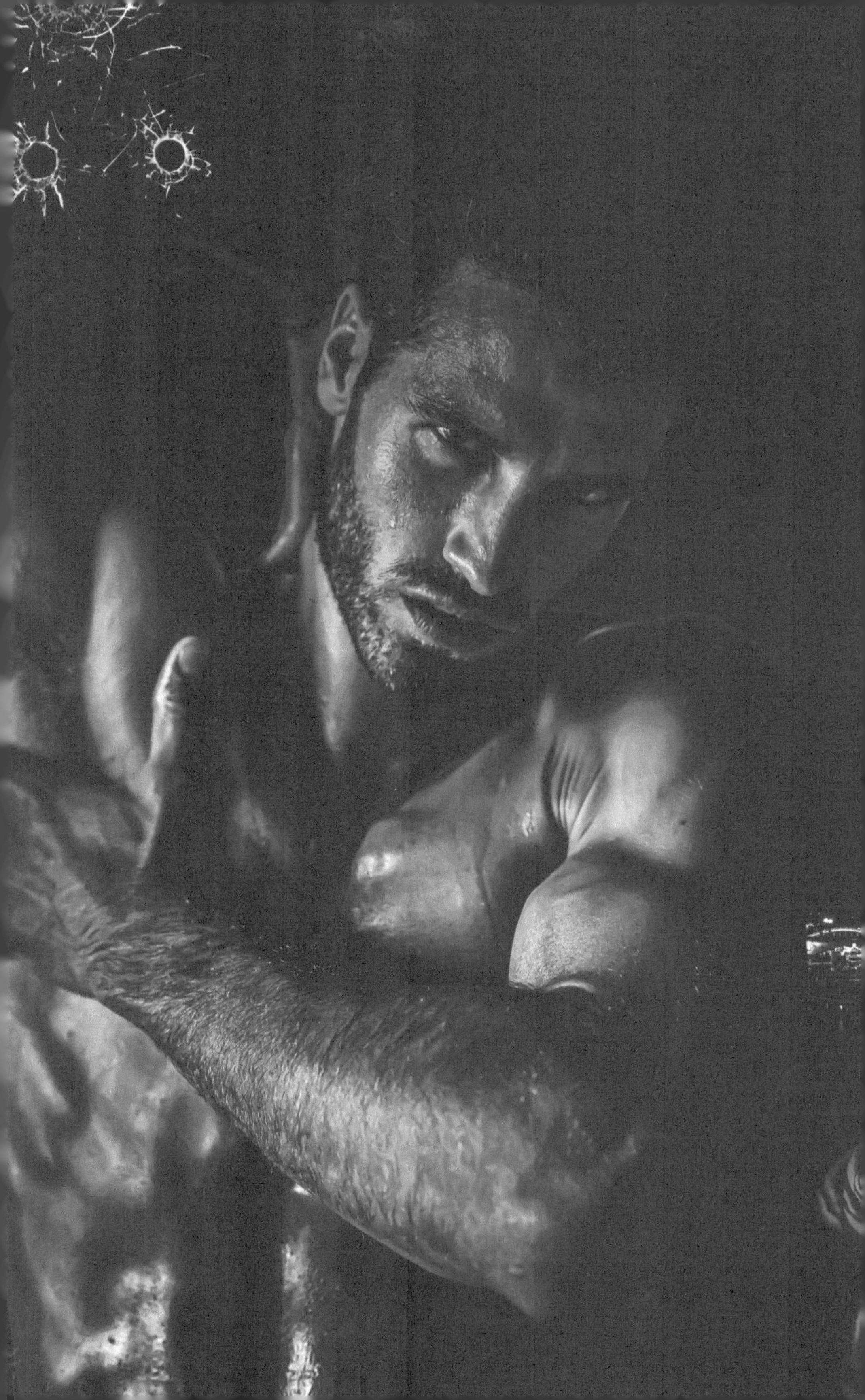

FIFTY-SEVEN
ENRICO

Four Months Later

Waves crashed against the shoreline. The beach was empty. The weather was still not warm enough to attract the crowds. Isla's small body pressed against mine as we sat on the cliffs. Each cool breeze from the sea had her pressing against me harder, her hands clutching for me like I was her lifeline.

It was fucking heaven.

Days, weeks, months had gone by and we had all settled into a routine. The paranoia refused to leave me, however, so I'd enhanced our security, scared to ever lose her again.

Kian and I had started teaching Isla self-defense too.

"If you get a cold, you still have to go to school."

My wife used her most stern voice, but the boys knew it was an empty threat. Nobody babied them like Isla. When Amadeo had come down with food poisoning, she insisted on holding his head as he puked his guts out. But I'd come to realize that they needed it. They needed a woman's touch. A gentle hand. And Isla fit perfectly into our family. The way I always knew she would.

Enzo and Amadeo swam in the cold sea, claiming it was warm. It wasn't. Their blue lips were proof, but they were stubborn as fuck. Just like my wife.

I wouldn't have it any other way.

The smell of coconuts hit my nose and my eyes found my wife. Her skin glowed golden. Her cuts had faded, but to the careful eye, the scars were still there. They were my reminder of her strength. Since that morning in the bathroom, we'd spent every waking moment outside. Highlights had even turned her ginger hair golden from all the sun.

As if to push all the darkness away from her.

I returned my attention to the horizon. To our home. There was something soothing about watching the sun dip low, the dancing rays across the surface of the sea giving us hope. For our future. For our happiness. For my family's safety.

"*Marito*." Isla's soft voice pulled my gaze from the horizon and to my wife. My thoughts were always with her. I leaned down and kissed her small nose.

"*Sì, dolcezza?*" Her Italian was improving. Konstantin hated it. I fucking loved it.

"Would you want a *bambino* or a *bambina*?" *Boy or a girl?* My heart stopped and the tiny bit of space that separated us disappeared as I pulled her on top of me. I could feel her soft breath on my lips.

"Are you saying what I think—" Jesus, my voice broke. So many emotions suffocated me.

She wrapped her arms around my neck, brushing her lips against mine. "I am."

I smashed my lips against hers. "*Davvero, amore mio?*"

She nodded her head. "Better believe it. You're going to be daddy to another boy or girl."

Fuck, I loved her so much. The way she always included the boys into our family. She was my light, illuminating every single inch of my dark soul. I had forced her into my life, but for the life of me, I couldn't regret the decision.

She had shown me what it was to live. To love. To be happy. All the lies and secrets were out in the open, yet she loved me anyway. *She was my happy ending.*

Her lips parted against mine, our mouths molding together. I brought my hand to her belly, holding it reverently.

"How long have you known?"

"I took the test earlier." She smiled against my mouth. "After what happened—" A dark cloud threatened to appear. "Donatella's dead, and we said we'd talk about children then. It was the reason I didn't opt for it when the doctor offered an alternative. For some reason, I forgot all about getting pregnant with everything else happening."

Anguish crawled into my chest. "*Amore*, do you want—"

Fuck, why was it so hard to utter those words out loud?

She closed the distance between us. "I want our baby. I love our family. You, the boys, the baby. I want it all."

Relief washed over me. "I want it all too. Just with you. Now how did you take the test? Where was I?"

She smiled sheepishly. "I made Manuel take me to the store." Before I could even frown, she quickly added, "Don't be upset with him. I threatened his life and told him if he said a word to you, I'd claw his eyes out." I sighed heavily. "I know I should see a doctor first, but I want us to go together."

I cupped her face. "*Grazie, dolcezza.*"

She scrunched her eyebrows. "For what?"

"For loving me."

She taught me to live in the moment. Live for the now. In the sunlight. Together.

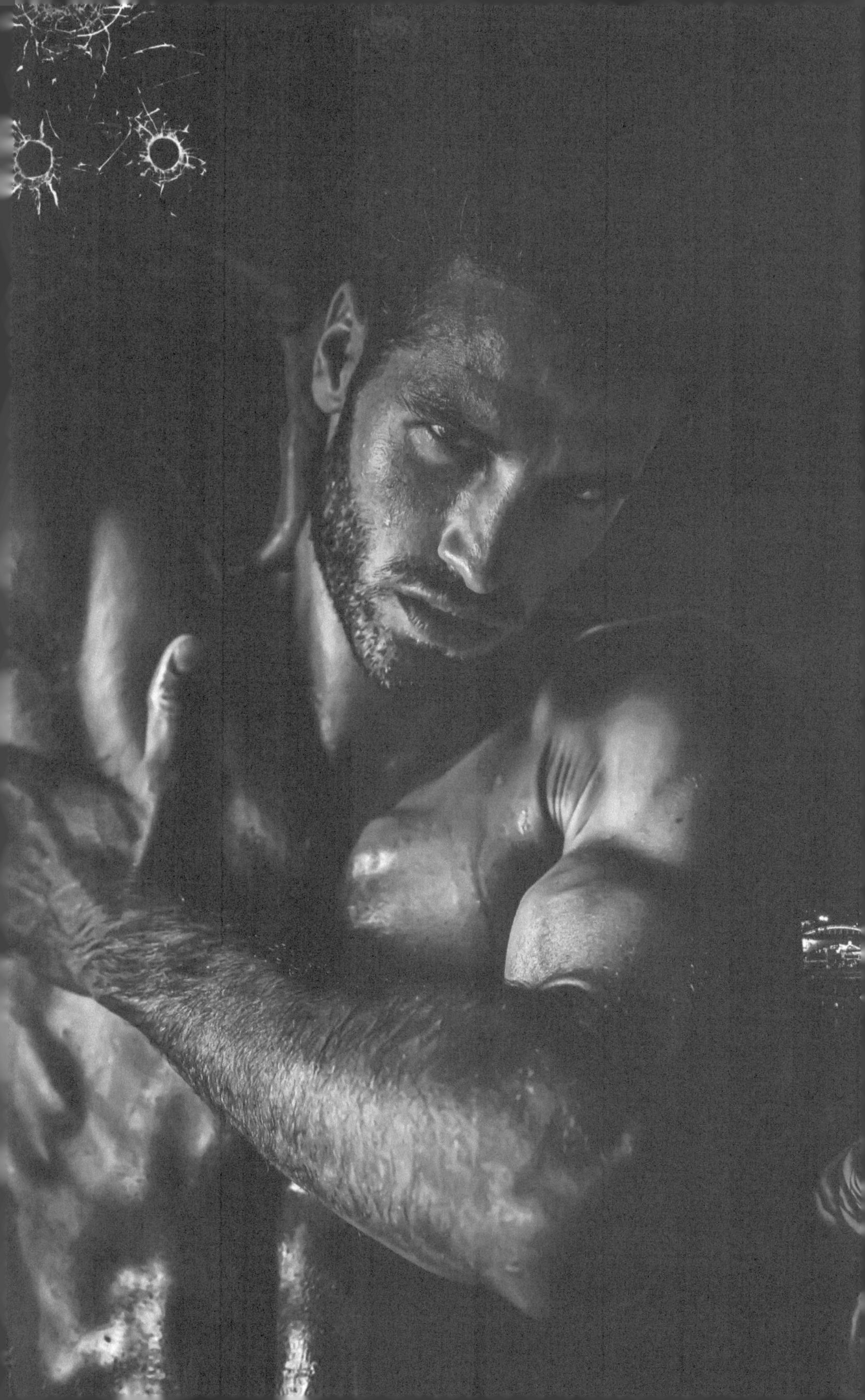

EPILOGUE
ENRICO

Four Years Later

From across the distance, I could see my wife and children making my heart swell. Two little heads full of red curls and one little head with a dark mane squealed happily, running through the garden.

Enzo and Amadeo were away at university—second and first year—and wouldn't be back until their summer break. They'd grown up into good men.

I was still unsure whether I deserved this happiness, but I selfishly kept it. It was ours. Isla's and mine, and I'd end anyone who tried to take it from me.

"It's about time we bury the hatchet with Luca DiMauro." Manuel pulled my attention back to the task at hand. Luca and his family were coming over. It wasn't until I had my daughters that I understood DiMauro's hesitancy to tie his daughter to my son. It wasn't until I'd opened my heart that I knew it was something I wanted for all my children.

It seemed a different lifetime—a different me—when Margaret

Callahan stepped foot into my territory and I arranged her safe passage but only on the condition of marrying her and Luca's child to my own. Of course, at that time, I didn't know that it was Luca's father, Benito, who'd set up the Callahans to cover his own traitorous ass.

"It will be good," I agreed. "And long overdue."

Manuel nodded. "Having daughters changes perspectives."

I couldn't agree more.

The door to my office swung open and my two-year-old, Inessa, appeared. Her green eyes darted over Manuel to me and her beautiful face lit up.

"Papà! Zio!" She put her small hands on her little hips and made a mad face that was way too adorable. Her vocabulary was advanced, and she definitely knew how to use it to get what she wanted. "I want gelato."

Much like her mother, Inessa loved her gelato. She could eat ice cream for breakfast, lunch, and dinner.

Manuel and I chuckled. He scooped her up and threw her into the air. She squealed happily, the sound of her voice making my chest expand.

I pushed back from the desk and stood up. "It's your papà's turn. Come here, *mio cuore*." *My heart*. My children and my wife had my heart. Without them, this life wouldn't be worth the hassle.

Manuel put her on her feet and she bolted toward me, her emerald eyes shining.

I opened my arms and she threw herself into me, knowing I'd always catch her.

"Can I have gelato now?" My youngest daughter was pure determination packaged in a small body. She was her mother, through and through. Our boy, Romeo, was a mirror image of his older brothers and me. But our girls were their mother's, much to my delight.

"Your mamma won't be happy."

She shrugged. "*È bene*." That's okay.

Manuel and I chuckled. "After dinner," I told her. "You can offer gelato to our guests."

She took my hand and twirled around. "Do I look pretty?"

I grinned. "Of course."

"But Mamma is the prettiest one of all," she finished for me.

"All my girls are beautiful."

She scrunched her nose. "I heard you tell Mamma she's your prettiest one in the world."

"Are you jealous?"

She stood on my feet and wrapped her small hands around my legs. "No. I think she's prettiest too."

My heart turned over. It wasn't her words that had my soul filling. It was the love in her voice. I scooped her up and brought her face up to mine.

"Now, where is my kiss, *principessa*?"

Her little arms wrapped around my neck and she pressed her lips to my cheek. *Smooch*.

Her eyes darted to Manuel, then back to me. "Are you done with work?"

"Almost."

"Mamma says you work too much."

"I know, *piccolina*. But we're almost done for today."

The voices of her siblings pulled her attention, and she darted through the French doors and joined them. If the DiMauro family didn't show up soon, my children's clothes would be covered in dirt.

"We're going to have our hands full with the young," Manuel said, chuckling as we both made our way out the door to join the family in the garden.

My eyes found my wife instinctively. Her red hair wild in the breeze, among the smell of the sea and lemon trees, our gazes met. It was a punch in the gut. Just the way it was the first time I saw her.

I went over to her and kissed her, placing my hand on her barely rounded belly. "*Amore mio*, you take my breath away every time."

She grinned, her eyes shining lighter under the blue sky. "As long as you don't stop breathing."

She still played the violin almost every day. She performed at the local orchestra and even taught music at the local high school. She helped run the Marchetti legal empire too. I didn't know where I'd be without her. I didn't even want to imagine it.

"*Ti amo, dolcezza.*" I brushed my mouth against her ear. "You have given me peace. Happiness."

"And you have given me family," she murmured. "I love you too."

Romeo and Iryna joined us along with Inessa. If Enzo and Amadeo were here, our family would be complete.

"Why do we have to have dinner with strangers?" Romeo grumbled, grabbing a handful of grass and throwing it at his sister.

I knelt down so we'd be eye to eye. "They won't be strangers for long."

He grabbed a handful of dirt this time and threw it in the air, creating a dust cloud overhead.

"Romeo, *basta*." Isla's stern voice scolded our son, warning him to stop. "You'll be a mess by the time our guests arrive."

He brushed his hands on his pants and Isla groaned, putting her hand on her forehead.

"*Che cazzo*," she hissed. I bit the inside of my cheek to stop from grinning. My wife had gotten really good at cursing in Italian. In fact, she'd perfected it so well, I was convinced she swore better in Italian than English. "Romeo, get your little butt here. Now."

"There they are!" Iryna exclaimed as a car pulled up in front of the gate. The guards approached the vehicle, assisting Luca and his family.

Iryna rushed to the gate, so eager to see new people, she climbed it and waved like she'd known them forever. "Hello," she yelled. "I'm Iryna."

Just like Inessa, she was too curious and too friendly.

I rose and shoved my hands in my trouser pockets, making my way to the gate with my wife by my side. My holster under my suit jacket, I studied Luca and his family. Just like mine, his had expanded over the years.

It was only then that I noticed my wife was barefoot, but there was no time to say anything about it because Luca stood in front of me.

"Luca," I greeted him. "Thank you for coming."

He tilted his head. "Marchetti." My gaze found his wife, Margaret. "Mrs. DiMauro, nice to see you again."

"You too." She smiled, her oldest daughter by her side and a small boy on her hip. Luca held a little boy's hand who looked to be Romeo's age.

Margaret's eyes darted to my wife. "My wife, Isla. And our children. Romeo. Iryna who already introduced herself. And Inessa. Enzo and Amadeo are not here."

I could have sworn Margaret breathed a relieved sigh.

"Damiano is my eldest son," Luca answered before tilting his chin at the boy that Margaret held. "Armani. And our Penelope."

I'd bet my life that he'd have preferred to keep Penelope hidden. She seemed to favor her mother's looks more than her father's. Thank fuck! Luca wasn't pretty at all. She was younger than Enzo by a good nine years. After all, Enzo and Amadeo attended their wedding.

"Welcome to our home." There weren't too many I invited to my castello. Luca knew it, and I hoped he'd see it as a symbol for our future. Together or not.

It was Luca who broke the tension, his eyes lowering to Isla's feet.

She followed his gaze and grinned. "My feet are killing me," she murmured. "It would seem my husband prefers me barefoot and pregnant." Then she extended her hand. "Nice to meet you, Luca." Then she bent slightly. "And you, Damiano. I really like your name."

Margaret chuckled. "It has to be something about Italian men. They insist on keeping their women pregnant." Luca and I groaned at the same time, but both women ignored us. "How far along are you?"

Isla glowed, happiness shining through her eyes. "Just three months." She flicked me a glance. "After this, we're done with children. We have six. That's more than plenty."

I wrapped my hand around her waist. "We shall see."

We had an early dinner out on the terrace with music, wine, and laughter. Manuel, Luca, and I discussed new products and routes for upcoming shipments. Isla and Margaret talked about motherhood, careers, and travel. They had quite a lot in common.

The children played. Little Armani, enthralled with Iryna and

Inessa, chased them around. Romeo and Damiano snuck into the garden and were probably killing Zia's lemon trees, while Penelope drifted around, touring the property.

It didn't escape me that Luca kept his attention on her. Almost as if he worried we'd kidnap her and marry her off to Enzo. She was still too young, for Christ's sake.

"How is your grandfather?" I asked Luca. "I heard his health worsened. I'm sorry to hear that."

Luca tilted his head in acknowledgement. "He's fighting it. He wants to live forever."

I smiled. "He has a lot to live for. It gave him purpose when you moved back."

He finally cracked a smile. "He never fails to remind me how I waited too long to move back."

"My old man used to say everything happens at just the right time," I told him.

Our server brought cognac and the three of us shared it. The women had dessert. The kids had gelato but refused to slow down and savor it. Instead, they ran around, happy and carefree with ice cream on their faces and dirt on their clothes.

"About the arrangement between our families—"

I wondered how long it'd take him to bring it up.

I met Luca's eyes. "I won't cancel it." Anger flashed across his face, but before he could say anything else, I continued, "But if our children don't grow to love each other, I'll be willing to reconsider."

Our wills battled. History danced. Ghosts lurked.

"*Va bene*," Luca answered, and we shook on it. "I'll take that, because I'm certain my daughter won't fall in love with your son."

I grinned. "We shall see."

It didn't matter. One way or another, my sixth sense told me, we'd connect our families. But that was to unfold in due time.

Right now, all I wanted to do was live for today. Just plain live and love every moment I'd been given on this planet with my family.

As if she could sense my thoughts, Isla's eyes found mine and she smiled. We still carried our scars, hers visible, mine below the surface but still just as telling of the trials that put them there. But with each day together as a family, they faded. Because of her—my wife. My entire world.

THE END

PREVIEW TO STOLEN EMPIRE TRILOGY- BITTER PRINCE

Once upon a time there sat a beautiful castle along the shore of the Gulf of Trieste. It was a magical place indeed, with views of the sea to the east and sprawling hills to the west. A savage king and his two sons lived amidst the darkness, slowly wilting right alongside everything in it. No amount of magic could save them.

Poppies, wild jasmine, gardenias, and violet plants filled the gardens. The soft breeze traveled the air and with it so many scents. The sea, flowers, fragrance of the citrus fruits all misted the air and attracted the butterflies, fluttering around us.

My sister and I gaped at the serenity of it all, her hand in mine. Dozens of people laughed, ate, and danced. A happy old Italian song, like the ones Papa loved, filled the air, and people chattered in Italian and English.

"It's so beautiful," I said as I signed to Mamma, Papà, and Phoenix. Lights flickered over my big sister's face, and for the first time in a long time, I saw an awed and happy expression passing across it.

"It's a magical home," Mamma chimed in, signing as well, but the expression on her face was grim. Papà's hand roamed her back, up and down, trying to soothe her.

"Romero, *sei arrivato*." A deep, stern voice had Mamma pulling both Phoenix and me closer to her. I didn't understand Italian. Papà mainly conversed in English with Mamma, so there was never a need. "I'm glad you both could make it. Both you and your lovely wife." The man switched to our native language, his blue eyes zeroing in on my sister then on me.

"Angelo, nice to see you," Papà greeted him. "Girls, this is Mr. Leone. He's our host." My sister and I leaned further into our mamma's skirt while Papà's hand wrapped around her waist. "This is my wife. Grace."

Mr. Leone's eyes shifted to our mother, and I saw a flicker of something I didn't understand. Something I didn't like.

He took Mamma's free hand and brought it to his lips.

"So nice to meet you, Mrs. Romero." I didn't like it. I wanted to yank my mother's hand from his grip and tell him she was mine. But I knew Papà would be displeased if I didn't show good manners. "You're even more breathtaking in person than on the screen."

Mamma was an actress, but she gave it up for Papà. And for Phoenix and me. She was beautiful, and when she smiled, everyone became mesmerized. Her soft blonde locks fell down her shoulders, bouncing with each move. She wore a red dress to show Papà how much she loved him; it was his favorite color. He loved her very much, but Mamma wasn't happy. I'd heard him tell her once that he would give her the moon and the stars so she'd be happy again.

Mamma's lips thinned as she watched Mr. Leone, in the same way they did when she didn't like something. Like when Grandma Diana told Mamma she was selfish. Like when the doctor told Mamma that Phoenix lost her hearing. She never cried; she never yelled. But Papà cried that day. I didn't understand any of it.

Papà took Mamma's hand. "Let's go dance, *amore mio*," he said, his eyes landing on my sister and me. "Want to go play?" We both nodded. "Go and have fun. Don't get in trouble."

"And don't get dirty," Mamma yelled after us as we both scurried away.

We walked through the gardens and grabbed two cannolis, only to shove them into our mouth and take two more. We giggled and ran off before someone could yell at us. Lots of Italian words were spoken. There were many curious glances thrown our way, but we kept to ourselves.

When we were tired of paying outside, we made our way inside the grand castle, roaming the empty rooms and avoiding other people and children. They all seemed to be laughing and talking like they'd known each other forever. They even talked to Papà in Italian, knowing Mamma didn't understand a single word.

We were foreigners here. But maybe not for long. Papà wanted to move us back to Italy, so this summer we'd spend it vacationing here. Mamma said it was a test, but I was unsure what we were testing.

"Hello?" I called out, my voice echoing across the long corridor. No answer. I shared a glance with my sister before turning back to the long hallway with perfectly slick marble floors.

An idea struck me, and when I met my big sister's eyes, I knew she had the same idea from the mischievous glimmer in her gaze. Papà said Phoenix and I had identical eyes. They were the color of a deep blue sea, like the bottoms of a lagoon.

"*Should we do it?*" I signed. Her eyes lowered to my feet. Mine lowered to hers. We wore matching dresses with frilly, lacy socks. This might be the best use for them yet.

She nodded and we kicked off the shoes that Mamma carefully selected for us.

I raised my hand. Three. Two. One.

We shot into a sprint, gliding over the marble floor of the mansion, Phoenix beside me. We giggled, falling over each other. We rolled over the cold, slick surface.

"*We'll be in trouble if we get caught,*" Phoenix signed.

"We won't get caught," I assured her. "I'll protect you."

We did it again and again, gliding like we were on ice. We bumped, ran, bumped again. It almost felt like flying.

Until... *Crash!*

We froze. Pieces of a large vase that looked to be from the Disney movie *Mulan* lay scattered on the floor. Our breaths sounded louder. My heart beat stronger, my pulse buzzing in my ears. Papà warned us to behave and not get in trouble before we came to the party.

"What the hell happened here?" A deep Italian voice startled me and I whimpered, causing Phoenix to do the same when I startled. The lion's eyes turned cold and cruel, staring us down. He took a step toward us, his form darkening over us like a raincloud. I took my sister's hand in mine and pushed her behind me. She was taller than me, but I was stronger. I'd bite him so she could run to get our Papa.

"Which one of you did this?" he hissed.

Panic rose inside me. We should run. We should scream. Yet my voice was stuck in my throat. A six-year-old girl against the evil king.

"It was me, Papà."

"No, Papà, it was me."

The voices of two boys answered in unison.

I followed the sound and found them standing in the corner. Two small shadows unmoving. Their eyes were locked on their father, not looking our way.

One boy looked like his father. Same coloring. Same dark brown—almost black—hair. Same harshness.

But the other... he was unlike any boy I had ever seen. His face had sharp angles. His skin was golden. His hair was darker than midnight and blue hues shone in its strands. His hooded eyes reflected the entire galaxy—a universe of its own—with stars buried deep within them.

When his gaze found mine, time came to a stop. It stood still, leaving us all alone in the world.

It felt like looking up at the black velvet of the night, letting your dream swallow you. There was no sun in his eyes. There was no moon. But there were stars.

Stars that would one day shine only for me.

PREVIEW TO THORNS OF SILENCE

I stood in front of the huge mansion in California where it seemed everything started all those years ago. It was the old Hollywood, something the Romero sisters were known for. There were several cameras placed at regular intervals, blinking red. The fence was high to keep intruders out. Although it never kept Reina and Phoenix in.

Old Hollywood and their old dragon of a grandmother protected them from the public. Their family kept them in a perfect little bubble. But it was all a lie.

There was no such thing as a perfect life. A perfect reality. Or a whole truth.

There were always people with agendas. Including the members of the Omertà. I was no exception. I wanted war. She wanted peace. I wanted to win, and she wanted to protect her sister.

It was how I made Reina agree to this farce of a wedding. I'd destroy her. She knew there was no way out. It was her or her beautiful sister.

Wrapped up in my brother, this Romero sister never saw me coming.

She underestimated me for the first and last time. I'd rip her apart, crush her bones, and watch the blood ooze from her wounds. And then, I'd still take her beautiful sister.

Deep blue eyes flashed in my mind, full of disapproval and scolding. I hated the hold *she* had over me. The silent sister. The deaf sister. The sister with lush lips and a warm touch that had been haunting me ever since she kissed me.

But there was no room for sentiment here. I had hardened my heart and my soul. Phoenix didn't matter, and her sister even less so.

It was time to make them suffer. It was time to make them pay.

When they committed their crime, they knew it'd come back to haunt them. They knew their time was limited on this earth.

They hid their secret for far too long. But not from me. *Never* from me.

Now, it was time to make them pay.

If the Leone bloodline would be erased from this world, so would the Romero family.

This was my revenge.

ABOUT THE AUTHOR

Curious about Eva's other books? You can check them out here. Eva Winners' Books https://bit.ly/3SMMsrN

Eva Winners writes anything and everything romance, from enemies to lovers to books with all the feels. Her heroes are sometimes villains because they need love too. Right? Her books are sprinkled with a touch of suspense, mystery, a healthy dose of angst, a hint of violence and darkness, and lots of steamy passion.

When she's not working and writing, she spends her days either in Croatia or Maryland daydreaming about the next story.

Find Eva below:

Visit www.evawinners.com and subscribe to my newsletter.

FB group: https://bit.ly/3gHEe0e
FB page: https://bit.ly/30DzP8Q
Insta: http://Instagram.com/evawinners
BookBub: https://www.bookbub.com/authors/eva-winners
Amazon: http://amazon.com/author/evawinners
Goodreads: http://goodreads.com/evawinners
Tiktok: https://vm.tiktok.com/ZMeETK7pq/

Made in United States
Troutdale, OR
02/21/2025